RIZZO'S DAUGHTER

Also by Lou Manfredo

Rizzo's Fire
Rizzo's War

LOU MANFREDO

RIZZO'S DAUGHTER

MINOTAUR BOOKS
NEW YORK

S

ISBN 978-0-312-53807-1

First Edition: March 2012

10 9 8 7 6 5 4 3 2 1

To my beloved grandson, Robert Basil Maull

ACKNOWLEDGMENTS

With deep gratitude to my dear muse, Joanne, for her creative assistance and inexhaustible patience.

And my thanks to Marie L. Basso-D'Agostino, whose grace and beauty equals that of the Italian language she has so expertly assisted me with.

But he had not that supreme gift of the artist, the knowledge of when to stop.

SHERLOCK HOLMES

"THE ADVENTURE OF THE NORWOOD BUILDER"

RIZZO'S DAUGHTER

CHAPTER ONE

March

LOUIS QUATTROPA knotted his black silk tie and slipped into his suit jacket. He eyed himself critically in the full-length mirror. Despite his seventy-one years, he cut an impressive figure. The custom-made Italian suit hung perfectly, contoured to his slim, sinewy frame. His black eyes held a dangerous glint beneath his near full shock of gray-brown hair. He found himself frowning at his image.

The Russians. Those goddamned Russians. As if he didn't have enough to worry about: the feds sniffing around constantly; the young kids coming up on all his crews, half of them druggies, half of them irrational violent psychos. And now the Russians.

He turned from the mirror. Brooklyn covered a lot of turf, and under Quattropa's regime, it included Staten Island. But now the Russians were shrinking things. They were too hungry, too aggressive. And with their well-earned reputation for violent reprisals against law enforcement, plenty of cops and feds were all too eager to focus on the Italian mob, discreetly turning blind eyes on any transgressions of the Russians. Every day, it seemed, Quattropa's grip on organized mob activities in Brooklyn grew more precarious, more perilous. And retirement was not an option.

No, Quattropa was old school, one of only a few such mobsters

1

still active. He would cling to his power with both hands until his death, natural or otherwise, or until the law caught up with him and exiled him to some Midwestern dungeon for his last few years on earth.

Quattropa left the bedroom and descended the staircase of his palatial Bay Ridge home. His wife of fifty-one years was seated at the kitchen table, sipping from a demitasse cup.

"Carlo is here," she said. "He's outside in the car."

Quattropa nodded. "I gotta take care of something," he said. "I won't be home late."

His wife rose, crossed to him, kissed him lightly on the cheek. "Alright. Be careful."

Quattropa patted her arm, returning the kiss. "Okay."

Louis Quattropa, known since childhood as "Louie the Chink" because of his tawny skin and almond-shaped eyes, left the house and climbed into the front passenger seat of the softly idling Lincoln. Carlo Lentini greeted him from behind the wheel. "All set, Louie?" he asked.

In the dimness of the interior, Quattropa nodded. "Yeah. Let's go. I wanna get there early, before this Russian prick shows up. I want him comin' to me, not the other way around."

Lentini pulled the car into gear, eased it around the circular driveway. "Smart," he said. "The way it should be."

"Yeah," Quattropa said. "But the way it should really be, this prick should be in the river with the fish eatin' his balls 'stead of gettin' a sit-down with me. Goddamn Russkie commie prick."

Carlo smiled. "Say the word. Just say the word."

Quattropa reached out and laid a hand on Lentini's shoulder. "It may happen, Carlo. Let's see how tonight plays out."

Carlo nodded, contemplating the brightness of his future. Only thirty-two years old and already working for the old man. True, he had to give up his crew, turn in his stripes, but a bump-up like this couldn't be refused. The old man trusted him as much as he trusted anyone, and that trust meant money. And money translated to power. Carlo knew it was possible for him to earn the big chair some day. Yes, Frankie Saverese, The Chink's first cousin, was technically next in line. But Saverese was only two years younger than The Chink, and once the old man was gone, who could say? Carlo had the respect of the captains and most of the soldiers. And, more important, he had their fear. Carlo Lentini was the most feared man in the Brooklyn mob outside of Quattropa and Saverese. And maybe that lunatic, Mikey. Mikey "The Hammer" Spano.

Lentini shrugged unconsciously as he drove. Bridges to cross, he thought. For another day.

The Hi-Fi Lounge had not changed much since it first opened in the 1960s. Most of its current patrons were only vaguely aware of what a hi-fi even was, but the business nevertheless did well. It was civilian owned by the same family from day one, and its current operator, Richie Maggio, played by the same rules that his father had established so long ago. Local gangsters were good for business. They were always welcome at the Hi-Fi and always treated well. In return, Maggio knew he'd never suffer at the hands of some two-bit stick-up man, nor would the local cops or Alcohol Beverage Control inspectors bother him much. Neighborhood folks knew they could stop by the Hi-Fi, double-park outside for as long as they needed to, and never be ticketed. They might even get to rub shoulders with a real wiseguy. And since the establishment held such a long tradition with the Brooklyn mob, it was understood that the place was off-limits for any business-related mayhem. It was a safe and neutral no-man's-land, and very lucrative for the Maggio family.

And so, when approached by Lentini, Maggio had readily agreed to his request. Louie the Chink would be conducting business at the Hi-Fi on this Tuesday night, March 10. The rear room of the bar would be closed to patrons, its eight tables and small pool table sitting idle until all business concluded.

Richie Maggio took almost a sense of pride from it all: most of The Chink's routine business was conducted at The Starlight Lounge, three blocks to the north of the Hi-Fi. The Starlight was anonymously owned by Quattropa. Without having to ask, Maggio understood: tonight's business, whatever it entailed, needed to be conducted on the Hi-Fi's neutral ground, and it must be very high level. Lentini told him to expect four men and to arrange a table accordingly. He prepared a corner table, using his best linens and finest place settings. Expensive Italian wine was chilling, Sambuca stood ready, and espresso awaited fresh brewing. An iced shrimp platter, covered in plastic wrap and fresh from the Thirteenth Avenue Fish Market, sat in the tiny kitchen.

Maggio, wearing his dark gray suit and best blue tie to mark the momentous nature of the evening, stood nervously in the large front barroom of the Hi-Fi. He eyed the room, noting how the cold, misty March evening had kept the bar crowd sparse. He smiled at the barmaid, known to most as Peggy Irish. She returned the smile while hustling to bring fresh beers to a couple of retired regulars at the bar's end. Jimmy Jam, always jammed up because of problems with local bookies and loan sharks, sat mid-bar, nursing a Seven and Seven. Two construction workers Maggio had seen once or twice before sat nearest him, still working on the "couple of beers" they had come in for some three hours earlier. At a small corner table, sipping what appeared to be gin or vodka cocktails, a young couple, perhaps in their late twenties, sat laughing into one another's eyes.

Just as Richie was about to turn and recheck the specially arranged table awaiting in the closed rear barroom, the front door swung sharply open. Louis Quattropa, his black felt fedora low on his brow, stepped in. Behind him, the burly figure of Carlo Lentini followed. Maggio glanced up at the clock fashioned into the Budweiser neon sign: seven-forty.

He moved across the barroom to meet Quattropa.

"Louie," he said, extending his hand. "You're early."

"Yeah," Quattropa said, unsmiling. "I'm early. You got a place set for us?"

Maggio half turned, extending his left arm, pointing toward the closed double doors at the rear of the room. "Of course, Louie, in the back. Just like I promised Carlo."

Maggio led the way, nodding a greeting over his shoulder to Lentini. He swung the doors open wide, ushering Quattropa and his bodyguard through. Quattropa eyed the corner setup, noted the soft lighting, the low tones of Sinatra piped in over the sound system. He smiled and turned to Maggio.

"You're a good kid, Richie. Like your old man taught you. How's he doing, by the way?"

Richie Maggio beamed. "Good, very good. Enjoying himself down in Florida. I'll tell him you were asking, he'll be happy to hear it."

Quattropa moved to the table, undoing his heavy outer coat. Lentini helped him out of it, and hung the coat and fedora on the rack against the wall.

"And your mother?" Quattropa asked.

"Good, thank God," Maggio said. "It looks like they got it all. She's feelin' good."

Quattropa screwed up his lips. "Fuckin' cancer," he said bitterly.

He sat, adjusting himself on the soft chair. Lentini took a seat to Quattropa's left where he could watch both the side-door street entrance and the double doors they had entered from.

"Lock that side door, Richie," Lentini said.

Maggio nodded. "It's locked. I locked it myself."

5

Lentini, his eyes dark, stood and crossed the room. He tried the doorknob and found it secure. He returned to his seat.

"What the fuck, Carlo," Quattropa said. "The man told ya it was locked."

Lentini shrugged. "Yeah. And he was right, too."

Quattropa turned to face Maggio. "I apologize. Sometimes Carlo goes too far." His tone was not the least apologetic.

"No problem, I understand. Can I get you gentlemen something? I've got shrimp on ice in the back, I'm putting up some espresso . . ."

Quattropa held up a hand. "No. Not yet. Listen, I'm expecting two guys. I tole 'em to check in with you at the bar. When they get here, come and tell us. Let 'em wait at the bar. Carlo'll come out to get 'em."

Maggio nodded, growing uncomfortable. He hadn't planned on personally participating in anything this evening. "Okay, Louie. You sure I can't get you anything? A drink? Carlo? Something for you?"

Quattropa declined. Lentini shook his head. "Not yet," he said.

Maggio backed away from the table. "Okay, then. I'll go out front, wait for . . . for your friends. Eight, you said, right? About eight o'clock?"

"Yeah," Quattropa replied, turning from Maggio, dismissing him. "That's what I said."

Maggio left, closing the double doors behind him.

Quattropa turned his eyes to Lentini. "Check it."

Lentini stood and moved to the coatrack. He removed an electronic scanner from his outer coat and returned to the table. After a thorough visual search of the table and its perimeter, he used the device to carefully scan the entire area.

"Clean," he said.

Quattropa pointed a finger, indicating the rack against the wall. "Put it away."

6

Lentini returned the scanner to his coat, then rejoined Quattropa. He placed his arms on the table and leaned forward. "So," he said, "how you figure this'll go tonight, boss?"

Quattropa sat back, inhaling and exhaling deeply. "This guy Oleg is a real greedy Russian prick. He's got Brighton Beach, he's got a hand in Gravesend and Gerritsen Beach and God knows where the fuck else. From what I hear, he's eyein' Canarsie and Flatlands, too."

Carlo Lentini shook his head. "And he's steppin' on Frankie's toes."

Quattropa leaned inward, closer to Lentini. His eyes were flat, slitted. "I love my cousin," he said softly. "But it's *my* fuckin' toes gettin' stepped on. Don't fuckin' forget that. Frankie Saverese runs his crews for me, not for himself, and never for some immigrant Russkie."

Lentini nodded. "Yeah, boss, yeah, I'm just sayin'. Maybe this guy, this Oleg, he figures he can muscle Frankie. Maybe he don't figure it's *you* he's fuckin' with. That's all I'm sayin'."

"Well, maybe the pope's got three balls, too, Carlo. So fuckin' what? Whatda I care what Oleg thinks? It's what he *does* worries me. Besides, this is what fuckin' Mikey Spano is supposed to be doin'. He's the middleman on this operation, he's the go-between for me and this Russian. Where's he on all this? I gotta hear about this shit from my cousin Frankie? Where the fuck was Mikey on this?"

Lentini remained silent for a moment, then raised his brows. "I been wonderin' about that myself lately. And I ain't got a good answer for ya."

Quattropa leaned back again, appeared to relax. "I don't need no answers. I got the answers. I meet with this guy tonight, we straighten all this shit out. He keeps Brighton, but he kicks up to me through Spano. He can hire his crew out to Frankie for muscle or monkey work in Frankie's territory. Frankie throws him a bone once in a while, lets him run some local shit in the Russkie sections. Sometimes we'll run a joint venture, like the one with Mikey. Period. If he don't agree to it tonight, I smile at him, say we'll sit down again after I talk to Frankie. Then Oleg goes away. Permanently."

Lentini's eyes widened. "You serious, Louie? The time'll be right?"

"I'm thinking it will be, if tonight don't go my way."

"I'm there for you, boss. If that's what it comes to."

Quattropa reached across the table, patted Lentini's cheek gently. "I know you are, kid. I'll remember that if this goes down. You can reach out to your old crew, whoever you figure you can count on, maybe that guy Pastore, and you get it done. We'll talk about it some more if it comes down to that. But keep this in mind: I don't trust Spano. He's gettin' too cozy with these fuckin' Russians, too palsy. Like Joey Gallo did with the dit-soons, back before your time, before you was even born. There ain't no equals. This is *our* thing. We stepped over the Irish, we stepped over the Jews, we chased the Jamaicans and the slopes that came from every shit hole in Asia. The Russians ain't changin' nothin'. Not while I'm breathin' they ain't."

The two men sat silently for a moment, then Lentini stood. "I'm gonna tell Peggy Irish to bring us some drinks. What can she get you?"

Quattropa looked up at him. "Sambuca, chilled. And tell Richie to get those shrimp now. Let's enjoy some of 'em before these two *gafones* get here and start pawing at 'em with their hairy fuckin' fingers."

AT 8:05, Peggy Irish, her long auburn hair glistening under the light of the back bar, noticed something odd. The young couple at the rear table stood up. The woman placed her large black shoulder bag onto the table. She then took both of the rock glasses, empty, that she and her male companion had been drinking from. Carefully, she placed them into her bag, along with the cocktail napkins they had been using. The man, tall, muscular-looking, turned and stepped quickly to the rear double doors, pushing one open. Peggy had worked and lived in Bensonhurst most of her life. She did not like what she was seeing.

"Hey, Richie . . ." she said.

From his seat at the bar, Richie Maggio turned to her, his brows raised in question.

At that same moment, Carlo Lentini looked up at the sound of the door opening. Expecting it to be Maggio announcing the arrival of the Russians, he glanced for an instant to his Rolex. The last thought he had was that these pricks were five minutes late . . .

After pumping two nine-millimeter rounds into Lentini's head, the intruder turned toward Quattropa. The old Mafioso was unarmed, seated in a corner. He knew he was out of options. He spoke quickly, surprising the gunman, causing him to hesitate.

"When you get to hell," Quattropa hissed at the young man, "I'll be waiting for you. Then I'll take your fuckin' eyes out with broken glass and piss in the sockets."

The silver automatic trembled slightly in the man's grasp, and sweat broke out on his forehead. He avoided the burning blackness of Louie the Chink's eyes and squeezed the trigger. A piece of Quattropa's cerebellum rode the steel-jacketed bullet to the wall behind the table and clung there. The shooter watched as the brain matter slid an inch, then stopped. He lowered the muzzle and fired again into Quattropa's face.

As he turned to leave, the half-closed door burst open and an irrational, red-faced Richie Maggio charged in, a long knife in his hand, anger throbbing in his neck.

"You can't do this here!" he screamed. "Not here! You can't . . .."

Startled, the shooter turned quickly and fired twice. Maggio's death was nearly instantaneous.

The man went to the side door and unlocked it, a thick wash towel in his hand to prevent prints. He stepped out onto Seventy-second Street as a dark blue Volvo slid up to the curb. He crossed and climbed into the rear of the car. The driver accelerated away.

The shooter's female companion from the bar table turned from the front passenger seat.

"It's done?" she asked.

Quattropa's final words and image were seared into the man's consciousness. He shivered slightly as he spoke.

"Yes. It's done."

CHAPTER TWO

TWENTY MINUTES AFTER Peggy Irish's frantic 911 call, and less than a mile from the Hi-Fi Lounge, Detective Sergeant Joe Rizzo stood in the den of his Bay Ridge home, scanning television listings. His wife, Jennifer, entered the room, a cup of coffee in her hand.

"Anything on?" she asked.

Rizzo shrugged. "Is there ever? The only thing catching my eye is some old rerun of the *Andy Griffith Show*. The one where Opie kills a mother bird, then he has to raise the babies to make up for it."

Jennifer shook her head. "Pass," she said. "You enjoy it. I'll grade some papers, then read for a while."

"Okay. Is Carol home yet?"

"Not yet." Jennifer sighed. "I cannot believe this. Thursday is her first day on patrol. I cannot friggin' believe this."

Rizzo dropped the listings onto the recliner. He took hold of his wife's shoulders. "Relax, Jen. Just relax. You've had six months of her being in the Academy to get used to this. We knew it was coming. Now it's here, so just relax. It'll be fine."

"And you're sure about the arrangements?"

11

Rizzo nodded, smiling at Jennifer. "I said I was, didn't I? Everything is set. I pulled some strings, got her into the Eight-Four. It's a good house, a little of this, a little of that. The best sectors cover Brooklyn Heights. Very artsy and civilized. And Thursday, she starts riding with Joey Esposito. He'll be her training officer. You remember Joey Esposito? He married Johnny Morelli's niece; we went to the wedding."

"Joey Esposito? Little Joey? He's a training officer?"

Rizzo laughed as he answered. "Yeah, Little Joey. He's like thirty-six now, been a sergeant for six years. I hear he'll get made off the lieutenants' list soon, maybe six more months."

Jennifer shook her head, placing the coffee cup on the table beside the recliner. She wrapped her arms around Rizzo and placed her face against his shoulder.

"My God, we're getting old."

"That we are, honey, that we are. Older and wiser." Rizzo leaned backward for a better angle to look into his wife's face. "And, in your case at least, better. Getting better every day."

She nodded. "Sure."

"Really. Would I lie?"

Jennifer extracted herself from his arms. "Yes. As a matter of fact, you would. Do you even want to go there?"

Rizzo sighed. "Don't start with that, Jen. We've been through this enough. I told you, I was absolutely committed to retiring, it was all set for seven months ago. But when we weren't able to talk Carol out of going on the cops, I couldn't leave. Believe me, people get forgotten real fast on this job. Real fast. If I retired, I'd be in no position to do anything for Carol. All the favors owed to me would get wiped clean. I couldn't help her, couldn't steer her along. I'd be 'Rizzo who?' every phone call I made. This way, I'm still around, they still gotta deal with me. That's why Carol is going to the Eight-Four, right here in Brooklyn. The patrol supervisor over there is an old partner of mine. You remember George Flynn? He set up this ride with Esposito. Carol will get the best deal available. She'll learn the right things from the right people, the way it's supposed to be. But without me around, without me stackin' the deck, she'd be at the mercy of the luck of the draw. You want her riding with some old drunk, some half-assed cowboy, some crooked fuck?"

"No, Joe, of course not. But this is all very far removed from what I want. What I *want* is for you to be retired, what I *want* is for my youngest daughter to still be in college, not starting out as a rookie cop. That's what I want."

Rizzo turned from her and dropped into the recliner. "I know. Me, too. But this is what we have. So let's deal with it."

Jennifer stood silently for a moment, then sat on the arm of the recliner. She placed a gentle hand on Rizzo's shoulder.

"I know, I know. And of course, you're right. You had to stay. It's just . . . I worry. About you. And now about Carol. She's just a kid, barely twenty-one. God knows what effect this job will have on her. Not to mention the physical danger. It's just one big mess."

Rizzo raised his eyes to hers. "It's not so bad. I've been at this for, what? About twenty-eight years? I've never fired a shot, not once. Never even been hurt."

Jennifer frowned. "Except for a broken finger, a bruised spleen, a knife wound, and God knows what else that I never knew about."

"Yeah, and your brother-in-law, the insurance guy, fell down the stairs in his office and herniated two discs. Shit happens, Jen. If it's meant to be, it's meant to be."

"Okay," she said. "But the mental stuff, the psychological stress and incessant negativity. The constant, toxic moral compromises. You can't deny—"

"Jennifer, listen to me: This job can't take Carol anywhere she isn't predisposed to or capable of going on her own. Yeah, if you've got a weakness, this job will find it. Find it and take it to the max. But

Carol is strong, she's a lot tougher than I ever realized. She showed us that with this whole cop thing. She beat us both, and she got what she wanted, what she figured was right for her. Let's give her that. We've got to give her that. Let's not shortchange her, okay?"

The telephone rang. Rizzo reached for it absently, studying his wife's grimly set face.

"Hello?" he said.

"Joe, it's me, Vince."

It was Rizzo's boss, the Sixty-second Precinct Detective Squad commander, Lieutenant Vincent D'Antonio.

"Hey, Vince. What's wrong?"

Rizzo heard D'Antonio's chuckle. "Funny how every time I call a cop, they figure something must be wrong. Well, relax, the world's still spinning. There's just one less scumbag in it. Two, actually. Somebody took out Louie the Chink and his fair-haired boy, Carlo Lentini. Less than an hour ago, over at the Hi-Fi Lounge."

Rizzo sat up straighter. "Tell me."

D'Antonio filled him in. As Rizzo listened, a curious mixture of conflicted emotions ran through him. He had known Quattropa for many years and harbored no misbegotten affections for the hardened gangster. Yet, oddly, something akin to sympathy resonated within him.

"The bad news is," D'Antonio went on, "a citizen went down, too. Richie Maggio, guy that owned the Hi-Fi."

Rizzo sighed. "Sloppy work. And a damn shame. I knew Richie, he was a decent guy. Little bit of a wannabe wiseguy, but an okay guy. I knew his old man, too."

"Yeah, so did I."

Rizzo furrowed his brow. "If the hit was in the Hi-Fi, we're clear here. That's on the west side of Thirteenth Avenue, the Six-Eight, not the Six-Two."

"I know," D'Antonio responded. "But there are complications.

14

Brooklyn South is involved, and the Plaza is sending OCCB and some Major Case guys over. Remember Lombardi? Dominick Lombardi, that lieutenant you fucked over with the Mallard case last year? Well, he's a captain now, with OCCB. He remembered you, knows this is your turf. He wants a local pair of eyes on this, a pair of eyes familiar with the cast of characters. He called me, asked me to have you head over there. I'll be there, too. Lombardi's on his way, and your old buddy, Jimmy Santori, from Brooklyn South. Hell, we'll all be in a bar, four guineas, we can have a few drinks and catch up. Like old frat boys at the reunion."

Rizzo laughed. "Yeah, sounds great." He glanced at his watch. "I can leave in a few minutes, be there in say, fifteen. Okay?"

"Yeah, sure. I'm in my car, almost there now. See you when you show."

Rizzo hung up. He raised his eyes to Jennifer. She sighed and stood, taking her coffee cup and moving toward the door.

"Don't even tell me," she said.

WHEN RIZZO entered the Hi-Fi, a faint odor of cordite touched his nostrils. He gazed across the barroom to the rear double doors. They were open, and Rizzo saw a body just inside the back room, covered with a blue plastic morgue sheet, an ugly red pool of blood surrounding what appeared to be the upper half. As he crossed the room, he wondered whose body it was.

"Maggio," Detective Lieutenant Jimmy Santori said, answering Rizzo's silent thoughts. Rizzo glanced toward the man.

"Hello, Jimmy," he said. "I didn't see you there."

Santori, the supervising field commander of the Brooklyn South Homicide Squad, spread his hands. "Must be fifteen cops in here, Joe. Guess we all look the same."

They shook hands and exchanged small talk. Then Rizzo turned to the business at hand.

"I'm not sure why I'm here. Vince told me an old acquaintance of ours, a captain from OCCB asked for me."

Santori nodded. "Yeah, that's right. Lombardi, Dom Lombardi. He went over to OCCB last year, when he made captain."

"When I last saw him, he was a lieutenant over at Major Case."

"Well, six a one, half dozen of another," Santori said indifferently. "Point is, when a boss like Quattropa gets whacked, Organized Crime Control is always on it. Nothin' ever gets cleared, but they usually figure out who was behind it. *Proving* it, now that's somethin' else."

Rizzo answered with a smile. "All they gotta do is wait and see whose head Frankie Saverese blows off. That'll be the guy that whacked Quattropa."

"Ain't gonna go that easy, brother," Santori said.

"Oh? Why's that? You figure it was Frankie who ordered the hit on Louie?"

"Nope. Frankie Saverese is no longer among the living. 'Bout seven o'clock tonight he was comin' out of his *goumada*'s place over in Sheepshead Bay. Imagine that? Fuckin' guy musta been seventy, he's still got a bimbo on the side. Fuckin' Viagra."

"Somebody whacked him?" Rizzo asked.

"Drive-by. Black car, two white males. And soon as word got out the vic was Saverese, all the witnesses forgot what they said they didn't see in the first place. You know how that goes."

Rizzo nodded. "Yeah, I know how that goes." He looked around the bar. "Where are all the citizens?"

"Couple doors down. We herded 'em over to Tony's. They're in the back with a coupla Six-Eight squad guys."

Tony was a retired police officer who now, in his mid-sixties, owned a small candy store two storefronts south of the Hi-Fi.

"Good idea," Rizzo said. "They must be shook up pretty good."

"Yeah, 'specially Peggy Irish. Richie Maggio was like a big brother to her. She's really freaking out."

Rizzo shook his head. "Sloppy fuckin' work, killin' a citizen. What happened here?"

Santori flipped open his notepad, glancing to it as he responded.

"According to the five guys who were at the bar when the shots went off, not a fuckin' thing happened. They didn't hear nothin', see nothin', or think nothin'. It's a mystery to them how those bodies got there. Musta got hit by lightning."

Rizzo smiled. "And Peggy Irish?"

"She says about seven-fifteen or so, this young couple came in. Male white, six feet, one-eighty, dark hair, black full-length leather coat. Female white, five-five, one-thirty, brown hair cut short, blue jogging suit under a heavy black cloth coat. Both appeared about twenty-five to thirty. They sat over there"—he indicated a corner table cordoned off with yellow crime scene tape—"and ordered vodka, neat. Had two each. Peggy says they were laughing, talking, having a good time. She figured by about eight, nine o'clock tonight, they'd be fuckin' each other's brains out."

"Tell me," Rizzo said.

"Quattropa and Lentini walk in around seven-thirty, seven-forty. They go in the back. Maggio's all decked out, wearin' a suit, kissin' The Chink's ass. He's got the back room closed off, shrimps on ice, good guinea wine chilling and that Sambuca The Chink likes. About eight o'clock, Peggy sees somethin' ain't kosher. The young broad at the table stands, picks up the glasses and napkins from the table and puts them in her bag. She heads for the front door and leaves. The guy heads toward the back. Peggy gets Maggio's attention, then the shots start goin' off. Four or five, according to Peggy. Maggio grabs a knife from behind the bar and goes running into the back like a dumb-ass fuck. Couple more shots, no more Maggio.

Peggy calls nine-one-one and runs over to take a look in the back. The side entrance is open, the shooter gone. Three bodies on the floor. Most gals woulda fainted. Peggy Irish came back out here, didn't let the other witnesses leave." Santori shrugged. "She meant well, but they won't tell us shit. Plus, now that Peggy's had some time to think about it, she's not too sure what she saw, either. Doesn't think she can I.D. the shooter or his girlfriend."

"Well, I don't know if I blame her much."

"No," Santori said. "Not so far as The Chink and Lentini goes. But we lost a citizen here, Joe. That pisses me off. That's what's wrong with this fuckin' country lately. Nobody takes pride in their work anymore."

Rizzo nodded. "Well, taking those glasses and napkins full of their DNA and prints, that's a pretty good work ethic."

"Yeah," Santori said. "And you can bet the CSU guys will find the table and chairs cleaner than Sister Mary Margaret's panties."

"There's a coupla screwy things here, Jimmy," Rizzo said. "Only one shooter for two targets? And a young shooter, not even thirty? And with a female accomplice? Somebody forgot to read the script on this one."

Santori agreed. "My thoughts exactly. Plus, every old goombah hood knows the Hi-Fi is neutral territory, off-limits for this kinda thing. That's the way it's been since I was a kid. It's exactly why The Chink picked it for a sit-down. Whoever this was, Joe, they ain't playing by the rules."

Rizzo thought for only a moment.

"The Russians?" he asked.

Santori shrugged. "Maybe. Or maybe somebody who wants it to look like the Russians. Somebody who could say, 'Hey, it wasn't me. I don't use women, I don't shoot in the Hi-Fi, I'm an old-school goombah.'"

"That could be anybody," Rizzo said.

"Yeah, and Frankie Saverese was next in line. If Quattropa died, Frankie boy would get his time in the sun. But then Saverese gets whacked, too."

Rizzo squinted as he spoke. "There's no clear-cut go-to guy after Saverese. The field is wide open."

Sanatori nodded. "Exactly. But I'm thinking the front runner is that psycho, Mikey Spano."

"The Hammer?"

"The one and only."

Rizzo considered it. "You know, about a year, year and a half ago, there were some rumors. Mikey wasn't too happy with The Chink, mighta been planning to make a move. Nothin' ever came of it, though."

"I hadn't heard anything like that," Santori said. "But Lombardi mentioned it to me tonight."

"Lombardi's here already?"

"Yeah, he's in the back with Vince and the CSU guys."

"Did he have anything to say about Spano?"

"Well, he said the word at OCCB is that Spano was gettin' real palsy with some Russian hood named Oleg Boklov over in Brighton Beach. The Chink was *very* old school—he figured, if you ain't Italian, you ain't in the club. You can earn, you can work, but you kick up and you shut up and you never move up. If that don't suit ya, you go in the river. Mikey, he maybe sees himself as a visionary, the younger generation, lookin' into the diversified future, buildin' bridges. A regular progressive. So, there coulda been some friction. But OCCB figured it was nothin' heavy, not enough to ruffle The Chink's feathers. If Quattropa heard those rumors a year ago, Spano's corpse would be pretty much decomposed by now."

Rizzo turned toward the rear. "Come on and show me the mess. I'm not on the meter. I don't wanna be here all night, there's no overtime in it."

CHAPTER THREE

"SIX-EIGHT'S THE PRECINCT OF JURISDICTION," Captain Dominick Lombardi said. "But they're out of the investigation. Organized Crime Control Bureau will be running this, with me in charge. We'll have support from Brooklyn South Homicide and Major Case resources and personnel, if necessary."

Lombardi, Vince D'Antonio, and Joe Rizzo were seated in D'Antonio's office at the Sixty-second Precinct Detective Squad in the Bath Beach section of Bensonhurst, Brooklyn. It was the morning following the murders of Louis Quattropa, Carlo Lentini, Frank Saverese, and the owner operator of the Hi-Fi Lounge, Richard Maggio.

D'Antonio, seated behind his desk in the cluttered office, responded.

"That's a lot of help, Dom. What do you need with us?"

"Well, I'm comfortable here. Reminds me of old times. Last time we were all together like this, right here in this office, the Mallard case had just broken. And Rizzo here, he was a big star. Remember? There are some people think that whole episode may have cost me a shot at a deputy inspector job over at the Plaza."

Rizzo spoke up. "But of course, Captain, *you* don't feel that way," he said casually. "Otherwise, I don't see us being all buddy-buddy on this Quattropa thing."

Lombardi laughed. "Relax, Joe. I'm not holding any grudges. It went down the way it did, end of story. Besides, I'll still get that job eventually. The way the city's under siege from the feds, I wouldn't be surprised if a few deputies handed in their papers and started running for the Sun Belt. Wouldn't be surprised in the least."

"You referrin' to the little scandal that just broke?" Rizzo asked. "Those federal indictments of the councilman and all those judges? You figure that's gonna work itself into the Plaza, boss?"

"You never know," Lombardi said with exaggerated thoughtfulness. "It just might." He paused for a moment. "That guy at the center of this, the councilman. He's from your neck of the woods, isn't he, Joe?"

"Yeah. Lives a dozen or so blocks from me. I hear he's a real prick."

D'Antonio shot a glance at Rizzo. "Let's stay on topic here, gentlemen. Like I asked, Dom: What do you need from us?"

"Not much. Just a place to hang my hat, desk space, maybe a coupla phones for my guys. A local base. And I'd like to borrow Rizzo for a day or two. Nothin' heavy, just as a familiar face. See, me and Santori are going to have a little chat with Mikey Spano tomorrow. Santori set it up. Spano's starting to look good on this already, and twenty-four hours hasn't even gone by yet. I had a coupla guys check out Spano's whereabouts yesterday and last night, and guess what? He was at his kid's school play from seven to eight-thirty, then out to dinner with the family till about eleven. He's got forty witnesses, at least, most of them upstanding citizens. He didn't kill anybody last night, and he can prove it."

"Very convenient," Rizzo said.

"Isn't it," Lombardi agreed. "What a stroke of luck for him."

"So why exactly are you borrowing Joe?" D'Antonio asked.

"Just as a courtesy to Spano. He may think he's the new breed, but he's just another gangster prick with all the usual bullshit protocols. I want to walk in with a local cop, a *paesan*, show Spano I respect him, I'm not some Manhattan hard-ass looking down my nose at him. It's politics, just bullshit, no different from those photo ops with the president playing with his dog. And to tell you the truth, I really can use a pair of eyes familiar with the local situation." He turned and faced Rizzo. "You knew The Chink. I understand you've done some business with him a few times."

Rizzo felt a flush of anger touch his face. "What?" he asked.

Lombardi held up a hand. "Take it easy, Joe. That was a bad choice of words. What I meant was, Quattropa musta been a resource for you, like all these old ginzo gangsters. Some old lady gets mugged in the neighborhood, they want to help out. Some young mother gets goosed, they'll take an interest, whatever. More politics, more bullshit. That's all I'm referrin' to."

Rizzo sat back in his seat, his anger subsiding. "Yeah. I knew The Chink. And yeah, he helped me clear a few cases. And I know Spano, too. Met him a few times over the years. He runs his crew in Canarsie and Marine Park. I don't get out there much, but I know him."

"So, okay," Lombardi said. "You take a little ride with me and Santori, we all talk to Spano. You know how this always works, Joe. Whoever arranged this hit is now dealing with a major fuckup. A *citizen* got caught up in it. Sure, Maggio was just plain stupid, he shoulda ducked under the bar and put his fingers in his ears instead of running in there like a goddamned fool. But that doesn't excuse what happened. I need Spano to know that. And if he's behind it, he's gotta pay the price."

D'Antonio leaned forward on his desk. "You looking for some payback here, Dom? Some street justice?"

Lombardi shrugged. "I'm just doing my job, that's all."

"And if Spano gets the message and takes out the hit man to make good for Maggio, you can live with it?"

"Sure. If it goes that way, it's not my responsibility. I couldn't give a shit if they all kill each other. But—and I want to be very clear here—that is not my primary intention. It would be interesting, though, wouldn't it? We lean on Spano about Maggio, and then we find a dead hood a few days later? A twenty-something-year-old six-footer with dark hair? A cop might take that to mean that Spano *is* our boy on this."

D'Antonio didn't respond. After a moment, he picked up a pen and made a point of turning to some paperwork on his desk. "Okay, Dom," he said casually. "See Sergeant Calder downstairs, tell her I said to find you a desk or two and a nail to hang your coat on. As to Joe here, it's his call. If you're ordering him, then I guess he's gotta do it. But if you ask him, it's up to him. His call. I'm not getting involved."

Lombardi stood and reached across the desk. He and D'Antonio shook hands.

"Thank you, Vince," he said. "I appreciate your attitude." He turned to Rizzo. "Joe, it's too early for lunch, but let me buy you a cup of coffee somewhere and we'll talk. Okay?"

Rizzo glanced to D'Antonio, saw his gesture of indifference and turned back to Lombardi.

"Sure thing," Rizzo said, standing. "But it'll cost you more than a cup of coffee. I'm not that cheap a date. You wanna fuck me, you gotta at least buy me breakfast first."

"YOU KNOW," Rizzo said as he cut into his ham and eggs, "when I was a kid, maybe twenty-one, twenty-two, I used to hang out at the Hi-Fi. Old man Maggio ran it back then, Richie's father. There was this Six-Two cop we all knew, guy named Monte. He was a real hard-ass. When we were teenagers hangin' around on Fifteenth Avenue makin' too much noise, once in a while somebody would call the cops on us. We were so scared of Monte, he never even had to say a word. The radio car would roll up on the corner, Monte would lower his window and just look at us. We'd start walkin', believe me. One time I saw him throw a nightstick at a guy. It skimmed along the sidewalk, bouncing end to end like it was running after the guy. Caught him in midstride, broke his fuckin' ankle. Monte took his time, walked over to the guy real slow. He picked up his stick, rebelted it, then stomped on the guy's busted ankle." Rizzo shook his head. "Monte. What a piece a work."

Lombardi sipped at his coffee. "What's he got to do with the Hi-Fi?"

Rizzo smiled. "He used to hang out there himself. One night he came in while I was there with a coupla my friends. We hear the bartender tell him, 'I'm so sorry, what a shame, it's terrible,' like that. So later on we ask the guy what happened. He tells us Monte's wife had just died a few days ago. Monte couldn't been more'n thirty, thirty-five at the time. Well, my friend Albee goes over to him, shakes his hand. Monte had smacked Albee around a few times when we were younger, kicked his ass for having some fireworks and once for a half-assed zip gun Albee made that shot pieces of vinyl flooring and razor blades. So Albee sits next to Monte, they start drinking. Now they're both tanked, all buddy-buddy, and Monte starts blubbering a little, talking about his wife. Albee, who was a real asshole, listens for a while, but then he's had enough. So, he leans over and says, 'You're probably better off without her. She was probably just a cunt, anyway.'"

"I bet that went over well," Lombardi said with a smile.

Rizzo laughed. "Yeah, Albee got off real cheap, though. Monte only knocked out two teeth when he jammed his gun into Albee's mouth. Took four of us to drag Monte off, calm him down." Rizzo shook his head. "Fuckin' idiot, Albee."

"See, Joe, see what I mean? You got roots here in this neighborhood. You know the history, warts and all. I can use that with this guy Spano. I wanna nail this prick. I know in my bones he whacked those hoods, he ordered it, and because of him, that poor bastard barkeeper is dead. Did you know Maggio has two kids in college? A wife? Now he's dead. And for what, Joe? So this scumbag Spano can wear the crown till somebody takes *his* ass out? Where does this shit stop?"

"Well, I don't know, Dom. But you're startin' to sound like a man on a mission, and I gotta say, you may be jumpin' the gun a little here. You don't know for sure it was Spano. Maybe in a week or so, if we see guys start kissin' his ring, then we'll have a better idea."

Lombardi shook his head. "It's him, alright. I hear what you're sayin', but it's Spano, Spano in concert with the Russians. He's the only guy in the lineup crazy enough to pull this shit. The feds are all over the Brooklyn mob, they're all on thin ice. If it wasn't for terrorist threats suckin' away their time, the feds woulda nailed Quattropa by now. He'd be in some jail cell instead of the morgue." He shook his head. "I don't know which end is more justice than the other."

"Justice?" Rizzo said, smiling. "You looking for justice, Dom? Go buy some fuckin' comic books."

"Yeah," Lombardi said bitterly. "Tell me about it. You know what I was thinking about when I looked down at Quattropa's body in the back of that bar? You know what was on my mind?"

"No, I guess I don't."

"I was thinking about my old man. My father. That man broke his ass working two jobs for thirty years to put food on the table and a roof over our heads. I got three brothers and four sisters, and we never wanted for one goddamned thing. So we all grew up, went out on our own, and my father finally gets to retire. Two months later, he's got colon cancer. Then he just rots away, dies a horrible fuckin' death. He was only seventy years old, about the same age as that prick Louie Quattropa, that murdering, lying, thieving son of a bitch. The exact opposite of my father. And how's The Chink get to die? In a split fuckin' instant, probably didn't feel a thing. And my old man, all the morphine they pumped into him those last two weeks didn't even help."

Lombardi broke off a piece of toast, stabbed it into his egg, then lifted his eyes to Rizzo's.

"Justice? No, Joe. I'm not looking for justice. I'm looking for some fuckin' revenge."

LATER THAT afternoon, Rizzo was once again seated in the privacy of Vince D'Antonio's office.

"So," D'Antonio said, "you gonna do it?"

"Yeah, I'm gonna do it," Rizzo answered. "What the hell, it's only one or two days, and maybe I owe The Chink that. In his own way, he helped keep a lid on things. There was some stability. God knows what will happen next. A new boss comin' in can get messy. Lombardi wants me to ride with him and Santori tomorrow when they go talk to Spano. He figures it'll ease the tension a little if Spano sees a familiar face. After that, we'll see."

"Maybe," D'Antonio said, unimpressed. "But I think Lombardi's reading this wrong."

"Why, you figure Spano is clear on this? You think it was the Russians actin' independent, or maybe one of the other capos?"

"No, no, Spano looks good to me. I'm just saying there *is* no tension far as Spano is concerned. He set up his alibi nice and neat with his kid's school play. He knew we'd be looking at him. Hell, Spano *wants* us lookin' at him. It gives him street cred with the other capos. Helps him get them in line. Last thing in the world he wants is for another wiseguy to get good press from this."

Rizzo nodded. "Yeah, I guess. And he really doesn't want the other goombahs lookin' at this as a Russian uprisin'. That would bring the whole city, not just Brooklyn, down on the Russkies. There'd be bodies all over the place."

"You know," D'Antonio said with a rueful smile, "I'm not sure who'd come out on top there."

"I hear you. Hollywood better start wrappin' up their wiseguy movies, or at least start castin' them with Boris and Natasha as the romantic leads instead of Rocco and Rosalie."

After a few more minutes of conversation relating to some outstanding Six-Two cases, Rizzo rose to leave. "See you later, boss. I've got some calls to make."

D'Antonio held up a hand, stopping Rizzo in mid-rise.

"Not yet. Sit for a minute. There's somethin' we need to discuss."

Rizzo sat back down, a tight smile forming on his lips. "And what's that, Vince?" he asked, his brows raised.

"I think you know."

Rizzo's smile faded. After a moment, he sighed. "We off the record here?"

"Absolutely."

"It's about Lombardi, right? That crack he made about me and The Chink doing business before."

D'Antonio nodded, remaining silent.

"Could be like he explained, Vince. Just a bad choice of words."

"Could be. But, you know, Lombardi was right: if he had gotten the credit for that Mallard case like he was angling to, he probably would have been paid off with a deputy inspector slot. You got in his way big time with that end run you pulled."

D'Antonio was referring to a case Rizzo and his former partner,

Priscilla Jackson, had solved fifteen months earlier involving the murder of a famous playwright, Avery Mallard. Dominick Lombardi, who at the time was a lieutenant with the Major Case Squad, had been the lead investigator on the high-profile, headline-gathering homicide.

"Yeah, well, shit happens, Vince. He'll just have to get over it. And, you know, he sounded like he already has."

"Maybe," D'Antonio said. "Or maybe not. Maybe after that little incident, he started nosin' around, looking in your closets. I know I.A.D. cleared you on that problem Morelli had a couple of years ago with Quattropa. But they never cleared Morelli. Far as I know, that case is still open."

John Morelli was a retired detective who shared a long history with Rizzo. They attended the Academy together, then served as uniformed partners. After a falling out, they had gone their separate ways, only to be reunited years later in the Sixty-second Precinct. In the interim, Morelli had deteriorated into an alcoholic and notorious gambler. Rumors had surfaced that in return for Quattropa erasing large gambling debts, Morelli had identified a soldier in the Brooklyn mob as an informer for OCCB. The soldier was subsequently found murdered, and when Internal Affairs began an investigation into Detective Morelli they also began looking at his partner, Joe Rizzo. The matter ultimately led to a second and final falling out between the two, and Rizzo had not seen or spoken to Morelli in nearly two years.

Rizzo shifted in his chair. After a few long moments, he spoke carefully.

"I'm clean on that. Hundred percent. I honestly don't know if Morelli gave that guy up or not. And to be truthful, I don't wanna know. I thought I did once, so I asked him. His answer wasn't a good one. He didn't admit to it, but he didn't deny it, either. That's when I walked away from him. End a story."

D'Antonio pursed his lips, considering his own choice of words with equal care.

"I know you, Joe. You might bend a rule here and there, maybe even piss on 'em sometimes. But I don't see you setting up a hit or going deaf and dumb if Morelli had." The lieutenant leaned forward, lowering his voice, his blue eyes steely and cold.

"But that ain't the point here. The point is Lombardi. You better watch him. If he's got a hard-on for you, now's the perfect time for him to make a play. You seem comfortable with the guy, maybe you even like him. He's got your guard down. Don't let him fuck you over. That's all I'm saying."

Rizzo stood, smiling across the desk at D'Antonio.

"Boss," he said, "thanks for the advice. But I haven't gotten fucked over since my old man died when I was nine years old."

Rizzo crossed the room to the door. Opening it, he turned for a last moment and faced D'Antonio.

"And that only happened because there wasn't a goddamned thing I could do about it."

CHAPTER FOUR

IT WAS THE FOLLOWING MORNING, Thursday, March 12, and Carol Rizzo sipped coffee behind the wheel of a blue-and-white. The car sat parked on the west end of Joralemon Street at the southern edge of Brooklyn Heights' Promenade, perched above the busy Brooklyn-Queens Expressway. Sounds of morning rush-hour traffic hummed faintly in the crisp air, and in the distance, across the mouth of the East River, Lower Manhattan glistened in the sunlight.

Carol had recently turned twenty-one. Tall and slim like her mother, her short brown hair more closely resembled that of her father's. Her dark blue patrol uniform was tailored over an athletic yet undeniably female body.

She turned to her training officer, Sergeant Joseph Esposito, thirty-six years old and a ten-year veteran of NYPD.

"So," she asked, "how long have you been a patrol supervisor?"

Esposito replied as he unwrapped the buttered bagel sitting on the impromptu shelf of the open glove compartment door.

"Since I came into the Eight-Four, 'bout two years ago. I came over from the Seven-Five."

"The Seven-Five? East New York?"

"Yeah," Esposito said. "You know it?"

"That was my father's first assignment as a rookie uniform. Back in the stone age."

"Don't let him hear you say that," Esposito said, smiling.

Carol shook her head. "The Seven-Five. That's a rough house. A few of the guys who graduated the Academy with me drew East New York. Guess they didn't have anybody pulling strings for them."

Esposito heard the resentment in her tone. "Is that what you think? That the old man got you assigned to the Eight-Four?"

"Of course. He wants to think he's doing me a favor, easing me in, but it doesn't work that way. You know that, and so should my father."

Esposito sipped coffee, considered it. "Well, I don't know about that. What I do know is he did talk to Flynn, my boss, and Flynn told me I'd be your training officer. At least at first. So your father did make at least one call for you, but as far as the initial assignment, the Academy is tough about that kinda stuff. I doubt your old man could've—"

"Oh, come on, Sarge, cut the shit. I know the whole story. You know my father, you married his old partner's niece. Are you saying you don't think he could get this done? I think, if we're gonna work together, we ought to get off on the right foot. Talk straight with me, Sarge, and I'll do the same."

Esposito nodded. "Okay. I'm telling you, I don't know how you drew the Eight-Four. It's a good house, sure, but it's no country club, kid. Yeah, this particular sector is sweet, right in the Heights. But we cover four very different residential areas, plus the government seat and about six different business sections. We got the Fulton Street strip to deal with, not to mention the Middle Eastern strip on Atlantic Avenue. And we got the municipal building and every one of the city, state, and federal courthouses and everything that goes with them: probation, parole, drug offender programs, all that shit. There are more skells per square yard around the Schermerhorn Street criminal courthouse than anywhere else in the borough. Believe me, Carol, you want some action, you'll get it. So far this week the Eight-Four had nineteen violent felonies and counting. Throw grand larceny and grand larceny auto into the mix, we do about two thousand felonies a year. I can't even guess how many misdemeanors. Then add a coupla lawyers a week strokin' out or havin' a heart attack on Court Street, two or three runs a week to back up the court officers at one of the courthouses, plus the thousands of transients moving through the precinct to and from Manhattan, and you got yourself some interesting tours. Believe me."

"Okay, Sarge, okay. Take it easy. I was just thinking out loud, that's all."

"Yeah, well, don't. Cops who think out loud say the wrong thing too many times. And while we're on the subject of thinkin', here's something to think about. You can forget half the bullshit they taught you in the Academy. The political bullshit, anyway."

"Like what, for instance?"

"Like profiling, for instance. Those freakin' people who get all fascinated by books about body language and Freudian slips and the real meaning behind facial expressions, they're the same people who deny the possibility that maybe, just maybe, an experienced cop can read some signs, too. And sometimes, when a cop sees a twenty-year-old kid with a heavy sag in his pocket, and the kid gets wide-eyed and starts his 'I ain't doin' nothin' walk away, maybe he *does* have a friggin' gun in his pocket. And if the kid happens to be black, maybe it's still just common sense and not racism."

Carol smiled. "I'll keep that in mind."

"Good."

After a moment, Carol finished her coffee and wedged the empty container between the seat and rocker panel.

"Any other tips, Sarge?" she asked.

"Plenty," Esposito answered, nodding. "But for now, I'll just give you the ones you'll need to get through the next few hours. First off, you ain't driving your civvies car here. You get behind some asshole, he looks in the mirror and sees a cop. He gets all nervous, no telling what he's gonna do: swerve out of your way, jam the brakes, whatever. And if you have to go into a store to buy something, I don't care if it's broad daylight or two in the morning, you look before you enter. Never walk into a place in uniform without lookin' first. You stumble blindly into an armed robbery, it's a good way to get killed. And with your gun still holstered. *Never*, and I mean *never*, walk in blind."

Carol smiled. "My father already told me that one."

"Good," Esposito said. "Did he tell you this? The most common ways to get jammed up on this job is, number one, not being *where* you're supposed to be *when* you're supposed to be there, and number two, just tryin' to do your job. The cops that usually get jammed up are the good ones, the active ones, the ones always trying to get the job done. You have to strike a balance. You see some guy smokin' a joint somewhere, you got to consider the possibilities. Are you willing to roll around with this guy, maybe wind up blowing him up? 'Cause if you're not, then just keep ridin'. You never know. You may be thinking 'summons—marijuana use,' and he may be thinking, 'I just threw my old lady into the wood chipper, and this cop knows about it. I better shoot her.' So, remember: when you commit to something, even the most minor bullshit, you're taking a risk. Once you start something, you have to get it done. If things start getting out of hand, you can't just say 'never mind' and walk away."

Before Carol could respond, the radio on the seat crackled to life.

"Dispatch, Eight-Four Charlie sector unit, vehicle on vehicle accident, Court and Atlantic, see the woman."

Esposito picked up the Motorola, keyed it. "Eight-Four sector super, dispatch, advise Charlie sector unit to disregard, this unit will respond."

"Ten-four, supervisor."

Esposito laid the radio down and drained his coffee cup. "Let's go," he said. "This will be your intro to the exciting world of street patrol. You can write up your first pain-in-the-ass accident report."

Carol pulled the car into gear, turning to back out of the dead-end street.

"Okay, Sarge," she said. "You're the boss."

THE YOUNGEST son of a sheepherder, Michele Spano had been born outside the town of Bronte, Sicily.

When he was two years old, his parents, Aldo and Silvia Spano, moved the family to the United States. As he grew up in America, the Italian pronunciation of his name, Mee-Kay-Lee, had evolved into "Mikey." Similarly, his brother Pietro had become Peter, and his sister Fiora, Flora.

When Aldo Spano first reached the United States, he found work as a janitor for a movie theater chain, each day riding buses and subways from one theater to the next, earning the money he needed to feed and house his family in a cramped, two-bedroom apartment in East Flatbush. Eventually, he managed to scrape together enough money to make a down payment on a small frame house in Canarsie.

The oldest Spano boy, Peter, grew up and became a New York City firefighter, eventually retiring as an assistant battalion chief. Then, from his home on Long Island, he began his second career as a licensed public fire adjuster.

The Spano's female child, Flora, first earned a master's degree and then her doctorate in romance languages and served as a full professor in the State University of New York system.

Young Mikey, however, gravitated from a very early age to a darker, more sinister prize offered up by his adopted homeland. By the time he was seventeen years old, Mikey had been disowned by his exasperated and heartbroken father. Despite tearful pleas from Silvia, Aldo banished their youngest child from the Spano household for all time.

Although he remained close to his siblings, Mikey had never again seen or spoken to his father, and only occasionally his mother. When both parents died within a few months of each other, it was only his mother's wake and funeral Mikey chose to attend.

Spano, now forty-four years old, had risen through the Brooklyn ranks of the old Gambino crime family, serving under a series of regime bosses. At a young age, by virtue of his natural ambition and instinctive brutality, he was anointed a capo, the boss of a large crew of associates and soldiers based in the Brooklyn neighborhoods of Canarsie and East Flatbush.

When Mikey was thirty-two, he earned the nickname "Mikey the Hammer," and had been so known ever since. Although nothing could ever be proven, the story was widely known by wiseguys and cops alike.

Spano's older brother, Peter, had fathered two daughters. One of them, a particular favorite of her uncle Mikey, had a bit of a wild streak. One night at age seventeen, she found herself at a drunken, drug-fueled party at an off-campus frat house near Hofstra University. Before the night ended, the girl had been beaten and raped by a college senior. Uncle Mikey did not take the news well.

The alleged rapist was from a solid Long Island family, and he had no prior criminal record. He was quickly arrested, and his distraught parents immediately posted bail. The young man was released.

Late one night the following week, he was leaving his part-time job at the local Home Depot. A black Mercedes pulled alongside him.

The young man's Nissan was found the next morning, still parked in the Home Depot lot, and he was never seen again. Eventually the family managed to have him declared legally dead, and their rather substantial bail was remitted.

His fate, initially known to only a few of Spano's soldiers, eventually made the gossip rounds among underworld characters and various law enforcement officers, Joe Rizzo among them.

After his abduction, the young man was taken to an auto body shop located on Flatlands Avenue and owned by a Spano associate. Once there, he was formally introduced to Mikey Spano.

"You raped my niece," Spano was alleged to have told the man. "You shouldn'ta done that."

Spano then proceeded to beat the man with brass-knuckled fists and, later, an aluminum baseball bat. With the man semiconscious, he was stripped naked. Spano and his crewmen then waited until he had revived sufficiently enough to stand and be fully cognizant of what was about to happen.

The man's hands were tied behind his back, his ankles duct-taped tightly together. Duct tape was also wrapped across his mouth. Then Mikey took up the ball-peen hammer that would bring him a hushed exaltation throughout the dark world of his peers.

Using what he recalled hearing his father refer to as "tenpenny nails," Spano individually nailed each testicle, then the man's penis, to the top of a heavy wooden table while his henchmen held the man standing in place. Once it was done, they released their grips. Mikey sat vigil over the next hours as the man struggled to maintain his footing, the tightly bound ankles the least of his obstacles.

Eventually, blood loss and pain, horror and exhaustion overcame the man. He fell heavily to the floor, a good portion of his genitals remaining affixed to the tabletop.

Mikey Spano, not at all a formally educated man, did possess a certain wealth of practical knowledge. One thing he had learned over the years was that a person who bled to death somehow experienced a sense of great euphoria in their last moments. Spano wasn't quite sure how that could be possible, but he was convinced it was factual information.

So when the man had finally fallen to the floor, blood streaming from his mutilated groin and the various wounds suffered in the beating he had endured, Spano stood, once again taking up the ball-peen hammer.

He used it to ensure that the man's final moments were anything but euphoric.

JOE RIZZO sat in the rear seat of Jimmy Santori's department Ford, Santori at the wheel, Dom Lombardi in the front passenger seat. They had picked Rizzo up at the Six-Two precinct and were now speeding east on the Belt Parkway. It was mid-morning, Thursday, March 12.

"See, the problem is, The Chink never really left a designated successor," Lombardi was saying. "Everyone just assumed it would be his cousin, Saverese. But Saverese was an old fuck, too. There should have been a backup named."

Rizzo spoke up. "The Chink didn't operate like that, Dom. First of all, he thought he would live to be a hundred, then die in his sleep. And he was a selfish bastard. He wouldn't care what happened after he was gone. There was enough money to take care of his wife till she died, more than enough, and his two kids are legit. One of 'em lives in California, the other one upstate someplace. If I know Louie, he figured as long as he didn't name a successor, any of the capos could think someday they had a shot at it. Louie just had to watch his back, make sure nobody got impatient and made a move. He figured they'd just bide their time, then scramble after he was gone, fight it out among themselves. Or Saverese would take over. I don't think Louie really gave a fuck."

Santori sounded in. "Well, if there was a problem between Mikey Hammer and The Chink, and Quattropa had seen it comin', he woulda taken Mikey out first."

"There were rumors," Lombardi said.

"Yeah, well, Louie was a greedy son of a bitch," Rizzo said. "Mikey was always a good earner—he put plenty a dough in Louie's pockets. That coulda blinded the old man a little."

After a few moments of silence, Rizzo spoke again, his tone reflective. "You know, it's kinda ironic. Word had it Quattropa was the shooter on the Joey Gallo hit back in the year of the flood. The old Mustache Petes runnin' things back then were pissed 'cause Gallo was gettin' too close to the black gangsters. Treatin' 'em like equals. Now the word is Mikey Spano's gettin' close to the Russkies. Maybe too fuckin' close from The Chink's point of view. And then maybe Mikey takes him out. Ironic."

Lombardi snorted. "Yeah, well, if we were writin' a fuckin' Greek tragedy here, maybe somebody'd give a damn about that. Otherwise, so fuckin' what?"

Rizzo laughed. "You got to entertain yourself a little here, Cap'n. Lightens the mood."

Santori angled the car toward the exit ramp for Rockaway Parkway and the Pompeii Social Club that served as Spano's base of operations.

"Nothin' lightens the mood more than a sit-down with Spano, Joe," he said bitterly. "Remind me to tell you about some of the corpses this guy's left layin' around for me to look at. He's a regular fuckin' Michelangelo of Mayhem, he is."

Rizzo, finally free of his near lifelong addiction to nicotine, popped two Chiclets into his mouth.

"Yeah," he said. "Michelangelo."

CAROL RIZZO returned to the radio car angled at the curb of the northwest corner intersecting Court Street and Atlantic Avenue, the car's red and white bar lights twinkling. The two vehicles involved in the collision, a red Maxima and a dark blue Ford, sat mashed together at the side of Atlantic Avenue, their drivers, unhurt, standing on the curb. Joey Esposito stood next to them, his arms folded across his chest, talking to the female driver of the Maxima who had called in the accident on her cell.

Carol dropped into the radio car's front passenger seat, leaving the door open. She arranged the two licenses, registrations, and insurance identification cards at the top of her clipboard. Removing an accident report form from the glove compartment, she slid it under the top clip of the board. As she reached for her pen, the radio she had placed on the seat came to life.

"Dispatch, all units, be advised: armed robbery, Seven-Six Precinct, female vic, corner Hoyt and Sackett. Suspect male black, twenty to twenty-five, medium build, dark complexion, blue jacket with unknown sport logo, black pants. Armed with silver handgun, possibly a revolver. Lone suspect fled scene late-model dark blue four-door, possibly a Ford, westbound on Sackett. Use caution, say again, suspect armed with handgun, K."

Carol returned her pen to the holder affixed to her gun belt. She looked through the windshield to the nervous-looking young black man standing next to his wrecked blue Ford. The man appeared to be a year or two older than Carol, and he wore a blue nylon NY Mets windbreaker and black pants.

Carol smiled. She put her clipboard down on the seat.

Under the guise of jotting down the plate number of the red

Maxima, Carol casually stepped behind the young man. She slipped her Glock from its holster. A surprised Esposito saw, stepped back, and reached for his own weapon.

"Hands on your head, now!" Carol barked, thrusting the gun forward in a two-handed combat grip, allowing the man to see her in his peripheral vision. "Gun! Gun!"

The suspect froze, fear replacing nervousness in his eyes. Esposito stepped forward quickly at the sound of Carol's shouted gun warning. He pulled his cuffs from their case and turned the man deftly, shoving him to the fender of the Ford. With a stiff leg, Esposito spread the man's legs wide, leaning him forward. He quickly applied the cuffs. Carol stepped forward, holstered her weapon and reached to the sagging right pocket of the suspect's Windbreaker. She slipped her hand in, extracting the snub-nose Smith & Wesson thirty-two. Her eyes met Esposito's.

"What the fuck, Carol?" the sergeant said.

Carol, suddenly aware of the heavy pounding in her ears, managed a small smile.

"My first accident report, Sarge. My very first one."

CHAPTER FIVE

MIKEY SPANO GREETED THE THREE COPS, motioning for them to take seats at a round, Formica-topped table that stood in the corner of the Pompeii Social Club's cheaply paneled back room. Moments earlier, Rizzo, Lombardi, and Santori had been ushered through the smoke-filled outer barroom by one of Spano's crew, a half dozen milling gangsters eyeing them indifferently.

Once they were seated, Spano beckoned to the only other person in the room, a tall, acned teenager. "Marco, bring the coffee and those pastries from Rispoli's, the ones in the refrigerator. Hurry it up."

The boy crossed quickly toward the small kitchen. "Okay, Mikey, comin' up."

Spano turned his small brown eyes to Captain Dominick Lombardi. He folded his hands on the tabletop and spoke in soft, pleasant tones.

"So, I got a captain, a lieutenant, and a sergeant. What happened to the admiral, he out on his battleship somewheres?"

Lombardi's eyes went hard. "We didn't come here for a stand-up comedy routine, Spano."

Rizzo saw anger flicker across Spano's face. He understood that

41

any pleasantries from Mikey Spano would be superficial and was prepared to undo the damage he suspected Lombardi was about to inflict.

After a slight pause, Spano smiled coldly. "So, what are you sayin'? You telling me you cleared this little chitchat through my lawyers? You saying you got some paper in your pocket says I can't throw the three of you the fuck outa here? Is that how it is, Lombardi?"

Lombardi shook his head. "No. The way it is, we got a right to ask you some questions. Maybe you got a right not to cooperate. Some people—me, for instance—might consider that obstruction. I'd have to talk to the D.A. about it."

Sitting back in his chair, Spano remained silent as Marco returned with a coffeepot and a large tray of assorted Italian pastries.

"Leave it. Then beat it," Spano said.

The boy turned and left, closing the French doors behind him, leaving the four men alone in the room.

Spano turned to Rizzo. "This guy's got shitty manners, Joe. Like a fuckin' immigrant. He came here on *your* ticket, but that don't mean he gets to stay."

Rizzo gave a studied gesture of frustration. He needed to placate Spano, give him his believed due, or the interview would be over.

Rizzo summoned up his street diplomacy. "Look, we're gettin' off on the wrong foot here. Captain Lombardi works outa Manhattan, he don't know how warm and cuddly we are over here in Brooklyn. Why don't we start over?"

After a moment, Spano shrugged. "Yeah. Let's start over." He turned his eyes to Lombardi.

The captain considered it, then let a small smile appear.

"How are the cannolis, Mikey? Any good?"

Spano picked up the coffeepot. He reached across the table and poured for them, speaking as he did so.

"Best in the city. They come from a place out in Bensonhurst, Joe's beat."

They each prepared their coffee and chose pastries, allowing the tension to ease. Rizzo caught Lombardi's eye and gave him a reprimanding twist of the lips. Lombardi shrugged slightly, averting his own eyes. They both knew Lombardi had initially misplayed his hand. Rizzo was grudgingly gratified by the captain's quick reversal.

After some small talk on the upcoming baseball season, Rizzo turned to business. He was careful to bring a practiced respect to his tone.

"So, Mikey. First off, our condolences on Quattropa and Saverese. We know you went back a long ways with them."

Spano nodded, his eyes flat. "Thanks."

Shifting in his chair slightly, Rizzo went on. "Now, don't take this personal, but we gotta get some shit out here. Put it right on your nice clean table."

"I figured," Spano said without emotion. "Say whatever you gotta say. Businesslike."

"See, that's just it," Rizzo said, seeing an opportunity. "Business is one thing. But we got a dead civilian here, Mikey. We lost us a citizen Tuesday night. Richie Maggio."

Spano sipped his coffee before replying. "Yeah, I read about that. It's a shame. But, I gotta say, I'm not too sure how much of a civilian he was. From what I read in the *News,* that joint of his was a hangout. Lots of undesirables in there. Matter a fact, I been in there a few times myself, and I tell ya, Joe, I seen some shady characters hangin' around."

Jimmy Santori joined in. "You mean like Louie and his driver, Lentini?"

Spano nodded. "Yeah. Like Lentini. I read in the paper he was a real tough guy. Gonna be the boss someday, maybe. Imagine that, he was, what? Thirty somethin'? And boss talk already." Spano broke off a piece of pastry and placed it into his mouth. Chewing slowly, he went on. "Musta been a real hard case. But, from what I read, he died same way as anybody else."

Lombardi leaned forward against the table, speaking softly. "Let's start puttin' some of that shit Joe mentioned out on the table now. Here's a theory some of the guys at OCCB have been kicking around. Quattropa was old, set in his ways. He still figures it's the good old days and he's got a clear field. You, on the other hand, maybe you see things a little different. You see these Russians makin' inroads, bringing fresh ideas and a whole lot of new customers with them. So you cozy up a little with this guy Boklov, Oleg Boklov. But you're out on a limb if The Chink decides he's had enough of it. And you know the other capos, they don't want any trouble. It's always easier for them to just go along with the guy on top. So Chink and his heir apparent, Saverese, get taken out. You and Boklov are still standing. You got more muscle and more money. Everybody else takes a look around, figures, what the fuck, Quattropa was an old man anyway. He lived his life. They make peace with you, you work things out with Boklov, and you all live happily ever after."

Spano nodded. "Yeah, I can see that makin' sense. *If* I was some kinda hood, that is. But, you should understand, I'm just a businessman. You know that big wholesale building supply outlet on Staten Island? The one out by Howland Hook? I own that. Hell, we sell material direct to the city contractors. Next time you're takin' a piss over in headquarters, you're probably pissin' into porcelain I sold to P.D. Plus, I own two hardware stores and a used car lot here in Brooklyn, on Flatbush Avenue, all three places. So you tell your buddies over at OCCB they got this all wrong. And tell them I said 'good luck.' I hope they find the son of a bitch killed Louie.

As for Saverese and Lentini, I don't give a fuck. But Quattropa, that was a shame."

Rizzo had been carefully monitoring Spano's demeanor, one of confident disregard for the three cops sitting opposite him. He found it vexing, and he was careful to modulate his tone as he spoke again. "You're forgettin' about Maggio, Mikey. The citizen."

Spano gestured with indifference. "Yeah. Him, too."

Lombardi took the opening. "About that. You can act as casual as you want, but you know same as I do the historical problem we have here. When one hood whacks another, we fill out the forms, ring some doorbells, and file everything away under 'who gives a fuck.' But this here changes things. This poor guy Maggio makes it real. Somebody has to fall for this, Mikey. And if it turns out to be you, everybody can live with that."

Spano ran his eyes across the three cops. He sighed.

"Maybe you should be talkin' to the Russians. Or maybe Tony Barone up in Greenpoint. Him and Quattropa first started pissin' at each other back on the boat comin' over here. Maybe you should be talkin' to Barone."

They sat in silence, picking at the pastries, sipping coffee. Rizzo now sensed some small discomfort dawning in Spano. He resisted an urge to smile. Santori broke the silence.

"We're talkin' to you, Mikey," he said softly.

Spano's eyes went dark. After a moment, he seemed to reach some decision, then responded. "That's a shame about Maggio. Papers said he's got a coupla kids in school. That's a shame." He paused, drained his coffee cup.

"Whoever shot the poor bastard musta been an asshole." Spano stood up, indicating the interview was over. He extended his hand to Lombardi. They shook.

"I hope whoever done it pays the price," Spano said, his voice an emotionless expression.

* * *

ONCE BACK in the car, Rizzo leaned forward and addressed Lombardi and Santori.

"You guys just signed the shooter's death warrant. And the broad that was with him, too. Spano as much as told us with that last remark of his. You might as well kill 'em yourselves."

Lombardi smiled. "It was gonna go like that anyway, Joe. Don't matter what we said or didn't say."

"Yeah," Santori added. "Standard operating procedure in a botched hit. They're probably dead already."

Rizzo sat back, unconvinced. He put Chiclets into his mouth and turned, looking out the window. Santori drove the car away, and they all remained silent.

SITTING ON the bench in Central Booking, Carol Rizzo turned to face Joey Esposito as he approached her.

"All set?" she asked.

"Yeah. He cleared the magnetometer, I locked him up. You gonna be okay with this? The paperwork, drawin' up the complaint with the A.D.A., all of that? You want me to send a guy over to help? I got two uniforms back at the house swattin' flies on light duty. I can send one of them."

"I'm fine," Carol said. "It's just filling out forms. I'm guessing where it says 'name' I put the guy's name, and where it says 'date of birth' I put his date of birth. I think I can manage."

Esposito stood. "Okay. But when you get back to the house, you and me are gonna have a little talk. You fucked this up big time, Carol. I know you're all hopped up, your first collar, and a heavy one, too. But you *ever* pull a gun on a guy without givin' me a heads-up first, without tellin' me what we're dealin' with, father or no father, I'll put my foot right up your ass. Believe me."

He turned and walked away. Carol turned to the forms in her hand.

Damn, she thought.

LATER THAT evening, Rizzo sat having dinner with Jennifer and Carol. The Rizzos' middle daughter, Jessica, had called to say she would be working late. Having graduated from Hunter College, Jessica had utilized her degree in art history to secure a job at the Brooklyn Museum as an assistant to the American art collection curator. The eldest Rizzo daughter, Marie, was currently serving an internship at New York-Presbyterian/Weill Cornell Medical Center, and no longer lived at home.

"Can you believe it?" Carol said happily. "My first day on the job and I lock a guy up for robbery in the first degree. It doesn't get much better than that." With her eyes twinkling, she addressed her father, irony in her tone. "So, what did you do today, Daddy?"

Rizzo winked at her as he replied. "Oh, I had coffee and pastry with some buddies of mine. Very civilized."

Jennifer slammed her utensils down on the kitchen table. "Enough. Let's get this clear from day one: no shop talk at the table. I've been hearing this stuff from your father long enough. I don't need it from both of you."

Rizzo reached out, patting her hand. "It's a deal, Jen. And it's a good idea, too." He turned to Carol. "Something you should keep in mind, kid. You can't live the job twenty-four seven. Let it rest."

Jennifer slipped her hand out from under her husband's and stood, moving toward the refrigerator.

"Please, Joe, stop," she said sharply. "You're still doing it, still talking shop."

Rizzo met Carol's eyes, then turned to his wife.

"Okay, you're right. I'm done."

Jennifer removed the butter dish from the refrigerator and slammed the door closed.

"Good," she said.

LATER, ALONE in the kitchen sipping coffee, Rizzo spoke softly to his daughter.

"Carol, if your mother is going to deal with this, we need to keep things on her terms. Let her pretend you spent the day helping kids cross the street down by the elementary school. In her heart, she'll know it's bullshit, and so will we, but it'll help her get through this."

She sighed. "Okay, Dad. But I'm not going to let her guilt me out about it. I don't want to be walking on eggs every time I'm around her."

"I know what you don't want. But get used to it, 'cause that's what you've got. I been doin' this through most of our marriage, just like every other cop. It comes with the territory."

"Well, maybe I should get my own place. If I don't come home a half hour after my tour ends, she'll be freaking out. I can't live like that."

Rizzo tapped her gently beneath her chin with a crooked finger.

"Relax, honey. No need to get dramatic. Save some money first, get yourself together a little. Then, decide what's best. There's no hurry with anything."

With another sigh, Carol stood up, glancing at the wall clock. "Ten hours ago I was drawing down on an armed felon. Now I'm being treated like Mommy and Daddy's little girl."

Rizzo smiled up at her.

"Just one more thing you better get used to. Because that's never gonna change."

★ ★ ★

"I REALLY don't think I can do this, Joe."

Rizzo turned in the darkness enveloping their bed. He could barely make out the features of Jennifer's face on the pillow beside his.

"You *can* do it," he said softly. "You can do it because you have no choice. We're temporarily out of options here."

"Temporarily? You call the next twenty-five years temporary?"

Rizzo shifted his body on the mattress, bracing himself up on his left arm. "It won't be for that long. She has to do some street time, learn the ropes, learn how to carry herself. For now, I stacked the deck as best I could. She's in a good house with a good training officer, and the patrol commander is watching out for her. That's as good as it gets for now."

"It's not good enough," Jennifer replied bitterly. "There are no good houses. Look at what she did today, her first damn day."

Rizzo stiffened his tone. "Well, it'll have to do. It's all we've got. Listen, I heard from Mike today, he called me at the squad. He just got made off the sergeant's list; he's now a detective-sergeant working the Plaza. Couple more years, he'll get his lieutenant's bars and start runnin' an office or a squad. I stick around till it happens, I keep an eye on Carol, make some calls for her here and there. Then I hand her off to Mike and I ride into the sunset. By then, she'll have had her fill of the streets, it'll be out of her system. When Mike moves to hook her up in some sweet spot, she'll jump at it. Then she'll be okay. Trust me here. I know what I'm doin'."

Rizzo had referred to a former young partner of his, Detective Mike McQueen. After working with Rizzo for a year, McQueen had landed a transfer to One Police Plaza, the headquarters building of NYPD. Circumstances had put the young cop's career on the fast track, and he was very much aware of the instrumental role Joe Rizzo had played in creating those circumstances. McQueen's future now looked unlimited.

Jennifer lay silent in the darkness, pondering it all.

"I know, Joe. I know you're on this. I just . . . I don't know. I just have a bad feeling. I can't help it."

Rizzo dropped his body back onto the mattress and turned away from his wife.

"Well, keep it to yourself," he said, his tone harsher than he had intended. "It's a fuckin' jinx to talk out loud about this shit."

CHAPTER SIX

AS THE DAY tour for Friday the thirteenth began, Detective First Grade Mark Ginsberg sat at his desk in the Sixty-second Precinct squad room, leafing idly through the day's *Daily News*. Ginsberg was forty-two years old and a twenty-year veteran of the NYPD. He had been a detective for eleven of those years, the last five spent in the Six-Two. When his partner George Parker had retired, Ginsberg had been teamed with fellow veteran Joe Rizzo for most of the last ten months.

Ginsberg waved a greeting as he saw Rizzo enter the squad room, then glanced up at the wall clock. It was exactly eight a.m.

Rizzo's morning was spent methodically working the phones and computers, culling through facts and speculations on a half dozen open cases he and Ginsberg were currently focusing on. After the previous day's interview with Spano, Lombardi had bade a casual farewell to Rizzo, mentioning only in passing that he may or may not request further assistance from Rizzo as the Quattropa homicide developed.

At eleven o'clock, the female witness to a street corner assault came into the precinct, and she and Ginsberg retired to the interview room to record her statement while Rizzo carefully read through the precinct situation reports, then the borough and city-wide reports. He learned that a rapist was operating in a near serial manner within the confines of Brooklyn's Sixty-seventh Precinct, and an outbreak of seemingly related burglaries was frustrating the detectives of Manhattan's Ninth Precinct. Citywide, a rash of commercial burglaries continued to occur with increasing regularity, the targets being cigarette jobbers and distribution facilities. Rizzo smiled at that one, wondering how many of the thousands of cartons of cigarettes stolen were his old favorites, Chesterfields.

At twelve-fifteen, with his witness interview concluded, Ginsberg approached Rizzo's desk.

"Up for some lunch, Joe?"

Rizzo looked up from the reports. "Yeah," he said, glancing at the clock. "How'd it go with the witness?"

Ginsberg shrugged. "Okay. Nothing too good, nothin' too bad. The usual."

Rizzo stood and stretched. "What'd ya have in mind for lunch?"

Before Ginsberg could answer, Vince D'Antonio appeared at the open doorway of his office. The lieutenant called to them.

"Hey, guys. Inside, stat. We got a situation."

Once seated in front of D'Antonio's desk, Rizzo spoke.

"Tell us," he said.

"Southwest corner, Eighty-sixth Street and Fourteenth Avenue. Three people waiting at the bus stop. Dark gray Lexus drives by, makes the right onto Fourteenth. Male white, early twenties gets out from the front passenger seat. He opens the rear door, unhooks a child seat, then puts it down on the sidewalk. There's a baby in the seat, maybe six, eight months old. Guy gets back in the car, it pulls away, southbound on Fourteenth."

"Who was driving?" Ginsberg asked.

"Witnesses were maybe forty, fifty feet away, and only one of 'em actually saw the entire incident. But it was a female driver."

"Who's there now?" Rizzo asked.

"Just uniforms. I got radio calls out to Dellosso, Schoenfeld, and Rossi. When they clear, they'll head over there. I need you guys there asap. Soon as I can get a uniform boss to babysit the squad room, I'll come over myself."

Ginsberg and Rizzo stood. "Okay, boss," Rizzo said. "We're on it."

Once at the location, Rizzo parked the black Ford at the Eighty-sixth Street bus stop behind three blue-and-whites. The two detectives crossed the sidewalk and approached uniform sergeant Wendall Tyler. Ginsberg let his partner take the lead. "Tell me," Rizzo said.

The sergeant, his ebony face glistening with perspiration in the unusually warm, humid March air, looked grim. He quickly filled them in.

"Did you secure the car seat, Wendall?"

"Sure. But at least two or three civilians were pawing at it, plus the first cops on the scene. And the kid was covered with a pink blanket hanging over the sides of the seat. I'd be damned surprised if they can lift a good print."

"Shit," Rizzo said.

"Damnest thing, Joe," Wendall continued. "But we mighta got lucky one way."

He jerked a thumb over his shoulder to a radio car parked on Fourteenth Avenue. "Young girl in that blue-and-white saw the guy dump the kid. She ran over there, on her cell at the time, and she snapped a picture of the Lexus. It was pretty far away by then, you can't read the plate." Tyler reached into his pants pocket, extracting a clear plastic evidence bag containing the cell phone. Rizzo took it.

"Get me a young cop, Wendall. Somebody good with this tech shit."

Tyler glanced around. "Hey, Dugan. Come over here."

53

Todd Dugan, a twenty-five-year-old Sixty-second Precinct patrol officer, walked over. "Yeah, Sarge?" he asked, nodding a greeting to Rizzo and Ginsberg.

Rizzo responded for Tyler. "Do me a favor, Dugan, take a look at this phone. There's a picture on it, a picture of the car dumped that kid. Show it to me. Should be the last shot in there."

Dugan removed the phone from the bag and examined it briefly. He punched at some buttons, then turned the phone around to face the detectives.

Rizzo and Ginsberg bent down. In the bright sunlight of the day, the camera had barely caught the rear of the Lexus as it moved southbound on Fourteenth Avenue. The car was so far away that only the color was identifiable. The plate appeared small, hardly recognizable as a New York license.

"Can you blow this thing up?" Tyler asked the cop.

He shook his head. "Not on that phone, no. But if I jack it into a computer with a USB cable I can."

Rizzo looked diagonally across the street to the sprawling funeral home on the far corner.

"Listen, kid," he said. "Take it over to that funeral parlor, they gotta have a computer in there. Is it likely they'd have a whatever-the-fuck cable? The one you need?"

Dugan nodded. "Yeah, they should have a USB cable, unless they got some stone-age freakin' piece a crap computer system."

Ginsberg spoke. "Come on, Dugan," he said. "Let's go. We're gonna commandeer their computer. You need to blow up that shot, get a make on the plate, then print out a hard copy. Can you do that?"

Dugan shrugged, a slight look of incredulousness on his face. "Of course. My six-year-old niece can do it."

Ginsberg took the phone from the young officer and dropped it back into the evidence bag. "Let's go."

A gray Ford rolled up and double-parked at the bus stop. Detectives Morris Schoenfeld and Nick Rossi, long-time Six-Two squad partners, climbed from the car and approached Rizzo. He and Sergeant Tyler ran it down for them.

"Where's the baby?" Schoenfeld asked Tyler.

"Back room of the real estate office across the street. I got a female uniform and some EMTs with her. We're waitin' on child services to show."

"And the other witnesses?" Rizzo asked. "Vince told me there were three people at the bus stop."

Tyler nodded. "There were. There's five witnesses now, countin' the kid that's sittin' in the blue-and-white. I got the other four in the real estate office, too. Owner's being real cooperative. I don't see 'im gettin' too many parkin' tickets in the near future."

Rizzo nodded. "Do me a favor, Mo," he said to Schoenfeld. "Can you and Nick talk to the witnesses? Dellosso is on his way, by himself, I think, and maybe Vince. I'll send Dellosso over to help when he shows. Me and Tyler will talk to the kid in the car."

Schoenfeld nodded. "You got it." He and Rossi moved away.

"Come introduce me to the kid, Wendall."

"Sure. But just so's you know, she was a little freaked out by all this. Can't be more'n fifteen."

Once seated in the radio car, introductions were made.

"Sara, this is Sergeant Joe Rizzo. He's a detective. Sergeant Rizzo, this is Sara Dalene. She's the young lady who had the presence of mind to snap that picture."

Rizzo smiled across the seat back from the front passenger side of the car. "That was pretty smart, Sara. That's really gonna help us out." He paused for a moment, leaving the smile on his lips. "How old are you?"

The girl, light-haired, freckled, responded in a small voice. Rizzo could hear the tension in her tone. "I was just fifteen in January."

"Okay," Rizzo said. "Tell me what happened, Sara. What you saw."

She hesitated. "How is the baby?"

Tyler, from the driver's side front seat, replied. "She's good. The EMTs checked her out, she hasn't been hurt, she's in good shape. Somebody been takin' good care of that child. Don't worry about the baby. She's fine."

Rizzo's smile began to fade. "Sara, listen to me. The faster we get to work here, the better off everyone will be. I need you to tell me what you saw." He softened his face, smiled again. "I know it's Friday the thirteenth, so we're havin' a little bad luck here. It's nothing we can't fix, though. But we need your help."

The girl bobbed her head. Rizzo saw resolve enter her eyes. She glanced at Tyler's face. The cop smiled at her. "My own girl is just about your age."

She looked back to Rizzo.

"Tell me," he said gently.

"Well, I was waiting for the bus. I was going to my grand-parents' house to feed their cat. They're on a trip. I was talking on my cell to my friend, Tina. I was looking this way, toward where we're parked here. I saw this shiny new Lexus pull up. It was gray, the same color as my uncle's. The car stopped and a guy got out. He opened the back door and put the baby on the sidewalk, in the car seat. The baby was crying or I would have thought it was a doll. The guy got back in the car. I told Tina what was happening, and I started going toward the baby. I was like, 'Oh my God, oh my God.' I saw the car driving away." Here, a sheepish look came over the girl. "To tell you the truth, it was Tina's idea."

"What was?"

Sara hesitated. "To take the picture. She was screaming, 'Take a picture, take a picture!' First I thought she meant of the baby,

56

then I finally got it. By that time, the car was almost down by Benson Avenue."

Rizzo reached into the backseat, patted the girl's arm. "You did just fine, Sara. And so did your friend, Tina. You guys make a good pair."

"Tell Sergeant Rizzo about the driver," Tyler said. "Like you told me."

"Well, it was a woman, and she was crying, too. She was older than the guy that got out of the car. Like, my mother's age."

Rizzo smiled. "That old, eh? What did she look like?"

"She had dark hair and she was crying. That's all I remember."

"What about the guy? Tell me about him."

Sara shrugged. "He was just a guy."

"You said he was younger than the woman. How old you figure he was?"

She thought for a moment. "Like about, like my brother. My brother Henry. Like, maybe around twenty."

"Can you tell me what he looked like?"

Another shrug. "He was pretty nasty-looking. Dirty. He had torn jeans and a raggedy old black T-shirt. His hair was blond, greasy like, and it was like standing up on his head. He looked like one of those old rock 'n' roll guys, the ones my aunt Camille likes. Punky, she calls them."

Rizzo nodded. He looked to Tyler. "Wendall?"

Tyler turned to the girl. "Sara, if we show you some pictures, do you think you'd recognize him?"

She cocked her head. "Well, I guess it depends on the pictures."

Rizzo chuckled. "Good answer." He ran a hand through his hair, thinking, then caught sight of Ginsberg and Dugan coming down the front steps of the funeral home.

"Excuse me a minute, Sara. Stay here with Sergeant Tyler. If you think of anything else, tell him."

With a nod of her head, the young girl spoke tentatively.

"Can I have my phone back?" she asked.

"Absolutely. As soon as possible. You can call Tina and tell her all about this. And thank her for us, too."

Rizzo joined Ginsberg and Dugan on the sidewalk behind the blue-and-white.

"Tell me," he said.

Ginsberg extended his arm. "The whiz kid here got us a good blowup." He handed a color hard copy to Rizzo. "Plate's as clear as day. I called it in, Vince ran it. Lexus GS. Comes back to a Linda Davis, twenty-six Harbor Lane, right off Shore Road in Bay Ridge."

"The high-rent district."

"Yeah, big bucks. Nothin' but mansions around there."

"Reported stolen?"

"No. Not yet. Vince ran the owner's name, no reports of her missing, nothin' unusual. He's tracking down next of kin now, trying to get us somebody to talk to and he'll get Legal to arrange an E-ZPass alert, see if the vehicle crosses a bridge somewhere."

"Any more info on this Davis woman?"

Ginsberg consulted his notes. "According to DMV records, five-ten, black hair, blue eyes, one-thirty, no glasses, thirty-two years old. Criminal run name and DOB comes back clean, no record. Vince is pokin' around some more, says for you to run things over here for now."

"We gotta APB that vehicle and check to see if it's GPS equipped, try to get a track on it."

"Done. We can figure maybe the car was headed down Fourteenth to the Belt Parkway. Coulda gone east, coulda gone west. It's a big fuckin' city."

"Or the car could still be local," Rizzo said.

Ginsberg shook his head. "I don't know what the fuck we're dealin' with here, Joe. Maybe postpartum stuff, or maybe some real evil shit. But whatever it is, if it was me, I'm not dumping the kid anywhere near the place I intend to ultimately wind up. That's why I say it's the Belt. I mentioned that to Vince, so he was going to scramble the highway patrol units, get all the blue-and-whites out on the Parkway. We could get lucky. What'd the eyeball say? The kid."

Rizzo filled him in. Ginsberg pursed his lips. "Sounds like a forcible abduction. Maybe a psycho brother or cousin of the Davis broad? Maybe some whacko carjack scenario?"

"Yes, yes, and yes. Could be any damn thing. We need to find Davis's husband or whoever. And we need to locate that car fast. If this is a jackin', she may turn up with her throat cut real soon."

Ginsberg nodded. "Thirty two, five-ten, one-thirty, black hair, blue eyes, and a pocket full of money—wouldn't surprise me if she's a looker. The skell coulda dumped the kid so he could rape mama in peace."

Rizzo glanced to the radio car and the young witness. "Stay on top of Vince. We need somebody to talk to. And do me a favor, Mark. I got Mo and Nick in the real estate office workin' the other eyeballs. See if they got anything to add yet. I'm gonna talk to the kid again. Maybe this wannabe rock 'n' roll asshole had a tattoo or something we can run through the computers."

"Okay."

As Rizzo turned back to the radio car, he glanced at Todd Dugan, the young uniformed cop. "Thanks, kid. You done good. I appreciate it."

The young officer beamed. "Piece a cake, Sarge. Glad to do it."

BACK AT the Six-Two squad room later that afternoon, all available detectives and uniformed officers gathered statements from the five witnesses and worked the computers and telephones. Sara Dalene's ashen-faced mother arrived, relieved to see that, yes, the police had told her the truth. Her daughter had not been harmed.

Vince D'Antonio, utilizing a reverse telephone directory, had contacted neighbors of the Davis woman. They, in turn, had provided the Wall Street work location of Jon Davis, the woman's husband. A blue-and-white raced, lights flashing, siren blaring, from Manhattan's First Precinct to deliver the man to the Six-Two.

Brooklyn Borough Command, acting on the assumption that an abduction had occurred, dispatched two police artists. Working with the witnesses, a computerized composite drawing was slowly developed. They then tapped into the computer's data banks searching for potential mugshot matches to the composite. The infant's car seat proved negative for useful fingerprints.

Rizzo and Ginsberg hastily gobbled down sandwiches in an interview room while discussing the case.

"If it's a kidnapping for ransom, this perp is some asshole," Rizzo said. "As soon as he dumped that kid, he tipped his hand. He can't contact Davis and make demands, he's gotta know the cops are already involved."

Ginsberg's face was grimly set. "I got a bad feeling here. This broad is already dead."

Rizzo finished his sandwich, washing the last of it, untasted, down his throat with a swig of cold coffee.

"Shake it off, Mark. Stay focused. If she is already dead, we can't change shit. But if she's still breathin', we gotta find her."

Ginsberg nodded. "Yeah."

The door opened. It was Detective Robert Dellosso, Bobby Dee to the squad.

"They found the car, guys."

Rizzo stood. "Body?"

Dellosso shook his head. "Not yet. Just the car. It was abandoned way the fuck out where the Mill Creek empties into Dead Horse Inlet. In the Six-One."

"Out by Plum Beach?" Rizzo asked.

"Yeah, just northeast of there, in the middle of nowhere. On one a them dirt roads running through the wetlands near Gateway National Park. Matter a fact, it was the federal park police found it. They notified the Six-One squad."

"Let's go," Ginsberg said.

"Bobby, tell Vince to get a forensic team out there," Rizzo said, gulping the last of his coffee.

"He already did. The Six-One has a radio car on the south side of the Belt, right near where the dirt road accesses the woods over there. Just drive east on the Belt, maybe a quarter mile passed Plum Beach. Look for the Six-One blue-and-white. Vince said he'll meet you out there when he can."

Ginsberg drove, Rizzo working his cell phone. The Six-One detective squad commander filled him in. The Lexus GS had been found partially burned, its paint blistered and cracked, but the car had never fully engulfed.

"The perp must have thrown some accelerant onto it, possibly gasoline, then lit it up. Guess the guy figured it'd go up in flames, but the gas just burned off and that was it. The interior never ignited. I got a feeling we ain't dealing with a criminal mastermind here," the commander concluded.

Ginsberg listened as Rizzo filled him in. "That could be a break, Joe. If the perp torched the car, he probably figured he left forensics behind and he wanted it destroyed. If that interior is intact, we got a shot at recovering something."

"Yeah," Rizzo said, punching another number into his cell. "The park police and the Six-One cops are searching the surrounding area for a body. But I'm thinking, if the perp whacked her, he'd a probably just left the body in the car. If he raped her first, he figures his DNA goes up in smoke. This woman might still be breathin'."

Ginsberg nodded. "What I'd like to know is, where'd they go? That area is desolate, basically a fuckin' wilderness. I read one time that when commercial photographers want to take pictures of an exotic location without spending any airfare, that's the place they shoot, near Plum Beach. Some parts of Dead Horse Inlet could pass for the African Serengeti."

Rizzo held up a hand to silence Ginsberg, his call having been answered on the second ring.

"Vince? It's me. Listen, somebody's gotta get on the horn to EMS. We're losin' light out here, by six o'clock it'll be dark. We need some floodlights around that Lexus."

D'Antonio responded. "Not a problem, Joe. The park police at the scene are federal. They got more equipment than they know what to do with. The C.O. out at Gateway made a few calls. It's done already. I'm leaving soon, I'll meet you out there."

"Any new developments? How's the woman's husband look?"

"He looks clean to me, or else he deserves a fuckin' Academy Award for best frantic performance in a starring role. The guy is really freaking out. . . . And on top of that, he's some hotshot investment banker. He's been pacing around the squad room on his cell phone calling in favors. I got two calls from the Plaza already. I'm waiting to hear from the fuckin' White House next. And the guy's wife isn't answering her cell phone. Verizon can't give us a location, either it's turned off or the perp disabled it."

Rizzo interjected. "Did anybody I.D. the last outgoing calls made from that phone?"

"I didn't just start this job yesterday, Joe," D'Antonio responded with annoyance in his tone. "We checked them and her husband

I.D.'d them. All familiar numbers, nobody the perp would have called."

Rizzo ignored the lieutenant's anger. "What was her schedule this morning?"

"The husband told me she had an appointment with the baby's pediatrician at noon. Doctor's office is in Park Slope, Ninth Street and Seventh Avenue. Before that, she was gonna run some errands. The baby was dropped at Fourteenth Avenue about noon, so it's unlikely she ever made it to the doctor, but I called the Seven-Eight squad. They'll check it out for us."

"Anything else?"

"The husband tells me there are no assholes running around the family, no nutty neighbors, no stalkers in the bushes. He hasn't gotten any call, no ransom demand, nothing. This is shaping up like a random act of stupidity."

Rizzo frowned, glancing at Ginsberg. "Random acts of stupidity are the toughest, Vince. No motive, no logic, no trail to sniff at."

Rizzo heard the frustration in D'Antonio's reply. "We'll see." The line went dead in Rizzo's ear.

As they rounded a sweeping left curve of the Belt Parkway, Plum Beach now to their right, the flashing light bar of the blue-and-white on the grassy shoulder came sharply into view. Ginsberg reached down, switching on the strobes of the Ford's grille lights and angled the car toward the shoulder. The door of the blue-and-white opened, and a young female cop stepped out into the rapidly darkening late afternoon.

She was just about Carol's age, Rizzo thought. Maybe a couple of years older.

He flipped open his cell once more. It was getting late, Jennifer would be wondering why he wasn't home yet. He needed to explain to her that it was very likely he wouldn't be home at all tonight.

CHAPTER SEVEN

DENISE MILLER, thirty-one years old and known around the neighborhood as Dirty Denise, reached out and smacked her latest boyfriend in the face.

"You goddamned stupid fuck," she hissed. "You stupid, stupid fuck!"

Kevin King, twenty-five, stumbled back a step. The PCP that had raged so demandingly in his brain for most of the past two days was finally easing its grip, and the situation was gradually becoming clearer.

"Shit," he said.

Denise ran a hand through her greasy brown hair. "And me no better. I shoulda left you out there in those fuckin' weeds, you and that rich bitch. What was I thinkin'?" She shook her head in amazement. "What the fuck was I thinkin'?"

Kevin stepped closer to her, reaching out a hand and placing it gently on her shoulder.

"You was just tryin' to help me out, honey, doin' right by me. I'da been screwed without you, baby."

Denise felt her anger begin to subside. She looked into the watery, bloodshot eyes of her man and saw what she thought to be sincerity. Of all the losers she had shared a bed with, this one, she believed, was different. She finally had one who was sincere.

And so, when Kevin called for help, she had taken the half gallon of gasoline from the shed out back and gotten into her battered, twelve-year-old Dodge. She had driven to the isolated dirt road near Plum Beach and met up with King.

Although he told her he had wiped the car clean of his prints, he wanted to burn it—just to be safe. Denise helped King torch the Lexus, then she drove him and the terrified rich woman back here, to her four-room one-bedroom hovel which she had recently offered as home to young Kevin King.

The abducted woman, tied hand and foot, duct tape securing her mouth, now sat on the floor in the cabin's small disheveled and darkened bedroom. She had been sobbing softly, her eyes wide with terror, when Denise had checked on her some minutes earlier.

Denise managed a small smile.

"Okay, baby," she said to King. "Okay, I'm glad I could be there for you. But, Jesus, what the fuck made you do this? What were you *thinking* about?"

Kevin King shook his head with his answer. "Damned if I know, Denise, damned if I know. It just seemed so *right* at the time, so fuckin' *smart*. Last night I brought Eddie's car back. We got to hangin' out a little, then he took out that goddamned angel dust and we started smokin' it. Next thing I remember, I'm out on the street in Bay Ridge, near that candy store Eddie lives over, by the parkin' lot on Fifth Avenue over there. I see this broad come outa the lot with her shiny new Lexus. See, Eddie, he was supposed to drive me home after I brought his car back, but somethin' happened, I don't remember what. I think the fuckin' battery went dead or some shit like that. I don't know how I wound up by the parking lot, honey, I swear, but, like I say, me and Eddie, we were blowin' on those PCP reefers all fuckin' night. It's his goddamned fault, that asshole, givin' me that shit. He knows it fucks me up, he shoulda never given it to me."

Denise stepped closer, putting her arms around Kevin and hugging him. "He ain't a real friend, fuckin' with you like that."

Kevin returned the hug and nestled his face into the crook of her neck. "Yeah, baby, you're right. You're always right."

After a moment, Kevin went on.

"I just got in her car, right in the front seat. I pulled my knife on her, told her to drive me home. But . . . I . . . I couldn't remember where I lived. So we drove around and around, her gettin' crazier and crazier by the minute. I swear I felt like bustin' her fuckin' mouth for her. I had a real bad headache and she was makin' it a lot worse. I felt like bustin' her fuckin' mouth."

Denise patted his back gently. "Poor baby," she said.

Kevin stiffened. "Oh, shit," he said.

Stepping back from him, Denise raised an eyebrow.

"What, Kevin? What's wrong?"

"There *was* a baby. *Her* fuckin' baby. I forgot all about that. The baby started crying, my headache and all . . . I made her pull over, shut the car off. I took the keys and got out. I think I dumped the kid there. See, by then I remembered where I lived, we were headed for the Belt, everything was gonna be okay, but then that fuckin' kid started wailing and the bitch started screamin' 'bout don't hurt the kid. So I left it on the sidewalk. By the park, I think."

Denise released Kevin and stepped farther back.

"Holy fuckin' shit," she said.

CHAPTER EIGHT

RIZZO AND GINSBERG stood beside the Lexus. A musty and pungent odor from the recent fire filled the rapidly cooling evening air. The entire scene was floodlit with United States Park Police equipment. A team of NYPD crime scene unit detectives were methodically examining the interior of the car and its surrounding area.

Captain Hal Woodside, the U.S. Park Police commanding officer for the detachment assigned to Gateway National Park, spoke to Joe Rizzo.

"The interior of the vehicle is pristine. Flames never touched it. Whoever torched the car didn't use enough accelerant."

Ginsberg sniffed at the air. "Smells like gasoline."

"Probably. But not enough. There's a pretty stiff wind coming in from the ocean, and it probably blew out the flames once the gas burned off. I figure the perp was attempting to destroy any prints he mighta left. Should be a slam dunk to I.D. this guy."

Rizzo nodded. "Yeah. Should be. What about these tire tracks, Cap'n?"

The three cops turned their attention to the soft, moist dirt and grass surrounding the car and then to the muddy dirt lane running northward away from the Lexus.

"Those multiple fat tracks, those must be ours from the four-by-fours we patrol in. Those other coupla sets off by the trees, they look old, dried out. Most likely kids. Lots of lovers' lane and party activity takes place around here after dark. Then you can see the Lexus tracks clear enough. These others, the ones that lead right up alongside the car, then go off along the road northbound? Those are interesting. Could be our perp called for somebody to meet him here, or maybe had it set up in advance. He put the woman in the accomplice's car, then torched the Lexus and off they went."

"Where's that road lead to, Captain?" Ginsberg asked.

"Hooks around in a semicircle, breaks out onto the south shoulder of the eastbound lanes of the parkway. It's the same road you came in on, just one big loop through the woods."

"Our guys check those tracks yet?" Rizzo asked.

"First thing they did. Photos and casts taken of all of them, even the ones we figure to be ours. Detective Winston, the black guy over there by the four-by-four, he did it. Says the wear pattern on the tracks next to the Lexus is very distinct, wheels all out of alignment. He says it'll be a piece of cake to match it up to the suspect's vehicle."

"First we gotta find one," Rizzo said.

"Well, yeah, let's hope for a print hit."

With that, a CSU investigator climbed from the front of the Lexus and approached the three cops.

"I'm Simpson, CSU. Who are the new guys, Captain?"

Introductions were made.

"This is my show till my lieutenant gets here," Rizzo said to the man. Then, indicating the two clear evidence bags the cop held, added, "Tell me."

"This here is a parking garage receipt for a municipal lot up on Eighty-sixth Street and Fifth Avenue, in your neck of the woods. It shows the Lexus entered the lot at ten-seventeen hours, exited eleven-eleven hours. Fifty-four minutes. It's dated today, this morning."

"What's that?" Ginsberg asked, indicating the second bag. Detective Simpson responded. "This is hair. I found it on the front passenger seat, nowhere else in the vehicle. Stood out clear as day against that gray leather."

Rizzo's eyes lit up. "If it's the perps, we got his DNA."

Simpson pursed his lips. "Well, Sarge, unless it was Mister-fuckin'-Ed or Flicker snatched the dame, this ain't gonna help us. This is horse hair."

Rizzo reached out, taking the bag. He and Ginsberg examined it.

"Howda you know that?" Rizzo asked.

The man shrugged. "Very distinctive stuff. Soft, but put it on its end, it'll stand up. Like straw. They make fancy shoe brushes outa this stuff. It's got a certain feel to it. I worked a homicide scene at Aqueduct maybe two years ago. Vic had this shit all over the lower part of his jeans, down around the inner calf. He'd been ridin' in those jeans quite a bit."

Rizzo took out his cell, punched the number of the Six-Two squad. He was surprised when the precinct commander, Captain Douglas Klupful, answered.

"Captain? It's Rizzo."

"What you got, Joe?"

"I'm at the scene. I need somebody to check out the municipal lot up on Fifth Avenue and Eighty-sixth, that indoor garage on the corner. Our vic had her gray Lexus GS in there this morning, ten-seventeen to eleven-eleven. We need a canvass and interviews with the lot attendants, store owners across the street, anybody coulda seen somethin'. Maybe she got jacked inside the lot or somewhere nearby."

"I'm on it. What else?"

"Check with the husband. I need to know if they ride horses, or if anyone they know who was recently in that Lexus rides. CSU found some horse hair in the car, passenger seat only. Coulda been left by the perp."

"Okay. We put out a regional hospital/morgue alert for the woman. Her husband's back home waiting on a possible ransom call from the perp. Vince sent Dellosso and two uniforms with him. Taps and wires are on the phone. The feds were notified. They'll monitor, come in if any ransom demand is made."

"If this is a carjackin', Captain, they can come in right now."

"I know that. They said they'd monitor. Carjackers keep the car, they don't try to burn it. The feds know we're all over this; Vince doesn't want them busting in and breaking our momentum. And neither do I."

"Okay."

"Has Vince shown out there yet?"

"No."

"Okay, Joe, it stays your show until he does. I'll get back to you asap on that parkin' lot and the horse hair. Anything else?"

"Yeah. The composite sketch got faxed regionally. Can you get the Queens cops to run it out to Acqueduct and Nassau P.D. to check at Belmont? Maybe the perp works the stables at one of the tracks."

"That'll best be done in the morning when the majority of workers start to come in, but we can try it now. Anything else?"

"Not yet, Cap. But there will be."

"Yeah. I hear you." The connection went dead.

Rizzo filled Ginsberg in, then turned back to Simpson.

"What about prints?"

Simpson looked grim. "Print guy is tryin'. But from the way the dust was all smeared on the passenger side dash, it looks to me like a wipe down. We'll see."

70

"Any cigarette butts in or around the car?" Ginsberg asked. "Chewin' gum, maybe?"

"Don't you wish. Not a fuckin' thing."

Vince D'Antonio arrived a few moments later. As they updated one another, Rizzo's cell phone rang. It was Detective Dellosso, calling from the home of Jon and Linda Davis.

"No horses in the picture," Bobby Dee said. "The husband can't imagine how that hair got there. Must be the perp's."

"Fuckin' cowboy, this guy," Rizzo said, bitterly addressing no one in particular as he closed the phone. He glanced around, saw a uniformed officer from the precinct which covered the location, the Sixty-first.

"Hey, guy," Rizzo called. "Let me ask you something."

The cop, a brawny, hard-faced man of about forty walked over. His eyes were watery, his bulbous nose crisscrossed with broken capillaries. He appeared hung over.

"What?" he said.

"This your sector? This area over here?"

"Sometimes. Why?"

"Well, I'm from over in the Six-Two," Rizzo said. "I don't know this turf too good. Tell me: if a local resident was into horses, any particular place he might frequent? I know there's a stable around here somewhere, a ridin' academy. One of my daughters used to go there years ago. Is it still here?"

"You mean the Gateway Ridin' Academy? The one offa the Belt in Bergen Beach, about a mile from here?"

"Yeah, that sounds like it. You familiar with it?"

"No. That's the Six-Three over there, not the Six-One. You need anything else?"

"Yeah, I do," Rizzo answered, anger touching his tone. "But I think I'll go ask a *cop*. Maybe I can find one around here somewheres."

Rizzo shouldered past the man, who glanced without expression at Ginsberg and D'Antonio, then shrugged slightly and walked away.

After conferring with detectives from the host Six-One precinct and Captain Woodside, Rizzo returned to D'Antonio and Ginsberg.

"I'm thinkin' here, Vince, we may be dealing with a local; a guy familiar with the area. Our perp knew about this road, and so did the buddy who picked him up. CSU guy just told me it looks like at least three people got into the getaway car, and casts were made of the footprints in that soft dirt. Woodside tells me a lot of horseback riding is done in this area. So, if the perps *are* local boys, what else we got? One of 'em leaves horse hair around—that points to this Gateway Academy, the only one anywhere near here. There's a possibility this spike-haired blond perp's been there, or maybe even boards a horse there. It gives us a place to start."

A grim-faced CSU detective approached. "Don't look good, guys. The fire ruined the exterior. Prints all over the interior, but none on the front passenger side. It was wiped down. We'll run the prints we lifted, but I'm bettin' they come back just the owner and her family. Looks like this asshole got careful for at least part of this little fuckup. He wiped down *and* tried to torch the car. I'll run the prints and let you know, but like I say, it doesn't look promisin'."

"Okay," D'Antonio said, handing the man his card. "Thanks."

Rizzo glanced at his Timex. It was seven forty-five. The woods around them had turned dark, the artificial glare from the floodlights not reaching around the eerie perimeter. The hum and buzz coming from nearby Belt Parkway traffic seemed oddly out of place. A brisk wind blew in from the Atlantic Ocean, a strong sea smell biting at the nostrils. After the unusual heat of the day, the new colder air seemed particularly harsh, raw. Rizzo shivered against it, buttoning his lightweight sport jacket and turning up its collar. A fleeting memory of the familiar Chesterfields he had long used crossed his mind. He shook the thought away.

Rizzo reached for his phone, obtained the number for the Gateway Riding Academy. The answering machine message told him they were sorry, but their hours on Fridays were ten a.m. to six p.m. and to please call back tomorrow morning at nine.

Rizzo turned his eyes to D'Antonio. "You know the number of the Six-Three, Vince? You, Mark?"

Neither did. Rizzo called information again and had himself connected. The Sixty-third Precinct desk transferred him to the detective squad. Rizzo quickly ran down his situation.

"Yeah," the Six-Three detective said. "That academy's been there thirty, forty years, probably. Family-run, I think."

"I need their emergency contact info. I gotta talk to somebody from the place asap."

"Yeah, let me put you on hold, I'll get it."

Less than a minute later, the cop was back on the line. "We got three contacts on file; primary, secondary, and the last one, the lawyer for the place."

"Give me all three."

In just moments, Rizzo was on the line with James Wilshire, owner-operator of the Gateway Riding Academy.

"Is everything all right, Detective?" the man asked. "Has there been a break-in? Oh, God, not a fire?"

"No, nothing like that, Mr. Wilshire." Rizzo gave the man a brief run-down, quickly getting to the point.

"Are you a hands-on owner, sir? Spend a lot of time at the business?"

The man chuckled. "Detective, sometimes I feel like I was born there. I took it over from my father, as my son will from me. I'm there ten, sometimes twelve hours a day, six or seven days a week."

"Okay, sir, then you're the man I need to talk to. We're looking for a white male, early-to-late twenties, about five-nine, dirty-looking guy with blond hair cut short in a spike style. Does any of that sound familiar, sir? One of your customers, maybe, a rider or a guy who boards a horse with you?"

The man's sigh came through the line. "Winky-Dink," the man said.

"What?"

"I don't know how old you are, Detective, but I'm sixty-seven. When I was very young, there was a cartoon character on TV named Winky-Dink. He had a star-shaped head, appearing very much like spikes. So that's what I nicknamed young Kevin. Winky-Dink. I must say, I'm not surprised to have the police calling about him. Is it drug-related? That's why I had to let him go, you see. The boy was a terrible drug abuser."

Rizzo raised his eyes to Ginsberg and winked. "Tell me," he said, smiling in the cold night air.

THIRTY MINUTES later, Rizzo and Ginsberg left the majestic home of James Wilshire, the second generation owner of the Gateway Riding Academy and Livery. The home stood in a tiny enclave of Mill Basin and backed up to the West Mill Basin inlet. The two detectives had noticed a good-size boat moored at the pier behind the house.

Wilshire, although not overly impressed with the likeness of the composite drawing Ginsberg had shown him, felt confident that it could be the recently fired employee of Gateway, Kevin King.

The three men rode silently to the nearby academy complex where Wilshire then disabled the alarm, allowing them to enter the rear office. Before beginning his search, he notified the night attendant of their presence. The academy boarded a large number of privately owned horses in addition to their own stock. The facility was manned twenty-four hours a day, every day of the year.

Rizzo and Ginsberg rummaged through the scant employee file Wilshire provided. Other than basic pedigree information such as Social Security number and date of birth, it wasn't much help. No relatives or emergency contacts were listed. Kevin King had lost his apartment some six months prior and been allowed to live on the Gateway premises for the last two months of his employment there. When the night manager had reported King's drug usage to Wilshire, the proprietor immediately terminated Kevin, along with his living arrangements.

"The last I saw of him was about two weeks ago, when he came to get Pal Joey. I had let him leave the horse here until he could make other arrangements."

"He owned a horse?" Rizzo asked.

"Yes. I believe it was a retired quarter horse from Belmont, or maybe it was Aqueduct. It was a reasonably stout gray stallion, past its prime perhaps, but still impressive."

"You say he picked it up?" Ginsberg asked.

"Yes, a week or so after I fired him, he showed up here with a young lady, although 'lady' may be a bit of a stretch. She was a dirty-looking, foul-mouthed little thing—suitable for Kevin, I suppose. They took the horse, and I haven't seen or heard from him since."

"How'd they take it?" Rizzo asked. "They ride it away?"

Wilshire smiled. "No. The young lady had some broken-down horse trailer hooked to her old car. They loaded Pal Joey and off they went." Wilshire shook his head at the memory. "I regret not going with my instincts, there."

"Which were?" Rizzo asked.

"Well, I was concerned for the welfare of the animal. God knows what they'd do with him. I was tempted to make an offer to buy him. He'd see some enjoyable years here as a mount for my young novices."

"So why didn't you?" Ginsberg questioned.

The man pursed his lips and appeared annoyed with himself. "Frankly, I was afraid to. Afraid Pal Joey would prove a magnet for Kevin, bring him back around Gateway. I wasn't comfortable with that idea. Actually, I was never comfortable with him in general. It was my son who hired Kevin. My son is a bit of a soft touch, an unfortunate liability in any business, especially one revolving around horses in New York City." Here the man smiled, looking from one cop to the other.

"You see, Brooklyn isn't a place which immediately springs to mind at the mention of horses. There are a number of horse lovers in Brooklyn, but let's just say some of them are a bit . . . peculiar. Yes, that's the word. Peculiar."

LINDA DAVIS sat on the floor in the pitch blackness of the tiny, malodorous room, rough ropes binding her wrists and ankles, chafing her skin raw. She was growing more and more desperate, wondering where her baby was, what had become of her. She wondered what her husband must think, what state he must be in. She had no idea what time it was or where on God's earth she was. And suddenly, with surprising ease, she made a decision that would normally have been unthinkable for her: she relaxed her painful, bloated bladder and urinated heavily into her silk panties and two-hundred-dollar Lucky Jeans.

As overwhelming physical relief washed over her, the warm wetness in her crotch devastated whatever last mental reserve she had managed to maintain. She broke into a shattering, sobbing hysteria, her gasps smothered behind the tightly wound duct tape covering her mouth. Her last conscious thought before falling into a blessed faint was of her beautiful little baby girl, whom she now believed, in the deepest recess of her heart, she would never see again.

★ ★ ★

MARK GINSBERG sat behind a borrowed desk in the Sixty-first Precinct detective squad room. He was on the phone with Vince D'Antonio. It was after nine p.m., and except for black coffee he hadn't had any sustenance since the hastily consumed sandwich so many hours earlier.

Ginsberg listened as D'Antonio gave him the latest news.

"King's last-known address from his rap sheet was a bust. Ex-landlord had no info on his whereabouts since he threw the guy out six, seven months ago. No leads to anybody, no family, no girl-friend, nothing. We found no listing for a telephone, no landline, no cell on record. This guy is shaping up like a ghost. I've got cops working the neighborhood looking for a lead. The canvass at the parking lot was also a dead end. The guys even managed to speak to the attendant who was on duty at eleven this morning. She didn't see anything unusual, had no memory of any particular Lexus. The prints lifted from the car are all accounted for: They belong to both Davises, Jon Davis's mother, and a friend of Linda Davis. The hair is definitely horse hair, and it's from two separate ani-mals. None of the witnesses have I.D.'d a mug shot yet."

"What about the tire tracks at the scene?" Ginsberg asked.

"The large ones match the make and model of the four-by-fours used by the park police. They're working to get a match on specific police vehicles to rule out a million-to-one shot the perp's buddy drove the same make and model the cops do. The dried out tracks near the woods are documented, origin unknown. Mixed brands, two Goodyears, one foreign, possibly Pirelli or Toyo. CSU is sure the worn set they casted right next to the Lexus belongs to our bad guy. You find a car, CSU tells me they can match it, abso-fuckin'-lutely. We just got to find the car."

"Workin' on it, boss. It doesn't belong to King. DMV has no rec-ord of him owning a car. He's got a New York driver's license listed at his former address."

"Yeah. I'll put out a national DMV search. Probably come back with a thousand Kevin Kings, but we'll cross check them with DOB and Social Security number. What's going on at your end, Mark?"

"Joe's on the horn. He's checkin' all the stables in the city to see if this nag Pal Joey's boarded anyplace by King. According to Wilshire, the trailer King and the unknown broad took the horse away in was red and white, very old. The car was old, too. Blue or black, maybe dark gray. Possibly a Chrysler product, maybe GM. No fuckin' help."

"Hold on a minute, Mark, I got Rossi on the other line."

A few moments elapsed, then D'Antonio came back on the phone. He was not happy. "Another fuckin' dead end. When we ran King's name through CIB, we found his three priors, all for CPCS. Two PCP, one cocaine. His last arrest was in the One-Oh-Four out in Queens. We checked the booking paperwork, specifically the call he made outa the precinct the night he got locked up. It was to some girl out in Springfield Gardens, an ex-girlfriend. Rossi just told me she hasn't seen King in almost a year. No idea where he is, and hopes he drops dead. Rossi went in heavy, with ESU and local backup, hopin' to find the Davis woman tied up in a closet. But it was a complete bust."

"What about the other two arrests, boss? Any calls on those?"

"First arrest, no call. Second and third both to this girl in Springfield Gardens."

"Fuck," Ginsberg said.

"Yeah, fuck, Mark. It's gonna be some miracle if we find this Linda Davis alive. She was probably dead two hours after she got snatched. Hell, it'll be a fuckin' miracle if we ever find this asshole, Kevin King."

Ginsberg heard a thud and looked up. Joe Rizzo had slammed down the phone receiver in mid-dial. His face was animated, his eyes bright. He stood, looking intently across the room at his partner.

A small smile came to Ginsberg's face. "Miracles do happen, Vince. In fact, I think I'm watchin' the Red Sea begin to part right now . . ."

"THIS IS what happens when I don't eat all day," Rizzo said. "I get stupid."

He and Ginsberg were in the black Ford, Rizzo at the wheel. They once again sped eastbound on the Belt Parkway, this time their destination the Seventy-fifth Precinct in the East New York section of Brooklyn. The late-Friday-night traffic was moderate, and Rizzo held the unmarked Ford steadily between seventy and eighty miles an hour, the grille lights flashing red and white, the siren piercing the air.

"I'm tellin' ya, Mark, if I had a plate of pasta and a few meatballs under my belt, I'da made the connection hours ago. Look at what we got here. A violent fucked-up PCP hop-head loser runnin' around in the middle of Brooklyn with a fuckin' horse and no money. It's so fuckin' obvious that if King wound up killin' this woman *after* we found out about the goddamned horse involvement, *I'm* as responsible for her death as he is. I swear, if that's what happened here, I'll find a way to kill this motherfucker before this is over, I fuckin' swear."

"Take it easy, Joe. Don't give me more info than I can convincingly lie to the Grand Jury about. Just relax. And watch where the fuck you're goin', you're drivin' like some rookie asshole who's seen too many movies. Slow the fuck down."

Rizzo held his speed as a blue minivan moved out of his way in the left-hand lane.

"I'll slow the fuck down when this is done."

CHAPTER NINE

WITHIN THE AREA OF BROOKLYN known as East New York, there exists a small subsection known to locals simply as "The Hole." This unique enclave of less than ten acres had been farmland before devolving into a vast dumping ground. Gradually it developed into a haven for working poor who shared an unlikely urban passion—horses. Among its few dozen shacks and converted trailers lived about forty horses housed communally or in individual backyard makeshift barns. The streets were narrow, mostly unpaved and usually submerged in stagnant, dirty water. The entire area nestled against a large expanse of project buildings, the effect giving The Hole an almost surreal, canyonlike ambiance. Its residents included a mix of races, creeds, and temperaments, their sole unifying trait a love for horses. Most lived in frontierlike austerity, isolation, and independence. And despite the common bond inbued by horseflesh, most remained standoffish and indifferent to one another, everyone tending to mind their own business.

As a rookie police officer decades earlier, Joe Rizzo's first assignment had been to the high-crime Seventy-fifth Precinct. His training officer, an ambitionless cop by the name of Sonny Carusso, had introduced young Rizzo to The Hole. "You'll never work this sector much, Joe," Carusso said as he slowly inched the old radio car along a battered and muddy stretch of Dumont Avenue. "But you gotta be familiar with it, so we drew it for our next four tours. I hope you don't mind the stink a horses."

Rizzo looked around, not quite believing what he was seeing. "Man, this is unreal. I've lived in Brooklyn since I was nine years old, I never even hearda this place."

Carusso nodded. "You won't find a hundred Brooklynites outside of East New York who have. But it's been here forever, and my money says it *stays* forever. It's a fuckin' swamp, basically. A swamp with horses and weirdos. Look around, you ever see anything like it? I never been down to Appalachia, but I bet it looks same as this."

Rizzo had been fascinated. Behind most of the widely spaced, beaten and weathered shacks stood small barnlike structures. Some were simply combined backyard sheds, others converted horse trailers, and they housed bright-eyed, lively looking horses. As the radio car rolled passed Eldert Lane, a magnificent black gelding with a diamond of white on its forehead trotted majestically by, a young woman in tattered clothing astride the animal.

"That is one beautiful horse," young Rizzo observed.

"Yeah," Carusso agreed. "Most of 'em are like that. These people around here, they live on beer nuts and cigarettes, but they always manage to come up with feed money. And they groom these animals, too. Look at the shine on that one. Fuckin' beautiful. Looks a hell of a lot better than the broad ridin' it." Carusso shook his head sadly. "That horse is perfect for the role nature gave it. Because nature itself is damn near perfect."

He turned and met Rizzo's eyes.

"Biggest mistake nature ever made was man," Carusso said. "Lettin' mankind get the upper hand with everything. That's what fucked it all up, kid."

After a few more moments, Rizzo spoke. "Why did you say I won't see much of this sector?"

Carusso grinned with his answer. "'Cause we got plenty of cops just as crazy as the people that live here. They *want* to ride this sector. They request it. We got guys in the Seven-Five rotating steady tours through here. Only time you'll have to do it is when somebody bangs out sick or goes annual leave and you come up on the wheel. Once in a blue fuckin' moon, and more likely never."

And now, so many years later, Rizzo sat before the shift commander's desk in the Seventy-fifth Precinct, shaking his head at the still vivid memory of Sonny Carusso.

"This all came back to me while I was callin' around the city to commercial stables. I just forgot all about working those coupla tours in The Hole so long ago. Once I heard this guy King owned a horse and didn't have two nickels in his hand, I shoulda put two and two together right then. Where else *could* the son of a bitch be?"

Roy Collins, the precinct shift commander, nodded. "Well, The Hole hasn't changed much. Gotten a little bit smaller, maybe. The city condemned some of the worst shacks, knocked them down. Then the guy next door would just expand his own turf, like a squatter."

"And you don't know of any spike-haired blond guy out there?" Ginsberg said to the lieutenant.

Collins shook his head. "No. Like the rest of the precinct, it's mixed. Predominantly African American and Hispanic, with West Indians and Caucasians rounding it off. I haven't been out there more than four, five times in the five years I've been working the Seven-Five. Most radio runs out there are for intox, once in a while a fight, domestic stuff, mostly lightweight. We had a horse theft about six months ago. That was the biggest thing."

"This guy Kevin King was rooming at the Gateway Academy up until about a month ago as part of his employment package. After he got the boot, he left his horse there for a while, then picked it up about two weeks ago. Some broad helped him. He may be very new to the area." Rizzo repeated the description of the woman Wilshire had provided, including vehicle and trailer information. Collins shrugged.

"Like I say, I don't get out there much. But that female's description, I gotta tell ya, Joe, could be any one of the white women out there. Aren't too many of them debutantes, if you know what I mean."

A knock sounded on the door, and a young uniformed sergeant entered the office. He held the composite drawing of the suspected kidnapper in his hand and returned it to Rizzo.

"Sorry. I showed it around. None of the guys here can I.D. it or ever heard of Kevin King. I'm callin' in the sector cars now, we can show it to the guys on patrol, see if they can make him. But your best bet is to talk to Perez and his partner, Tyson. They work The Hole steady, they like it out there."

"Yeah," Rizzo said. "I remember there were guys like that even way back when. Where are Perez and Tyson now?"

The sergeant shrugged, glancing at the wall clock. "Well, it's almost ten o'clock, they worked a day tour today and are scheduled for one tomorrow. They're married guys, got kids. I'd say they're probably at home."

The shift commander opened his desk drawer, removed the precinct directory, and reached for the telephone.

Officer Geraldo Perez listened as Rizzo filled him in and described the composite sketch. The man's voice sounded clearly through the speakerphone.

"You know, Sarge, there's been a new white boy out there last coupla weeks. And he's got blond spiked hair, too. Could be your guy. I've seen him riding a good-looking gray stallion. Keeps it in the double shed behind Dirty Denise's place." The man chuckled. "If he's her new live-in squeeze, you better move fast, Sarge. Dirty

Denise changes her men a whole lot faster than she changes her underwear."

Ginsberg, excitement pushing his fatigue away, spoke into the speakerphone. "What's her address, Perez?" he asked.

There was a pause. "I don't know the number, guy. But it's the broken-down white shack, mid–four hundred block on the west side of Opal Street."

"Is there a trailer there?" Rizzo asked. "A horse trailer at the address?"

"Yeah. Matter a fact, 'bout a month ago, I tagged it. Expired reggy. I guess it belongs to Denise."

"What color is it?"

"Red, I think. Yeah, red and white. The top of it's white. At least, the part that isn't rusted."

Rizzo exchanged glances with Ginsberg, then turned back to the phone. "Does this Dirty Denise have a car? And a last name?"

"I only know her first name. But she's got a car, old black Plymouth, maybe a Dodge. Parks it next to the horse shed. She's got a nice size patch of ground, maybe seventy-five by a hundred. Plus the lots on each side are vacant. North side lot is just an empty mud hole people dump junk into. The south side lot had an abandoned cabin on it, but the city knocked it down about a year ago. You can't miss Denise's place, Sarge. Picture *Little House on the Prairie*, horror-movie style."

"Where you live, Perez?" Rizzo asked.

"Brentwood. Out in Suffolk County."

Rizzo frowned. "Take you, what?, an hour to get here?"

"If I keep my foot down, forty-five minutes."

"What about your partner, Tyson?"

"He's farther away than me."

"No good. Too long. We'll have to I.D. this place without you."

"Whatever you want, Sarge. You tell me."

"Thanks, Perez. Go to bed. Do your tour tomorrow. Thank you, you've been a big help."

"Okay, Sarge. Good luck." The connection was broken.

Rizzo stood. "How many detectives you got upstairs?" he asked Collins.

"If nobody's out in the field, four."

"We need to get up there, Lieutenant. I'll need some extra hands on this."

Collins stood.

"Let's go," he said.

KEVIN KING drew deeply on the hash pipe, holding in its harsh smoke and then passing the pipe to Dirty Denise. The Valium she gave him had taken some of the edge off his PCP hangover, and he hoped the hashish would do the rest. He slowly let remnants of smoke leak from his mouth and leaned closer to Denise. They sat on a worn couch in the cramped front room of the cabin. His eyes were mere slits in the dimness of the room.

"We got to do it, Denise," he said softly. "What else can we do? She can make me to the cops, make you, too. And probably lead 'em right here. What choice we got? We torched the car, the cops got shit, no prints, no nothin'. I used my prepaid to call you, not her cell. Without her, the cops'll never find us."

Denise, despite her fear, felt an odd stirring of excitement. Kevin *needed* her, really needed her, even more than Wendy, her roan mare, needed her. Beautiful, graceful, magnificent Wendy. But this . . . this felt different. This was Kevin. This was a *person*. And he *needed her*.

"I don't know, Kevin. I'm scared . . . *kill* her? I . . . I don't know."

He nestled her breasts, taking the hash pipe from her hand. "Yeah, baby," he purred. "Sure you do. We can do it at midnight, that'll be so cool, won't it, baby? At midnight, like in those spooky movies you like. Then we can wrap her up in some garbage bags and that old rug out in the shed. We'll take her to Queens, to the wetlands by the airport, and we'll dump her there. It'll be fine, baby. Trust me."

He took another hit on the pipe and smiled at her.

"This is *real*, baby, what we got together is *real*. I don't wanna fuck this up. *Please*, don't make me have to fuck this up. I *love* you, Denise. We can get married, we can live here forever. Just you and me and Pal Joey and Wendy, together *forever*."

He smiled at her again, raising the pipe to her mouth.

"Please, baby. I *love* you."

U.S. POSTAL Inspector Hank Larson listened from the other end of the phone as Rizzo explained the situation.

"Whatdya need me to do, Sarge?" he asked.

"I need you to find an addressee for me. Female, first name Denise, four hundred block of Opal Street."

"Where the fuck is Opal Street?"

Rizzo shook his head, angry with himself. He'd been working for over fourteen hours straight and had consumed nothing but black coffee since early that afternoon. He was not thinking clearly.

"I'm sorry. It's in Brooklyn, East New York. Right by the Queens border."

"Give me a minute, I'm at a computer . . . hold on."

Rizzo could hear the man tapping the keyboard. As he waited, he eyed the second hand sweeping around the face of the Seven-Five squad room's wall clock. It seemed to be moving much too quickly. Rizzo shook his head clear again and looked away from the clock.

"I've got it, Sarge," Larson said. "Four hundred block. Four-four-six Opal Street. There are only three other delivery addresses

on that block. Denise Miller is her name. The house is between Dumont Avenue and Linden Boulevard."

"Inspector, you enjoy the rest of your night. You may have just
saved a life. Or if not, maybe you helped us catch a murderer."

"Well, let's hope you save her, Sarge."

"Yeah. Let's hope." Rizzo hung up, waited a second for a dial
tone, then punched in the Six-Two squad number.

"D'Antonio, Six-Two detectives."

"Vince? It's me . . ."

THE COPS were now gathered in the second-floor detective squad
room of the Seventy-fifth Precinct. D'Antonio shook his head an-
grily at Lieutenant Roy Collins.

"I don't give a fuck *whose* precinct it is, this is *my* fuckin' case.
I'll call the shots."

Collins replied in an equally harsh tone. "You're not kickin' in
some citizen's door on my watch. We get the fuckin' warrant first.
End of story."

Rizzo glanced at his Timex. "It's eleven o'clock, we don't have
time for this. The law is clear here. We have reasonable cause to
believe a dangerously violent felon is holed up in that house. The
tax record search shows only Denise Miller on the deed. It's not
King's residence. We have reasonable cause to believe King has an
accomplice, but we don't know who it is. Let's assume it's some
whacked-out angel dust asshole buddy of his and not Dirty Denise.
That means we may have *two* women in serious and imminent
danger: Davis *and* Miller. That mandates us to act fast *and* hard.
Even the chief ball-breaker at the ACLU would agree, especially if
one of those women was *his* daughter or *his* wife. We don't have
time to run down to night court and convince some half-drunk
judge to sign a fuckin' warrant."

"Rizzo is one hundred percent correct, Collins," D'Antonio

said. "We're taking that house now. You get me some uniforms, stat."

"When we get the *warrant,* I'll get the *uniforms.* It's *my* fuckin' precinct."

"Hey, Collins," Ginsberg said. "I bet you did real good on the part of the lieutenants' test that asked, 'How much red tape bullshit does it take to make one asshole a boss?'"

Collins turned, moving toward the seated Ginsberg, who quickly rose and stepped forward. Rizzo pushed in front of his partner and held out a blocking hand to Collins's chest.

"Knock this shit off, guys," he said. "We're all tired, we're all pissed. Let's remember who the enemy is."

Collins, his face flushed, addressed Ginsberg. "We'll finish this later, Ginsberg."

Mark shrugged. "Just remember to leave your rank on the desk."

D'Antonio pulled his cell phone and punched at the speed dial. Captain Klupful answered on the first ring. D'Antonio filled him in, then a tight smile came to his lips and he held the phone out to the still red-faced Collins.

"My captain wants to speak to you."

Collins took the cell, his eyes still on Mark Ginsberg. "Collins, Seven-Five."

Klupful, known at the Six-Two for being succinct, spoke.

"Fuck the warrant, Collins. Give D'Antonio as many uniforms as he needs and hit that fuckin' house. I'll take responsibility for whatever goes down. *That* is an *order.*"

Collins averted his eyes from Ginsberg, glancing first to Rizzo, then D'Antonio.

"Yes, sir."

"YOU KNOW, Joe, I think we're stretchin' this a little," D'Antonio said as he, Ginsberg, and Rizzo climbed into the black Ford.

"Klupful is under the gun because the vic's husband has political juice."

Rizzo nodded. "I know, boss. The criminal check on this Miller dame shows five priors—three drugs, two assaults. Odds are she's the co-conspirator and in her own legal residence. But we don't know anything for sure, and besides, we're out of fuckin' time. With no ransom demand after nearly twelve hours, this Davis woman is either dead already or about to become dead. If there's any chance left here, we gotta move fast. Let the fuckin' lawyers work it out tomorrow."

"Yeah," Ginsberg said to D'Antonio. "And thank God you've still got the balls you were born with. Sometimes they snip 'em off when they hand a guy those gold bars."

"Yeah," D'Antonio said, hooking his shoulder belt. "Sometimes."

RIZZO, GINSBERG, and D'Antonio stood huddled in the darkness of Dumont Avenue, one block west of Opal Street. This particular stretch of Dumont was narrow, barely wide enough to accommodate two-way traffic. The asphalt was badly broken, with long, muddy expanses. Low spots held pools of stagnant water. Lighting was sparse, and Rizzo had noted the complete lack of streetlights and sidewalks on each narrow lane crossing Dumont. The moon was obscured behind cloud cover, making this night the darkest Rizzo had ever seen within city boundaries. The faint hum of traffic from Linden Boulevard was the only sound heard.

The few cabins and shacks along the avenue where the police and their vehicles stood were mostly darkened, and it was difficult to distinguish the inhabited ones from the abandoned. Horse manure lined the roadside, its pungent odor permeating the air.

Lieutenant Collins approached the three Six-Two cops.

"Okay," he said. "I had one of my plainclothes guys take a walk down Opal. He made the house. There's no way we can drive down there without tipping our hand. The fuckin' street is nothin' more than a dirt lane, only wide enough for one car at a time. We'll have to wade through all this horseshit and mud, just walk over there."

"Good thing none of us are wearing our fancy Italian loafers," Rizzo said. "Did your guy see any activity at the house?"

"No. He said there's a small light on in the front room and the shade is up a little, maybe six inches. If we get into the yard, we can take a look inside, see what we got."

"What's our current body count?" D'Antonio asked.

"I got four uniforms and two plainclothes street-crime cops, plus the four of us."

"Should be more than enough to hit the place *and* cover the back and sides," Ginsberg offered.

Collins pointedly ignored him, addressing D'Antonio. "I think we need to get EMS down here before we make a move. They have the equipment; all we have is one half-assed mini-ram that might not be heavy enough to take the front door."

Rizzo shook his head. "Bullshit, boss. Take a look at these places: give me a hammer and a screwdriver, I can knock a whole shack down in fifteen minutes. I say we go right now." He depressed a button to illuminate the face of his Timex. "It's almost eleven forty-five. Let's wrap this up while it's still Friday."

Collins looked grim. "I say we wait."

They looked to D'Antonio. After a moment, he shrugged.

"Let's do it. By the time EMS gets here, somebody's gonna notice all of us standing around. Word may spread; we can spook King. Let's just fuckin' do it."

Collins raised his hands, palms outward. "Fine, long as you're on record with that. If this was my show, I'd have a warrant *and* EMS. Just so we're clear."

"Don't worry, boss," Ginsberg said. "We'll write you a note to give the teacher."

Even in the darkness of the night, Collins's flush was visible. "I told you, Ginsberg . . . later."

D'Antonio shot an angry glance at Ginsberg. "Knock it the fuck off, Mark, or get back in the car and sit this out. I got enough goin' on, I don't need this adolescent shit. So just knock it off."

Ginsberg smiled. "Sure, boss. No problem."

Now Rizzo had a thought. "I got an idea." He addressed Collins. "Can you get Perez on the horn again? Ask him if he knows the name of any of Dirty Denise's neighbors. A name and a rough description of the person: age, race, accent, anything like that."

"Why?"

"I'm thinkin', maybe we all sneak up on the house, then one guy just knocks on the door. He says, 'Hey, Denise, it's me. Crazy Dexter from across the street. Open up, there's a problem with your horse. Open up.' We watch through that front window. If somebody inside looks out and sees us, then it's just, 'Fuck it, use the ram.' But if they get distracted, scared for the horses, maybe they'll get sloppy and open the door."

Collins seemed unconvinced. "What about your theory that Miller is a hostage same as Davis? What about that?"

Rizzo shrugged. "Yeah, well, King has his horse out back, too. So *he'll* open the door. It's worth a shot."

D'Antonio looked to Collins. "Make the phone call, Roy. It could work."

Four minutes later, Collins closed his cell. "There's an old black man everybody calls Willie the Shoe. He's about eighty years old, lives down at the south end of Opal. Perez says he's seen the guy talking to Denise a few times."

Rizzo looked around, saw a black plainclothesman. He approached the man.

"How are you at impersonations, guy? Think you can do the voice of an old black man . . . ?"

OPAL STREET was even narrower than Dumont, just remnants of a one-lane blacktop, now mostly mud and weeds. With no streetlights, the eerie glow from Linden Boulevard far to the south was the nearest illumination.

Four forty-six Opal Street stood mid-block on the west shoulder, set back some thirty feet from the roadway. The small, battered shack was surrounded on each side by vacant lots, the north lot strewn with rusting appliances, old tires, and discarded household furnishings; the south lot a tangled mass of dead or dying vegetation. The shack's host lot was equally overrun, appearing more like an abandoned property than an occupied residence.

To the rear of the shack, some forty feet away, stood a large, shedlike structure closed against the cold night air, surrounded by a split-rail fence enclosing the paddock area. In contrast to the rest of the property, the shed and paddock were well maintained, appearing almost pristine within the general shoddy environment.

Next to the shed, a horse trailer and old Dodge were parked, their colors unidentifiable in the near total blackness.

Joe Rizzo, snub-nose Colt revolver gripped in his two hands, crouched in the mud and weeds beneath the dimly lit front window of the shack. He raised his head cautiously and peered in. Kevin King and Denise Miller sat cuddling and giggling on the couch, drug paraphernalia spread out on a low table before them. The room was cluttered, disheveled, quite small. Rizzo lowered his head and looked to the small front porch with its three rickety steps. He thrust his right hand forward, two fingers held high, then formed a fist and gave it three sharp pumps.

Police Officer Reggie Powell returned the fist pump, thumb extended skyward, then turned toward the front door. With a nine-millimeter Glock clutched in his right hand, he used his left to knock sharply on the front door.

"Yo, hey, Denise, my girl," he said, his voice garbled, deep. "Open up, you got a problem. Your horse, open quick, girl, you got a problem. It's me, Willie, Willie the Shoe. Open up, girl."

Rizzo had been carefully peering through the dirty, cracked glass of the window pane. He watched as King leapt to his feet at the sound of the knock at the door. He stumbled, unsteady, the drugs working heavily on him. Denise rose as well, stabilized him and turned toward the front door. From his position, Rizzo could make out her words.

"Oh, God, oh, shit, Wendy!" Then, releasing King, she shouted across the room. "I'm comin', Willie, I'm comin'. Hold on."

Rizzo turned his eyes back to the front porch, lowering his head from the window. He pumped an extended pointer finger sharply at the cops who massed around the sides of the door.

When it opened from within, Rizzo sprang to his feet and rushed up the three steps. Ginsberg, D'Antonio, Collins, and Powell rushed into the room.

Mark Ginsberg grabbed Dirty Denise by her shirt and twisted the shocked young woman around, forcing her to the floor. Shouting instructions and threats, the other cops rushed to the surprised, still standing, Kevin King. In a moment, he was facedown on the floor, rear cuffed, a gun trained on him.

Rizzo ran through the room to a closed door in the corner. D'Antonio appeared beside him, his weapon extended forward in a combat grip. A uniform cop peered tentatively into the small bathroom, then turned and yelled, "Clear!" Collins quickly scanned the tiny kitchen to the right of the front room. "Clear!" he shouted.

"Take it," D'Antonio said, indicating the closed door with the muzzle of his weapon.

Rizzo darted forward, his Colt extended, carefully staying out of D'Antonio's line of fire. He kicked brutally at the door, shattering the dried, peeling paint of the ancient doorframe. The door flew open wide. From the sanctuary of the wall beside the doorway, Rizzo chanced a quick glance into the darkened room. He could hear a muffled, terrified, and tearful whimpering. As someone switched on an overhead light in the front of the house, a slight illumination spilled into the tiny bedroom. Rizzo again looked into the room, scanning it quickly in the anemic light. A doorless closet at the rear wall was uninhabited, and there seemed to be only one person in the room.

Linda Davis, her eyes wide and bloodshot, tears flowing freely, a wild look of sheer terror on her face, sat bound and trussed on the floor in the corner. Beside her stood a small table and an unmade bed. From behind the dirty tape covering her mouth, she was screaming. Rizzo reached into the room, feeling around for a light switch. Finding it, he flicked it on, fully illuminating the bedroom. He dropped to one knee and looked beneath the bed, then quickly regained his footing.

"Clear!" he hollered, holstering his weapon and crossing the room toward the woman. She cringed in horror and balled her body up, pressing farther backward into the corner, her muffled screams growing more horrified.

Rizzo held his badge out to her, crouching slightly to appear less ominous, less looming.

"It's okay, Mrs. Davis, it's okay. We're cops, we're here to help you. It's okay, it's over. It's all over now."

The bedside digital clock sitting atop the small table next to Linda Davis caught Rizzo's eye as it clicked over.

Midnight.

SOME FIFTEEN minutes later, as the EMTs entered the small bedroom, Joe Rizzo stepped out into the front room. Kevin King and

Denise Miller sat rear cuffed on the sofa guarded by Reggie Powell, the Seven-Five cop who had announced himself as neighbor, Willie the Shoe. Rizzo glanced to the stunned, scared-looking couple, blood running copiously from King's nose, spilling over his chin and onto his dirty black T-shirt.

"What happened to him?" Rizzo asked Powell.

The man's face was void of expression as he answered.

"Oh, he fell."

Ginsberg appeared beside Rizzo. "Yeah," he said with low tones into Rizzo's ear. "Twice."

Rizzo nodded. Suddenly, the bitter stench that permeated the room reminded him of the acrid, sour odor of the urine that had drenched Linda Davis. He turned toward the front door.

"I'm goin' out for some air," he said to Ginsberg. "I think I'd rather smell the horseshit than the inside of this fuckin' place."

CHAPTER TEN

AT SIX A.M. Saturday morning, Rizzo, Ginsberg, and D'Antonio sat in the lieutenant's office, sipping coffee. D'Antonio had taken a bottle of bourbon from his desk drawer and liberally laced each cup. They drank in final toast to a very long night. It was just over twenty-two hours since the three cops had reported to work the previous day.

Rizzo had left the ramshackle cabin in The Hole at twelve-thirty and followed the ambulance carrying Linda Davis and a female patrol officer to the hospital. Collins and his men had returned to the Seventy-fifth Precinct while D'Antonio and Ginsberg transported King and Miller to the Six-Two.

Once there, the two cops interrogated Dirty Denise Miller in a small interview room. Detectives Robert Dellosso and Angela Paulson grilled Kevin King in a second room.

King, still reeling under the aftereffects of Valium and hashish, gave a rambling, nearly incoherent account of how he had merely been trying to hitchhike a ride home and had every intention of releasing Ms. Davis. He had no idea how things had gotten so out of hand. He told Dellosso that he and Denise had finalized a plan just moments before the police had broken in: they decided to drive

Davis to the wetlands near John F. Kennedy Airport and release her there. Then he, Denise, and their two horses would ride away in Denise's car and trailer, heading for big sky country out west. Once there, Kevin would get a job on a ranch and they would live in peaceful harmony for all time.

Detective Angela Paulson sat silently as Dellosso recorded the statement. When he was finished, Paulson leaned over the small table, speaking directly to King.

"You know, Kevin, you are one stupid motherfucker. Anybody ever mention that to you before?"

At the same time, Dirty Denise gave a somewhat different account. She reported to Ginsberg and D'Antonio that Kevin had misled her from the onset, calling to tell her that he had run out of gas just off the Belt Parkway, could she come and help him? Once there, he took the gasoline she had so thoughtfully brought for his car and used it to burn the Lexus. Then he forced her to take the rich lady back to the cabin, where he then threatened to kill Denise if she didn't continue to help him.

"Help him how?" D'Antonio asked.

"Help him to kill the lady and dump her by the airport. He wanted to kill her as soon as it got dark, but I was able to stall him. I figured if I got him stoned, maybe he'd fall asleep, then I could call the cops. I saved that woman's *life*. You should be kissin' my ass 'stead a lockin' me up. I'm a fuckin' *hero*, that's what I am."

Dirty Denise, it seemed, was considerably smarter than Kevin.

"You might be able to sell that story to some spaced-out jury that's seen too many bullshit movies, but you're not sellin' it here, Denise," Ginsberg told her.

He was about to leave and get coffee for him and D'Antonio, but before exiting the room, he turned with an evil smile.

"And as for kissin' your ass, lady, I wouldn't go near your ass if my fuckin' pension depended on it."

Meanwhile at the hospital, Linda Davis had been examined, cleaned up, and mildly sedated. After being cleared for discharge by the emergency room doctor, Rizzo sped the grateful woman back home to her husband and infant daughter. He returned to the Six-Two just as the sun began to rise over the city.

Now, the three cops sat sipping their spiked coffee.

Kevin King was locked in a basement holding cell, Denise Miller held in a small cage just off the squad room. The preliminary arrest paperwork was complete, and the two felons awaited arrival of the day tour when D'Antonio would assign officers to transport them to Central Booking and complete the process. They would probably be arraigned that afternoon, just over twenty-four hours since the abduction.

Rizzo shook his head. "Stupid fuckin' dust head didn't even have a plan in mind. All this grief 'cause he needed a ride back to that shit-hole. Unbelievable."

"I stopped using the word 'unbelievable' a long time ago, Joe," Ginsberg said. "Although, I gotta say, it *is* almost unbelievable we found the vic alive."

"Yeah," D'Antonio agreed. "As this thing moved along, I was convinced King was our boy, but I thought for sure we'd find Linda Davis out in the woods somewhere, at Plum Beach or Gateway Park, with her throat slashed."

Rizzo joined in. "We'da had some good case against King, though. Tire and foot tracks, maybe one of the witnesses I.D.-ing him. They coulda matched Pal Joey and the other horse through DNA from that hair we pulled outa the Lexus. And with all the crying, sweatin', and pissin' Davis did in the corner of that bedroom, we'da had her DNA, too."

"Well," D'Antonio said, pouring more coffee into his cup with another splash of bourbon, "thank God it went this way."

"*A*-fuckin'-*men*," Ginsberg said, raising his cup in toast.

"What a break we caught," Rizzo said. "Imagine if I'da never worked the Seven-Five? We'd *never* have found that shack."

D'Antonio nodded. "Twenty years I been assigned to Brooklyn, I never even heard of that place."

"Yeah," Ginsberg said. "And if you stood in front of Dirty Denise's shack and threw a rock, it'd land in Queens. I worked Queens nine years, same story: never hearda The Hole."

Rizzo drained his cup and stood. Even though he had eaten an egg on a roll, his stomach felt empty and cold. The bourbon seemed to have just bypassed it, going straight to his head instead.

"I'm gonna get washed up, then head for home. You can give me a wake-up call, Vince: say about a quarter to Monday o'clock."

"Okay, you got it. And thanks. You did a hell of a job. Incredible. I'm puttin' you in for a meritorious service commendation."

Ginsberg laughed. "Gee, I wish I had been there, Vince."

D'Antonio stood, extending his hand across the desk, shaking both their hands.

"You, too, Mark. You too." He grinned. "I don't wanna catch any grief from your friggin' rabbi."

AT SEVEN a.m., Rizzo pulled his car into the driveway, parking next to Carol's Civic near the two-car garage.

As he climbed out, the side door of the house opened, and Carol, uniform suitbag slung over her shoulder, stepped out. She smiled at her father and went to him.

"Mom's been keeping me posted," she said, kissing his cheek. "Way to go, Dad. Sounds like quite a story. You'll have to tell me all about it tonight. I don't think Mom will object to a little shop talk this time, not on this case."

Rizzo returned the kiss, giving his daughter a quick hug.

"Okay, kiddo. Go to work. Don't be late and embarrass me."

Carol shook out her short brown hair and moved toward the Civic.

"No way, Daddy. Never."

As she climbed into the car, Rizzo turned and took a step to the house. Then, pausing, he turned to look at his daughter. He called to her.

"Hey, Carol."

She looked up, met his eyes.

"Yeah, Dad?"

He hesitated for a moment before speaking.

"Do this job the best you can," he said, his voice soft. "*Always* do this job as best you can. 'Cause if you don't, you'll never get a good night's sleep. Believe me." Rizzo began to turn away, then looked back and spoke one last time. "Best you *can*. Remember that."

CHAPTER ELEVEN

RETIRED DETECTIVE JOHN MORELLI shifted painfully in the bed he had been confined to for five seemingly endless days. The cramped hospital room was dismal and claustrophobic despite afternoon sunlight at the window and the superficial efforts made to cheer up the place.

The soft pastels of the painted walls. The artificial flowers on the small table. The hand-drawn smiley face on the dry erase board that proclaimed his nurse for the shift to be "Tammi," his tech "James."

Morelli sighed and turned red-rimmed eyes to his wife, seated stiffly in a hard-backed chair beside the bed. Today was her only visit to the hospital. And the first time Morelli had seen her in nearly six months.

"Please, Teresa. You've gotta do this for me."

Teresa Morelli had been estranged from her husband for five years and out of love with him for many more. Looking at him now, ravaged by disease, withering away, she tried to recall the feelings of animosity she had harbored for so long, but she felt her heart softening. As she held his watery, agonized eyes, she saw not the alcoholic, compulsive gambling liar and fraud he had become. Instead, she saw the kind, compassionate, loving man he had once been, the man she had loved throughout her youth and for so many years: the man she had married. Johnny lay there, dying, physical death hovering in the room, waiting to claim him at last from the spiritual and moral death he had wallowed in for the last fifteen years. Despite her best efforts to stay strong for him, Teresa's eyes welled with tears. Tears of loss and regret, pity and emptiness.

She placed a gentle hand on Morelli's and offered a weak smile.

"I think *you* should do it, Johnny. I'll put the phone on the bed. I think it should be you making the call."

Morelli shook his head, the slight motion brushing aside the morphine with arrogance and sending bolts of pain throughout his ravaged body. He summoned his strength, trying to speak forcefully to the woman he had shared so much of his life with, the woman whose love and respect he had so relentlessly squandered.

"I can't, Teresa. I'm afraid he'll hang up on me, shut me down. If I make the call, he won't come. Joe's done with me, sweetheart. He said I was dead to him. He told me right to my face. He never says anything he doesn't mean."

"But you two were so close, such good friends, partners. . . . I can't believe he wouldn't come now."

Again, despite the searing pain, Morelli shifted his body and pushed it closer to the bed's edge, closer to his wife. "Maybe he will if *you* ask him. If you say it's important to *you*. Maybe he'll do it for old times' sake, for when we were so close, the four of us. Remember? You and Jennifer, me and Joe?"

"Yes. I remember."

Now the physical pain raging in his eyes was challenged by a deeper, more reflective pain, one even more devastating.

"I know what I've put you through. I know what I've put the kids through. You deserved so much better, honey, and I got no right to ask anything of you now; I know that. But I really *need* you to do this one last thing for me. I need you to make this call."

Morelli's eyes filled with tears. With his time so close at hand, he saw the impossibility of making amends, of righting his wrongs, and it saddened him deeply and imposed a pleading tone on his words.

"It's the *last* thing I'll ever ask of you, Teresa. Please."

Teresa Morelli, her tears now breaking free, running slowly across her cheek, gently squeezed her husband's hand.

"Okay. Tonight. I'll call Joe tonight." Teresa feared if she made the call from her husband's bedside and Joe Rizzo simply hung up on her, she could not bear to see the impact on the man she had loved for so much of her life. In honesty, she doubted her own ability to handle that kind of rejection right now.

AS TERESA Morelli was gathering her belongings and preparing to leave the hospital, Joe Rizzo walked into the Sixty-second Precinct building. It was just before four p.m., Monday, March 16.

"Hey, Joe, wait up."

Rizzo turned, saw Dom Lombardi emerge from the Ready Room buttoning his overcoat, going home for the day. It had been six days since the gangland murders at the Hi-Fi Lounge had taken place, and the OCCB captain was still using the Six-Two as a temporary base of operations.

Lombardi extended a hand. "Congratulations, Joe. I heard all about the Davis case. Matter a fact, the husband has a few important friends. He made some calls already. Fuckin' guy is on a quest to get you beatified."

"That's good," Rizzo said as he shook the captain's hand. "I can always use another hooked up ass-kisser on my side."

Lombardi laughed. "Yeah, can't we all? But seriously, D'Antonio filled me in. That was one beautiful job you did, Joe. Beautiful."

Rizzo shrugged. "You know how it works. We had cops from five or six different precincts, plus CSU and the lab guys and the park police. Team effort, boss, like always. Musta been fifty cops all over that case."

"Yeah," Lombardi said. "And forty-nine of 'em were interchangeable with any forty-nine others. You were the spark plug there, so don't play blushin' rose with me. I remember how you work, buddy. I still got the splinters in my ass to prove it."

"Yeah, I'm a fuckin' genius," Rizzo said, smiling. "And a saint, too."

Lombardi nodded. "I can use some of that, Joe. Any time you wanna make a move over to OCCB, just say the word."

"Well, you know, Dom, now that you mention it, I got a daughter just came on the job. After she runs up some miles over the next year or so, you and me can talk. Work out some kinda package deal, maybe."

Lombardi gave a knowing nod. "Doable. Just say when."

"I will. And thanks for the offer. How're things goin' with the Quattropa hit?"

"There's some light at the end of the tunnel," Lombardi said, lowering his voice and discreetly glancing around to confirm that no one was within earshot. "It's a fifteen-watt bulb and a two-mile tunnel, but the light's there."

"No kiddin'?"

"No. We've been working Peggy Irish for more cooperation. And we've been rousting wiseguys, looking for a weak link or some discontented potential rat. But the big news is, we got us one of Spano's soldiers, guy over in Canarsie. He's been running junk in through Canada, workin' with some Afghan warlord asshole. The feds are on the Afghan for a possible terrorist angle, and they threw us a bone with this Brooklyn wiseguy. I'm anglin' things now with the FBI, trying to work out an arrangement where they'll let me squeeze the guy's nuts a little. Use him to get a wire into a high-end sit-down, maybe." Lombardi shrugged. "Like I say, it's a long shot. But if I gotta spend every fuckin' minute of my life to nail this prick Spano, I'll do it. I'd pawn one of my balls to bust that scumbag, Joe."

As Lombardi was speaking, Rizzo noticed the man's face flushing and the artery in his neck rapidly pulsating. He smiled at the captain.

"Take it easy, boss. You seem to be takin' this a little too personal. Remember, it's just business, just all us kids playin' tag in the schoolyard. Don't stroke out over it."

Lombardi shook his head. "Bullshit. I'm sick a these wiseguy assholes. I'm *rooting* for the goddamn Russians to take over. Let *them* live with this shit, let *their* kids deal with it. Every fuckin' TV show, every goddamn movie or book, guinea gangsters runnin' wild. Never an Italian doctor, scientist, not even a freakin' opera star. You need a doctor for your TV show? Cast a black guy. You need a scientist? How 'bout that WASP woman over there. You need some psycho mobster? Grab the first actor looks Italian. I'm sick of it, and it's causa guys like Louie The Chink and Mikey Spano. We get rid of them, we're all better off."

Rizzo shrugged. "My girls laugh that shit off. They think it's funny. Far as I'm concerned, I couldn't give a fuck. This country'd be a hell of a lot worse off without the Italians. Hell of a lot worse."

"But a hell of a lot *better* off without guys like Spano. I'm gonna nail him. You watch. I'm gonna get a wire into that Pompeii Club, and I'm gonna do it so Spano can de-bug all the fuck he wants. I'm gonna get one in *after* he de-bugs. You watch me."

"Okay, Dom. Good luck with it. Anything I can help with, you know where to find me."

Lombardi nodded, his face still tight with anger.

"Yeah. I know where to find you."

* * *

AT FIVE-THIRTY, Rizzo's direct line rang. He picked it up absent-mindedly as he read a DD-5 report on the Davis abduction case prepared by one of the Seventy-fifth Precinct Detective Squad.

"Rizzo, Six-Two squad."

There was a pause. "Joe? Joe, it's me, Teresa. Teresa Morelli."

Rizzo stiffened, placing the report down on his messy desk. He frowned into the mouthpiece.

"What's wrong, Teresa? Tell me."

Another pause. "He's dying, Joe. The doctors want to discharge him, say they can't help him. They think in a few days, maybe a week . . ."

Rizzo sighed. "Yeah, I heard he was sick. I'm sorry, Teresa. I really am."

"Johnny wants to see you. He just about begged me to call you. He didn't think you'd come if he called. He wants to see you one last time. It's very important to him, Joe. It's his last wish."

Rizzo hesitated before responding. "Not gonna happen, Teresa. I'm sorry, but he died on me a long time ago. I already buried him, and I can't visit a ghost. I don't believe in ghosts."

"Please, Joe," she said, tears in her voice. "Do it for me. Please. I just want to erase it all. I just want to bury my husband. The husband I had once. The friend you had, the *partner* you had, once. I don't know what happened between you two, he never told me. I know you had a falling out back when you were still in uniform, but I never knew why. All of a sudden, you and Jen were just out of our lives, and I never understood it. Neither did Jen. And that was back when Johnny was good, when he was . . . when he was still Johnny Morelli, a good husband, a good father, a good cop. Later on, with the booze and the gambling, after you two patched it up when he went to the Six-Two, I thought, 'Joe will straighten him out, Joe will fix it.' I was so hopeful."

"Yeah. I know. And how'd that work out? I mishandled it, and then he almost got me fired and railroaded off to jail. I'm sorry, Teresa, I can't. I told you. I can't talk to a ghost."

Rizzo heard her muffled sobs coming through the line, and he steeled his resolve, searching for a way to end the call and hang up. After a moment, composing herself, Teresa's voice became cool, businesslike.

"He's in Downtown Hospital, in the city. Room four-twenty. He's expecting you, Joe. He believed you'd agree to come for *my* sake. I guess maybe he was wrong." The line was silent for a moment. "I guess you've stayed a cop for too long. You gave it a chance to take your heart. Just like it took his."

The line went dead. Rizzo sat there for nearly a full minute, remembering. Then he dropped the phone into its cradle and stood up. He saw Vince D'Antonio come out of his office and go to the copy machine in the far corner. Rizzo crossed the squad room to his boss.

"Vince, I need some personal time. Maybe a coupla hours."

D'Antonio turned, casually eyeing Rizzo. "Oh?" he asked.

"Yeah," Rizzo said with a grim look on his face. "It's Morelli. Johnny Morelli. He needs me."

As HE made his way slowly through the Brooklyn streets and toward lower Manhattan, Rizzo's mind drifted back in time. Back to memories and emotions he had spent many years suppressing.

As he reflected, a part of his mind marveled at how clear it all seemed, how recent. As if two decades had melted away.

Joe Rizzo and John Morelli had met on the first day they reported as cadets to the New York City Police Academy. During their initial few days together, they discovered much in common.

Rizzo was raised in Bensonhurst, Morelli in the nearby Brooklyn neighborhood of Gravesend. Rizzo was recently discharged from the Army and dating his former high school girlfriend, Jennifer Falco. John Morelli was newly married to his own high school sweetheart, Teresa McGinn, and he, too, was an Army veteran. Morelli and Rizzo developed an easy, familiar friendship, double dating, spending much time together as couples.

After graduation, Rizzo drew assignment to the high-crime Seventy-fifth Precinct, Morelli to the equally tough Eighty-first. Although their conflicting work schedules limited opportunities to see one another, they managed to maintain a close bond over the next couple of years. Then, coincidentally and much to their liking, both were reassigned to Bushwick's Eighty-third Precinct. It was during a very bad period in Brooklyn's history, drug-driven crime and violence increasing at an alarming rate. In fact, New York City itself seemed under siege, and in response to media and public outcry, the police department organized Neighborhood Stabilization Units. Young, energetic officers were drawn from all sources within the department and funneled into the hottest spots, the Eighty-third being one such location.

Rizzo recalled how shortly after being assigned there, he and Morelli requested to be partnered. They would eventually ride together for two years.

Soon after graduating from the Academy, Rizzo had married Jennifer Falco. By the time he and Morelli became partners, Rizzo had a daughter, Morelli a son and a second child on the way.

The two young cops grew closer with each exciting, dangerous tour. They soon led the precinct in gun collars and stayed in the top tier for felony arrests, and Rizzo remembered how both men had leaned heavily on one another for support under the strains of fatherhood and the job. They created a pocket of security and trust in a treacherous, pressure-cooker-type environment. After a very short time together, Joe and Johnny shared a special bond known only to combat soldiers and street cops in high-crime areas. Each held the other's life in his hands, and each stood willing to sacrifice his own to save the other.

Now, as he watched the sky darken above the city, Rizzo thought back to the dark, rain-swept night shortly after the birth of his second daughter, when his loyalty was put to the test. The two cops responded to a call of a report of screams coming from the basement of an abandoned building on a battered strip of Gates Street. Upon arrival at the location, it appeared deserted, quiet. The two cops, service revolvers in hand and held discreetly out of the rain beneath their coats, entered the dark basement.

When first they came across the huddled mass, they thought it a doll or a store mannequin. The sharp beams of their flashlights soon revealed otherwise.

They later learned the girl had been only thirteen, raped and then brutally murdered by knife. It was a sight neither young man would ever forget.

A sound from their right surprised them and both cops dropped quickly into crouches, turning in the darkness toward the movement in the shadows. A figure materialized, that of a knife-wielding man, his eyes wild, a wide, insane grin on his face. The man raised his weapon, stepping closer. Rizzo leveled his firearm at the man, now less than ten feet away.

"Drop it! Drop the fuckin' knife! Now!"

The man, seemingly puzzled by Rizzo's harsh tone, dropped it.

"Take it easy, motherfucker," he said, giggling crazily. "Take it . . ."

Rizzo saw a flash blazing the area into a split second of light. Then, as the cold, dank basement returned to near blackness, he heard the deafening gunshot. Morelli, quaking with fear, anger, and tension, had fired. He had seen the wild, animated lunacy in the man's face and he jerked the trigger; not squeezing it as his training had dictated, but just jerking it in blind, crippling anger.

Even now, so many years later, Rizzo wondered at how the entire incident had taken only seconds. The semi-wadcutter .38 caliber bullet struck the man's chest, expanding under the impact and slamming into the heart like a brick. By the time Rizzo, his ears ringing and muffled from the gunshot, reached him, the man was merely moments from death.

Joe Rizzo turned and raised wide, frightened eyes to his partner. Morelli, his weapon now dangling in his hand, stepped backward, his legs weakening. He propped himself against the damp, mildew-stained concrete wall, the sound of driving rain gradually returning to his ears, now recovered from the sharp crack of the gunshot.

"Jesus, Joe . . . I thought . . . I thought he was closer. I saw the knife, saw his face . . . crazy son of a bitch, I thought . . . I thought he was closer to you. Jesus, Joe . . ."

After their reports were duly reviewed and filed, and the Grand Jury heard both cops' sworn testimony, the shooting was ruled justified and Officer John Morelli was awarded a commendation for saving his partner from the crack-addicted, knife-wielding murderer who had been about to kill Joe Rizzo with the same bloody weapon he had used to butcher the young girl.

Morelli and Rizzo had never spoken of the incident again.

Someone had once told Rizzo that there is only one thing that could tear even loving brothers apart, and that one thing was a woman. And the manner and nature in which that might occur took on many different forms.

Reluctantly, as he reached the Manhattan-bound ramp of the Brooklyn Bridge, Rizzo allowed his recollections to continue.

Under the enormous pressures of a dangerous, unforgiving job, coupled with financial and emotional burdens of marriage, family, and home-ownership, Joe Rizzo weakened. He became involved with a young nurse, Cathy Andersen, and they carried on a short but passionate affair with each, against all logic, envisioning a future together. Rizzo managed to rationalize away his guilt and shame by pushing it down into the mire of his work, pushing it into some recess of his psyche that was inaccessible to him. It sometimes seemed as though he were two separate men, two distinct beings leading independent, unconnected lives. And incredibly, it all made sense to him. He believed he saw it quite clearly.

But Rizzo remembered that John Morelli had not. After exhausting all efforts to dissuade Rizzo from continuing the affair, Morelli made a decision that would rupture their friendship for nearly twenty years: he went directly to Cathy Andersen.

As it turned out, the young woman did truly love Joe Rizzo. Hers was not a casual involvement, but rather one based on strong, if illicit, feelings. She listened to Morelli, his sad brown eyes imploring her. Let go of Joe, he told her. Set him free to his wife, his daughters, his future. John knew that his friend and partner was not thinking clearly. Rizzo seemed incapable of breaking it off with Cathy. He felt he was truly in love. But his *real* love, his *real* life, was back home with Jennifer and the girls in the small, handyman's special they shared on a quiet, tree-lined street in Bay Ridge.

"Send him back there, Cathy," Morelli told her. "If you really love him, send him back where he belongs. Give him back his future."

The next day Cathy did just that; she broke it off with a fierce and determined finality.

With crystal clarity of memory, Rizzo saw himself storm into the precinct to find Morelli in the Ready Room, awaiting roll call for their four-to-midnight tour.

Rizzo waded into John. It took four other cops to finally tear them apart.

They would never again ride together in uniform. In fact, they hadn't spoken to one another for many, many years; not until they were reunited as detectives in the Six-Two.

John Morelli was one of few people who truly knew Joe Rizzo well enough to foresee Joe's reaction to his influencing Cathy: Morelli believed Rizzo would never forgive him. But Rizzo had come to understand that John was at total peace with that. Morelli knew in his heart that he had done the right thing, the right thing for his friend. And that was all that mattered to him.

Now, so many years later as he drove into Manhattan, Rizzo had allowed those years to run through the vision of his memory, his lips pressed tightly, a tension furrowing his brow.

He had never been able to grasp what caused his friend's downward spiral. John Morelli—the once noble, idealistic, eager-to-help young cop Rizzo had known—had somehow deteriorated into a bitter, drunken, and corrupt gambler. Over the years, Rizzo had heard the stories and innuendos. He'd been a cop long enough to understand that smoke meant fire: his old partner had become a rogue heading for a bad end. It added to the guilt Rizzo still harbored; guilt for turning on his friend, devastating him, a man he had once loved as a brother. It was one of the few great regrets Joe Rizzo had, a dishonor that somehow remained immune to his usually deft, pragmatic, cleansing logic.

Much like his affair with Cathy Andersen.

And so, when the battered, broken John Morelli was transferred into the Six-Two to serve his last few years before retirement, Rizzo recalled seeing it as an opportunity to redeem himself, expunge some of the guilt. Again, he took Morelli on as a partner, and they rode the streets of Brooklyn for the second time in their careers.

This time, though, it was quite different: Morelli's behavior—drunk nearly every tour, chasing gambling debts with borrowed betting money, irrationally believing he would "get even"—wore on Rizzo like a recurring nightmare. Still Rizzo felt his debt to

Morelli was so great, his influence so crucial, that he refused to allow himself to see things clearly. He never imagined the bad end he feared for Morelli could very well become his own. Instead, for four years, he covered, excused, and lied to protect his friend. And he worked harder and longer than ever before, clearing cases with virtually no assistance from the distracted, muddled man living behind Morelli's badge. As far as department statistics were concerned, John Morelli had suddenly morphed from a dangerously useless drunk into one half of the borough's leading team of aggressive investigators.

But the situation with Louie Quattropa had ended all of that.

Just prior to Joe Rizzo's having been partnered with young Mike McQueen, Morelli had discreetly retired. The Internal Affairs Division had been looking very closely at him, and if they had managed to prosecute him while he was still active, he would have risked forfeiting his pension. On the advice of Detective's Endowment Association lawyers, Morelli put in his papers and retired into the vodka bottle he was never very far from.

Morelli had finally cornered himself: he owed over thirty thousand dollars to a variety of bookies and loan sharks throughout Brooklyn. In the past, for far lesser amounts, he simply exchanged information or warnings of pending police action in return for having debts wiped away. But this time it was different. This time, the money was too big, the debt too great. The matter had been referred to Quattropa, the boss of the Brooklyn mob.

Quattropa was known for settling debts one way or another: you paid up, or you disappeared. There were no other options.

But Internal Affairs believed Morelli *had* found an option as he suddenly appeared debt-free. There were no more late-night phone calls and ominous messages left for him at the precinct. And at the same time, Quattropa was faring better as well. A Brooklyn soldier and low-level thug working for a crew in Williamsburg had turned up brutally executed in the traditional mob style reserved for rats. His death was very fortuitous for Louie Quattropa.

The soldier had been recently compromised by OCCB and agreed to provide damaging information about the Brooklyn organization. Details of his wiring up were being worked out. OCCB saw it as a path to Quattropa's downfall in the not so distant future.

But suddenly that possibility died along with the soldier, and OCCB turned angry eyes toward Morelli.

Now Rizzo, approaching the hospital, shook his head, memories and images rushing over him, almost dizzying him as he drove. *How* had he not seen it? *How* had he not realized it when it was happening right in front of him? Or had he seen it and simply chosen to ignore it? Had it been somehow more subtle than that? Had he subconsciously *forced* himself to not see it, the way he had done with Cathy Andersen? Had he once again become two separate men, one so removed and disconnected from the other that he could simply live two separate lives, with separate values and standards and beliefs?

Had it all been some malevolent, twisted replay of that long ago night in the dank, bitter air of that abandoned basement in Bushwick: a pressing—no, crushing—burden of loyalty, of right and wrong, good and evil, moral and immoral?

Rizzo had no idea. As he drove slowly on Manhattan's Beekman Street, he felt lost, uncharacteristically floundering and unsure. He no longer *knew* what he *knew*. How could that be possible? Ultimately, it had been by virtue of his own deft maneuvering and skillful exploitation of the system that he managed to avoid his own destructive end from the Quattropa affair. And in the midst of it all, he had written John Morelli off as dead, pushed him once more from his life, and turned to his new, young, and fresh partner, Mike McQueen.

Yet here he was on this night, with the March evening as dark as his mood, going to New York Downtown Hospital, going to his friend.

His partner.

CHAPTER TWELVE

FROM THE DIMNESS surrounding his sterile hospital bed, John Morelli smiled up weakly at Rizzo.

"I knew you'd come, Joe. A guy can always count on Joe Rizzo. No matter what."

Rizzo slid a chair closer to the bed and sat down.

"Hello, Johnny," he said, his face neutral, the horror he felt from the sight before him concealed, guarded.

Morelli, still smiling, nodded. "I know, I know. I look like I should be in a specimen jar somewheres, don't I?"

Rizzo forced a laugh. "I've seen ya lookin' better, yeah." He paused, allowing a lightness into his tone as he went on. "Besides, what's the difference? An old cop once told me that we all wind up just a bunch of faded photographs somebody throws out."

"Yeah," Morelli said, a hint of the old spirited cop Rizzo remembered briefly evident in his voice. "When they're cleaning out the house. After the fuckin' funeral."

They sat in silence for a moment, each with his own reflection. They had last seen one another two years earlier, in a dismal, last-stop bar on the Lower East Side. The meeting had not gone well and ended with Rizzo telling Morelli their friendship was over.

Now, looking at the ashen, emasculated man before him, Rizzo found it oddly puzzling. How, he wondered, could such strong animosities arise? With the inevitability of death awaiting everyone, how could anything ever seem important enough to generate such feelings?

Rizzo shook his head slightly, clearing it and refocusing on Morelli.

"What are we lookin' to accomplish here, Johnny?"

Morelli held Rizzo's eyes, pondering it. "How's Jen? And the girls?"

"Good. Everybody is good. We gonna chitchat, Johnny? Make small talk, like we're waitin' for somebody to bring us dinner? Is that what you had in mind? A fuckin' first date?"

Despite the pain it caused, Morelli laughed. "Yeah, my kids are okay, too. Teresa was even able to talk them into coming up to see me one last time. And I guess she did the same with you. So, okay, let's do it. We always were pretty straight with each other, considerin'. So okay."

A few moments passed, Morelli shifting slightly, searching for the least uncomfortable position. Rizzo averted his eyes and pretended not to notice the painful wincing in his former partner's eyes.

Once resettled against the pillows beneath his head and shoulders, Morelli began.

"Last time you saw me was in that dive I hung out in. You asked me about the business with Quattropa. Out and out asked me. The only time you ever did. You remember what I said?"

Rizzo nodded. "Yeah. You told me to take my I.A.D. wire outa there and go fuck myself."

Morelli smiled. "Yeah. I was pretty drunk, but I remember it that way, too. Pretty ballsy, eh? Tellin' a guy like you to go fuck himself."

"I wasn't wired, Johnny. I would never have done that to you."

"Never say never. It's never that simple."

"Yeah, John, sometimes it is."

After a few moments of uncomfortable silence, Morelli spoke.

"I wanted you to come here so we could clear the air. I don't wanna die without that. I want it okay between us. Maybe not like it was, like it shoulda stayed. I know that's probably gone. But at least . . . okay."

"It's not necessary, Johnny. Things are good enough. We can just let it go."

"No, we can't. *I* can't."

More uncomfortable silence, this time broken by Rizzo. "I never knew. I never really knew where or why you went bad. Or *how* you went bad. I never knew."

"Is that what you think? Sure you knew, Joe. The job made me wrong, it was always wrong for me, from day one. You remember how I was. Christ, I was like some bleedin' heart goddamned social worker, tryin' to save the world, one scumbag at a time. I just wanted to help, that's all I wanted to do. I shoulda been a teacher or a counselor or a fuckin' priest, never a cop. That's what went wrong. I couldn't handle it. I wasn't strong enough, I wasn't tough enough. Not like you, Joe. Not nearly like you."

Rizzo contemplated it, remembering. "You were a good man once. A gentle man. But you always had balls, you coulda survived it." Now Rizzo ran a hand through his thinning brown hair, his eyes falling from Morelli's.

"Maybe, John," he said, his voice soft, "maybe if I'da been around, if we still . . . if I hadn't . . . after that time with Cathy, when you saved my marriage, saved my whole life for me. Maybe if I hadn't been such a thick-headed son of a bitch, things woulda gone different."

Morelli winced, from pain or memories, Rizzo couldn't tell.

"Funny, Joe. But I got a medal once for savin' your life. Remember? Remember that bullshit story we both swore to, the one that saved my ass? Do you realize we never talked about that, not once? Not from when the Grand Jury cleared me right to this second. Not one fuckin' conversation."

"Some things don't need talkin' about. Some things just need forgetting."

Morelli nodded. "Yeah. But you see, that's where it all started. For both of us. In that fuckin' basement, the second I let that round go. That bullet killed me just the same as it killed that skell."

"That's foolish, Johnny. It was just a bad call, a mistake. You think everything woulda turned out better if we had let them lock you up for wastin' that guy? Is that what you think?"

"Bad call? Joe, I saw that kid, that butchered-up kid . . . layin' there on that wet basement floor. Then I saw that fuckin guy, saw him grinnin' . . . and I saw him drop the knife. I can still see it hit the floor, same as I can still see that dead girl. Then I *killed* that fuck. I *executed* him."

After a few seconds, Rizzo shrugged. "Maybe you did. Maybe you didn't. What's the fuckin' difference?"

"See, that's exactly why I wanted you to come here, why I had to see you one last time. I know you, Joe, I know you real good. Yeah, you're a tough guy, tougher than I could ever be, and stronger, too. But down in your heart, you're a good man. You got a real noble streak in you. And that night in the basement, you and me took a step. A *big* fuckin' step. Back when we were just kids, when we were so close we were like one person, with one brain, one heart, one fuckin' soul. Remember how it was, Joe? That night in the basement we *both* knew *exactly* what I'd done. And we looked each other in the eye, and we made our first lousy decision. And you're still making them, all these years later. Yeah, you get the job done, even get justice once in a while. And then you start thinking you're special, maybe better than the law. So you go on autopilot, flying along. And then, one day, you fuck up—and it's too late. You're over the line, and you never even seen it coming. You want the truth, Joe? I'll give you the truth, I'll tell you what you already know. Yeah, I made that deal with Quattropa. I found out about The Chink's problem, and suddenly, I saw the answer plain as day. No big deal, just another day on the job. Doin' business with Quattropa was no different than shooting that psycho in the basement and then lyin' my way into a hero's medal. With Quattropa, I just did what I had to do, and it made perfect sense to me. It still does. The thing is, if you'd be honest with yourself, you'd admit it makes perfect sense to you, too. Just like back in that basement."

Rizzo shook his head. "Apples and oranges. You're talking crazy."

"It *started* in the basement, Joe. The compromising, the cutting corners, bending the rules, all of it. Don't you see, it *always* seems right, always makes sense at the time. Then, after years and years of it, *nothing* seems right or wrong anymore, *nothing* makes sense anymore."

Rizzo's heartbeat rapidly increased with his response. He suddenly felt trapped, claustrophobic. He wanted out of that room and away from the sunken, haunted gaze of whoever this man laying prostrate before him was.

"Blah-blah-blah, Johnny. It's the morphine talkin' now."

"No. It's me talking, Johnny Morelli. The Johnny Morelli you first suited up with in that locker room way back in the Academy. Of all times for him to decide to come back. It'll be the final irony: *he'll* be the one goin' to hell, not the fuckin' drunk who ruined his life."

Rizzo stood slowly, bending down to the bed, speaking softly and evenly.

"Okay, so the old Johnny is back? Well, then, listen to this. Yeah, we bent some rules, we learned to see things different from the way citizens do. But we're *cops,* Johnny. We don't get the luxury of screwy hipster theories and pop-psych bullshit. We get *real,* and that's all we ever get. My conscience is clear. Don't tell me we're the same. I don't give a fuck what I've done or haven't done, it's got nothin' to do with you setting up some guy to get murdered for no reason other than to save your own ass. Nothin' at all."

John Morelli smiled weakly. He reached out a heavily veined, black-and-blue hand, an I.V. taped to it. He laid the hand on Rizzo's forearm and squeezed gently.

"You're wrong, Joe. It's all the same. By the time I got to the Quattropa setup, it just wasn't a big deal. Just another scheme, another angle, another street deal. That rat was a hood, a murderer himself. If he helps nail The Chink, he goes into witness protection and lives out his life in Sunny Crotch, Arizona, and gets to die in bed an old man. A week after Quattropa goes away, somebody else takes his place and it's business as usual. And me? I'm still screwed. I still owe money I can never repay. So I turn up dead somewhere. But . . . if I give up the rat, *he* gets whacked. A death sentence for a murderer. Justice, right? And then I'm off the hook for the thirty g's and The Chink still has his throne. Life goes on.

"See, Joe, a deal. Just another deal, same as the others we worked over the years, same as the ones you're still working. And you know what, partner? You can't be a little bit pregnant. You either are or you aren't . . ."

Rizzo stepped back from the bed, out from under the cold, ugly hand, further away from the unsettling sunken eyes.

"Get out before you wake up someday and see it all clearly," Morelli said softly. "Then you'll start frying *your* liver in vodka, like I did. Once you see it clear, you find out you can't live with it, so you got to blur it up again. Get out, Joe. Get out before you start seein' it all too clear."

Rizzo held Morelli's eyes, seeing the plea they bore, seeing the anguish. A slight throbbing began at his temples, and he felt his throat tightening. He moved nearer the bed and bent slightly, his face close to Morelli's. He laid a gentle hand on his partner's shoulder. A near ravaging despair washed over him as he spoke.

"I'm sorry, John," he said, his voice steady, surprising him. "Whatever happened, happened. We can just put it behind us."

Morelli smiled weakly. "You know, Joe, if I've ever learned anything it's this: there are only two times in life you're really happy. One is when you're doin' something you shouldn't do. The other is when you're making believe something good is going to last forever."

He raised his own hand and placed it over Joe's, patting gently as he spoke again. "Here's your chance to cover both bases, Joe. Tell me you forgive me. Tell me we're friends again."

CAROL RIZZO rapped sharply on the steel-plated door.

"Hello, Mrs. Borkowski? It's the police, ma'am. Open the door, please. It's the police, Mrs. Borkowski."

From somewhere inside the apartment, a mumbling distant voice sounded, the words unintelligible.

Carol glanced to Esposito. "Could you make that out, Sarge?"

Esposito shook his head, stepping closer. "No," he said, slipping a short day stick from his gun belt and banging it against the door. "Open up, Mrs. Borkowski, or we're coming in. Can you hear me? This is Sergeant Esposito, Eighty-fourth Precinct. Open up, ma'am."

Again, the indistinguishable voice came from somewhere behind the door.

"Go ahead, open it," Esposito said to the building superintendent.

The man unhooked a massive key ring from his belt and quickly undid the three locks. Tentatively, he turned the doorknob and pushed inward. The door opened three inches before stopping against a safety chain.

"Step back, please, sir," Carol said, ushering the man to the side of the doorway. Esposito stepped in even closer, peering in through the gap.

"Hello? Mrs. Borkowski? You okay, ma'am?"

This time, with the door ajar, the woman's voice carried clearly to the front of the apartment.

"I fell! I'm in the bathroom. I'm stuck in the bathtub."

Esposito stepped back, raising his right foot, then threw his weight forward, kicking heavily at the door just below the level of the security chain. A sharp tearing of metal and splintering wood sounded as the door crashed inward and open.

"Wait out here for now," Esposito said to the super. He entered the apartment, one hand on the grip of his holstered Glock.

Eleanor Borkowski, an elderly woman well into her eighties, had been preparing to venture out from her State Street apartment to run some errands. That morning, as usual, she sat on the side edge of the free-standing porcelain tub squatted in the cramped bathroom of her four-room apartment. She reached to the floor, picking up her Nike, then sat back, swinging her right leg up toward her lap. Not quite making it, she wobbled a bit on the edge of the tub and considered bending to don the Nike and do up its laces. But then she decided no, that would be too old-lady-like. So once again, she swung the leg, this time giving it a mighty heave.

The woman tottered backward, balancing herself for a brief, valiant moment before tumbling backward into the tub. Instinctively, Eleanor pushed her head forward, her chin nearly touching her chest, preventing a potentially damaging blow to the back of her skull; it was her shoulders which took the impact from the unforgiving tile bathroom wall. Even so, the blow stunned her and rattled the newly installed bridgework in her mouth. After a moment, she composed herself, attempting to free her small body. Her buttocks rested on the bottom of the tub, her legs splayed upward and draped over the tub side. The light spring dress she wore had ridden up to her waist to reveal a long-legged corset and knee-high nylons.

She was completely stuck. After a few fruitless minutes of continued effort, she sighed. Reaching into the front neckline of her blouse, she removed a plastic pendant and pressed its raised, red button.

Shaking her head and frowning, Eleanor tried to relax. It may take a while, she thought, for someone to get there. Idly, she wondered how they would get into the apartment, guarded so well by its multiple locks.

With her head still shaking, she smiled slightly.

"Just like a damned old lady," she said aloud. "A damned little old lady."

Now, from her awkward and uncomfortable position, she watched as a good-looking young cop took a tentative peek into the room. Eleanor smiled at him, attempting to push her skirt downward to cover herself, but it seemed to be stuck under her body somewhere.

"You can come in, son," she said. "I won't bite you."

Esposito entered, followed by Carol. Eleanor Borkowski, despite her physical discomfort, was amused by the situation. She peered at Carol Rizzo, noting the young woman's unadorned good looks, then addressed the tough-looking sergeant.

"Bet you'd prefer to see your partner stuck in this position instead of an old hag like me, eh, Sarge?"

Esposito laughed. "Well, I'd *rather* be on the beach in Hawaii, ma'am. But here I am."

"Are you okay, Mrs. Borkowski?" Carol asked, stepping forward. "How long have you been stuck here like this?"

"I'm not sure, honey. What time is it?"

Carol glanced at her watch. "Just about eight-fifteen."

Eleanor nodded. "You people got here pretty fast. I couldn't a fell more than twenty minutes ago."

Esposito and Carol questioned and examined the woman, satisfying themselves she had not been injured. They extricated her from the tub and sat her atop the toilet seat. Despite Eleanor's protests, Carol Rizzo placed a radio call requesting an ambulance.

"We'll just have the EMTs take a look at you, Mrs. Borkowski," Carol said. "Make sure you're okay, that's all."

The woman consented reluctantly. She thanked the newly present super for his help, and the man excused himself and left. Eleanor turned her sharp, intelligent eyes to Carol.

"You know, young lady, when I was a girl, I thought about signing on as a police matron. In those days, that's all a woman could be in the police department. But I couldn't imagine myself typing forms and getting coffee for a bunch of"—she shot a quick, amused glance at Esposito—"no offense, Sergeant, a bunch of lazy old men cops, so I never did join. Later on, though, long before you two were born, things finally changed. Women quit just bitchin' behind closed doors and went public. Now, you see plenty a girl cops around. Plenty."

Carol smiled. "Only we like to think of ourselves as all grown up now, Mrs. B. Not *girl* cops, exactly."

Eleanor nodded. "Damn right," she said. "*Women* cops."

A telephone rang from the front of the apartment. Eleanor Borkowski turned to Esposito. "That'd be my son. Musta just got the message from the Live-Free-Alert company. He's checkin' up on me. Can you get that, tell him I'm okay? My legs are still a little shaky from being up in the air."

"Sure," Esposito said, turning and leaving the room. While he was gone, Eleanor, still perched on the toilet seat, beckoned in a conspiratorial manner to Carol.

Carol crossed the room, bending down as directed. Eleanor spoke to her in a low tone.

"That's one good-lookin' boss you have there, honey. Is he single? He'd make a hell of a catch for a nice young woman like you!"

BACK IN the car, Carol sat in the passenger seat, known as the "recorder" position. She jotted down notes for the aided card she would complete later on. Esposito sat behind the wheel. He pointed to the copy of a mug shot taped to the car's instrument panel.

"Don't forget to keep your eyes open for that guy. He likes to hang around this sector of the precinct. Guy's a real asshole, I'd love to lock him up. Guaranteed those last two purse snatchings on Fulton Street were his. Guaranteed."

Carol nodded. "Okay, Sarge. You drive, I look. No problem."

Esposito pulled the car away. "This sector is a lot different from The Heights. Very mixed area here. Lots of older people, like Borkowski, a few yuppies working on gentrifying the place. But the heart of the sector is the criminal courthouse on Schermerhorn Street, and like I told you your first day, it's a friggin' magnet: every skell in Brooklyn shows up here one time or another. The court officers handle the building and the perimeter, but the rest is our problem. Plenty a he-say she-say spillover issues between the courthouse and the surrounding area, especially the bus stops and subways and local coffee shops and bars. That's usually where the vic runs across the perp and things get a little tense. Especially when they all got their families and friends with them. We usually have very busy day tours around here, and night court runs until at least one a.m., so the morning tour starts out hectic, too."

"Noted, boss," Carol said. As she picked up the recorder sheet and began documenting the Borkowski run, the radio crackled to life. Listening, she picked it up and gave a short, "ten-four."

"That's us, Sarge," she said.

"Yeah. Like I said, it's busy around here."

Esposito sped toward the job located on a litter-strewn, run-down stretch of Pacific Street. Halfway down the block, a blue-and-white with its bar lights flashing, sat double-parked. The car bore the markings of a New York State Court Officer patrol vehicle. Two uniformed officers stood on the sidewalk before what appeared to be an abandoned commercial storefront.

"What's up, guys?" Esposito asked.

The taller officer, a muscular, athletic-appearing black man of about twenty-five, responded.

"We were cruising along heading back to court. Citizens waved us down, told us about this guy." The officer gestured into the open doorway of the old building. A young, apparently Hispanic male lay on the ground amid the rubble, on his back, arms folded across his chest, eyes rolled up in his skull, only the bloodshot whites showing. Spittle encircled his open mouth, drool oozing out, running across his jaw and pooling on the dirty, tiled entry floor.

The second court officer, a white male about thirty, spoke up.

"We checked for a pulse. I think he's dead." The man gestured with his radio toward the prostrate body. "Tracks on both arms. Looks like an O.D., but I don't see a needle anywhere."

Esposito nodded. "You call for a bus?"

"Yeah. Should be here in a few minutes."

"Well, then, guys, looks like it's yours," Esposito said. "Come on, Rizzo."

The black court officer, his head shaking, a smile on his face, reached out to touch Esposito's arm.

"Not so fast, Sarge. We're a long ways from the courthouse. Only reason we were passing by here was 'cause some witness got threatened, and the judge wanted the guy escorted home. We're due over at Jay Street to transfer drug evidence back to the Property Clerk. My boss told me to wait for P.D., then leave, and that's what we're gonna do. This dead junkie can lay here till the rats eat 'im, far as I'm concerned. We gotta go."

Esposito compressed his lips. "Yeah. I had a feeling it wasn't gonna be that easy."

The court officer shrugged. "Sorry, Sarge. You know how it is."

The two men walked off, climbed into their car and pulled away. Carol turned to some curious local residents, moving them along, then rejoined Esposito beside the body.

"Think he's really dead?" she asked.

Esposito shrugged. "Well, he's the color of newsprint, I don't see his chest moving, and the court officer couldn't find a pulse. I'd say, yeah, he's dead. We'll wait for the EMTs. Don't touch the guy. Between the spit and the snot, he's gotta be an infectious time bomb. Stay clear."

Moments later, a New York City paramedic ambulance slid to the curb. Two young EMTs got out, one with a clipboard in his hand, the other a heavy medical box.

"Good mornin', guys," one said to the two cops. "What da we got here?"

"Dead junkie," Esposito said. "Probably O.D."

The EMT with the medical kit moved into the building's alcove and knelt beside the body.

"Yeah," he said, peering carefully at the man's eyes and visually searching the neck area for signs of a heartbeat. "He's dead, alright." The EMT then turned from the body, looking upward over his own shoulder to the two cops. "How long has he been here?"

Before Esposito could respond, Carol Rizzo let out a gasp and stepped backward, her hand moving to her mouth. Esposito's eyes widened and moved suddenly away from the face of the kneeling EMT.

Puzzled, the young paramedic turned back toward the body.

"Fuck!" he yelled, jumping to his feet, stumbling over the medical box and reaching out a hand to stabilize himself against the building wall.

The Hispanic man had sat up silently, the whites of his eyes moving slowly downward to reveal large, black fixated pupils. Drool still oozing from his mouth, he gradually focused on the cops and EMTs hovering before him.

"Shit, man," he slurred, his body bending deeply forward as if in slow motion. "Am I fuckin' busted, or what?"

CHAPTER THIRTEEN
April

HAROLD ZITZMANN was twenty-two years old and known locally by his middle name, Gunther. He had dropped out of New Utrecht High School six years earlier to work full-time at the Bath Beach Speed Shop, a small, specialized garage on Bensonhurst's Harway Avenue. There, he pursued his one and only passion: fast street cars. By the time he reached the legal driving age of seventeen, Zitzmann had built himself a truly unique hot rod.

He first rebuilt a salvaged Pontiac 421-cubic-inch performance engine and somehow fit it into the front compartment of an ancient, resurrected 1966 Pontiac GTO. He painted the car in flat black primer, and except for its deep, angry rumble and telltale chrome header pipes, the car appeared completely innocuous. But Gunther and his GTO, known throughout the subculture of Brooklyn hot-rodding as the "Tin Goat," were widely respected as the fastest street rod racers in the borough, if not the entire metropolitan area.

And Gunther was as equally known to the police as to hot-rodders.

Harold Gunther Zitzmann stood five feet eight, two hundred pounds of hard-packed muscle. His torso was covered in blue and red tattoos ranging in nature from a suffering, thorny crowned Christ head to a naked dancer whose hairless vagina appeared to pulsate when Gunther flexed his left bicep. His scalp was shaven clean, and his eyes, the left one blue, the right one gray, were small and set close in a seemingly permanent scrowl.

On those occasions when the officers of the Sixty-second Precinct had found themselves dealing with a belligerent Gunther, they had done so with nightsticks and mace canisters in hand.

If it could somehow be argued that Gunther was capable of any form of human emotions, they seemed strictly limited to a love of his GTO and a seething underlying anger with everything else. Gunther lived rent free in his parents' apartment above a Thirteenth Avenue candy store, while his prized GTO luxuriated in an obscenely expensive climate-controlled storage garage on Cropsey Avenue. Gunther would drive his battered Toyota to the garage, park on the street, then, with great ceremony, back the Tin Goat out for a spring or summer or early fall evening of prowling and racing. The car was a familiar sight at the illegal pickup drag strips of Brooklyn's waterfront First Avenue or the wide, sparsely trafficked stretch of Cross Bay Boulevard in Queens, as well as the remote outlands of Staten Island's Port Ivory. In those places, Gunther reigned supreme, racing money challengers from throughout the city and such areas the provincial, untraveled Gunther considered far-flung, such as neighboring Nassau, Suffolk, or Westchester counties. He had even won handsome sums beating cars towed in from the foreign and exotic state of New Jersey.

Gunther's most serious transgression with the laws of the land had come from shattering the jaw of a fellow racer with a baseball bat. The victim had, after losing a two-hundred-dollar drag race to Gunther, expressed his disdain for the Tin Goat.

"Runs okay," the young man had commented. "But it looks like shit."

He had then spat at the ground near the GTO. Unfortunately, a sudden wind gust carried some spittle, depositing it on a shiny steel racing wheel. Gunther had reacted poorly and paid dearly with eight months on Riker's Island.

Since his release over a year ago, Gunther had given his time in jail little thought. Now, just before midnight, he eased the GTO to a stop in front of the Seventy-second Street home of Janine Tedoro, his latest girlfriend. He sounded the horn and watched as Janine bounded down the steps and climbed into the car.

She kissed him, her eyes wide with excitement. "You gonna race Nicky Waves tonight, Guntha?" she asked breathlessly. "*Finally?*"

Gunther slipped the GTO into gear, eased off the clutch, and let the five hundred horses under the hood draw in a precise mixture of air and racing gasoline.

"Yeah. Son a bitch gets his shot tonight. I'm gonna shut him the fuck up."

JOHN BOITINI, a.k.a Jackie Boy, had stolen dozens of automobiles in his life, but tonight was his first Corvette. With residential Sixteenth Avenue stretching deserted and straight before the low-slung hood, he pressed heavily on the accelerator. Keeping one eye on the road, he watched in amazement as the backlit speedometer rushed rapidly to nearly one hundred miles per hour. There was, Jackie Boy realized, plenty more where this came from. As he flew through the intersection at Seventy-fourth Street, he pressed down a bit harder.

Gunther stopped at the corner of Seventy-second and Sixteenth, glancing casually to his left. He noticed low-slung headlights two blocks away as he rolled the GTO through the stop sign, turning right. It was a warm, near moonless April night. The working-class neighborhood was quiet, the streets empty. He eased the car onto the avenue, accelerating gently.

The sounds of a blaring horn and screeching tires caught Gunther off-guard, and he yanked the wheel instinctively to the right. Headlights washed the GTO's interior, lighting the panic-stricken face of Janine as she screamed in fright. Gunther saw the low-slung Corvette fly past the GTO on the left, fishtailing wildly into the empty oncoming traffic lane, verging on complete loss of control.

Gunther watched with a detached and nearly professional admiration as the other driver wrestled the 'Vette under control, its tires smoking under the strain. The multiple red taillights flashed on and off as the driver pumped the brake pedal, downshifted, and slowed the car, muscling it back onto a straight track. Gunther estimated the car's speed now at about eighty miles per hour as it roared away, shrinking in the distance.

"Jesus, that fuckin' guy coulda killed us!" Janine shrieked, pounding the top dash with a fist.

"Take it easy," Gunther said calmly. "You punch that dashboard again, I'll break your fuckin' arm off."

Janine blanched and dropped her hands to her lap. "I'm . . . I'm just sayin'. He coulda wrecked us, wrecked the Goat."

Gunther shrugged. "Well, he didn't. My fuckin' fault, anyhow: I shoulda seen the guy was punchin' out that 'Vette, shoulda let him clear." He shrugged again. "Shoulda seen it."

"Yeah, well, what the fuck, the guy's crazy. He musta been doin' a hundred."

Gunther nodded, driving casually, the Tin Goat in second gear, his right hand resting in his lap. "Better'n that."

Gunther rolled the GTO along, stopping for the red light at Sixty-fifth Street. The Corvette sat before him, also waiting for the light. Gunther switched on his left blinker and glanced at his watch. His money race with Nicky Waves was set for one a.m. Plenty of time to snake the GTO under the Gowanus Expressway, then swing west two blocks to First Avenue. Plenty of time.

The driver's door of the Corvette began to open. Gunther watched with hooded eyes as the driver climbed out.

"That's him," Janine said, interrupting her lipstick application, pointing through the GTO's tinted windshield. "That's the god-damn asshole almost killed us."

Jackie Boy, a small twenty-two automatic dangling in his right hand, approached the GTO driver's side. Gunther glanced out the open window at the gun.

"You fuckin' idiot!" Jackie Boy said, the vein in his forehead beating sharply, his face flushing. He raised the gun and pointed it at Gunther. Janine screamed and threw herself down into the cramped area in front of the passenger bucket seat. "Oh, Jesus, oh, Jesus, oh shit," she wailed.

"I should blow your fuckin' brains out," Jackie yelled. "I should fucking kill you!"

Gunther looked into the muzzle of the gun, then turned his eyes upward to meet Jackie's. He assessed what he saw there, then reached for the door handle.

"Yeah, well, you didn't," he said, pushing the door open, press-ing it against the now surprised Jackie Boy. "And I'm thinkin' you're a pussy motherfucker, and you ain't shootin' nobody. If you had any balls, you'da done it by now. So get the fuck back in your car before I shove that gun up your ass."

Jackie Boy backed away, raising his left hand to the gun, trying to steady it in his now trembling right hand. This was not going the way he had imagined. Not at all.

"Get back!" Jackie Boy said, backing away as he spoke. "I'll fuckin' shoot you, I swear!"

Gunther kept walking forward, a small, ugly smile forming on his lips. He craned his neck, looking around the gun-wielding man and into the Corvette. A young, pretty blonde, about Gunther's age, was looking back over her shoulder and through the rear window of the Corvette, her face illuminated by the GTO's headlights. Gunther's smile broadened. Casually, he pushed Jackie Boy aside, passing him and approaching the driver's side of the Corvette. He bent to the open window and peered in at the blonde. She wore a red halter top over ample breasts, her nipples pressing visibly against the thin material. Her legs were long and pale under tight black shorts.

With his back to the stammering, baffled Jackie Boy, Gunther reached into the car and tweaked the blonde's left nipple.

"Anytime you feel like suckin' a real dick, sweetheart, you look me up." He flipped a quick, derisive look at Jackie Boy. "Piece a ass like you shouldn't be hangin' with this limp-dick jerk-off."

The young woman, terror in her eyes, shrunk against the door, holding her breath in fear.

Gunther suddenly stood straight up, turning with great speed. He grabbed Jackie's gun hand and twisted it sharply, pulling the man violently forward and slamming the man into the car's roof, dazing him with the impact. The gun fell to the pavement. Gunther turned Jackie Boy around and kneed him viciously in the groin. Jackie sputtered and fell to the ground, grabbing at himself. The blonde in the Corvette screamed.

"Kill the prick, Gunther, kill him!" Janine hollered from where she now stood beside the GTO. "Kill him!"

Gunther looked at her, considering it. He glanced at his watch, mindful of his race with Nicky Waves, then bent down and picked up the small automatic, tucking it into the back pocket of his Wranglers.

"Last time I used a baseball bat," he said softly to Jackie Boy. "My lawyer tole me if I'da just used my fist, I'da probably got probation." He shrugged. "I don't know if he was bullshittin' me or what."

Gunther bent to the squirming, stunned Jackie Boy and took

hold of his shirt collar, then twisted him around and lined him up. Gunther leaned slightly backward before lurching forward with a crashing, crushing right fist, throwing his body weight behind the punch. He thought he could actually feel bones breaking under the blow.

He got back into the GTO and slipped it into gear. The light at Sixty-fifth Street was green, and he swung the Tin Goat around the idling Corvette, making the left onto Sixty-fifth and accelerating away.

There was still more than enough time to make the race. More than enough.

Gunther liked to be punctual.

SOME TWO hours after Jackie Boy's run-in with Gunther, Mark Ginsberg crossed the squad room to the only other detective present, Sergeant Joe Rizzo. He pulled a chair alongside Rizzo's desk and placed a large plastic bag atop the clutter.

"Dinner's ready, dear," he said, rummaging through the bag. "One corned beef on club, heavy on the mustard for you, one pastrami on rye for me. Two potato salads, two Doctor Brown cream sodas."

Rizzo took the generous sandwich wrapped in greasy white paper. "You get extra pickles?"

Ginsberg nodded. "Sure. What good would eatin' this shit at two in the morning be without extra pickles? If we're gonna kill ourselves, we might as well do it right."

They ate at Rizzo's desk, Bath Avenue standing dark and deserted outside the grimy second-story window beside them.

"You hear anything new on the Quattropa hit?" Ginsberg asked. "Since Lombardi moved the task force back into the Plaza, it's like it never happened."

"I haven't heard anything. I was half expecting him to reach out to me again for help, but he never did. Just as well—it's been what, five weeks? Those two shooters are probably part of some skyscraper's foundation by now." Rizzo bit into his sandwich before continuing. "Lombardi's on a cold trail. Good luck."

"So," Ginsberg asked, picking at his potato salad, "how's Carol making out? She clean up Dodge City yet?"

Rizzo smiled. "Yeah, like all the rookies do. She had that rob one collar her first tour, but it's been downhill from there. All routine stuff."

"Good. Routine is good."

"Yeah," Rizzo agreed. "Boring is good, too. And I still can't get my mind around this whole thing. Imagine? My baby girl a *cop*? It just don't compute."

Ginsberg laughed. "Yeah, Joe, I hear you. My mother felt the same way about me. Can you picture it? My brother's an accountant, my little sister is a pharmacist. Me, I become a cop, a freakin' Jewish cop. I can relate to Carol, believe me. The shit I hadta hear from my parents, you wouldn't believe it—like I told 'em I was gonna enlist in the fuckin' Palestinian Paratroopers."

"I can imagine," Rizzo said.

"No," Ginsberg said, shaking his head. "You *can't*. One time, about seventeen, eighteen years ago, I was just married. My old man buys four front-row-center tickets for Jackie Mason on Broadway. You remember him, the old Jewish shtick comedian? My old man and my mother and me and Paula, we all go. So Mason comes out, starts his routine, and I notice he keeps glancing down at us, me mostly, while he's doin' his act. Then, after about a half hour, he walks over to the edge of the stage and looks at me, right in the eye. 'Can I ask you something?' he says. 'Sure,' I say. Then he says, 'I'm looking at you all night—first row, most expensive seats in the place. And I'm looking at your jacket and I'm thinking, what?, a Kmart jacket? Mister Fancy Shmancy front-row-seat big shot, and in a twenty-dollar jacket? I'm looking at your girl there, you both look Jewish. Am I right? You Jewish?' So I tell him, 'Yeah, I'm Jewish. So what?'"

Rizzo smiled. "What was he gettin' at?"

"He says, 'So you're Jewish, you got some money, you sit in the front row. But, bubby, that jacket? It hurts my eyes. Go for a few bucks, spend, buy something nice you wanna come sit under my nose, front-row fancy, shmancy.'

"So, I tell him, 'Hey, what can I say? This is all I can afford.' Mason does a double take, smacks his forehead. 'What?" he says. 'All you can afford? What the hell you do for a living?'

"So I tell him, 'I'm a cop,' and he starts laughing. 'A cop? A Jewish cop? Oh, now I understand. Somebody is getting mugged outside, so you ran in here to hide.' He taps his temple with a finger. 'Smart,' he says. 'Don't get involved, be smart.'"

Ginsberg smiled and shook his head at the memory. "My mother almost hid under the seat. My old man wanted to wait by the stage door for Mason to come out so he could tell the guy about my brother and sister. Save face." Ginsberg shook his head again, biting into his sandwich. "I'll never forget that. So, be careful with this Carol thing. Watch what you say, watch how you act. She'll remember it long after you forget."

"Yeah," Rizzo conceded. "I guess. But you know, I think I'm okay with it. It's a little weird, yeah, I still think of her as a baby, just a young kid playing teatime with me. But, I gotta say, in a way, I'm kinda happy about it. My grandfather was a cop, then me, now Carol. It's kinda nice." Rizzo paused, sipping at his Dr. Brown. "Tell you the truth, I probably could have done more to keep her off the job. When I saw she wasn't changing her mind, I coulda steered her to the feds like I told Jen I would if worse came to worst. I did talk to this guy I know, over in Newark. He's a boss with ICE. He told me to send her over, he'd set up an interview. Piece a cake.

But I never followed up on it. I even lied to Jen, told her the guy was retiring and couldn't help me. At the time, I told myself it was because, hey, Carol was an adult. She had a right to do what she wanted regardless of what her parents said. But the fact is, on some level, I'm damn proud of her. Another Rizzo to carry the torch after I go buy some yellow pants and white shoes and move to Prostate Estates in Florida somewheres." He shook his head. "It's weird, though, Mark. Really."

Ginsberg shrugged. "Good for you. You *should* be proud. Carol's a good kid, she'll make a good cop. Half these young kids today, they're walkin' around with their heads up their asses. My wife's nephew is twenty-eight, he still lives at home. He's been in college long enough to collect a fuckin' pension from the professors' union. At least Carol knew what she wanted and went out and got it."

"Yeah. I hope it pans out for her. Tomorrow's her first court date, a preliminary hearing on that gun collar from a month ago. We'll see how she likes gettin' slapped around by some wiseass, latte-suckin' Legal Aide asshole."

"Man, how time passes," Ginsberg said. "I just cracked my twentieth year on the job, and I still remember my first court date like it was yesterday. I was down at the old Grand Jury on Centre Street in Manhattan. I asked one of the court officers if there was a nonpublic toilet I could use, so he walked me up to his locker room. We got to talking and I told him it was my first court appearance. The guy was about fifty-five, working soft detail in Grand Jury, waiting to retire. He pointed at one of the toilet bowls. 'Kid,' he said to me. 'You see that water in the bowl?' 'Yeah,' I said. 'I see it.' 'Well,' he says, 'remember somethin'. That water is the only thing on the level in this whole fuckin' joint.'"

Rizzo smiled. "Amen to that."

"Which reminds me, Joe. Didn't you work that missing

princess case coupla years ago? The city councilman, Bill Daily's daughter?"

Rizzo nodded. "Yeah. Me and McQueen."

"I thought so. I heard on the radio he's pleading out. Cut himself a deal with the U.S. Attorney for the Eastern District. He's turning over some evidence he had on those six judges the feds indicted along with him. Plus a bunch of other pricks; even another councilman and some other wheels. He's gonna save his own ass as best he can and fuck all his buddies."

"Sounds about right," Rizzo said, his tone neutral. "I didn't know the guy, only met him once, but he seemed like a real arrogant prick. But the feds don't play around. He can give up his mother, they'll still slap him with some jail time. Guaranteed."

"Well, from what I hear, he's copping to three of the twelve counts in the indictment and agreeing to testify in current and future cases from any new indictments related to this. He'll probably do, what?, six, seven years maybe?"

Rizzo shrugged. "I don't know, depends on what he pleads to."

A uniformed officer appeared at the top of the stairs that serviced the squad room. "Hey, guys, got a minute?"

"Yeah, Randy," Rizzo said. "What's up?"

"There's somebody downstairs says he needs to talk to the detectives. Says somethin' went down tonight." The cop held up a small automatic pistol in a plastic evidence bag. "Handed this over."

Rizzo crumpled the wrappings from his meal and drained his soda can. "Anybody pat the guy down, make sure that's the only iron he's carrying?"

"Yeah, I did it myself." The cop looked sheepish. "Thing is, Joe, this guy . . . it's that fuckin' whacko, Gunther. Gunther Zitzmann."

Ginsberg grunted. "Great. As if this fuckin' pastrami isn't gonna give me enough agita, now I gotta deal with that nazi cocksucker?"

Smiling, Rizzo gestured to Randy. "Send 'im up. Let's hear his story."

Shortly, Rizzo and Ginsberg sat opposite Gunther in an interview room off the squad room. Gunther related a modified version of the events from earlier that night. Rizzo gazed across at the stoic, evil-looking young man.

"What time was this again?"

"'Bout midnight, quarter to, like that."

Ginsberg joined in. "So the guy almost crashes into you, then walks up at a light and points a gun at you?"

"Yeah."

"And he tells you to get out of the car?"

"Yeah."

"*So*," Rizzo interjected, "you get out. Then you figure the guy is gonna shoot you, and you make a play for the gun."

"Yeah."

Ginsberg: "And somehow, you twist the gun outa his hand. It falls on the street, and you bust the guy in the face."

"Yeah."

Rizzo: "The guy runs back to his car and takes off. You pick up the gun."

"Yeah."

Rizzo: "And where'd this happen again?"

"I'm not sure a the corner. On Sixty-fifth Street someplace. Around Nineteenth Avenue, maybe. I don't remember," Gunther shrugged, deliberately misstating the location.

Ginsberg: "Then, you toss the piece in your car and go race Nicky Waves for money." Ginsberg smiled at Gunther. "Who won?"

"Me."

Ginsberg nodded. "I guess you drive better than you bullshit, Gunther, 'cause I gotta tell ya, this is some weak shit I'm hearing from you."

141

"Yeah, Gunther," Rizzo added. "A little weak."

The man shrugged silently.

"And you were alone in your car? And he was alone in his?" Rizzo asked.

"Yeah," Gunther lied.

"And far as you know, no witnesses?"

"Yeah."

"And other than the 'Vette being a new blue coupe, no other info. No plate? No partial plate?"

"Yeah."

"'Yeah,' what?" Ginsberg asked. "Yeah, it was a blue coupe, or yeah, you know a plate, or yeah, you don't know a plate?"

"It was a blue coupe."

Rizzo and Ginsberg exchanged looks. "Why you tellin' us this, Gunther?" Rizzo asked. "Why not just ditch the piece and go home to bed? What's the angle?"

"No angle. I don't want this guy walkin' in here tomorrow with a cracked face talkin' shit about me. I'm telling ya what happened. You're the cops, check it out. I wanna be on record here, that's all."

Both Rizzo and Ginsberg knew that under New York State law, a person was considered in lawful possession of a firearm if that person had found or otherwise come into sudden possession of that firearm and was in the process of safeguarding or delivering the weapon to an authority legally authorized to accept such delivery. Although both cops had serious doubts about the story Gunther presented to them, they were without legal grounds to detain him. The two detectives once again exchanged looks.

"Okay, Gunther," Rizzo said. "You're on record. You handed in the weapon. We'll check it out. How bad you figure this guy was hurt?"

Gunther shrugged. "I busted his face for him. I tagged him good."

Rizzo nodded. "Okay. Come in tomorrow whenever you get up. Give your statement to the day tour. We'll leave our report on the catch pile."

Gunther stood, his mismatched eyes flat. "You really gonna check this out?"

Ginsberg stood as well. "Yeah, we're really gonna check it out."

Gunther seemed to consider it for a while. "Okay. Just remember: I was here first. I told you first." He turned to leave, pausing at the door and turning back to face them.

"*I* was here first."

THERE ARE at least two dozen Brooklyn hospitals that provide around-the-clock emergency care. Rizzo and Ginsberg divided the list in half, then starting with those within or nearest the Sixty-second Precinct, they systematically called each emergency room.

"We're looking for a white male," Ginsberg said on his third call, "about five-ten, one-seventy with dark hair. He'd have injuries consistent with a hard blow to the front of his face. Anybody match that tonight?"

The supervising ER nurse paused briefly before replying.

"As a matter of fact, Detective, yes. Some guy came in a while ago. We cleaned him up and put him on pain meds. We're just waiting to get a CT of his skull."

Ginsberg waved a hand to get Rizzo's attention. "No kidding?" Ginsberg said, taking up a pen. "What's the guy's name?"

The nurse chuckled. "Gee, I guess this must be your first day on the job, Detective. Otherwise you'd never ask me to violate patient privacy."

"Yeah, well, you're right. I just started this morning, so you're gonna have to bear with me a little."

"What was your name again, Detective?"

"Ginsberg, Mark Ginsberg. Six-Two detective squad."

Rizzo reached Ginsberg's desk and dropped into a chair, raising his eyebrows in question. Ginsberg covered the mouthpiece.

"Community Hospital, over on Kings Highway," he said in a low voice. "Guy's there now. What precinct is that?"

Rizzo spread both hands and shrugged. "I dunno, I'll find out." He rose and returned to his desk.

When the nurse finished admonishing him, Ginsberg smiled as he replied. "I'm very sorry about all that. Tell you what, you keep him there for another fifteen, twenty minutes, I'll make it up to you. How do you like your coffee?"

"My coffee? I like my coffee on the beach in Aruba. Black, no sugar. I'll start packin'."

"All right," Ginsberg replied, laughing. "Don't forget your sunblock. They probably got some topless beaches down there, and I wouldn't want you hurtin' yourself."

"No, Mark. I'm sure you wouldn't."

RIZZO CALLED the Seventieth Precinct and spoke to the shift commander who consented to dispatch a sector car to Community Hospital and wait there for the Six-Two detectives. The uniformed officers were instructed to detain the white male patient matching the suspect's description should he try to leave before Rizzo and Ginsberg arrived.

The serial number of the gun revealed it had been reported stolen two years earlier in a residential burglary on Long Island.

Taking the bagged twenty-two automatic with them, Rizzo and Ginsberg left the precinct for the fifteen-minute drive to the hospital. Ginsberg insisted on stopping at an all-night convenience store where he picked up a large black coffee and a box of tropical fruit–flavored Mike and Ikes candy.

Arriving at Community, Rizzo thanked the two Seven-O uniforms and sent them on their way. Ginsberg smiled at the fortyish, far from unattractive, nursing supervisor he had spoken to on the phone.

"Best I could do," he said, handing her the coffee and candy. "I'm afraid you're gonna have to use your imagination."

She smiled and opened the box of candy, putting a mango-flavored Mike and Ike into her mouth. "Hmmm," she said, closing her eyes. "I feel just like I'm on Manchebo Beach."

Rizzo grunted. "I hate to break this up, but I got a question: How much dope is this guy on? If we talk to him, is it gonna be an issue? Is he in control of his faculties?"

The nurse shrugged. "If he is normally, he is now. Just some Tylenol with codeine, and that was almost two hours ago. He's okay."

"When did he come in?"

She glanced at the chart on the nursing station counter beside her. "Zero one-twenty. He said he tried to stop the nosebleed himself, but the pain and swelling got too bad, so he came in."

"What'd he say happened to him?"

The nurse smiled at Rizzo, sipping at her coffee. "Guess you just started the job this morning, too, like your nice sweet partner here. The guy's in cubicle nine. Why don't you go ask *him*?"

Rizzo nodded. "Okay, we will."

He and Ginsberg turned to enter the treatment area of the ER. As they did so, the nurse called to them.

"What'd he do?" she asked.

Ginsberg turned and smiled at her over his shoulder. "He didn't *do* anything. He's *alleged* to have done something."

He winked at her twisted lip expression.

"And that, I'm afraid, is confidential."

"I NEVER seen that gun in my life," said John Boitini, known on the street as Jackie Boy. "I'm tellin' ya, I fell down the steps in my mother's house. Go ask her. I busted my fuckin' nose, and now that dot-head doctor tole me I mighta cracked my cheekbone, too."

The man's nose was heavily bandaged, surgical tape pressed across his discolored, bloated cheeks. Both his eyes were swollen almost completely closed and surrounded by dark rings of purple and yellow.

Ginsberg slipped the bagged gun back into his coat pocket, nodding at Jackie Boy. "Okay. So, I'm guessing your prints won't be all over it, then. That'll clear things up once and for all."

Jackie furrowed his brow. "Prints?"

Rizzo slid a chair close to the bed and sat down. Ginsberg remained standing. Rizzo leaned closer to Jackie as he spoke.

"Yeah. Fingerprints. Of course, a coupla people been pawin' at that gun, so the outer prints may not be too identifiable."

Jackie Boy smiled. "Well, too bad, I guess."

Rizzo nodded. "Yeah, but, lucky for us, this is an automatic. Nobody pawed at the clip holding the rounds. We can lift a good set of prints off it and see who loaded the weapon. That'll be good enough to prove possession. But, like you already told us, you never saw the gun before, so it can't be you who loaded it. Right?"

Jackie looked from one cop to the other, the throbbing pain in his face no longer his most pressing concern.

"Okay," he said. "Maybe I seen it. I found it a week ago, about a week ago. I mighta even took the clip out, to check if it was loaded. Yeah, I think I did. Maybe that's the same gun. I threw it away a few days ago. I threw it in a Dumpster over by Sixty-fifth Street and . . . and someplace over there, near that big whatdya-call-it? Salumeria. The one with all the cheeses hangin' in the window."

Ginsberg brushed some lint from the sheet at the corner of the bed and sat lightly. "You drive a blue Corvette, John?"

"Jackie," the man said, stalling, his heart rate increasing. "Everybody calls me Jackie. Jackie Boy."

"You drive a blue Corvette, Jackie Boy?"

He shook his head. "No."

"Whatdya drive?"

"A Chevy. My mother's old Chevy. It's white."

Rizzo stood. "Excuse me a minute, Jackie. I gotta go make a call. You relax, talk to Detective Ginsberg here. I'll be back in a minute."

Jackie Boy frowned. "I . . . I rather not talk too much. It hurts a lot when I talk."

Ginsberg reached out and patted Jackie's sheet-covered knee. "No problem. *I'll* do the talking till Sergeant Rizzo gets back. You like to play baseball, Jackie? Me, I was pretty good. When I was in college, I played first base. Let me tell you about this big game I was in . . ."

Rizzo crossed the outer emergency room and exited into the darkness of the street. He glanced at his Timex, noted it was three-thirty a.m., then took out his cell and called the Six-Two squad. Reading from his notes, he gave John Boitini's, a.k.a. Jackie Boy's, pedigree information to the plainclothes officer who answered the phone. Then, with a fleeting thought of his old Chesterfields passing through his mind, he took a casual stroll along the nearly deserted main thoroughfare of King's Highway. Parked just off the corner of East Twenty-eighth Street, he saw a shiny new blue Corvette sitting at the curb. Despite the darkness, he was able to peer through the driver's side window and see drying blood on the seat and steering wheel. He jotted down the license number, then copied the VIN from the dash plate and made a second call to the Six-Two.

Ten minutes later, he returned to Jackie Boy's bedside. "Can I see you a minute, Mark?"

Ginsberg stood. "Sure." He turned back to Jackie and smiled coolly. "You sit tight, buddy. When I come back, I'll tell ya about the big game we played against Fordham."

Once outside the treatment room area, Rizzo filled Ginsberg in.

"Our boy has four priors, three grand larceny auto, one CPW. I found the Corvette a block and a half from here. Plate comes back to an unregistered Buick owned by Miriam Boitini, forty-eight, same address as Jackie. Probably his mother. The VIN comes back registered to an Angelo Luperto, Seventy-eighth Street offa Sixteenth. The car hasn't been reported stolen yet, but if Jackie boosted it outa the guy's driveway just before midnight, Luperto probably doesn't even realize it's gone yet."

"Imagine this?" Ginsberg said, shaking his head. "You think that psycho Gunther was on the level? He's telling us the truth, and *he's* the friggin' victim here?"

Rizzo shrugged. "Well, 'on the level' may be overstatin' Gunther's case a little. But, yeah, he's probably telling us most of the truth. We'll arrest Jackie for GLA, then get the twenty-two dusted. Assumin' the prints come back Jackie's, we'll add a CPW. Then we can talk to Gunther and see what he wants to do, which will probably be nothin'. My money says he'll want to let sleeping dogs lie and just wash his end of this."

"Okay, Joe, I'll call the house, get a uniform down here to sit on Jackie until the docs clear him. Then the day tour can lock him up. And I'll call for an impound vehicle to come get the 'Vette."

"Okay. I'll go inside and burst this guy's little red balloon."

SOME HOURS later, at seven forty-five, fifteen minutes before their morning tour was to end, Lieutenant Vince D'Antonio called across the squad room to Ginsberg and Rizzo.

"Can I see you guys? I need a few minutes."

Once seated with the office door closed, D'Antonio addressed Rizzo.

"First off, Joe, I got some bad news for you."

"Tell me," Rizzo said, a heart stopping image of Carol flashing before his eyes.

"John Morelli died last night. It came in on the morning fax sheet. I know you guys were close once. I'm sorry."

Rizzo felt his pulse slow and his tumbling stomach settle.

"I got a kid on the job, Vince. Next time you got bad news, word it different."

D'Antonio's eyes widened with sudden realization. "Jesus, holy fuck, I'm sorry, I wasn't thinking."

Rizzo nodded. "No problem. It's new to me, too." He sighed. "As for Johnny, the doctors had him dead a month ago. It's amazing he lasted this long. Probably for the best he's gone. It musta been hell these last few weeks."

"Yeah," D'Antonio said. "Musta been."

Ginsberg reached out and gave a slight, backhanded slap at Rizzo's arm. "Sorry, buddy. I hope he rests in peace."

After a few silent moments, D'Antonio went on.

"Now, I know you guys are almost off the clock, so I'll keep this short. Two developments. One, you know those citywide burglary jobs, the ones taking down the tobacco distributors? Well, they're getting closer. Last night around one-thirty, a jobber in the Six-Six got hit. That's right next door to us. The pattern shows these guys work a borough, then move on. They've hit places in Manhattan, The Bronx, and Queens. Looks like it's Brooklyn's turn. We got three likely targets in this precinct: Gabber's Wholesale on New Utrecht Avenue, Carchessio's Tobacco Jobber on Benson Avenue, and J and D's Confectionery Warehouse on McDonald Avenue. I'm talking to Borough about it. I need some manpower, maybe some uniforms from the street crime units. I want to set up a stakeout. Maybe we can get lucky and nail these guys in the act. There's no question they're pros, in and out like ghosts, moving hundreds of cartons of tax-stamped product on every job. You know the retail cost on just a single *pack* of smokes? You know the total street value we're talking here? They've already walked away with close to two million dollars in swag."

"Okay, Vince, go get 'em," Ginsberg said. "What's me and Joe's involvement?"

"If I use young uniforms, I need supervision on all three sites. I'm thinking you work one team, Joe works the other, maybe Bobby Dee on the third. We invest a week, ten days, steady six-to-six tours. These pros are getting a lot of attention, maybe the Six-Two can break the case and get some ink. It'll make us look good, get the squad a little positive recognition."

Rizzo laughed. "You still anglin' for that liaison spot at Brooklyn South, boss? Is *that* what this is?"

"Exactly," D'Antonio said pleasantly. "It can't always be *you* putting us on the map."

"Well, sounds like a plan. But, just speakin' for myself and not for Mark, I'm not interested. Sittin' in some warehouse with a buncha anxious rookies wielding shotguns is not my idea of a perfect evening. And six-to-six steadies? What am I, a fuckin' milkman? Not to mention how ten days off the streets would kill our stats. But, like I say, I'm not trying to speak for Mark."

D'Antonio turned to Ginsberg. "Well, Mark?"

"I don't know. Let me think about it. Six-to-six can translate into a vacation. I can let the rookies watch the windows while I sleep, then I go home and have the whole day free. Think of how thrilled my kids would be to have me around the house all day. I gotta think about it."

"Okay," D'Antonio said with a nod. "Let me know, but by tomorrow, okay? Joe, you definitely out?"

"Yeah. I'm gonna pass."

"All right. One more thing before you go. Something else came

150

in on the morning fax: looks like Mikey Spano made good for that dead citizen, Richie Maggio. The cops in the Six-Seven found two dead Russians in a car parked near the Long Island Railroad right-of-way. They fit the male-female shooting team from the Hi-Fi Lounge. The bodies were very publicly dumped: Mikey didn't want them to just go missing. He wanted to make sure Lombardi got the message. I wish Captain Lombardi was still rentin' office space downstairs, I'da liked to have seen his face when he heard. I bet the son of a bitch is real happy about this."

Rizzo shrugged. "Tell you the truth, I won't be losing any sleep over the two of 'em, either."

"Yeah, two dead hoods, who gives a fuck? But that's different from being *happy* about it, Joe. And God forbid Mikey just whacked those two without a sanction from Oleg Boklov. We could wind up with a war on our hands, maybe some more collateral damage citizens, too. All because Lombardi engineered this. Maybe without him and Santori leaning on Mikey Spano, it all woulda ended at the Hi-Fi that night. Fuckin' Lombardi's got some blood on his hands here far as I'm concerned."

Rizzo stood, a sudden weariness from his long night at work, from the surprisingly painful loss of Morelli, and the whole conversation, washing over him.

"Yeah, well, I was once told this job can be a slippery slope, boss. I guess maybe Lombardi lost his footing a little bit. What the fuck, he's got my sympathy, the poor bastard."

CHAPTER FOURTEEN

FRIDAY AFTERNOON, Carol Rizzo stood in the gutter, her back to the crowd of onlookers congregated on the sidewalk. Joey Esposito was to her right, speaking into the Motorola he held. The block's buildings were crisscrossed by swirling lights from the multitude of emergency vehicles haphazardly scattered along the street. Carol raised her eyes skyward.

A man stood tightly against the building's wall on a ledge ten floors up, his arms extended outward at his sides and pressed into the bricks behind him. Five feet to his right, a window was open wide, a patrol officer Carol recognized from around the precinct leaning out and talking to the man.

Esposito completed his radio transmission and turned his attention to Carol.

"Can you believe this?" he said in frustration. "EMS has another jumper all the way the fuck out in Brownsville. They just got there and started inflating the crash bag. They'll never get here."

Carol looked back up to the man on the ledge. "I don't know, Sarge. This guy looks pretty determined. Is that the only bag in the borough?"

Esposito shrugged. "I don't know. Fire has a few. We got a call

out to them and to Manhattan." He glanced at his watch. "I'm trying to get us relieved. It's almost three-thirty, and I was planning
on quitting at four: I'm taking my son to his Little League tryout
in Dyker Park. It's the Saint Bernadette Junior League. He's only
six years old, this is the biggest thing in his life right now, and I'm
stuck here because of this asshole."

Carol smiled. "You know, in the Academy they taught us that
empathy was the most important tool a cop has. Did you miss that
class, Sarge?"

"Yeah, empathy. Let me tell you somethin', Carol. If this guy
really intended to jump, he'da opened the fuckin' window and
dove out. Look at him, he's scared shitless. He's frozen. If he was
able to, he'd walk his ass along that ledge and climb right back inside, believe me. Some ESU guy or firefighter's gonna have to risk
their own neck to go out there and get this guy. Dispatch said fire
is sending a hook and ladder. Mark my words, this guy isn't gonna
jump."

Gasps from the crowd caused the two cops to look upward.
The man had stepped away from the wall, the tips of his sneakers
now protruding four inches over the edge of the foot-deep ledge.

"On the other hand, I could be wrong," Esposito said reflectively.
He put a hand on Carol's shoulder, and she turned her eyes to his.

"Listen," he said. "If this guy *does* go off that ledge, don't watch
him fall. Do *not* watch him fall. I know you're gonna be tempted,
but I'm tellin' you, don't. Just look away. Believe me, you'll hear the
impact, and you'll have to see what's left of him, but listen to me,
Carol, you do not want to see this asshole when he actually hits
the pavement. Just trust me on this."

"I guess you've seen it before?"

"Yeah, like lots of cops, I've seen it *once*, but I'll *never* see it twice.
You can learn the easy way by just listening to me, or the hard way
by ignoring me. It's your choice."

153

Carol looked up toward the now desperate, panic-stricken man so very high above them, and a shiver passed through her.

"You know what, Sarge? I think I'm gonna take your advice."

ON THE afternoon of Saturday, April 18, Joe Rizzo stood before the full-length mirror in his bedroom, adjusting the knot of his black tie. He shot the shirt cuffs through the sleeves of his dark gray suit jacket and turned to Jennifer, who sat on the edge of the bed slipping into her black pumps.

"I guess we're the only two dinosaurs who still get dressed up to go to a wake," he said. "Half the cops there will show up in jogging suits, and the civilians'll look like they're at some backyard birthday party."

Jennifer stood and crossed to him, laying a hand on his arm.

"How are you doing with this, Joe? I know it can't be easy for you. You don't have to be the big tough guy here, you know."

"I don't?" He smiled sadly. "Jeez, I thought that's why you married me. I wish you'da told me this twenty-six, twenty-seven years ago."

"Okay. Stay in character if it makes you feel better. I just want you to know, I'm here. That's all I'm saying."

Rizzo looked into her dark eyes. He sighed.

"I know you didn't care much for him those last four years we worked together. I know how pissed you were about that I.A.D. jam-up and how you blamed him for getting me involved. Yeah, Johnny was a screw-up, a drunk, a gambler, and God knows what else. But I knew the guy from way back, before all that. We were rookies together, just kids, really. We had each other's back. I owed him. I owed him more than you'll ever know." He paused, putting a hand on each of her shoulders, smiling at her. "Believe me, I *owed* him." He let his hands slide from her.

"We *both* owed him."

Jennifer held his eyes, searching them, and appeared about to say something. Instead, she simply returned his smile with one of her own; a weak, tired smile.

"Okay, Joe," she said finally. "We'll go pay your respects." She turned to leave the room, speaking one last time without turning.

"*Both* our respects."

THE DELANCY Street funeral home on Manhattan's Lower East Side presented itself as a local family-run institution but was, in fact, part of a national chain owned by a corporation based in Europe.

Joe Rizzo sat on a couch against the wall of the room, gazing across to the pasty, reconstructed face of John Morelli, twenty-five feet away. Jennifer Rizzo sat in the front row of viewing chairs, speaking softly to Teresa Morelli. The Morellis' adult children and their spouses sat scattered in the first two rows. The room held a sprinkling of casually dressed men Rizzo recognized as cops. He nodded greetings as they wandered past him, and exchanged polite comments, but had so far successfully avoided any prolonged conversations.

He watched as Jennifer and Teresa stood and walked together toward the rear doorway of the room, presumably heading out for some air or perhaps to the downstairs powder room. When they were gone, Rizzo rose slowly and approached the plain coffin, a folded American flag propped at Morelli's side. He moved his eyes to the highly polished mahogany table standing beside the coffin. It held an eight and a half by eleven color photograph of a twenty-three-year-old rookie police officer, Johnny Morelli. Rizzo met the clear, twinkling eyes in the photo, remembered the honest, hopeful smile.

He turned from the picture, dropping his knees to the padded kneeler before the coffin. Silently, he made the sign of the cross and looked at the battered, ravaged face that had once belonged to his most cherished friend.

"No more, partner," he said softly. "You don't have to deal with it anymore. None of it. God bless you, Johnny."

Rizzo crossed himself again, then stood. After a moment of looking down into the casket, he turned and walked across the room and out into the hall. He would wait there for Jennifer to return. They were done here. It was time to leave.

"DID YOU ever find out, Joe? For sure, I mean? Did you ever find out if Johnny was responsible for that whole mess with Quattropa?"

Rizzo and his wife sat at a corner table in the small Italian restaurant on Hester Street in Little Italy. In the dim lighting of the room, a candle flickering on the tabletop highlighted Jennifer's dark good looks, her face belying her age. Rizzo smiled across to her and reached for his wineglass.

"You look beautiful. You can pass for thirty, thirty-five, you're so beautiful."

Jennifer nodded, her face solemn. "Good, I'd settle for forty-five, but okay. You didn't answer me. Was Johnny responsible for that hoodlum getting killed?"

Rizzo sipped his wine, then put the glass down and shook his head. "I don't know," he lied. "I never knew for sure. But, if I had to bet, I'd say no. It *looked* like he did it, but the Johnny Morelli I knew coulda never done something like that. So, I'd say no, he didn't."

Jennifer considered it, holding Rizzo's eyes.

"What about the Johnny Morelli you didn't *want* to know? What about him? Could *he* have done it?"

After a moment, Rizzo replied, his voice soft but firm. "The man is dead, Jen. Dead in that box. You just saw him there. Let him rest in peace, okay? Just let it go."

Jennifer hesitated, then nodded. "You're right. I'm sorry. He should rest in peace." She sipped at her own wine, then let a smile come back to her face.

"His kids turned out well, though, didn't they? God knows how Teresa managed that. But she was always such a good mother, from when they were infants and we'd be together all the time. Remember?"

"Yeah, I remember."

"The oldest boy has his own insurance brokerage, and the younger one's an engineer—computers, I think. Mary, the daughter, married a boy from college; they live in Pennsylvania. She teaches school there."

"Like you do."

"Yes. Three nice kids."

Rizzo smiled. "Like we have."

"Yes, thank God."

"No," Rizzo said. "Thank *you*. Talk about a good mother."

"Don't sell yourself short, Joe. The girls hang on every word you say. I'm waiting for one of them to marry some Joe Rizzo clone. Seriously."

The waiter served their meals, and they dined in pleasant, easy conversation. Taking her last sip of espresso, Jennifer, her eyes twinkling with the evening's red wine, leaned across the small table to her husband.

"Tell me again how beautiful I am. It just might get you lucky tonight."

CHAPTER FIFTEEN

"YOUR FIRST JUMPER'S always tough," Rizzo said to Carol as they sat in the living room on Sunday afternoon. Jennifer and the middle Rizzo daughter, Jessica, were both out.

Carol sipped at a can of soda, her eyes guarded as she responded.

"I thought I was prepared for the sight, Dad, but, damn: I never imagined it could be that messy."

Rizzo nodded. "Well, the head is a heavy body part, it tends to hit the street first and absorb most of the impact. Physics, I guess. And the street always wins that battle." He smiled weakly across the room, trying to gauge the depth of Carol's despondency. "I hope somebody thought enough to tell you not to watch, to look away before the guy hit."

"Yeah, Espo did. He was pretty adamant about it, too. I've got a feeling it's good that I listened to him." She shuddered slightly, sipped more soda. "But I sure as hell heard it. The impact, I mean."

"Yeah," Rizzo said sadly. "Very unique sound. It'll stay with you a while, kiddo. Just try not to let it get you down too much."

They sat in silence for a few moments, Rizzo discreetly studying the creases around his daughter's faraway eyes, Carol recalling the events from Friday.

"How could anyone do something like that, Dad? I mean, I know people jump from ledges, but to actually *see* someone, what could possibly make a person do something like that?"

"I don't know," Rizzo replied, carefully screening his thoughts, aware of the significance of this moment. "Lots of things piling up on a guy, then workin' on whatever weakness, mental problems he already had."

"I guess. But like I said, knowing these things happen, that's one thing. *Seeing* it . . ."

Rizzo resisted the urge to stand and cross the room, cradle his daughter, tell her not to be sad, not to cry, everything was going to be all right.

But everything wasn't going to be all right. This was not a childhood disappointment, a birthday party uninvited to, a boy teasing her, a skinned knee. This was not a little girl.

This was a cop. A fellow cop.

"Lesson learned," he said gently. "See, that's the difference, honey, between us and the rest of the citizens. Everybody's *aware* of suicide, aware murders are committed, *aware* of child abuse. . . . But cops, we actually get to *see* it. That's a very major difference."

"Yeah, Dad, I know. I'm finding that out."

"Good. Just keep one thing in mind, kid: the world didn't start fallin' apart the second you put that uniform on. Fact, the world hasn't changed one iota since then. What's changed is *you*, your perspective. Truth is, Carol, the world just evolves, modifies itself. You look back in history to the Romans, the English kings, the friggin' Dark Ages, the Crusades, things have gotten a hell of a lot better over the centuries.

"You'll be seeing plenty of the dark side in the next years, honey. Just try and remember it's nothing new, and it's not going to change any time soon, not in our lifetimes. But, God willing, with our help . . . it'll keep improvin'. One step at a time."

Carol smiled sadly. "You planning on motivational speaking as a second career, Dad?"

He laughed. "No, I'm planning on pizza and beer on the beach as my second career. Just remember, you won't see much of it on your street tours, but there are still plenty a puppies in this world, cute little kids and sunrises and sunsets, lots of hardworking, loving people. What *you'll* see is the stuff that's jumped the tracks, people who were in the wrong place at the wrong time, and you'll see it day in and day out. But you should never forget—that's not all there is. Sometimes it can start to look that way, but it isn't. And if there ever comes a day you find yourself unable to believe that anymore, that's the day you quit this job."

Carol looked into her father's eyes. She visualized the pulpy, unrecognizable skull of the jumper, glistening vividly red and gray against the dull black asphalt, and she heard the hollow, vapid thud of the impact and shivered once more.

Rizzo rose and crossed to Carol. He knelt and hugged her to him, his face pressed to her short brown hair. He remembered coming in late after night tours and going to his daughters' rooms, kissing them as they slept, their hair smelling like baby shampoo, each breathing softly, safe and secure in their beds. He drew back from her and met her eyes, smiling as he spoke.

"Remember when we used to talk about Shrek?"

She tried to return the smile. "Yes, Daddy. I remember."

"SO, TEN twelve-hour tours I'm in that friggin' tobacco warehouse, racking up overtime, smelling all those cigarettes that woulda drove you back to the habit, and nothing comes of it. All of a sudden, these guys decide to break their pattern."

Rizzo wove the Ford through the midday traffic on Bay Parkway. He glanced to his partner and winked.

"I figure you were asleep at least seven hours of those tours, Mark, so I don't know how many cigarettes you got to smell."

Ginsberg shrugged with his reply. "Yeah, well, I had those street crime unit kids watchin' my back. I was in good hands."

"So Vince figures the stakeouts are a dead issue now?"

"Absolutely," Ginsberg answered. "The overtime wasn't reauthorized. The guys hitting those jobbers used to be just like clockwork: two, three jobs in a row, over maybe a week or two, all in one borough. Once they hit that joint over in the Six-Six, Vince thought for sure they'd strike again, and probably in the Six-Two. It was a good idea, it just didn't pan out."

"Well, I'm glad to have you back, partner. I've been workin' our cases with temps from uniform. More trouble than they're worth."

"I hear you, Joe, I've been there. So catch me up on the personal stuff. How's Carol makin' out?"

"Okay, I guess. She's gettin' a little ragged around the edges. You know, rookie shell shock. But she'll be okay. She's pretty tough."

"Like her old man. Is she just as thick-headed?"

"What can I tell you, it's the Calabrese in me. But Carol will be all right; she's still riding with Joey Esposito. He's a good kid."

"Yeah, I ran into Espo at Morelli's wake a coupla weeks back," Ginsberg said. "He's married to Johnny's niece. But, the guy's no kid, Joe; he's been around a while. He's even got two kids of his own. He was telling me about his son, the kid is six or seven, plays Little League ball already. And he's got a daughter about ten, I think. We're all getting older, none of us are kids anymore."

Rizzo turned onto Bay Ridge Parkway. "No, I guess not. My last partner, you remember her, Priscilla Jackson? She just got her stripes off the same list as McQueen. Imagine that? When Mike McQueen first started working with me, he looked like he was about twelve years old."

Ginsberg nodded. "Best thing ever happened to both of 'em, working with you. Let's see, McQueen's at the Plaza, Jackson got into that sex crimes unit in Manhattan she wanted, so whatdya have planned for me? How 'bout chief of detectives? I can do *all* my sleeping on the job, like I was doing on the stakeout. Whatdya say? Think you can swing it?"

"I'll see what I can do. Actually, I was talkin' to Vince this morning. Lombardi's not getting anywhere with that hit on The Chink. Last I heard he was still trying to work a rat to wire up for him, but Vince said it hasn't happened yet. I'm thinking of giving Lombardi a call, see if I can help him out again."

"Really? Why would you wanna do that?"

"Well, my plan was to let Carol get her sea legs, work the street for a year or so. I figured by then McQueen would have enough juice at The Plaza to hook her up with something safe and clean. But now I'm thinking, why wait? If I stroke Lombardi a little, help him out with this vendetta he seems to be wagin' against Mikey the Hammer, maybe he can step up for Carol sooner. Then, once she's set, I can finally put my friggin' papers in. I been promising Jen for a couple a years now, she's anxious to see me get out."

"Is that what you want, Joe? To get out?"

"Yeah," Rizzo said. "It is, I think. I've had enough. I'm getting close to overstaying my welcome. And what the hell." He turned to Ginsberg and smiled. "I always wanted to be the first cop to retire while he's still a fuckin' virgin. I don't think I should push my luck any further. You know what I mean?"

Chapter Sixteen

OLEG BOKLOV SHOOK HIS HEAD, a weary smile touching his lips. He gazed across the desk to his associate, Afansi Gorban.

"Dear Afansi, please. Try to understand. We are no longer in the alleyways of Vladimir. We are in America. We must do things correctly here."

"Correctly? Is this what it is you call it? Correct? I think it is not so correct. I think it is—forgive me—cowardly. I think you have let the Italians gut you. Forgive me."

Now Oleg frowned. His long history with this cold, hard man seated before him justified many liberties between them. But there were limits.

"If you refer to me in that manner again, Afansi, we will see who the coward is. And I ask not for your forgiveness, I ask for your loyalty. For your cooperation. And, most important, your obedience. Am I understood?"

Afansi held the steely cold eyes of his boss. After a moment, he gave a barely perceptible nod of his head.

"As always."

"Good. Now I will explain this to you. One time, I will explain it to you. You have done well. And you have been rewarded most

163

generously for your efforts. And you will continue to receive such rewards. But if you are thrown into an American prison, if you perhaps compromise my own security in the process, you will be rewarded in quite a different manner. Again, I ask you: Am I understood?"

"Yes, Oleg."

Boklov nodded. "Good. Now listen to me, and perhaps you will learn. You have established what the American police or, for that matter, the Soviet police would identify as a 'pattern.' It is therefore necessary to break that pattern, to diminish the probability of a policeman anticipating your next venture. Anticipating it and then terminating it with your arrest or execution. And so, for now, you will collect no further cigarettes. You will, as my American friends say, 'take a break.' "

Afansi was displeased. Oleg, he believed, was becoming a bit too familiar with the American way of life, a bit too comfortable with it. Afansi was beginning to suspect that Oleg was *becoming* an American, or perhaps even an *Italian*. And he wasn't sure which concept revolted him more.

"And so," Afansi said, "I will not earn? I cannot put food on my table? Why should I 'break'? Why can I not continue—move operations from Brooklyn—perhaps strike in Staten Island or Long Island? That would alter this pattern you fear. Why must I sit idle?"

"Afansi, Afansi, put food on your table?" Oleg again shook his head, patience beginning to fray. "You have taken enough money from my hands to feed an army through a hundred winters. Do you deny that?"

Afansi did, in fact, deny a part of it. He denied the inference as to whose hands the money rightfully belonged in.

But he had known Oleg Boklov since they were children stealing bread from the State Store in Vladimir. He recognized the familiar and frightening look that was beginning to dawn in Oleg's eyes.

"No, Oleg," he said. "Of course I will not deny it. But this is *America*. In America, it is *never* enough, there must *always* be more. You tell me time and time again how I should be an American, how I should adapt to the ways of this country. I am merely attempting to do so. I want *more*, Oleg. Always more. Like a *good* American."

Now Boklov smiled, his anger subsiding. In so many ways, Afansi was still that small, hungry young boy from Vladimir, that same poor wretch Oleg had mentored for most of his life.

"And you shall have more. I promise you. Take this break, temporarily, stop your operations. The Italians are growing fat from our labors. They control the network, and they have the means necessary to retail these cigarettes in massive quantities. They are living well on the profits, and they, too, are good Americans. They want more as well. And so, when there *is* no more, when their supply begins to run low, they will come to me. 'Oleg,' they will say, 'where are the cases of cigarette cartons? When will the next shipment arrive?' And then, I will shrug. 'I can't say,' I will tell them. 'Perhaps, if the price were higher, perhaps if the price per case increased by, say, twenty percent, then it might be feasible for me to once again motivate my people.'"

Oleg sat back in his seat, reaching for a bottle of Pertsovka vodka on the desk. He slid a glass toward Afansi, then placed one before himself. He poured generously into each glass. Both men took the liquor up, toasting one another silently. They drank, then Oleg wiped a stubby, powerful hand covered in coarse black hair across his mouth. He smiled at Afansi.

"And then, dear friend, after much bickering and complaining, they will agree to pay ten, perhaps even twelve percent higher."

He reached for the bottle a second time, once more pouring generous drinks for them both.

"Then you will be able to fill your table. You will be able to fill it with the blackest of caviar, as though you were a minister of

Moscow. You will understand, then, Afansi. And I will not be required to explain my actions to you ever again."

"THIS IS not good," Vadim Pilkin said.

Afansi sipped at his vodka. "No. It is not good."

The two men sat at the end of the bar farthest from the tavern's front entrance. It was a small place, sparsely furnished. Except for the thin, worn-looking bleached blond barmaid sitting solidly out of earshot, they were alone.

The bar and building housing it, owned by Afansi, sat on a busy corner of West End Avenue in the old seaside Brooklyn neighborhood of Brighton Beach.

It was Monday afternoon, May 4, three days since Afansi's terse meeting with Oleg Boklov.

"Why is he so insistent, Afansi? Did you try to reason with him? Try to explain . . ."

Afansi slammed the heavy rock glass down on the worn Formica bar top. "Perhaps *you* would like to try. Perhaps *you* can sway the czar, convince the premier, as he sits there on his throne and looks down on us peasants. Call him. Here, you may use my cell. I would like to hear it."

Vadim dropped his eyes from Afansi's angry glare. Meekly, he reached for his drink.

"No, Afansi. I meant no offense. I'm sure he is not to be reasoned with."

"No, he is not. Our dear old friend Oleg is very sure of himself, very confident. He and his new friend both, the Italian from Canarsie, the new boss of bosses. Both so confident." Afansi bent to his left and spat at the floor. "Bosses. I shit on them in Russia. I will shit on them here as well."

Vadim glanced with nervous eyes around the near empty room.

"Be *careful,* Afansi. Even in your own place the walls may have ears."

"Yes, I must be careful. Always so careful. Even now, in America, where Oleg told me we would be free, the place where we would be safe to conduct our business and prosper. Even here I must be always so careful. And, my friend, do you know why? Do you know why I must be so careful?"

Vadim sipped his vodka and shrugged. "Because you are alive. When you are alive, you must be careful."

"Yes, that is true. But I must be *extra* careful. Because I am a stepchild, Vadim. Never a son, never a brother. Always a stepchild."

Afansi turned his eyes to Vadim. When he spoke again, it was in the coarse dialect of a Russian peasant.

"Go, my friend. Go to Gleb and tell him of our new orders. Tell him to sit idle and await our next commands from the czar. But tell Gleb this as well: we will soon be done waiting. You see, I know of another stepchild, another man who sits at the feet of his master and waits for a scrap of meat to fall from the table so that he may eat: the Irishman. The Irishman in Sheepshead Bay."

"What are you planning, Afansi?"

Afansi's smile was dark. "Oleg has signed a pact with the Italians. He signed it with the blood of Albert and Vera on the day he allowed them to be murdered solely to protect the Italian in Canarsie. But I choose not to honor that pact. I choose instead to be free. Oleg insists I adopt the ways of the Americans. Well, so be it. Americans pride themselves on their great freedom."

He drained his vodka, then glanced to the barmaid, waving for another.

"We shall start small, Vadim. We will take baby steps. And at first, it will be just you and Gleb and I. But as we grow in strength, as we grow in confidence, others will join us. And we will grow fat as well, we will grow stronger. Then we shall see who is czar. And someday, we will spit in the eye of the Italian.

"And then we will be truly free, Vadim. Like real Americans."

As his fresh drink arrived, Afansi raised it in toast.

"Like real Americans," he said, this time employing his accented, gutteral English.

CHAPTER SEVENTEEN

TUESDAY, MAY 12, was a dreary, rainy day. Late into her four-to-midnight tour, Carol Rizzo shifted the nightstick affixed to her belt and took a seat on the old, worn sofa. She smiled at the middle-aged Hispanic woman beside her.

"You okay now, Rosa? Calmed down some?"

"Yes, thank you, yes. I'm . . . I'm sorry to have troubled you with all this." The woman dropped her eyes, embarrassment and shame bringing color beneath her olive complexion.

"He never did anything like this before, never," she said. "Twenty-six years we're married, never once did he raise his hands."

"Well, I guess with losing his job, plus a little too much to drink . . . but that's no excuse." Carol leaned over closer to the woman and laid a gentle hand on her arm. "There's *never* an excuse for it, Rosa. No matter what, he's gotta keep his hands to himself. Maybe a night in jail and a visit to the Domestic Violence part in criminal court is just what he needs."

"No, Officer, no. That is not what I want. He's sorry, truly sorry, and I swear on my grandchild, he never once did anything like this before. Please, don't arrest him."

Carol shook her head. "It's not him I'm worried about here. It's you. Besides, policy is pretty clear with domestic incidents. In cases like this, we have to follow certain procedures. I'm afraid you don't get much of a say once you've called the police. It's designed like that specifically to protect battered spouses, the ones who repeatedly have problems . . ."

"Yes, yes, I know, but this is not like that. My cousin, Carla, she was abused for years. Her husband was a bum, good for nothing. Finally, thank God, she got smart and put him out once and for all. But my Ricardo, he's not that kind of man. He's a good husband, a good father, a very proud man. When he lost his job, he was so . . . so ashamed. He *never* comes home drunk. A beer with the baseball on TV, some rum at a party, maybe, but that's it. Please, don't arrest him. I beg you not to."

Carol stood. "Let me talk to my sergeant, see what he says. Everything'll be okay. Trust me."

The woman smiled up at Carol. "Yes, I do trust you. You are a very nice girl. Thank you."

Ricardo Munoz sat dejectedly on the edge of the bed in the rear room, which overlooked Warren Street. He held his head in his hands and sobbed. Sergeant Joey Esposito stood before him, his arms folded across his chest, looking down at the man.

"Chill out, Ricardo, take it easy. Once the booze runs its course, you'll feel a lot better. Just calm down."

The man raised teary, bloodshot eyes. "I *hit* my wife! I *hit* her! How can a man calm down after doing that? How?"

Esposito pursed his lips. "Yeah, I know. But it's not like you knocked her teeth out. She says you barely slapped her. It was stupid; you were drunk. You just need to talk to somebody about it, work through it. Just relax, okay?"

Carol stuck her head into the room. "Can I get a word with you, Sarge?"

Esposito turned. "Yeah. Excuse me, Ricardo. You sit tight, okay? Don't get up. I don't wanna see you walkin' out of this room, understand?"

Munoz, his face once again buried in his hands, answered without looking up. "Yes, Sergeant. I will stay here."

In the small foyer, Carol spoke in low tones.

"What are we gonna do here, Sarge?"

"Lock 'im up," Esposito said with a shrug. "The nine-one-one call was made, and they both admit there was a blow struck. We lock him up."

"Is that carved in stone, boss?"

Esposito shrugged again. "Only thing carved in stone on this job, kid, is every fourteen days you get a paycheck. The rest is subject to environmental considerations."

"Okay. In this environment, what are our options?"

"Why you looking for options?"

"Humor me, Sarge. What are they?"

"Well, we can walk the guy to the outside hallway, pat him down for his house keys, then drive him to a coffee shop someplace. We tell him to have some coffee, go for a walk in the rain, chill out. Then, when he comes back home, he can't get into the building or his apartment with no keys. It's up to Rosa: she wants to let him back in, she does. If not, he finds a friend's place to crash in."

"I'm convinced this was a onetime thing, Joey. And Rosa doesn't want to press charges. I think lockin' this guy up is a waste of time and won't serve anyone."

Esposito shook his head. "We don't need her to press charges in DV; we can lock him up anyway. Let the judge and the social engineers work it out tomorrow in court. Besides," he glanced at his wristwatch, "it's almost eleven. We got just over an hour left on straight time tonight. We lock this guy up and you run him through the system, you'll pick up three, four hours overtime at least."

"Yeah," Carol said. "I know all about collars for dollars. My father's been a cop for a hundred years. I seem to remember how, when my sisters and I were kids, he'd get real active making arrests in October and November, what with Christmas coming and all. I'm not looking for OT here, Sarge. I'm just looking to do the right thing."

Amused, Esposito responded. "Oh, the *right* thing. Yeah, okay, Officer Rizzo, tell me: What's the *right* thing?"

Carol thought a moment before responding. "Let's get him that coffee. Let him cool off, think things through. He seems sorry as hell about this. We'll take his keys, like you said, and get him outa here for a while. I say he comes back later on with his tail between his legs, and nothing like this ever happens again. Okay?"

Esposito considered it, his lips pursed. Then he smiled at his young partner.

"Okay, kid. I guess not havin' a mortgage nut to crack helps with doing this *right* thing you're talkin' about. I'll go tell him, you tell the wife. If you're wrong, and he comes back later and throws her out the window, we can read about it in tomorrow's paper. We're off tomorrow, right?"

"You bet we're off, Sarge. All day."

AFANSI GORBAN sat parked in the driver's seat of the black van and contemplated the nature of his night's work. He watched as the heavy rain slashed across the windshield and pounded the nearly deserted stretch of Atlantic Avenue. The weather forecast had been accurate, and Afansi viewed it as a good omen. His planning, as always, was proving impeccable. Heavy rain meant little traffic, fewer still pedestrians, both conducive to his needs.

Tonight's work was of crucial importance, but not for its monetary outcome, a few thousand at best—minimal by Afansi's standards. No, money was not the issue here.

This night was about Afansi Gorban defining himself, establishing once and for all in the minds of his underlings that he was a man to be reckoned with, a man afraid of no other man, a man not pressed beneath the thumb of another.

Tonight, Afansi would demonstrate his independence and courage by defying Oleg Boklov despite the grave risk of deadly consequences usually associated with such action. And even though tonight would initially remain secret and unknown to Boklov, the implication would be clear. Both Vadim and Gleb would know they were working for a man of vision and daring, a man both willing and able to take what he believed to be his.

In the long run, this would prove far more valuable to Afansi than a few cases of cigarettes and some ready cash ever would.

And no less important, the Irishman in Sheepshead Bay would know as well. This small, private side-job arrangement was simply a down payment on what could someday be an independent syndicate with great profit potential, free from the kickups and tariffs of Oleg Boklov and the Italian in Canarsie. With time Afansi would grow his following, nurture more and more disgruntled minions of Oleg. The day would soon come when he possessed the resources and manpower to strike and sever Oleg Boklov completely.

And that would give Afansi control over the entire operation. Then he could finally turn an angry, jealous, and murderous gaze upon the Italians.

Afansi's eyes narrowed as he watched the rearview mirror with little interest, while headlights pulled to the curb some thirty feet behind the van. On some not-too-distant day, after he had reduced the Italians to errand boys and messengers, it would be he, Afansi Gorban, who ruled the nest. He, Afansi Gorban, as far removed from the dismal, putrid back alleyways of Vladimir as a man could ever get.

Oleg Boklov had told Afansi to break his pattern. He would soon get his wish.

Afansi smiled into the watery windshield, the streetlights and distant glitter of the moon liquid reflections in the glass.

Soon, he thought. Very soon.

"OKAY, HON," Esposito said into his cell phone. "Yeah, figure about twelve-thirty. No, I'm not hungry. I ate late, don't fix anything. I'll see you later." He paused, listening. "I won't forget. Matter of fact, I'll pick it up right now, there's an all-night place a few blocks from here." He closed the phone.

Carol glanced over from behind the wheel of the blue-and-white.

"Everything okay, Sarge?"

"Yeah, fine. My son ate all the cornflakes before he went to bed, and the only thing my daughter will eat for breakfast is, guess what?, cornflakes. Drive down to Anwar's, I'll pick up a box." He glanced at his watch. "Perfect timing, twenty to midnight. We'll make this quick stop, then head for the house and sign out."

Carol swung the radio car to the left, going westbound toward the largely Middle Eastern stretch of Atlantic Avenue. Anwar's was a sprawling beer and soda distributorship with a small convenience store attached to the front of the warehouse. The business, one of many commercial establishments in the mixed Muslim-Christian neighborhood, was owned and operated by second generation Lebanese Christians.

Carol drifted the car slowly to her right, pulling it to the curb near the storefront. The block, with most businesses closed for the night, was sparsely scattered with parked, darkened vehicles. She stopped the radio car some thirty feet behind a black panel van. She put the car into park just as the rain, already steady and heavy, came down with a new vengeance, drumming furiously against the body of the car.

"Figures," Esposito said, turning up the collar of his nylon uniform jacket and pulling his cap down low on his brow. "I'm gonna get more soaked than I already am."

He opened the door and stepped out, sprinting diagonally across the sidewalk to the store.

Carol pursed her lips as she watched him. So much for that, she thought: Esposito ran straight through the door without first looking into the storefront, as he had repeatedly preached to his new rookie partner. Carol picked up the recorder sheet, clicking her pen in preparation of closing out the sheet for the tour. She made a mental note to chastise her training officer for his carelessness as soon as he returned.

Joey Esposito dashed into the convenience store, slamming the door behind him to shield the driving rain. He stamped his feet, brushed water from his jacket sleeves, then raised his eyes.

As his gaze met that of the ski-masked man with the large automatic pointing at him, Esposito's last thought was of his daughter and her breakfast.

The bullet entered his face, tearing upward through the cheekbone and into his brain. He died with his own weapon still holstered.

In her peripheral vision, Carol saw the bright, unnatural flash of light coming from the storefront, heard the horribly unmistakable shot. She fumbled on the seat, grasping the Motorola, a cold terror seeping rapidly into her chest.

"Eight-Four sector super seven-Bravo, shots fired, shots fired! Backup, get me backup!"

She threw the car door open, jamming the radio into her belt, pulling her Glock free. As she began to run around the front of the radio car, rain tearing at her face, she saw the squat, darkly masked gunman inside the storefront, standing over the body of her sergeant.

Their eyes met. Carol raised the Glock and squeezed the trigger. The crashing boom stunned her out from the dangerous, almost robotic state she had fallen into. Suddenly, she felt her pounding heart, the slashing rain, her painfully clenched arm and shoulder muscles. The storefront window shattered under the bullet's impact, and the masked man dropped into a crouch and fired back. Carol thought she heard the round whiz by her in the wet air. She dropped behind the fender of the radio car, her training telling her to keep the engine block between her and the shooter. The Motorola at her waist was crackling with a tense, excited male voice.

"What's your twenty, Eight-Four super? What's your twenty? Where are you, Eight-Four super? Where are you, what's your fuckin' location?"

Carol fumbled once again for the radio, trying to keep a grip on the Glock at the same time, her hands trembling, her mind detached, almost blank, instincts alone governing her actions.

She realized she didn't know the address of the store and couldn't make it out through the wetness in her eyes. She felt running eye shadow sting at those eyes. Eye shadow? Why the *fuck* had she put on eye shadow?

"Atlantic Avenue, west of Henry, north side, north side, west of Henry."

Afansi tried to control his anger as he opened the driver's door of the van. What were these goddamned cops doing here at this hour? They should be closer to the precinct, a half mile away, in anticipation of the change of tours. Bad goddamned luck, he thought as he circled the van and moved toward the young female cop crouched behind the police car in the pouring rain, screaming into her radio. He approached from her blind side.

Carol saw him too late, turning to her left, exposing her chest to him. He fired his handgun.

Carol's Kevlar body armor took the heavy round, just below her left breast, flattening and stopping the bullet. The effect was as though she had been kicked by a mule, the impact breaking two of her ribs. She flew backward, bouncing off the front quarter panel of the car and landing on her right side in the street, her Glock sliding away. She gasped for air, her lungs emptied by the blow to her chest, and a searing pain from the broken ribs screamed at her.

Afansi watched her gasp, then glanced at the storefront. He saw Gleb and Vadim, their faces still cloaked in ski masks, running toward the van.

He turned his eyes back to Carol while lowering the gun and leveling it. He fired a second time.

The bullet grazed the split seam of her body armor and drove through the Velcro fastener, tearing into Carol Rizzo's flesh. A new piercing, burning pain exploded with vicious intensity and she collapsed into unconsciousness.

Afansi ran to the van and climbed in behind the wheel.

"Goddamn it to hell!" he screamed to Gleb in Russian. "We fucked up! We fucked up!"

As the van sped the short half block to the Brooklyn-Queens Expressway and up the ramp with its escape, the Motorola lying in the rain in the street beside the bleeding, unconscious Carol Rizzo continued to squawk.

"Eight-Four supervisor—what's going on? Eight-Four super, we're on the way, talk to me. What's going on . . ."

Seconds later, a blue-and-white slid a harsh right turn off Court Street and onto Atlantic Avenue, its siren blaring, light bars flashing, engine roaring under full acceleration. A second car flew out from Henry Street against the one-way traffic, turning brutally left onto Atlantic, its driver barely holding it under control on the slippery, oily blacktop. Both cars raced west, the officers within grasping their Glocks tightly, breathing in short, shallow breaths.

It was just before midnight, May 12. Exactly two months had elapsed since Carol Rizzo had ridden her first tour on patrol.

Chapter Eighteen

"STAY WITH ME GIRL, stay with me. Carol, Carol, listen up—talk to me, Carol, come on girl, talk to me."

Police Office Deshawn Starke, his large body wedged before the radio car's rear seat upon which Carol Rizzo was now sprawled, implored her. Starke's heart raced as Carol's eyes, unfocused and flat in the dim lighting, began to roll upward in her skull. He shook the young woman harshly, raising his voice.

"Carol! Carol, goddamn it, don't you fuckin' give in! Carol, talk to me!" He turned sharply over his shoulder, spitting words at his partner.

"Faster, Danny, goose this fuckin' thing! Faster!"

Officer Danny Faulkner, his hands slippery with Carol Rizzo's blood, mashed the accelerator to the floor. The car rocketed along Atlantic Avenue, covering the short distance to Hicks Street. Faulkner stood on the brake pedal, the screech of the tires sounding an eerie backdrop to the piercing scream of the siren. He wrestled the car into a hard turn, throwing it against traffic onto the narrow one-way Hicks, then again mashing the accelerator. The engine roared under the effort, the car flying past Pacific Street and through a solid red signal light at Amity. Long Island College Hospital, just three blocks from Atlantic, loomed brightly in the car's windshield. A trauma team, sheltered from the rain under the ER's ambulance entrance, awaited the police car's arrival. Faulkner slid the car to a brutal halt, its rear doors yanked open by trauma team nurses even before the vehicle had fully stopped.

Deshawn Starke, his dark blue uniform stained and glistening under the harsh hospital lights with Carol Rizzo's blood, jumped clear of the car, allowing the medical team access.

"What's her name?" a focused, intense-looking nurse asked over her shoulder as she bent into the car.

"Carol," Starke said. "Carol Rizzo."

Starke felt a sudden weakness come into his legs, a light-headedness touching him. He shook it off and steadied himself with an outstretched hand, touching the cold, wet metal of the radio car.

"Her name is Carol Rizzo," he repeated, to no one in particular.

JOE AND Jennifer Rizzo had spent a pleasant evening at home, nestled on their double recliner, a bowl of popcorn between them, a pay-per-view movie on the Sony flat screen.

Just after eleven o'clock, they had retired to bed.

The jarring ring of the phone woke them both. Rizzo glanced to the red digital at his bedside: one-fifteen a.m. He forced his mind blank and reached for the night-light.

The caller I.D. pierced his eyes like a laser:

NYPD 84 PCT CMDR

"Fuck," Rizzo said.

Jennifer, now bolt upright in the bed, raised a hand to her mouth.

"Oh God, Joe! Oh my God!"

Rizzo listened to the Eight-Four precinct shift commander's words and felt his heart tear inside his chest.

THIRTY MINUTES later, Jennifer, Joe, and Jessica Rizzo sat at a small table in the private consult room of the hospital triage area. They wore hastily thrown-on clothing, their hair still tousled from sleeping. A dark growth of whiskers dabbled in gray covered Rizzo's face. Jennifer and Jessica, red-eyed and breathing in labored effort, each trembled uncontrollably.

A tall young doctor entered the room. "I'm Dr. Melner, one of the ER physicians. I can tell you what we know so far."

"Tell us," Rizzo said. Jennifer leaned forward, a tightly balled fist clutching a damp handkerchief pressed to her mouth. Jessica, pale and suddenly trembling more acutely, sat beside her mother, her arm draped tightly around Jennifer's shoulders.

"We were able to stem the blood loss, but it was already significant. Your daughter appears to have one bullet wound to her left side in the area of the spleen and pancreas. From the amount of bleeding, it's probable one or both organs were compromised, but we don't know that for sure yet. Or at least, *I* don't know. She's been taken up to the O.R., and the surgical team undoubtedly knows more than I do. There was a second bullet that struck her in the left chest below the breast, in the vicinity of the diaphragm. The body armor she wore stopped that round, but it may still have inflicted some blunt trauma damage. If it did, it probably isn't life-threatening or, at any rate, not the biggest problem we have here."

Rizzo, his eyes hard, addressed the young doctor. "My oldest daughter's an intern at New York-Presbyterian. Is it possible to get Carol transferred over there? Have they actually started operating yet?"

Dr. Melner shook his head. "I don't know if they've begun

surgery, but I do know she can't be moved. We were lucky to even stabilize her; she was almost gone when they brought her in."

"Oh, Jesus," Jennifer said, suddenly wracked by uncontrollable choking sobs. Jessica, her own tears running freely, attempted to comfort her mother, but found her voice inoperative, her throat seemingly paralyzed.

Rizzo stood. "Thank you, Doctor. But this place isn't exactly an experienced gunshot trauma hospital, and in the middle of the night, I don't want some surgical resident . . ."

The young doctor smiled, raising a calming hand to Rizzo.

"I understand, Mr. Rizzo. I'd feel the same way. But less than twenty minutes after Carol was brought in, Dr. Sanders arrived. He lives nearby, on Montague Place in the Heights. You won't do any better than him anywhere. Years ago, he enlisted in the Army Reserve Medical Corps. Now he's a colonel and regimental surgeon. He's done at least two tours in combat zones and one at the main U.S. Army hospital in Germany. About three months ago, he returned from a seven-month tour at Bethesda. He's one of the top projectile trauma surgeons in the Northeast, probably in the whole country. Your daughter's in the best place she can be right now. If there's one good thing about this entire ordeal, it's Dr. Sanders being here. The ER triage nurse called him as soon as we were notified a shot police officer was coming in."

Rizzo held the man's eyes, weighing it. He eased his tensed muscles and allowed himself to drop back into the chair. He reached a hand out to Jennifer, rubbing her back gently, trying to ease the wracking sobs.

"Okay, Doc. Thanks. Nothin' personal."

"Of course not, Mr. Rizzo. Would anyone like something? Maybe something to help calm your nerves a little?"

Rizzo answered for them. "Maybe some Xanax, Doc? My wife's used it in the past."

He nodded. "I'll send a nurse in. And just so you know, there are police officers all over the hospital. They want to give blood, help out any way they can."

Rizzo nodded. "Thanks."

The doctor smiled and turned to leave. "I'll keep you informed, of course, but I'd say we're looking at a long wait. Don't let the amount of time that passes frighten you. It could be an hour or two or it could be all night. I promise to keep you posted."

After the doctor left, the sounds of Jennifer's gentle sobbing and Jessica's soft, comforting words lent a strange backdrop to the burning rage beginning to smolder in Rizzo's mind.

Moments later a nurse appeared and gave Jennifer .5 milligrams of Xanax. Joe and Jessica both declined her offer.

The Rizzos sat. Waiting.

VINCE D'ANTONIO stood in a corner of the ER's lobby with Eighty-fourth Precinct patrol commander Lieutenant George Flynn and Brooklyn South Homicide Squad detective sergeant Art Rosen. It was three a.m. They spoke in hushed tones.

"Espo was dead at the scene. Probably never knew what hit him," Rosen said.

"How the fuck could a vet like Espo walk blind into this shit?" Flynn said, his face flushed in anger. "You tell me, how the fuck!"

D'Antonio shrugged. "We've all done it once or twice, George, we've all slipped up. Sometimes this is how it breaks. Goddamn it."

Rosen checked his notes. "Esposito took a head shot. This motherfucker shooter wasn't taking any chances. He wanted Espo dead."

"Same shooter on the Rizzo girl?"

Rosen shook his head. "No, doesn't look that way. Rizzo got one shot off, either it grazed the inside shooter or the guy took some flying glass. There was blood on the floor near Espo that probably wasn't his; the stains trailed out to the sidewalk under the awning.

We had a dog walker about half a block away who saw Carol fire a shot, then duck behind the radio car. A guy got out of a black van and blindsided her. The dog walker saw the guy fire two shots at Rizzo."

"Son of a bitch," Flynn said, shaking his head. "Two shooters, both stone-cold motherfuckers."

"Any description of them?" D'Antonio asked.

"Not much. White males, three all together, average height. Nothin' on the van, either. After the shots, it took off east on the BQE. We've got twenty cops canvassing for witnesses, maybe something else will turn up."

D'Antonio ran a hand through his hair. "However it goes with Carol, Rizzo is gonna want in on this. He'll want to track these guys down, you can bet on that."

Rosen shook his head. "Well, we all know better, Vince, *including* Rizzo. He can't be within a mile of this, and he knows why: any evidence he found, or even touched, would be contaminated beyond belief. Rizzo *never* works this case, Vince, not even answering phones on a tip line. No fuckin' way. This is a cop killing, and a task force is already forming. We'll find these pricks, and we'll get a conviction. But *not* if Rizzo starts fuckin' with it. After he thinks about it, he'll understand."

Flynn shook his head. "I rode with Joe, we partnered years ago. I remember how he was with those girls of his. Joe Rizzo's not thinking about convictions here, guys. You *know* what Joe Rizzo is thinking."

"Yeah," Rosen said. "Same thing we'd all be thinking. Another reason for him to sit on the bench. In fact, the PC will issue a directive. That's SOP for situations like this."

D'Antonio glanced at his watch. "I'm gonna go find somebody who maybe knows what's going on with the kid. Then I'll talk to

Joe. Jesus, his wife must be half nuts. They had a whole thing about Carol comin' on the job. Now look, just two months and maybe this kid is . . . Two fuckin' months."

Flynn shook his head. "Between the three of us, we got, what, maybe sixty years on the job? I fired my gun once, one fuckin' time. And I missed the son of a bitch. Either of you guys ever shoot? Ever take a bullet?"

They both shook their heads.

Flynn reached into his inner jacket pocket, slipping out a small black flask. He unscrewed the top, offered it, was declined, and took a long pull of the whiskey it held. He replaced the cap and shook his head.

"Go figure," he said sadly. "Go fuckin' figure."

"THANKS FOR coming down, Vince, but it wasn't necessary."

D'Antonio shook Rizzo's hand. "I came as soon as Flynn called me. He's outside with Brooklyn South. I think he's afraid to come in here. He said he was supposed to be watching out for Carol, he can't believe this happened."

"It was meant to be," Rizzo said, standing outside the consult room. He glanced through the window of the closed door; Jennifer was still seated inside, staring into space, her eyes red-rimmed and bloodshot, Jessica sitting beside her. Rizzo sighed.

"I arranged Carol's Eight-Four assignment, Vince. I figured she'd be safe there. Now look. What a fuckin' mess. If *anybody's* at fault, it's me."

"Well, that's just it. It's nobody's fault. Like you said, it's like it was meant to be. Don't beat yourself up."

Rizzo turned suddenly cold, hard eyes away from the window, away from his wife and daughter. He leaned slightly inward to D'Antonio as he spoke, his voice lowering.

"Actually, it *is* somebody's fault. The scumbag that shot my daughter, it's *his* fuckin' fault. And he ain't walking away on this. You mark my fuckin' words."

D'Antonio nodded. "I won't insult you by saying I know how you feel. No one can know, no one who hasn't been where you are now. But . . . I can *imagine* how you feel, and I can *imagine* how Espo's widow feels, how his two kids feel. But you gotta step away from this, Joe; let Brooklyn South and the task force handle it. They'll get these fuckin' guys, believe me. Coupla shit-bag junkies, probably, knocking over a store to score a dime or two."

"Yeah."

"I'm putting you out on leave, effective immediately. I'll clear it tomorrow through the PC's office. Administrative leave, at least two weeks. It won't be charged to your annual, you can just stay home and take care of Carol while she's recovering." D'Antonio looked through the glass discreetly, noting the pale, lifeless face of Jennifer Rizzo and the slumped boneless appearance of her body. "You take care of your daughters. And your *wife*."

He nodded. "Okay, boss."

D'Antonio looked carefully at Rizzo, noting the determined hatred burning in his eyes.

"I'm serious, Joe. Listen to me: you gotta stay out of this. That's an order."

"Yeah," Rizzo said, turning to reenter the room. "Whatever you say, boss. You and the fuckin' PC."

Later, at four a.m., with coffee sitting on the small table before them, Rizzo addressed his middle child. They had spent the last hour in near silence, each with their own thoughts, memories, fears. Rizzo had forced practicality to the forefront of his mind. He knew that his daughter's shooting would make the morning news.

"Jessica, do me a favor, honey," he said. "I think you should call your big sister at her place. She'll be getting up soon to start her shift at the hospital. I don't want her learning about Carol on the news. Are you up to that, or do you want me to handle it?"

Jessica stood and began rummaging through her bag for her cell phone.

"Sure, Daddy, I'll call Marie. You stay with Mom." She picked up her coffee and left the room, closing the door gently behind her.

Rizzo slid his chair closer to Jennifer. He draped an arm around her.

"Carol's gonna be fine, Jen. We got very lucky with this Sanders guy. You see what they've done with those kids from the war, patching them up good as new—and from a lot worse than a single gunshot. She'll be fine, I know it. Trust me, baby. She'll be fine."

Jennifer turned dull eyes to her husband. "Trust you. You want me to *trust* you? After the way you've betrayed me?"

Rizzo blinked in surprise. "Betrayed you? What are you talking about? How did I betray you?"

"You betrayed me with Carol. You've been *glad* she's a cop; you've been happy about it. Until tonight, maybe, now that you see how it's turning out."

"What? What are you talking about?"

"You've been secretly happy and proud all the while, ever since she first brought it up years ago. And I don't think you've done *everything* you could to dissuade her, like you led me to believe. You said if worse came to worst, you'd steer her to a federal agency like Customs, anything to keep her off the streets as a cop. So what happened to that, Joe?"

Rizzo felt his ears redden. He struggled to hold the icy gaze glaring from his wife.

"I told you, Jen. The guy I knew retired, he lost his juice. He couldn't help, he said . . ."

"Oh stop it. Just stop it. You're glad she wanted to be a cop: That father-son macho experience you thought you missed out on.

You were *happy* about it, and now look what's happened. My baby, my little girl, shot . . . shot in the street, in the rain, like an animal, like a rabid dog!"

"Knock it off!" Rizzo said harshly. "She's *my* daughter, too, and don't forget that. How dare you compare her to a rabid fuckin' dog—she's a *cop,* goddamn it, and the rabid dog is the son of a bitch that shot her."

Jennifer lowered her eyes from his, dropping her hands gently into her lap. When she next spoke, it was in a soft, detached voice. It sounded to Joe as though she were almost talking to herself, alone in the room. Alone in the world.

"You've betrayed me for the second time. I'm not stupid now, and I wasn't stupid then. Marie was a toddler, Jessica just an infant, and I was so busy. I was distracted and totally dependent upon you. But I was never stupid, Joe. Yes, I found out about your little friend, the nurse. You were having quite a time for yourself, playing cops and robbers with Morelli all day and screwing your girlfriend all night. No wonder you and that bum were so close. I bet you had plenty of laughs, the two of you. Laughs at my expense."

Rizzo sat back in his seat, his mind suddenly reeling. If only she knew, he thought, if only she knew the truth about Johnny Morelli. How it had been he who made the nurse break things off with Joe. But, Rizzo realized, he could never exonerate Morelli without damning himself at the same time.

"Jen, I don't know what you're talking about, you're talking crazy. It's all the stress, the Xanax. I . . ."

Jennifer shook his arm from her and sat back sharply, returning her eyes to his. And when she spoke this time it was not to herself; she spoke directly to Rizzo.

"Twice. You've betrayed me twice now. And I don't know which time was worse. But I assure you there won't be a third time."

Rizzo stared at his wife, a new fear tormenting him, the sensation of an inescapable living nightmare swirling around him. The darkly intense look in Jennifer's eyes shivered him. He desperately sought words, thoughts, something, anything to snap him from his evil sleep, end this nightmare, wake him back into his life.

A knock sounded and Vince D'Antonio pushed open the door. He smiled at the Rizzos.

"The mayor is here," he said. "And the PC. They'd like to say hello and offer their support."

The strained look on Rizzo's face and the cold, alien body language of Jennifer suddenly registered on the lieutenant. He stammered as he continued.

"Is . . . is it . . . is this a bad time, Joe?"

Rizzo's eyes narrowed with his response.

"Yeah, it is. Tell them they'll have to wait. They're just gonna have to wait."

LATER, RIZZO once again shook the mayor's hand, this time thanking him for coming and bidding him farewell. He turned to the police commissioner and did the same. The two men walked off toward the hospital conference room where they would prepare their statements for the growing crowd of news reporters gathering in the lobby.

"Shall I meet with your wife and daughter now, Joe?" police chaplain Father Alex Lynn asked.

"Yeah, sure, Father. They'd like that. They're down the hall in consult room three. I need to talk to a guy I know, Father. You go ahead. Don't wait for me. I may be a while."

"All right. Stay positive, the doctors all seem very optimistic."

Rizzo nodded. His last hourly update on Carol's surgery, now under way for more than three hours, seemed neutral to him, noncommittal at best. But Rizzo had no desire to debate it with the priest. Instead, he sought solitude in a way he never remembered having sought it before.

He came across a small, nondenominational chapel. He went in and took a seat.

Looking around, he grew reflective. The room was softly illuminated and had two sets of four pews with an altarlike structure at the front. The air felt cool and fresh.

Rizzo crossed himself then raised his eyes toward the altar some twenty-five feet away. He imagined someone sitting there, a vague presence, indistinguishable, waiting for some*thing* or some*one*.

"Don't take my little girl," Rizzo said softly. "Don't let Carol die. Don't hurt her, don't hurt my wife and my daughters to get to me. If you're pissed about something, whatever it is, take it out on me. Whatever I've done, it's *my* baggage. Make *me* pay for it."

Suddenly Rizzo stood, his eyes still fixed on the altar, anger now stirring in his heart.

"Don't do this. Be a man about it. Deal with *me,* man-to-man. *Don't* fuckin' do this."

His eyes suddenly welled with tears, and he fell heavily back into the seat, weeping gently. He cradled his face in his hands, rocking forward and back, now sobbing intensely.

"Please. Please don't take my little girl."

"THOSE FIRST cops on the scene really used their heads, Joe," Mark Ginsberg said. The sun was just rising over the city, and he and Rizzo stood together on Congress Street, sipping coffee from cardboard containers. "One of the nurses told me if they had waited for an ambulance, it mighta been a lot worse. She seemed *positive* Carol was gonna be fine. And she had no reason to bullshit me. It's gonna be okay, Joe. Believe me."

Rizzo dragged deeply on the Marlboro he had bummed from an ambulance attendant and nodded.

"Yeah."

Ginsberg shot a sideward glance at his partner. "Try and relax. Try to hold it together a little longer. Pretty soon they'll be telling you she's okay. You'll see, just a little longer."

Rizzo expelled smoke and turned to Ginsberg. "Do I look like I'm about to lose it, Mark?"

"No," Ginsberg said, shaking his head. "Not at all. That's what's got me worried. You seem a little *too* cool. The way a guy looks sometimes just before he does somethin' real stupid. You know the look I'm talking about. You've seen it on lots a guys over the years."

Rizzo nodded. "Yeah." He dragged again on his Marlboro. "I ever tell you about my parakeet, Mark?"

"Parakeet?" Ginsberg asked, his brow creasing. "A bird?"

"Yeah, a bird."

"No. You never told me about your parakeet."

"My mother got it for me right after my father died and we moved in with my grandparents. The parakeet was for the both of us, me and my sister, but it was really more like my bird. I took care of it. Cleaned the cage, fed it, gave it water. I used to buy these hard, white biscuitlike things that I'd clip onto the inside of the cage, right near the perch. Luigi, that was the bird's name, he loved those things. He'd sit there on that perch for hours just scraping and pecking on that biscuit, opening his beak, his fat little tongue coming out. It was like the highlight of his life."

Rizzo raised the cigarette to his lips, drew on it.

"So one day, I come home from school, and the cage is empty. My grandfather's home, musta been working a morning tour. So I say, 'Hey, Grandpa, where's Luigi?' He takes me over to the window and points to the fire escape. Something is out there wrapped in newspaper. 'Sorry, kid,' he says. 'The bird is dead . . .'"

Rizzo shook his head with the memory. "He coulda eased me into it a little, but that's what he did. 'The bird is dead.' I went totally bonkers, hysterical. I was about twelve years old by then, not really a kid anymore. But I couldn't stop cryin'. Eventually, I put Luigi in an old mayonnaise jar and screwed on the top. Then I put the jar into a shoe box and buried him in the backyard. I cried for a fuckin' week. If a kid reacted like that today, they'd have him jacked up on Wellbutrin and talking to a shrink. My grandfather used a different approach."

Ginsberg smiled. "Yeah. I'll bet."

"He told me I wasn't crying about the bird. He said I really didn't give a damn about the bird. He said I was cryin' for my father. The dead bird reminded me about my dead father."

"Probably what a shrink would tell a kid today," Ginsberg shrugged. "Same answer, minus the two-fifty-an-hour fee."

Rizzo smiled briefly. "Yeah." After a moment he took a final drag on the cigarette and flicked the butt toward the curb. "But you know, years later, my mother told me I never cried at my father's wake. Not even at the funeral. I don't really remember that myself, but that's what she said."

"Yeah, well, I don't know what the fuck you think you're sayin' here, Joe, but take a little advice, okay? Don't get all morbid and bleak. Let's keep our eyes on the ball, stay positive. Carol's gonna be fine. You can buy *her* a fuckin' parakeet on her next birthday."

"I'll tell you what I'm saying, Mark. When that bird died, something in me died, too. Years later, when I lost my grandmother, then a year or two later, my grandfather, I took it all in stride. When they died, I got depressed 'cause I *wasn't* feeling depressed. And all these years, back of my head somewhere, I've been a little afraid that maybe I couldn't fully feel loss. Not since Luigi."

He turned, heading back toward the hospital, Ginsberg walking beside him.

"But I know better now. I do feel. I guess I always have, just never knew for sure. Not until this."

Rizzo stopped, turning to face his partner before speaking again.

"What a fuckin' way to find out."

"HELLO, I'M Dr. Sanders."

All four Rizzos stood: Joe, Jennifer, Jessica, and the oldest Rizzo girl, Marie. Joe spoke.

"Tell us, Doctor."

The man smiled. "Carol is stable. We have her listed as acute critical, but that has more to do with hospital protocol than medical consideration." He turned his eyes to Marie. "I understand you're interning at New York Hospital, so I know you understand my point. After I leave, you can make it clearer to your family." The doctor turned to Jennifer. "Your daughter should be fine. The bullet fractured on impact. We removed her spleen, which had taken the brunt of the damage, but that isn't a life-threatening or even life-altering consideration. The pancreas was pierced, as was the left kidney, and both have been repaired. The risk of infection is now our most immediate concern, but I assure you, I've seen very similar wounds and treated them under far less ideal circumstances. If infection were to develop, we'll handle it. I honestly believe she'll recover fully, but she's had a tremendous loss of blood and great trauma, both from the initial gunshot and the subsequent surgery. A second round was stopped by her vest, and it broke two ribs; very painful, but not serious. She's very weak and not conscious. It will be quite a few hours before you can even see her, let alone speak to her."

"Is there any permanent damage, Doctor?" Rizzo asked.

He hesitated. "From my perspective, no. But I called for a surgical assist from Dr. LaGrassi. He specializes in reproductive tract surgeries. Your daughter's left fallopian tube was utterly destroyed, and we removed it. Her uterus had been pierced as well, and Dr. LaGrassi repaired it. You'll speak to him later on, perhaps to-morrow; he has surgeries scheduled all this morning. He tells me it's possible, *possible* mind you, that she may, in the future, should she choose to have children, find it difficult to sustain a pregnancy. All of that remains to be seen and isn't something to concern your-selves with now. Let's just see her through the next few days. If there are to be any complications, that's when they'll begin to manifest themselves. I've brought in Dr. Sangal as her internist, he'll oversee things. And, of course, I will maintain involvement for as long as necessary." He glanced at his watch. "I need to get going, I'm afraid. I have a scheduled procedure in forty minutes, and I should get something to eat. It's been a very long night for everyone."

They all thanked him, and he excused himself.

"Come on, Mom," Jessica said. "Let's go home. You need to eat something, too, and get some rest. Carol's gonna be okay now, thank God."

"Yes, Mom," Marie said. "I'll stick around for a while. I want to take a look at Carol's chart and speak with her internist."

Rizzo glanced at Jennifer. Her expression, though relieved, still reflected pain and shock.

"Go, hon," he said to her gently. "I'll get one of the cops to drive you and Jessica. I want to talk to the guys, see if they have any leads. Me and Marie will be along in a little while."

"All right," Jennifer said, her voice flat. "Whatever you say, Joe."

Chapter Nineteen

SALVATORE SEXTON was fifty years old, known throughout the Brooklyn underworld as Sally Clams.

Sally had been born in the Bath Beach section of Bensonhurst, the only child of an Italian mother and an Irish immigrant day laborer. As a young man, Sally had earned leadership ranking in the Bath Beach Boys, a loosely organized youth street gang serving as unofficial training ground for would-be wiseguys. Sally had, at the relatively early age of twenty, graduated to membership in the local gangland crew of Raphael Riccio, then the boss of Bath Beach. There he thrived as a foot soldier but, because of his half Irish blood, had never risen to full associate status. Despite two successful contract killings, one reputedly at the behest of the late Louie the Chink Quattropa, Sally hadn't gotten any closer to becoming a made man. It was, he came to realize, his destiny to labor in the chorus with no hope of a starring, or even a featured, role in the production.

So Sally had utilized a newly discovered talent for independent, innovative, and nearly legitimate ventures. Years earlier, when the once thriving restaurant and business strip along Sheepshead Bay had fallen into disrepute, and Emmons Avenue stood lined with

195

abandoned, shuttered properties, Sally had purchased a number of them very cheaply. In one, he opened a twenty-four-hour convenience store, and the surrounding Sheepshead Bay neighborhood had responded to it well. Word had gotten around that the place was mobbed up, and robberies would pose no threat. People knew they could double-park in front of the store at any hour of the day or night, run in and buy their milk or bread or cigarettes, and return safely to their cars. They also knew that a discreet wager could be placed on the daily number, a horserace, or any type of sporting event.

Sally had reaped nice profits from his enterprise. He rented out his other properties as storage or temporary space to area businesses, and all his mortgages were paid in a timely fashion.

Using his profits from the first store, Sally Sexton expanded slowly, eventually coming to own ten such convenience stores throughout Brooklyn with three additional ones on Staten Island. His legitimate income nearly equaled that of his illegitimate, and some of the sting he had suffered as a result of his second-class mob citizenship was now offset by his newly found favored-son status with the local Chamber of Commerce.

And then an amazing thing happened. Sheepshead Bay, with its fleet of commercial and sport fishing vessels tied to piers perpendicular to Emmons Avenue, began a renaissance. Lundy's, the hundred-year-old fabled seafood restaurant at Emmons and Ocean avenues, reopened after many idle years. Visitors began arriving from various gentrified areas of the borough in their shiny new Audis and BMWs; they gradually displaced the battered Chevys and Dodges of the diehard fish fanciers who never stopped coming to the bay to greet the fishing boats returning from their daily outings and hawking their catches on ice-covered tables along the waterfront.

Eventually the entire strip was reborn with upscale shops and fine restaurants, eclectic in nationality but mostly bound together by seafood themes. And many such properties were purchased or leased from Sally Sexton.

So, when a trendy Manhattan chef found himself dangerously in debt to a Tribeca loan shark, Sally stepped in. With the chef now completely in *his* debt, Sally opened a fine-dining seafood restaurant on the bay. Yuppies and judges, wiseguys and professionals dined side by side in gleeful ignorance or fascinated tolerance of one another, Sally Sexton pocketing the cash.

A number of the newer establishments were owned and operated by recently arrived Russian immigrants, mostly legitimate businesspeople freed from the stifling, initiative-destroying Soviet system of heavy-handed socialism. And they thrived in their new environment.

But others, Sally discovered, like Afansi Gorban, were not so legitimate.

Sally, with his new street name of Sally Clams, was nothing if not an astute student of capitalism. He was very much aware of a basic rule of business: the less you paid for a product and the more you sold it for, the higher the profits. He saw this most clearly on his liquor sales with their legitimate three and four hundred percent markup. Sally made proportionately more money selling drinks than clams and lobsters. In his convenience stores, he also turned a nice profit on cigarettes and often dreamed about what those gains could be with a markup similar to that of liquor. Indeed, as taxation had increased the cost of a single pack of cigarettes to an almost unsustainable level, Sally realized what he needed to do.

Afansi Gorban, the leader of a loosely associated band of professional burglars, had been consulted and details worked out. The plan required kickups to go from Afansi to his boss, Oleg Boklov, and from Sally to his, Mikey Spano. Spano, in turn, would kickup to Louis Quattropa, although that aspect had recently changed permanently with The Chink's death. And Sally couldn't imagine Boklov was required to kickup to anyone because, according to Afansi, Boklov was The Czar.

And so, through his restaurant and thirteen convenience stores, Sally now sold cigarettes for which he himself had paid a mere fraction of tax-free wholesale. He would sell each pack at full market value, pocketing not only that portion of the price representing the product profit but most of the taxes as well. Eventually, Sally found himself with so many cigarette cases that he began anonymously moving some through mob-owned vending machines throughout the city. Eventually he found it necessary to wholesale the excess, thus branching out his operation far to the north Bronx and eastern Queens.

It was a pleasant operation, fully protected by its openness with the respective local bosses with the bulk of risk falling to Afansi and his thugs. Sally Clams, as he recently told his twenty-five-year-old fourth wife, "had the world by the balls." The only real peril Sally could envision was being found out by the ruling Manhattan mob, but even there, with Quattropa's involvement, Sally felt insulated and safe.

But now on this Wednesday afternoon, sitting at his desk in the rear of Polipo, his fine Sheepshead Bay restaurant, Sally felt a sinking, sickly feeling in the pit of his stomach; almost as though someone suddenly had *him* by the balls.

"Jesus Christ, Afansi. Holy fuck! That was *you*? You killed that fuckin' cop? Oh, shit."

Afansi told his half truth sheepishly. "It was Gleb. He shot the one who died. Vadim shot the woman. But in all fairness to them, it could not be avoided."

Sally shook his head. "This ain't the fuckin' boondocks in Siberia, 'Fansi. This is *Brooklyn*. You shoot two cops in Brooklyn, you better have a bulletproof skull."

"I don't think there are any boondocks in Siberia, Sally," Afansi said calmly. "And I am not afraid of your American police."

"Well, good for you. But listen to me, I ain't talkin' about any cops. I'm talkin' about Mikey the fuckin' Hammer. And Oleg. They find out we went independent on them, workin' a side job got all fucked up, they'll be servin' *us* for dinner in this fuckin' joint. We'll be *inside* the fish when they're done feedin' on *us*." Sally ran a hand through his hair. "Jesus Christ."

Afansi shrugged. "Looking back, perhaps it was not wise. Not our arrangement, no; that was good, that was justice. After all, it is we who take the chances, we who do the work. Why not cut the bosses out on occasion?" He leaned over and spat at the floor.

"That is for the bosses."

Sally frowned. "This ain't some shit-hole in Moscow, 'Fansi. Don't fuckin' spit on my floor."

"I am sorry. But I am angry. As you, too, are angry, with these so-called bosses."

"Why the fuck didja hit a store that was still open for business, for God's sake, with a clerk there? What were ya gonna pull, two bills and ten cartons? What the hell were you thinkin' about?"

"The basic concept seemed sound," Afansi said. "I checked the place some days ago. There were many cases of cigarettes there, in the back, with the beer and soda. They wholesale some of them. A small job, yes, compared to what we usually do. But, Sally, you'll only be able to move small additional amounts discreetly without drawing attention from Spano; and the fact that it was not a warehouse, not a jobber—it would not draw Oleg's eye. He would not suspect it was me—us—behind such a job if he were to even hear of it. Nor will the police. They will round up the usual assortment of drug addicts, street thugs, and stickup men. They may even arrest one, and that will be the end of it."

"So why you here, tellin' me all this shit? I'da rather stayed ignorant, for Christ's sake. I don't need to hear this."

"Ah, yes, my friend, but you do. We are, after all, partners. We share the profit, we share the risk. Besides, I am a man of my word. I told you I would have at least twenty cases for you today, and surely you deserve an explanation. I would tarnish my honor by doing anything less."

Sally frowned across the desk. "You better hope Mikey don't get wise to this, Afansi; you better fuckin' *pray* he don't get wise to it. 'Cause if he does, it ain't gonna be your honor gettin' tarnished, it's gonna be your fuckin' brains gettin' smeared—all over the street in Canarsie."

"SO, JOE, how's Carol doing?"

Rizzo sat across the desk from Brooklyn South homicide lieutenant Jimmy Santori. It was Saturday afternoon, May 16, four days since the shooting.

"Coming along, thanks. They've got her off the critical list, and they think she's out of danger."

"Good," Santori said. "Any idea when she might go home?"

"Not yet. My oldest girl's in daily contact with the internist overseein' Carol's case. He wants to take it one day at a time. Marie tells me it'll probably be another four, five days. We'll see."

"Okay." Santori ran his eyes over Rizzo's dark suit and black tie. "You heading over to the Esposito wake?"

Rizzo nodded. "Yeah. Jen's gonna sit this one out. She's had enough death and stress for a while. Her time is better spent at the hospital with Carol."

"I'll try to go by this afternoon, too," Jimmy said. "If not, I'll go tonight. When's the funeral?"

"Monday."

They sat in silence for a few moments, then Santori cleared his throat. "So, Joe, what can I do for you?"

Rizzo sat back in his seat and casually crossed a leg. "Well, you can fill me in. I've got a feeling I'm not gettin' the whole story from the newspapers. What's really going on?"

"Unfortunately, the papers got it pretty covered. There's really not much else I can give you. This ain't goin' that well."

"Tell me."

Santori reached across his desk, pulling a thick folder in front of him. He flipped it open and scanned the contents as he spoke.

"You know about the witness, the dog walker. He was no real help, other than to tell us there were three perps and they escaped in what he believes was a black panel van. Carol told us the inside perp took a shot at her. We dug a slug out of a car parked across Atlantic. It matches the gun that killed Espo. Blood traces at the scene that weren't Espo's were sampled and run through DNA banks. Negative result for an I.D., blood was male, that's all we know there. The slug from Carol's nine was dug out from the rear wall and tested negative for trace blood, so the perp probably got cut up by flying glass from the front window. But it's still a possibility the round clipped him. They can't be sure. Negative for tristate area hospital inquiries on matching wound cases. We had some interesting bleeders at a few hospitals, but they all checked out alibied and negative. Forensics on the scene also negative, there were a million prints all over the place, but the store clerk vic told us the perps wore ski masks *and* gloves. Two white males, both five-eight, -nine, one guy one-fifty, the other guy a little heavier. They didn't talk much, but the clerk said one guy had an accent, he couldn't be sure from where." Santori shrugged. "Fuckin' clerk is a third cousin of the store's owners, just got here from Lebanon about six months ago. He barely speaks English himself."

"What's the task force doing?"

"Carl Douglas, the inspector from Manhattan North, is runnin' it. He tracked down the last cop killer, that guy up in Riverside. He put his team together and added me and Rosen, plus some of my other guys from Brooklyn South. Task force is based downstairs in the Operations office."

"What are they doing?" Rizzo repeated.

"Grunt work mostly. Checking those hospitals, like I mentioned, plus rounding up stickup guys and junkies."

"Junkies?" Rizzo asked. "Ski masks, gloves, a driver and escape vehicle outside watchin' their backs, and the task force is roustin' *junkies*? Are you fuckin' kidding me, Jimmy?"

"I know, Joe, I know. It plays a little like pros, sure, but why would pros be knockin' over a two-bit twenty-four-hour joint sellin' milk and newspapers? It doesn't necessarily compute, so we still need to check out the usual assholes."

Rizzo thought for a moment. "Anybody run the Middle Eastern angle?"

Santori nodded. "Sure. FBI gives the whole family a clean bill. Plus they're Christians, not Muslims. Far as we know, they ain't jihadin' types. This looks like a straight-up armed robbery."

"Yeah?" Rizzo said. "Timed at the change of shift on a wet, rainy night? If these guys are junkies, they're the smartest fuckin' users I've ever heard about."

"We see that. Believe me. We're on this, buddy. We just don't have much yet. Every snitch in the city knows this is the ultimate 'Get out of Jail Free' card. We got a hotline eight hundred number, plus hand-picked P.A.A.s monitoring lines in every precinct. If a call does come in, we'll jump on it. In the meantime, we just keep pluggin'. And Joe, you don't have to chase me down for info. If I hear anything, good or bad, I promise I'll let you know asap. The less you show your face around this investigation, the better it'll be. For *all* of us. Including you. Your presence risks contaminating and compromising any evidence that turns up. We don't want to hand any ammunition to some fuckin' defense lawyer."

Rizzo sighed. "I know, Jimmy, I know. But, goddamn it, I'm like a caged tiger here. I've got so many ideas about how I'd be runnin' this, my fuckin' head's gonna explode."

"Sure, of course. But listen to me: relax. Go to Esposito's wake, go to the hospital, take care of your family. That's what you need to get your head on. Leave the rest of it to us. We'll get these guys, believe me." Santori leaned forward, a dark smile slowly forming.

"When was the last time we let a cop killer get away, Joe?"

After a moment, Rizzo nodded. He stood and extended a hand to shake Santori's, both their grasps firm and dry.

"Okay, Jimmy. Thanks. You keep me posted."

He turned and walked out of the office, Santori watching the door close slowly behind Rizzo.

Jimmy Santori didn't know much about caged tigers. But he knew plenty about Joe Rizzo.

A caged Joe Rizzo was a very dangerous thing.

RIZZO ENTERED his daughter's hospital room, the sight of Little Joey Esposito prone in his coffin and the sobs of his widow still fresh in his mind. He sat down next to Carol and smiled.

"Mom around?" he asked.

"She just left for dinner. She's been here all day," Carol said, her voice still raspy from the breathing tube and harsh anesthetic drugs.

"Oh, okay. So how you doin' today?"

Carol smiled weakly. "How do I look like I'm doing?"

"You look like you're doin' fine, honey. Just fine." Rizzo reached out and gently patted her bare arm. "And you're gonna be totally up and around real soon. Fully recovered."

"These broken ribs are killing me, Dad. They're worse than the postsurgical pain."

"They just need time, that's all. You want me to call a nurse, get you something? I see the morphine drip is gone."

"Yeah, they stopped it last night. But no, I'm okay. They gave me something about an hour ago."

Rizzo nodded, rubbing gently at her arm. "You tired, Carol? Would you rather I come back later?"

She shook her head. "No. Stay a while." Her eyes fell away from his face. Idly, she started to pick at a loose thread in the bedsheet. Rizzo watched her for some moments, then reached a hand out to her face, placing it softly under her chin. He raised her face to his.

"What, honey?" he asked gently. "Tell me."

Carol hesitated before responding. "We haven't discussed it, Dad."

"Discussed what?"

Despite the pain and drugs clouding her eyes, Rizzo saw a flash of anger begin to pass through them.

"The Met game. What else? Oh yeah, maybe the *shooting*. Maybe I meant the shooting."

Rizzo had expected and dreaded this moment. He understood the guilt, illogical as it may be, that tortured a cop who lost a partner. The haunting, internally whispered, "what ifs" that sounded in their ears and wakened them at night.

And this time it wasn't just a fellow cop. This time it was his daughter.

"You wanna discuss it?" he asked gently. "Fine. But before you say anything, let me tell you what I already know. You went to that store because *Espo* needed to go there. Then he screwed up and ran in on a robbery in progress and had the bad luck to get shot. You immediately called for backup and got out of the car, returning fire and drawin' blood from the perp. Then you got ganged up on and

204

blindsided. So if you're gonna tell me you think anybody blames you on this, just let it go. Okay? This whole thing was written in the stars, Carol, and nobody coulda changed one friggin' thing about it. Not you, not me, not anybody. This was *not* your fault."

Carol's eyes welled. "Joey wanted us to lock a guy up, Dad. Just before this happened. He wanted to lock up a guy who had a few drinks and got into a domestic. I talked him out of it. Joey woulda been typing reports in the precinct at midnight instead of lying on the floor dead. He coulda picked up the damn cornflakes later, on his way home, picked them up somewhere else."

"Carol, please. How far back you wanna go with that logic? If Joey had never studied for the sergeant's test, he'da never become your training officer, so he wouldn't of been at the store at all. If his old man had gotten killed in Vietnam, he'da never even been born. You can't —"

"I was trying to do the *right* thing," Carol said, tears running across her pale cheeks, her face suddenly morphing before Rizzo's eyes into that of a young, scared, disappointed child. *His* young child. He stood and moved close to her, cradling her in his arms, softly stroking her head.

"I know, Carol. I know."

She raised agonized eyes to her father. "I was just trying to do what was *right,* Dad. And look at what it turned into."

Rizzo, as helpless and impotent here as he was in the investigation, found himself unable to respond with any semblance of insight.

"I know, Carol."

The *right* thing, he thought. The right fucking thing.

JOE RIZZO sat in the small, cluttered office at the rear corner of Anwar's Quick Pick and Beer and Soda Palace. Behind the desk were Barry Anwar, adult son of the owner, and his recently arrived third cousin, Said Malouf. Rizzo took a notepad and pen from the inner pocket of his suit jacket. With that one simple action, one he had taken thousands of times before, he solidified his resolve. This was *his* investigation.

"Thanks, Mr. Anwar. It'll be much easier to do this with you interpreting." He turned to Malouf. "I understand, Said, that your English isn't perfect yet."

"No," Said responded. "It not perfect."

Rizzo nodded, jotting in his pad. "I know you've been through this a couple a times already, so I'll try to keep it short."

Rizzo turned back to Anwar. "I'll ask you the question, then you just repeat it to him exactly the way I said it. When he answers, you just tell me exactly what he said, okay? You don't have to say, 'He said . . .' every time, and please, don't paraphrase or try to correct something you think he's misstated. Just tell me *exactly* what he says, even if you think he meant to say something else, okay?"

"Sergeant," Anwar said pleasantly. "I spend half my time at holidays translating. Believe me, I know what you want from me. Please, begin whenever you are ready."

"Thank you." Rizzo turned to Malouf.

"You were alone here the night of the robbery?"

"Yes. I came in at eleven, I was to work until six a.m."

"Tell me what happened."

"Two men came into the store. One stayed near the door, the second approached me at the register, a gun in his hand. They both wore masks, woolen masks, garishly colored. I was very frightened, the gun was pointed at my chest. The man gestured I should move, come out from behind the counter."

"He didn't speak?"

"No. Just pointed with the gun. I understood what he wanted. I followed his instructions."

"What were his instructions?"

"He pushed me toward the rear area where all the cases are stacked, where we distribute the beer and soda cases. We went behind a stack. He had me face the wall."

"Then what?"

"The second man appeared."

"Had anyone opened the register yet?"

"No. I would have heard it."

"Go on."

"The first man bound my wrists with tape, the heavy tape of a workman. Then he made me sit on the ground."

"Neither man had said anything to you yet?"

"No, not a word."

"You told other detectives that one of the men had an accent and didn't sound like a native of this county, but you couldn't place the accent."

"Yes, that is all correct."

"So at some point, you did hear them speak?"

"Yes. To each other."

"What did they say?"

"The first man, the thinner of the two, he said to the other, 'Go and find them.'"

"Go and find who?"

Malouf shrugged. "I don't know. There was no one else here. As I told your colleagues, it made little sense to me."

Rizzo, a twitch at his right eye nagging him, thought for a moment.

"After the first man said 'Go and find them,' what did the second man do?"

Once again Malouf shrugged. "He walked away, some feet away, to the side. Then he simply stood there, looking."

"Looking at what?"

"I don't know. The wall? I don't know."

Rizzo stood. "Please, show me. Let's go out into the store. Show me where the man stood."

When they left the office and crossed the cool, musty warehouselike room piled high with beverage cases, Malouf stopped and pointed.

"Here. He stood here."

Rizzo moved to the spot indicated.

"Which way did he face?"

"That way. Toward the wall."

Rizzo turned, following Malouf's pointing finger.

His eyes fell upon neatly stacked, sorted by brand, cases of cigarettes. He counted: Five Marlboro red, three Marlboro light, two extra lights. Four Parliaments, one Kool, one Newport, six other single cases of various brands, twenty-two in total. Rizzo smiled grimly. No Chesterfields.

"What happened after the second man stood here?"

"After a moment, he looked around. Then he went that way." He pointed. Rizzo once again followed the pointing finger, this time with his sight only. His gaze fell on a large, well-used hand truck tucked into a small alcove in the far wall. He turned back to Malouf.

"Have you told all this to the other police who interviewed you?"

Malouf shrugged with his answer. "I have answered all their questions."

"But did you tell them about where the man stood, which way he faced, where he seemed to be going after that?"

After a moment of consideration, Malouf again, through the interpreter, Anwar, responded. "This they did not ask, I think. Yes, they did not ask these questions."

"Did the thieves ever ask you if you had a safe on the premises?"

"No."

"Is there one?"

"Yes. In the office."

Rizzo turned to Anwar, addressing him directly. "What's in the safe?"

"Legal papers, copies of our beer and wine license, some tax documents, and so forth. And, perhaps, a thousand or so dollars. For unexpected expenses, petty cash, whatever."

Rizzo turned back to Malouf.

"Okay. So the second man stands there, looks toward those cigarettes, then starts to head in the direction of the hand truck. What happens next?"

"The front door of the store opened. It opened harshly, I heard the brass bells above it clamoring loudly, and I heard the door hit the wall. One of the men looked that way, then hurried toward the front. From where I sat on the floor, I could see no more. I heard a shot. The second man, the one who guarded me, he swore, then ran to the front also. I heard another shot and glass breaking. Then, more shots. All was still for a very short time, then I heard sirens. After a few moments, two policemen appeared before me, their guns extended. I think when they saw me, they were startled. I believe one of them almost fired. He looked very tense, very angry. I think he *wanted* to fire."

"Yeah," Rizzo said, jotting in his pad. "I wouldn't doubt it."

LATER THAT night, Rizzo stood in the shadows of Fourteenth Avenue, looking diagonally across the street to the funeral home on the corner. He leaned on what he knew to be the parked department Ford of Jimmy Santori.

After almost an hour, Rizzo saw the lean figure of Santori exit through the gold-gilted doors and walk slowly down the steps. He watched as the man crossed the street toward the Ford.

"Joe," Santori said. "What the hell you doing here? Why didn't you come inside?"

"I went this afternoon, Jimmy. Actually, I'm here to see you. Why don't we sit in the car? I'll explain."

A few moments later, Santori punched at the steering wheel.

"Are you fuckin' crazy? Do you realize what you've done? You contaminated the eye-fuckin'-witness. You bullheaded fuckin' idiot, I told you to stay away . . ."

"Yeah, well, I didn't, so let's not waste time with the drama, okay?"

"Drama? You think this is fuckin' drama? You got *me* involved in this mess now. You *know* I gotta go straight to Inspector Douglas and tell him about this. You're looking at an obstruction charge here, Joe, an official misconduct, God knows what the fuck else. Are you really this goddamned stupid?"

"Cut the shit, okay? You ain't going nowhere. You rat me out on this, I can lose the job, the pension, everything. You know you're not gonna talk to Douglas, so just hear me out, okay? That's all I'm asking."

"You got some balls, Rizzo. Don't take me for granted here, you're makin' a big mistake."

Rizzo leaned closer to him and lowered his voice.

"No, Jimmy. I'm not. We go back too far, you and me. We both know where too many bodies are buried. I'm not making a mistake. Don't you make one, either."

After a long tense moment, Santori averted his eyes first. Rizzo smiled.

"That was a pretty short pissin' contest," he said. "I was prepared for a lot worse."

Santori, his eyes cold, answered. "I'm gettin' old. I know which fights to fight. This ain't one of them."

Rizzo nodded. "Good. Two old friends, we shouldn't fight. Now, you ready to hear me?"

Santori, his anger slowly evolving into a working, familiar prag-matism, nodded. "Yeah."

Rizzo gave him all the details of his interview with Said Ma-louf. When he was finished, Santori responded.

"So you're seeing some half-assed connection to the cigarette ring that's been boosting butts all over the city? Is that it?"

"Yes."

Santori shook his head. "The M.O.s are on two different plan-ets. The cigarette burglars hit unoccupied warehouses and disable sophisticated alarm systems. And from the bulletins I've seen, they're walking away with two, three hundred grand in street value product per job. This Anwar's, it's completely different. Open for business, clerk on duty, weapons involved, and for what? A few cartons of smokes layin' around?"

"No. I counted twenty-two cases, Jimmy. Ballpark that at a street value of over fifty grand. And you wanna talk about pros? These guys were pros."

"No, they were assholes. They hit a freakin' convenience store and wound up killing a cop and nearly killing another one, then they barely beat the first ten-thirteen car away from the scene. These guys are assholes."

"Yeah, are they? You got one eyewitness inside the store, he can only tell you they were two white guys, maybe one had some kinda accent. No forensics left except for blood the perps couldn't an-ticipate and which you can't even I.D. The outside eyeball knows even less than the vic. They hit that store around midnight, change of shift, heavy rain falling, the streets deserted, anybody who *was* out was walking fast with their eyes down and an umbrella in front of their face. And look at the target location: a stone's throw from the entrance to the BQE. In minutes they're in Manhattan or halfway to Queens or Staten Island or a dozen other places within

211

Brooklyn. It was just their bad luck that Espo walked in at *exactly* the wrong moment. Seconds later, the perp woulda had his mask off, Espo wouldn't a known anything was going down."

Santori interjected. "I'm not impressed. Assholes."

"Just hear me out. The plan was to tape that clerk up, stick him behind some cases of beer. Then they take off their masks. They load the hand truck, two, tops three quick runs out to the van, they're done. If anybody does wander in for a container of milk, they sell it to him. Who the fuck robs a cash register joint in a panel van? Come on, Jimmy, open your eyes, look at it, look at the fact pattern and stop being distracted by imagining the PC's crackin' your nuts 'cause I talked to the eyeball. Look at it, Jimmy."

Santori reflected a moment. "So, okay. It's a possibility, but a very remote one. Why, all of a sudden, do these guys go low tech and become strong-arm gunslingers and for a fraction of the dough? Come on, Joe, admit it: a million-to-one shot. *You're* the one dis-tracted, not me. Your daughter was shot, so you're pissed. I get that. I understand that. But you're letting it fuck with your logic."

"All I'm saying is take a look. You can spare a coupla guys from shaking down street skells and junkies and steer them this way. Just check it out. There was a safe in the office, these two guys never even asked about a safe, never once touched the cash register. Their only target was the cigarettes, right from the jump. *That's* why there were three guys, a driver and two loaders; that's why they used a van."

"You don't *know* one of those things to be a fact, Joe, not one. It was a two-bit job, even if you're right and they were after the smokes. You know how many jobbers we got in this city? Not to mention Nassau, Suffolk, Westchester, wherever? If it's cigarettes they're after, they could knock over a joint a week all year before they'd have to start grabbing mom-and-pop opportunities."

"Okay, then consider this," Rizzo pressed. "A while ago, my boss set up a stakeout on three joints in the Six-Two these guys maybe would target. And guess what? They never showed. And they haven't hit anywhere else, either. Maybe they decided to rewrite the script, go sustaining level and bide their time. Pull some small jobs until the heat's off, then start hitting the jobbers again. Or maybe these three guys decided to do a little part-time work on their own. They can't handle the alarms, so they need a business that's open. Or maybe they've flooded the market, demand for the product is a little off. So they're doin' like the oil cartels, turning the taps down some, jacking the price up again by producing less product."

"Yeah, and maybe when I get home, my wife'll look like Megan Fox." Santori ran a hand across his face. "Look, if anything, maybe these are copycats, but even if it is the burglary ring, there's a separate task force working that case. And far as I know, they got shit."

"Exactly, Jimmy. Far as *you* know. All I'm saying is check it out, coordinate with that task force. You don't know what they have. Jesus, how hard could it be to crack that ring? They're moving thousands of packs of cigarettes, hundreds of cartons, they gotta have some kind of network in place to do that. Tommy Boy Tomasulo in Little Italy's been running smokes from down south for twenty fuckin' years. You think he doesn't know something about this? The cop killing changes the rules here, Jimmy, you know that. There *ain't* no fuckin' rules, and everybody, including the wiseguys, knows that. The task force can confront Tommy now, harass and threaten his ass, make him into more trouble than he's worth. He gives up some names or maybe the old ginzo runnin' Manhattan says, 'Hey, throw Tommy Boy in the fuckin' wood chipper, he's bringing too much heat down on us.'"

Santori pondered it. After a minute, he sighed.

"You should really be sellin' life insurance, Joe, or maybe used cars. This conversation started off with me gettin' you fired. Now it's ending with me starting to buy into this bullshit."

Rizzo smiled in the dark interior of the car. "No way. If I ever decided to become some sleazy snake oil salesman, I'd do it the right way. On Wall Street, or better yet, in fuckin' Washington."

CHAPTER TWENTY

MONDAY WAS A BUSY DAY for Rizzo. Following the church service and burial of Joey Esposito, he spent the balance of the morning and early afternoon by his daughter's bedside. He believed that Carol had probably not picked up on the cool, detached aura now hovering over her parents, and if she had noticed, she most likely attributed it to the ongoing friction with regard to her career decision and not Jennifer's accusations. He could not imagine Carol knowing anything about that.

By twenty minutes to four, Rizzo milled around the Ready Room of the Seventy-sixth Precinct house on Union Street, one of three precincts that bordered the Eighty-fourth. The night Carol and Esposito had been shot, cars from all three houses, as well as three additional nearby precincts, had responded to the "shots fired—officer needs assistance" radio call.

Now, uniformed officers began trickling into the room in preparation for their pre–night tour roll call. Rizzo, the detective sergeant badge dangling from a heavy silver chain on his neck, eyed them as they entered. A tall, muscular black cop and an equally tall but leaner, redheaded officer walked in together, laughing among themselves to some private joke. Rizzo crossed the room and intercepted them.

"I took a wild guess here," he said, extending his hand. "You're Starke, and this is Faulkner, am I right?"

Deshawn Starke eyed the badge, then the extended hand. He raised his eyes to Rizzo's face. After the briefest instant, recognition came into his eyes and he took Rizzo's hand, shaking it firmly.

"You're the father, right? The father of that cop got shot last week."

"Yeah. I was with my wife and my other daughter at the hospital that night. A nurse pointed you guys out to me, but I never got a chance to come over and thank you."

Starke shrugged. "No need, Sarge. We were just helpin' out a sister cop best we could, that's all."

Rizzo nodded. "Yeah. I get that. But the doctor said if you two had waited at the scene for an ambulance, Carol probably woulda bled out. You guys saved her life."

Faulkner responded as he took Rizzo's hand. "We figured it was best not to waste any time. Your daughter looked like she was hurt pretty bad. How's she doin'? We stopped by to see her last night, she seemed pretty good."

"Yeah, she's coming along. Another coupla days we should be bringin' her home." Rizzo's eyes darkened. "I was at the other cop's funeral this morning. Coulda been hers, too. I owe you guys."

"Your girl woulda done the same for us, Sarge," Starke said. "You don't owe us a thing."

"Yeah," Faulkner added, then smiled. "Maybe buy us a cup a coffee some day."

Rizzo reached into his suit pocket and extracted two cards. He handed one to each officer.

"That's where you can reach me. I wrote my personal cell number on the back. You guys ever need *anything,* you call me. You ever get jammed up, if you ever can use a hand with something, call me. I been around the job since you guys were gettin' weaned offa Pampers. Not too many things I can't help out with."

The two young cops studied the card, then each slipped it into his memo book.

"Sounds good, boss," Faulkner said. "You may just get that call someday."

"Yeah," Starke answered. "Could happen."

Rizzo extended his hand and they all shook again.

"Good. I like to keep my books square." He moved to leave, then turned and spoke once more. "And do me a favor: Be *careful,* okay? *All* the time."

They both nodded at him, cocky smiles on their faces.

"We're nothin' but, Sarge," Starke said. "Nothin' but."

Rizzo pursed his lips, then nodded. He turned and left the Ready Room, glancing at his watch. Plenty of time to get to the restaurant. It was only about two dozen blocks away.

DETECTIVE SERGEANTS Mike McQueen and Priscilla Jackson, fresh from visiting Carol, raised their glasses in a toast.

"To Carol," McQueen said. "She looks great, Joe. Strong and healthy."

"Yeah," Priscilla said. "And she seems to be holdin' up to it all, too."

Rizzo sipped his Dewar's. "I guess. It's gotta be tough enough losin' a partner, but for a rookie, Jesus, I can't even imagine. She was just *looking* for excuses to blame herself. *Looking* for them."

"We talked about that some," Priscilla said. "The three of us talked it all out. She's okay, trust me. This kid's got your genes, Joe, no doubt about that. She's tough as nails."

McQueen smiled. "But a hell of a lot better-looking. Guess Jennifer managed to slip some DNA through."

"I'm sure Carol was glad to see you guys," Rizzo said. "Thanks for going up. It was just family allowed the first few days, I hope you understand."

"Freakin' hospital," Priscilla said with distaste. "We're *all* family. They oughta know that."

The three cops sat eating their early dinners and catching up on one another's lives. McQueen was in a serious relationship with a woman he had met a year earlier at the pharmaceutical company where she was employed. He had been giving a seminar on security and antiterrorist measures in the workplace. It was part of McQueen's responsibilities in his new role with Community Relations out of Police Plaza.

"In fact," Mike said, as he told them about her, "I've been looking at engagement rings."

Priscilla again raised her glass. "Good for you. It's time you settled down."

Rizzo turned. "And what about you, Cil?"

"Same old same old," she shrugged. "Me and Karen are still over at our place on East Thirty-ninth Street. She's been making 'I wanna be a mommy' noises for a while. We may start looking into it very soon."

"Adoption?" Rizzo asked.

"Possibly, or maybe Karen will get inseminated. She's been thinking about going that route."

"Well, good luck with it, Cil," Rizzo said, a disturbing thought of Carol's damaged womb flashing through him, tempering his happiness for his former partner's plans. "You'd make a great, what, mother? Father? How's that work?"

Priscilla laughed, shaking her head. "It's good to see you still live inside that cave, Joe. Renews my faith in the order of things."

"Always glad to be of help," Rizzo said, the dark thoughts fading. "But really, good luck with that. I think it's great."

Later, when their espressos arrived and the server had left them, Rizzo glanced around. The rear corner of the Queen Italian Ristorante where they sat was empty, with only a few diners scattered near the front of the dining room. Soon, Rizzo knew, the place would begin to fill with its usual heavy crowd of local Heights residents, attorneys and judges from nearby courthouses, and blue-collar workers from outlying neighborhoods. He leaned inward on the table and lowered his voice as he spoke.

"Remember back when, Mike, how you tapped the computers at the Plaza and helped me and Cil crack that homicide case?"

"Sure, I remember. The ink we got from that helped me get the P.R. gig I have now. That scheme of yours worked out for all of us."

Rizzo nodded. "Yes, it did. Well, I need your help again. But this time, it's more for me. And for Carol . . . and Joey Esposito."

McQueen glanced at Priscilla. Her face was without expression as she met his eyes. McQueen turned back to Rizzo.

"Tell me, Joe. What can I do?"

IT WAS after ten p.m. when Joe and Jennifer Rizzo entered the kitchen of the house they had shared for most of their long marriage, leaving Carol in her hospital bed some twenty minutes earlier. The drive home had been mostly silent.

Rizzo went to the refrigerator and removed two bottles of water. He crossed to the table, where Jennifer sat idly going through the day's mail, and placed a bottle before her. He sat down and twisted the cap off his bottle. He waited for Jennifer to raise her eyes to his. When, at last she did, he spoke.

"We've got to straighten this out, Jen. We need to clear the air. I know it's hard to imagine, with Carol still in the hospital and me wearin' this goddamn funeral suit, but listen to me: things *can* return to normal, *can* be good again. It just depends on how we handle it. We can roll over and die, or we can build on it. It's up to us."

Jennifer pondered it before replying. Her eyes were hostile when she spoke. "Oh? And what shall we handle first? What you did with Carol, or what you did with your girlfriend?"

Rizzo ran a hand through his hair, then sipped at his water. He sighed.

"Jen, I already told you. There *was* no girlfriend. I don't know what crazy idea you've been harboring all these years, but if you were so convinced I *had* cheated, you seem to have made some kinda peace with it. I thought we had a damn good life together so far. Now you're gonna wrap it up into one big mess because of some plot you think I ran on you about Carol becoming a cop? I'm gettin' my ass kicked here while my daughter's in a hospital bed recovering from a near-fatal shooting. Gettin' my ass kicked for *two* things I never even did, for Christ's sake. So, Jennifer, explain it to me."

"Is that how you intend to 'straighten this out'? With more lies?"

"They aren't lies, Jen. How do I prove something didn't happen over twenty years ago? How do I *prove* what I was *feeling* about Carol coming on the job? You've got me in an impossible situation here. You tell me: How do I prove anything to you?"

Jennifer stood, looking down into her husband's face. Her own face was drawn, stress sitting heavily upon it.

"Suppose I asked you to swear on Carol's life? What would you do then, Joe? All your repressed old-world bullshit superstitions would rise up and bite you right on the tongue, wouldn't they? So what would you do? I'll tell you *exactly* what you'd do. You'd stand up and walk out of the room without saying a word. *That's* what you would do."

Jennifer turned and walked away. Even from the kitchen where he sat, Rizzo could hear the slam of their upstairs bedroom door.

He remained there for a while, staring at the wall, drinking his water.

* * *

AT MIDNIGHT, Rizzo went down and took a seat at the desk in his small basement office. Spread before him were copies of various department faxes and bulletins regarding the recent past rash of tobacco warehouse burglaries. By sheer strength of will, he had pushed any thoughts of Jennifer from his consciousness. He would deal with that later.

Now, he had a more pressing concern. Somewhere out there in the night, the man who had shot his daughter was breathing air. Somewhere out there in the night, the man who had killed Esposito was breathing air.

It was Joe Rizzo's intention to change all that. And soon.

CHAPTER TWENTY-ONE

THE STREETS surrounding One Police Plaza in lower Manhattan were lined with official and private vehicles of police department headquarters personnel. Rizzo's generic NYPD plaque would not suffice, so he parked his Camry at a no standing zone on Broadway and walked toward Police Plaza, some three blocks away.

As he walked, Rizzo pondered his situation.

Officially, his hands were tied. Since the case involved a family member, he was barred from involvement and keenly aware of the logic behind it. Any evidence he produced would be called into question and challenged before and during any trial as biased; and if, in the unlikely event there was a street confrontation with an armed suspect, any action Rizzo took would be subject to skeptical review.

And so now, after nearly an entire career playing angles to benefit countless other victims, Rizzo was cornered and stymied in a case that involved his own flesh and blood.

But, of course, that was in an official sense.

As he walked along Chambers Street, Rizzo ran his options through the forefront of his mind. He couldn't risk any further fieldwork, having pushed his luck far enough by his interview with

Said Malouf. He instead needed to perch on the shoulders of the official investigators, monitor all their moves, become privy to each of their suspicions and attuned to their thought patterns. And from that perch, he would somehow have to find a way to subtly nudge and guide them in whatever direction he believed would prove most fruitful. It would be a difficult, but not impossible, task; he had already directed Santori's next move toward possible coordination of the two separate task forces.

Rizzo felt confident that if the shootings had resulted from botched efforts by common street criminals or junkies, the homicide task force would take them down soon enough. He knew that such cases were usually solved not so much by police investigatory efforts, but rather by skillfully leveraged pressure exerted across the appropriate criminal population. Eventually, some low-life street thief or junkie, in order to shift pressure from himself, would inform on the perpetrators.

But Rizzo wasn't too concerned with that. In fact, his instincts, coupled with the formidably circumstantial evidence elicited from Malouf, told Rizzo that it wasn't some junkie or two bit stickup man he was after.

No. It was someone bigger, someone smarter. And probably someone a lot more dangerous.

With the usual tools of his trade now denied him, Rizzo needed to draw upon other resources to learn the identities of the perpetrators. He had done it before. And he would do it again—one final time.

As he reached the guarded entrance of Police Plaza and dug his shield and I.D. card from his pocket, his thoughts turned for the uncounted time to that second shot, the shot that had pierced his daughter's flesh. The shot that had nearly killed her and may have robbed her of a child of her own some day.

Rizzo had listened to Santori's verbal report, committing to memory every word. The dog-walking witness had been very clear. The first shot had knocked Carol to the ground, and the cops who found his daughter lying there recovered her Glock nine millimeter from ten feet away on the wet pavement beneath the radio car. The doctors at the hospital had explained how, after receiving such a devastating first blow in the vicinity of her diaphragm that resulted in two broken ribs, Carol would have been breathless, her lungs unable to inflate *or* deflate, her diaphragm most likely paralyzed. She almost certainly would have passed out, and that sudden and complete relaxation would have released the diaphragm and restarted the breathing process.

For all practical purposes, that first shot had sufficiently disarmed and disabled her, thus allowing the shooter freedom to make his escape.

Joe Rizzo had been a professional police officer most of his adult life. He now believed he was hunting for an equally skilled professional criminal.

The first shot was professional business: a criminal shooting a cop in order to make good his escape.

But that second shot had made it personal. Personal to Rizzo.

And that's exactly how Rizzo intended to deal with all of this. Personally.

MIKE MCQUEEN spread his arms above his desk as he addressed his former mentor and partner.

"So, Joe, how cool is this? My own office, with a door *and* a window."

"Yeah, very cool. But I think I got a closet in my house a little bigger than this."

McQueen laughed. "You might, at that. But I'm young yet. Wait."

Rizzo nodded. "I'm sorry to get you involved in all this, Mike. I don't have a lot of other options."

McQueen's face became somber, his steely blue eyes narrowing the slightest bit before he replied.

"Yeah, well, I don't mind helping out. But I wanna know something, and I need the hundred percent truth. What exactly *are* you getting me involved in here? You're not planning on doing anything stupid, are you, Joe?"

"Have I ever?" Rizzo replied lightly. "I'm not goin' vigilante here, buddy, so relax. Yeah, it crossed my mind, and more than once. But, no, you don't have to worry about bein' an accessory to stupidity. Relax."

McQueen nodded. "Okay. I'm relaxed. So what is this, then? What's your angle?"

"No real angle. I just know how this stuff works. They got two separate task forces, each headed up by some prima donna who's looking to move up the food chain. Neither boss probably trusts the other, most likely they don't even *like* each other. I believe there's a very good chance the cigarette boosters are also the shooters on Carol and Espo. I put that theory to Santori, so now it might get to each task force boss. Maybe then they'll put their heads together and keep their eyes on the big picture. Or, maybe they won't, maybe each guy officially blows the concept off, then ignores it or starts working it separately. Then they start stepping on each other's toes and fuckin' up the whole thing, CIA-FBI style. I don't want a nine-eleven here, Mike. I want those shooters."

McQueen considered it. "Or maybe they'll remember they're cops and go after the shooters together."

With a skeptical gesture, Rizzo replied. "Yeah. Maybe."

The two detectives sat in silence for a while. "So, I give you the file on the cigarette case, and you do what with it? If you get caught doing fieldwork on this, you're in a jam. A big jam. Plus, you might wind up collapsing the whole thing on your head, causing an acquittal or even dropped charges on any suspects you do manage to round up."

"Yeah, that could happen. *If* I was stupid. Look, I'm not lookin' to kill this guy, and I sure don't want to jeopardize a life sentence for him. All I'm looking to do is keep one eye on each task force. This way, if I see something that looks promising, I feed it to Santori, and he follows up. If it goes anywhere, this Inspector Douglas will get all the credit, and if I turn out to be right and the two cases *are* related, Douglas will move to combine the task forces and make it one joint force with guess who in charge? Douglas will set the stage to become the hero. The other boss running the cigarette case, *he* gets an 'atta boy' and a backseat. And I don't give a rat's ass how the politics work out, I just want that fuckin' shooter."

McQueen held Rizzo's eyes, then after a moment seemed to relax, a smile touching his face.

"Okay, Joe. I just needed to hear you say it out loud."

Rizzo nodded. "And you were right to. So, now I said it."

McQueen reached down behind his desk and extracted a large manila folder from a drawer. He tossed it onto the desk.

"This is what they have so far on the cigarettes. The last DD-five entries were posted last night, everything's right up to date."

Rizzo reached to the folder and flipped it open casually. "You look through this at all?"

"Yeah. After I printed it off the computer."

"Anything catch your eye?"

"Well, they figure anybody moving nearly two million dollars worth of cigarettes must have some kinda sales network in place. Initially the task force focused on a wiseguy in Manhattan, Tommy Tomasulo. You know him?"

"Never had the pleasure, but I've heard of him. He runs cigarettes up from Virginia and the Carolinas. Been doing it since back when they were two bucks a pack."

McQueen shrugged. "Still does, according to the file. But the interesting thing is, he convinced the cops he's as pissed about these burglaries as they are, probably more so. Whoever's knocking over those jobbers is putting a big dent in Tomasulo's bottom line. See, Tomasulo brings in merchandise that's unstamped. He can't move it through legitimate outlets like stores or vending machines without having a New York tax stamp. So most of his stuff has to go outa the trunk of a car in dribs and drabs. He does counterfeit the stamp on some product, but the trouble is he needs to do that on each individual pack. That means opening every carton and stamping one pack at a time. Very time consuming and expensive, not to mention risky. If some shopkeeper gets busted because of a phony tax stamp, odds are he'd give up his source, somebody could track it all back to Tomasulo."

"That's a big marketing advantage for our burglars," Rizzo said. "The cases they steal are already legit, already officially tax stamped. No wonder Tomasulo is hurtin', *if* he's being straight with the task force. And that's a very big if."

"Well, yeah. But they've invested lots of hours into him, even staked out his place a few nights. Anytime a jobber got hit, they'd monitor Tomasulo's crew. They saw no activity connecting things. They're convinced Tomasulo's clean on this."

Rizzo again reached to the file, closing it. He picked it up as he stood.

"You got a big envelope I can put this in?"

McQueen produced one. "All ready for you."

They shook hands, the young cop rising behind his desk.

"Thanks, Mike. I'll look this over tonight. I'd appreciate it if you kept me current on any developments. Anything at all, even if you don't think it's important."

"You got it. I backdoored my access, same as I did on that homicide last time. I'll get dailys and send them over to you."

"At my *house*."

McQueen smiled. "Of course. I haven't known you these last few years without learning a thing or two."

Rizzo turned to leave. "Kiss that girlfriend a yours for me. I wanna meet her soon."

"Sure, Joe. Maybe you and Jen can join us for dinner once things get back to normal with Carol."

Rizzo turned. "Yeah," he said, a sadness in his voice which surprised him. "I'll mention it to Jen."

RIZZO SAT back in his seat, an overhead buzz of fluorescent lighting the only sound in his basement office.

He considered what he had gleaned from his two thorough readings of the file McQueen had provided him.

The task force had gravitated to a theory of organized crime involvement in the jobber warehouse burglaries. It was common knowledge that many of the candy stores and bodegas in the city served as fronts for numbers taking, sports betting, and localized loan-sharking operations. They would also provide an ideal outlet for purloined cigarettes. For as far back as any police authority could remember, the bulk of bootleg tobacco trade was rooted in Manhattan's Italian mob. So the task force had centered its efforts there, beginning with Tommy Tomasulo.

Detectives had also taken a good look at the competing activities of Chinese gangs. Some Chinatown outlets appeared to be retailing more cigarettes than they had legitimately purchased. But thorough examination of their books seemed to reveal no discrepancies. The after-hours clubs and smoky, illicit casinos operated by the Chinese had also been investigated. And although they were clearly benefiting from a steady flow of tobacco product, its source remained hidden.

The investigators next began to entertain the theory that independent operators were channeling their ill-gotten gains to one of the mobs for a fraction of its retail value. That theory led the cops to the independently operating Irish criminals of Hell's Kitchen. But after much effort and many man hours, the detectives had once again become frustrated.

Rizzo found a small, passing mention of the possible involvement of Brooklyn operators, but it had received scant follow-up. Scrawled in the margin of the DD-5 report, a supervisor noted that the Brooklyn Italian mob would never dare to intrude upon what had traditionally been the exclusive domain of Manhattan. An attached report detailed the results of a cursory interview with Brooklyn mob boss Louis Quattropa, who had convinced the detectives the last thing he would ever want to do was foster bad blood between the families by muscling in on anyone's tobacco trade. Much too dangerous and not nearly profitable enough, Quattropa had reportedly said.

Rizzo rubbed at his eyes. Too dangerous? That was some months prior to The Chink's assassination.

He turned tired eyes back to the file.

As part of the follow-up on the ultimately discounted Brooklyn angle, one investigator had speculated on the possible involvement of the Brighton Beach Russian mob. After yet another cursory review, that aspect had also been abandoned. The Brooklyn Russians, it was determined, lacked the networking and refinement of execution necessary to conduct such an operation. The only way they could hope to succeed in such an endeavor would be in joint venture with the Italians. And since no link existed between the Brooklyn Russians and the Manhattan Italians, all that was left was Brooklyn's organization headed by Louie Quattropa. But that angle had been explored and discounted. Additionally, the Russians were notoriously close ranked. It was only in the most superficial and perfunctory manner that they involved themselves with the Italians, and then only out of a discreet, self-preserving fear, which, among themselves, they referred to as "respect." It was clear to the task force investigators that the Russians, as a matter of policy, did not easily enter into joint ventures with any other ethnic groups, but were simply compelled to a pragmatic and tenuous working relationship with the dominant Italians.

And so, the investigation had gone full circle, leading back to where it had begun, and no closer to a solution.

Rizzo fingered the DD-5 in his hand, considering it all. If this *were* independents, he thought, it would fit his theory well. Independents were far more likely to lower their sights on occasion and hit a place like Anwar's. But if they were independents, where were the cigarettes going? How were they being marketed?

Rizzo dropped the report, once again rubbing at his eyes. While doing so, his sight fell onto the filing cabinet resting against the near wall. His lips turned down.

Now was as good a time as any. Slowly, he rose from the desk chair, taking a key ring from the pocket of his pants. He crossed to the cabinet, unlocking and opening the second drawer. He reached in and extracted the tightly bundled face towel and its content, returning to his desk and dropping into the leather chair. He stared at the towel for some time before slowly and deliberately unwrapping it.

The shiny stainless-steel Ruger revolver, with its pearly white bone handle grips, glistened beneath the fluorescents.

A pimp's gun, Johnny Morelli had once called it, laughing at the gaudy bone grips.

Rizzo's throwaway piece. The only one he had ever carried.

It had been common practice back then, when Rizzo first came on the job. The streets of Brooklyn were wild, crime-infested whirl-winds, tormented by a crack epidemic and a decaying, crumbling city economy. Shootings were commonplace, shootings involving police no less so. And in the pit of their heart, each street cop harbored a sinister dread: a lightning flash instant of fear and terror and the accidental shooting of an unarmed citizen. More than one young cop, swept up in the hypocritical, criminally cynical, and unjust winds generated by crooked, lying, conniving politicians, had found himself facing homicide charges from just such an accident. Charges brought about and wielded with cruel vigor despite the mitigating and extraneous circumstances which had caused the accident to occur.

And so most young street cops carried concealed in a coat pocket or wedged into their belts at the small of their backs, a throwaway. A street gun untraceable to them, fully loaded and wiped clean of their own fingerprints, ready to be discreetly tossed beside the body of an unarmed suspect as he lay dying on the pavement.

A throwaway.

Rizzo reached to the weapon he had never needed to use and took it into his hand, its inanimate, comforting heft once again imbuing him with a chilling and conflicted sense of both comfort and dread.

The Ruger had been untraceable when it had served a rookie Joe Rizzo.

It remained so today.

CHAPTER TWENTY-TWO

RIZZO GLANCED at his watch. "One week ago, almost to the exact hour, Dr. Sanders walked in and told us you were going to be okay."

"Only a week?" Carol said from where she sat, propped in her hospital bed. "I swear, it feels like I've been here a month. At least."

Rizzo smiled at his daughter. "I'll bet. How are you feeling this morning?"

"Great. The pills take the edge off the pain, I'm hardly aware of it, actually. I feel good, Dad. You can stop worrying."

"Yeah. Stop worrying." Rizzo caught himself before saying, "Wait till you have kids . . ." Instead, he shifted in his seat, his eyes dropping for a moment from Carol's face. Then he smiled at her again.

"Well, you look great, kid, you got all your color back. The doctor says you should be out of here tomorrow, by Friday the latest."

"Are you still out on administrative, Dad?"

"Yeah. I'm going in to have a talk with Vince when I leave here. I'm ready to go back, but he said two weeks." He shrugged. "We'll see."

"I'm glad Mom went back to work. I don't think sitting here all day was doing her any good, and she mentioned finals are coming

232

up. She's needed more at school than here." Carol hesitated before continuing. "Is she . . . is she okay? I mean, she didn't go to Espo's funeral, and she seems a little spacey lately. I know this has been hard on her, I know how dead set against my going on the job she was . . ."

"Your mother will be fine. Just worry about yourself. Just get well and get out of this hospital. Come home."

Carol swung her legs over the side of the bed, steadying herself with a downward pressed palm. She addressed her father softly, but her underlying tone was firm.

"As soon as the department surgeon clears me, I'm going back to work. I thought maybe you were wondering about that, or maybe Mom was getting all hopeful I'd quit. I think it's best to straighten it out now, just clear the air. I *will* be going back to work."

Rizzo sat silently, considering it. He saw the determination in his daughter's eyes.

"It's your call, Carol. Always was. Always will be."

She smiled. "Besides, I've already got the hard part over with. I got shot, what are the odds of *that* happening twice." Her expression changed almost instantly, all self-imposed lightheartedness fleeing from her face.

"*And* I lost a partner. The worst has got to be behind me."

Her flat tone registered with Rizzo, a sudden melancholy settling on him. He gave a barely perceptible shake of his head and forced a casual smile.

"You talk all of that over with anyone?"

"Yes, I've discussed it with Mike and Cil. Plus, the department shrink was here. Twice."

"What'd he have to say?"

"She. It was a she. And good news: I'm handling the situation well, I have it in perspective, any self-imposed feelings of false guilt have abated, and, best of all, I don't have any *Daddy* issues."

Lou Manfredo

Rizzo laughed. "You made that last one up."

"No, Dad, it's true. The shrink didn't say it, I just *know* it."

Rizzo patted his daughter's knee. "Good for you."

After a moment, Carol spoke, her voice once again taking a formal tone.

"I know something else, too. I know you and Mom are having problems."

Rizzo felt his ears flush, his poker face, so sharply honed and reliable after nearly three decades of police work, almost failing him.

"What do you *think* you know?" he asked.

"I know you guys are barely speaking. I know your attitudes toward one another are strained. And I know why."

"Tell me."

"Because of me. My going on the job. I think Mom has it in her head to blame it on you somehow. I even mentioned it to the shrink. Wanna know what she said?"

"Not particularly."

Carol laughed. "It's called transference. Mom is actually mad at me, but because I've been hurt, her maternal instincts won't allow her to manifest any hostile feelings toward me. But she still *has* those feelings. And so, she turns them against you."

"Blah-blah-blah," Rizzo said lightly. "I'd like to see the bill she submits for that horseshit. Your mother is mad, all right, at *both* of us. But she'll get over it."

"I'm sorry for all of this, Dad. But it *is* what I want. What I *really* want. I hope Mom can come to terms with it."

Rizzo stood, then bent to Carol, kissing her on top of her head. Her hair carried the scent of strawberries, and it invoked memories in him of the childhood scent of baby shampoo. He smiled warmly as he spoke.

234

"She will, honey. And *I* already have. It'll work out fine. You just get well and get out of here, okay?" He glanced at his watch. "I've gotta get going. I wanna see Vince, then I've got a few things I need to take care of. You just rest up. Get well. I'll see you later."

"Okay, Daddy," Carol said, a strange intensity showing in her eyes and not unnoticed by Rizzo.

"Just be careful," she said softly.

He turned and left.

"SO, VINCE, how much longer you going to keep me benched?"

The two cops sat in D'Antonio's office, the door closed behind Rizzo. The lieutenant shrugged.

"Depends. When you figure Carol will be home?"

"Maybe tomorrow, more likely Friday."

"So what's your hurry? The initial authorization was for two weeks. You've barely got the first week done. Besides, Carol may need you once she gets home. Is Jen back to work yet?"

"Yeah. There's about four, five weeks left of the school year."

"That's good. Carol should be out LOD at least through the summer, so Jen can be home with her." D'Antonio thought for a moment. "Is she planning on coming back? Carol, I mean, to the job?"

"Yeah. She just told me."

"Okay, then."

After a few moments, Rizzo spoke.

"So, Vince, what's new around here? How's Mark gettin' along without me?"

"Okay. He's workin' your caseload with that street crime unit kid, Jenkins. Kid'll make a good detective someday."

"Good. Anything new on the Quattropa hit?"

"Actually, I spoke to Lombardi a coupla days ago. He may be

movin' his operation out of the Plaza and over to the Six-Nine. Same as when he set up shop here."

"The Six-Nine? Canarsie? How come?"

"Well, he's workin' some soldier out of the old Grassi crew out there. He's been tryin' to wire the guy up and maybe take down Mikey Spano. Lombardi's on a mission."

Rizzo shook his head. "Tough workin' a case with a hard-on. It tends to get in the way and screw things up."

"Yeah."

"Who's the hood in Canarsie? Anybody we know?"

D'Antonio shrugged. "I didn't ask, and he didn't say."

"No further jobber takedowns, Vince? Maybe it's time for you to set up another stakeout."

"Well, the department is curtailing overtime money for the task force on that. We're pretty much out of it, Joe. Far as I know, there haven't been any burglaries since that lone Brooklyn job back in April."

"Maybe they went to ground, figured they'd wait out the heat a little."

"Yeah, whatever. I got enough on my plate here without looking for more shit."

Rizzo stood, shaking hands with D'Antonio. "Alright, I'm outa here. Tell Mark I was asking about him. I guess I'll take that second week off, not that it looks like I got a say in it. But, you're right, Carol may need me around the house the first few days she's home. Thanks, Vince. I appreciate all you've done."

"Sure, give my best to Jen. If I hear anything on the shooters, I'll let you know."

"Thanks." Rizzo turned to leave. He was stopped at the door by his boss's voice.

"Funny, Joe. You specifically asked about the Chink hit, you asked about the cigarette boosters, but you never asked about the shooters. Strikes me as being a little odd."

Rizzo turned and looked into D'Antonio's face. Its sheer lack of expression carried inquiry.

"Yeah, well, I spoke to Santori about that. He promised to keep me posted. I haven't heard from him, so I'm assumin' no news yet. Right?"

After a moment, D'Antonio responded. "Yeah, Joe. Right."

"WHAT I was thinking, Dom, is maybe after Carol's back at work, puts in a little more time on the street, maybe you can do something for her, like we discussed before. I wouldn't mind seein' her working the Plaza, if you want the truth."

Captain Dominick Lombardi smiled across his desk at Rizzo. "Don't be shy. You just say what's on your mind."

"Okay, boss," Rizzo said, laughing. "Maybe I'm a little out of line. But this isn't some guy did me a favor. This is my *daughter*. She already took a bullet, so I'm not lookin' to waste any more time here."

"I understand. Let her come back to work, get some more street time, then we'll see."

"I can pay the freight, Dom. I know you're after Mikey Spano, maybe I can help you with that like you first suggested. Brooklyn's my turf, I been dealin' with the wiseguys there for a lot of years. I'm just sayin', I can help, maybe. And then, if you can see it clear, Carol can find a home somewhere. Not even necessarily here at the Plaza, but there's a big wide world out there besides a radio car seat."

Lombardi pondered it. "I did like the way you handled yourself around Spano, I gotta admit. And I think he respects you, figures you're a square deal for him. Let me think about it; you still got time left on your admin leave. Use it. I got a little something cooking with a wiseguy in the Six-Nine. I may just take that prick Spano down *without* any help."

"No shit? Is that the same guy you were gonna wire up back in March? The guy the feds handed you? Anybody I know? Maybe I can give you a hand with 'im."

"Yeah, it's the same guy. Problem is the feds are workin' him, and he's been able to jerk us both off for two months, but he's runnin' outa time. I figure another coupla weeks, he either wires up or he goes down on those drug charges we're sittin' on. The guy's name is Ralphy Avena. You familiar with him?"

Rizzo smiled. "No, I'm not. But I did notice you've cooled a little, boss."

"Cooled?" Lombardi asked, his brow furrowed. "Cooled how?"

"Well, back when I ran into you at the Six-Two, after me and Mark cracked that abduction case, you were all gung-ho to get me on board with OCCB. Plus, you said helpin' my daughter was— how'd you put it—doable, I think. Yeah, that was the word: doable."

Now it was Lombardi smiling. "You got a good memory, I better remember that. Yeah, I wanted you on board with this Spano thing, sure. You said you'd think about it. But you been thinkin' for a long fuckin' time, and I ain't gettin' any younger. As for your daughter, you said she'd get some street time first, maybe a year or so. It's barely two months. That's how *I* remember our conversation."

"Okay, boss. I hear you. When I get back to work, I'll give you a call. You still need help with Mikey Spano, I'll see what I can do. How long you figure before you wire up that hood?"

"Maybe a coupla more weeks, a month at the most. We'll see."

Rizzo rose and extended his hand. "Okay, I'll let you get back to work. Sorry if I overstepped with my kid, but this shooting, it shook me pretty bad. I'd like her off the streets asap."

Lombardi nodded. "Part of the job, Joe. We were all there."

"Yeah. We were. I'll be in touch."

"Okay. Give my best to your daughter."

THE SMALL bar on Sixth Avenue in the Park Slope neighborhood was dimly lit and warmly decorated. Catering to the upscale brownstone crowd, Rizzo thought the drinks appropriately overpriced. He smiled as he addressed Jimmy Santori.

"Nice place, Jimmy. I didn't know you were a fuckin' yuppie."

Santori shrugged. "So now you know. Actually, this place is just far enough from the Seven-Eight and just expensive enough to keep it relatively cop-free. I come here for a change of scenery."

Rizzo looked around. "These friggin' ferns should help keep the cops out, too. I feel like I'm inside one of them exhibits at the natural history museum: 'Twenty-first Century Man in Bar.' Jesus."

"So, Joe, you want the update?"

"Sure. What's new?"

"The cigarette task force says no way the shooters are their guys. The M.O.s are too different, the score's not big enough. They're convinced their perps are somehow mobbed up, but these shooters are just independent assholes. Inspector Douglas agrees."

"How 'bout you?"

"I don't know. It sounded good when you were pitchin' it to me, but now, I dunno. I'm thinking, no. Two separate issues. Besides, the Manhattan task force has squat on those boosters, nothing at all. Even if they *were* our shooters, that task force's got nothing to bring to our table. We'll nab the shooters long before they get their guys, and we won't have them riding our coattails. Watch."

"What have you guys developed, Jimmy?"

"Coupla leads to a stickup crew works outa Greenpoint. Lots a Polish up there, some just off the boat. That could explain the accent. Fact they were white, even the escape route. East on the BQE will lead you right out to Greenpoint."

"Yeah, and twenty other places."

Santori shrugged. "We're followin' it up. Checkin' the where-abouts of the Polacks, runnin' alibis as we hear them. So far, nothing. But it's not dead yet."

Rizzo drained his Dewar's and waved for another. "At these prices, two more drinks, I coulda bought my own bottle."

"Yeah," Santori said. "But you'd have to drink them without the ferns. *That's* what you're payin' for here, buddy. It's call ambiance."

CHAPTER TWENTY-THREE

"WHEN'D YOU SWEEP this room last, Mikey?" Rizzo asked. It was later that night, near eleven o'clock, Wednesday, May 20.

Mikey Spano glanced at his watch. "Less than two hours ago when I got here. It's clean. I been in here the whole time. You can say what you gotta say."

Rizzo sat back, both hands on the tabletop, slowly rotating the rock glass of single malt scotch. Except for him and Spano, the back room of the Pompeii Social Club was empty.

Rizzo knew the time was right. The theory gestating quietly in his mind since his interview of Said Malouf, the store clerk at Anwar's, was now sharply in focus. File reviews and carefully cloaked conversations with cops and crooks had brought the theory to life.

It was time to play it all out.

"You've got a problem, Mikey."

"Yeah?" Spano asked, his brows raised. "And what's that?"

"Lombardi. The OCCB cop me and Jimmy Santori was here with a coupla months ago."

Spano's smile was dark. "Cops ain't a problem. Cops are just a pain in the ass."

"Yeah, well, Lombardi wants you. He figures you're smearin' the good name of Italian Americans everywhere. He figures guys like you should die of cancer, not guys like his father." Rizzo shrugged. "That kinda attitude moves him out of the 'pain in the ass' class. He goes to the head of the 'problem' class."

Spano sipped his drink, then puffed at his cigar. After a moment, he leaned his weight onto his arms on the table closer to Rizzo.

"So tell me, Joe: What's my problem with him?"

"Well, it's like this. So's we don't get off on the wrong foot here. And so there's no misunderstandings, I'll talk straight. See, *I* got a problem, too. And wasn't for *my* problem, I couldn't really give a fuck about yours. So, you help me with my problem, then I help you with yours. Strictly business, no need to blood-brother-up here."

Spano sat back, considering Rizzo's words and tone before answering.

"So, what's *your* problem, Joe?"

"Some cold-blooded cocksucker shot my daughter. I want him."

After a moment, Spano's eyes widened. "Jesus Christ, that cop, that cop got shot . . . that was your *daughter*?"

"Yeah. You heard about that, did you?"

"Yeah, sure, it was all over the news, TV, papers, everywhere. I didn't make the connection, but yeah. I heard about it. How's she doin'?"

"Good, thanks. But let's stay on topic. I want the shooter."

Spano spread his arms. "What the fuck you comin' to me for? How would I know some junkie asshole stickup man?"

"Okay, Mikey, I'm gonna lay this out for you. I'm the only person looking at this from three separate angles. One, The Chink hit. Two, a citywide burglary operation takin' down tobacco jobbers. Three, the stickup and shooting at Anwar's."

Spano's eyes narrowed. "Are you fuckin' kiddin' me? You came in here with some half-assed idea *I* had something to do with get-tin' your kid shot? Is that what the fuck this is?"

"No. Hear me out. I'm gonna give you some facts and some theories, all from the three cases I mentioned. When I'm done, we'll hash it out. Okay?"

Spano twisted his lips. "And what's this got to do with *my* prob-lem? 'Cause, you wanna talk straight, I ain't that fuckin' interested in yours, see?"

"Hear me out, Mikey."

After a moment, Spano silently nodded.

"First, the burglaries. The cops workin' them feel they're tied to organization, and I agree. It takes a network to move two mil-lion dollars in cigarettes, you think a cigarettes, you think Man-hattan and Tommy Tomasulo. But Tommy checks out clean. In fact, he's actually gettin' hurt by this competition. So, if Tommy's not in the loop, the task force figures the entire Italian mob is out of the loop, 'cause who'd wanna step on Manhattan's toes? Tom-my's one thing, but the *old man*? Who'd have big enough balls to fuck with him?"

"Nobody, I hear," Spano said calmly.

"Yeah, that's what I hear, too. The task force looks at the Chi-nese next. They seem to have some extra product, but what could they do with a whole load? Nothin', 'cause they can't get their reach two blocks outa Chinatown. So it looks like they're just buying from whoever is sellin'. Now, cross-check that info against the shooting case. The eyeball inside the store makes the perps as two white males. He saw enough a their eyes through the openings in those ski masks to tell an Asian from a Caucasian. Plus, even this immigrant Arab witness could tell the difference between a Chi-nese accent and a Western one. So, I'm thinkin' the Chinese are clean here, too, just buyin' product from whoever's sellin' it. Now, maybe it's some renegade bunch, like the Irish in Hell's Kitchen.

But they got the same problem: How do they move the product? Plus, every time they piss off the Italians, the police boats start plucking Leprechauns outa the Hudson River. No, the micks wouldn't wanna cross Tommy Tomasula, let alone the big boss. Next the task force starts rousting the Polacks up in Greenpoint. Now cross-check them with the shooters: white males, accent, so Greenpoint's a possibility. But those guys have no network, either, or at least not a very good one. So once again if they were the perps, they'd have to be partnered with *somebody*. And you know, those Polacks are just frustrated blue-collar workers, not real criminals. Open a shoe factory up in North Brooklyn, they'd all be workin' double shifts and carryin' lunch pails. No way they'd ever gun down two cops."

"So, Joe, I'm thinkin' you figure the burglars and the shooters are the same guys."

"Yeah, that's what I'm figurin'. Now, you tell me something. Who are white males with accents, organized but without extensive networking in place, and cold-stone killers to boot? Any group come to mind, Mikey?"

"You're talking about the Russians. Okay, I can see that. So why can't the task force?"

"Because they're not seeing all three cases as connected. Everybody's working from their own little cubicle, eyes on their desks and fingers up their asses."

"Maybe you better tell me what the fuck you're saying here, Rizzo, before I start to forget you're a fuckin' cop."

"Sure, Mikey. The cigarette task force ruled out the Russians 'cause they work strictly on their own, they don't play well with the other cretins. Fact, only one they *do* play with is you. And maybe The Chink through you, and now he's dead. But like I said, the task force has decided no Italian crew would touch it, including you."

Now Spano laughed. "Jesus, Joe, you had me there for a minute, you really fuckin' had me. I thought you were serious, you figured I'm workin' with the Russkies and I killed Quattropa."

"I *am* serious, Mikey."

"Yeah, sure. It was me knocked over that store for a couple a C-notes. Let's see, last time I did that I was, what, sixteen? Yeah, I think I was sixteen."

"I don't mean you personally. If I thought it *was,* you'd be on the floor ten minutes already with three fuckin' bullets in your head."

Spano's face went dark. "I think you better get to the point, Rizzo. Now. And don't forget who the fuck you're talkin' to."

"Okay, Mikey. By combining aspects of all three seemingly unrelated cases, this is what I came up with. You been livin' next door to the Russians for years. It's easy for the other bosses to talk tough and look down at the Russkies. But you, *you* have to actually deal with them, day in, day out, nose to nose. So, you get a little palsy with somebody over there, maybe the boss. The Russkies wanna grab smokes by the truckload. You ever meet a fuckin' Russian wasn't a chain-smoker? But what to do with all those cases? So they approach you. You like the idea, but what about Manhattan? On the scale the Russkies are talkin', this definitely steps on Tomasulo's toes. If his kickup to the old man on Mulberry Street starts droppin' off, questions are gonna get asked. So you take it to The Chink. He was a greedy bastard, you wave some dough at him and he'd sell his wife's ass on the street corner. Plus, he always felt he shoulda got the big chair, Manhattan, not just Brooklyn. So he okays the deal, long as you guarantee it stays quiet. Somehow you convince him you could move millions in product without Mulberry Street tracking it to you *or* Quattropa. So the Russians get green-lighted. They start the jobs off in Manhattan, then the Bronx. People start looking at Tomasulo. Queens gets hit. By then, everybody figures it's citywide, so when Brooklyn finally gets hit, it's not a big deal. Nobody makes it for a Brooklyn-based show." Rizzo paused, examining Spano's face carefully. He smiled at the gangster.

"How'm I doin' so far, Mikey?"

Spano remained silent. Rizzo continued.

"Then one day, maybe The Chink calls you in. 'It's over,' he tells you. He wants to terminate the operation, stop pushin' his luck. If Manhattan gets wise, it's possible The Chink catches a bullet. So he calls you in like a fuckin' waiter and pulls the rug out from under you. He wants *you* to go tell the Russians. But, like I say, he's a greedy old fuck. You convince him it would be in his best financial interest to sit down with the Russians, probably Boklov himself. That's his name, right? Boklov? Truth is, though, you know you *can't* go to Boklov and call off the operation. If he sees you standin' with your tail between your legs, you got a problem. If Boklov decides Chink can push your face into the dog shit, he figures *he* can, too. That wouldn't be such a good next-door neighbor for you to have, Mikey. I can understand that.

"So, you've already had enough of that old prick Quattropa anyway. I heard that rumor long ago. And you're sick of Savarese, too, the guy who's had you jumpin' through hoops for twenty years. So you pretend to do what Chink says: you go to Boklov, but not to end the operation. No, you go to him to help you set up the hit. With just one move, you get the big chair for yourself, plus you get a heavy message through to Boklov nice and clear: *nobody* puts Mikey the Hammer's nose in dog shit. *Nobody.*"

After a brief moment of unsettling stillness, Spano smiled.

"If any of that's true, I come out lookin' like a pretty smart motherfucker, don't I?"

Rizzo nodded. "You do, yeah, you do. In fact, your balls get so big that after Lombardi comes to you and threatens to make your life miserable on account of a citizen got clipped in the Hi-Fi, you got enough juice to go back to Boklov and say, 'Your people fucked up, and *I'm* catchin' the heat for it. We have to even it off. They gotta go.' And Boklov, he figures he better agree. Maybe even *that* sick bastard isn't crazy enough to want to fuck with you now, Mikey. So the two Hi-Fi shooters get a very public murder." Rizzo paused, smiling across the table coldly. He raised his rock glass in toast. "Salute, Michele."

"Salute," Spano answered.

After a moment, Spano spoke.

"Question, Joe. How'd a big-shot Mafiosa like me get involved in a two-bit stickup? You got an explanation for that?"

"Yeah, actually I do. See, the burglaries have stopped. Either you or Boklov called them off. Maybe you're just letting things cool off, maybe you're flexin' some muscle with Boklov, showing him who's boss, or maybe *he's* squeezing *you* for a bigger slice, I don't know. But the operation has stopped. So, somewhere, somebody is bitchin'. 'Where's my product? Where's my shipment? I got orders I gotta fill.' As one of my daughter's college professors would say, a real capitalistic conundrum, a real problem. And whenever capitalism hits a snag, some enterprising young man or woman usually steps right up. That's why we all got two cars and air-conditioning and the ticket lines are a thousand miles long to get into this country. So some small-fry asshole from the chorus gets an inspiration. There were twenty-two cases of cigarettes in Anwar's. *That* was the target, the cigarettes, not the cash register like when you were sixteen tryin' to score some blow-job money. The *cigarettes*. And once those Russian renegades went off the reservation making an end run around you, they fucked it up. *They* fucked it up, and *my daughter* paid the price. Her and her partner paid the price."

"You're fuckin' nuts with this, Rizzo."

"Okay, Mikey. Let me tell you this first, then you can call for the removal team from King's County Psych. Lombardi's coming to get you. You squared it for Maggio gettin' caught up in The Chink hit, so Lombardi stopped rousting your capos to put direct pressure on you, he's playing by the rules. But he's still comin' after you, and he's got exactly what he needs to do it. You're drownin' in the ocean, paesan, and *I'm* holding the fuckin' life preserver. And time is running out real fast."

Rizzo stood, draining his glass and placing it gently on the table. He dug his car keys from his pocket.

"You think it over. I'll be in touch. Today is Wednesday, why don't we figure I'll stop by on Friday night, around this time. You can give me the two shooters' names. And the other asshole in the store, too. They drove a black panel van, two of 'em about five-eight, at least one had an accent. We got DNA evidence, so it better be the right guys. You give me their names, I give you the information you need to save your ass. And you make damn sure to keep this whole arrangement just between us. I don't want Lombardi or any other cop hearin' about it from one of your flunkies. If you need to sell it to your people, you sell it like it's a way to keep everybody in line, like you got resources that give you information about what's going on in your world. If you confide too much, it could all get back to Lombardi. Just keep all this between you and your go-to guy, Davilla. The rest of your little band of merry men may not be as loyal as you think. But this whole thing can still work to your advantage— can show the troops just how deep your resources are, how nobody gets over on you. Consider this a favor I'm doin' you. Then, someday, maybe you and me can sit down for another drink together."

Rizzo pushed past the table and headed for the French doors.

"In hell."

"I'M GONNA ask you some questions, Sally," Mikey Spano said. "And you're gonna give me straight-up answers. Do you understand me?"

248

Sally Sexton, a.k.a. Sally Clams, sat in the same seat Joe Rizzo had occupied the night before. Also seated at the small table, black coffee before him, was Herc Davilla, Spano's number one enforcer.

Sally Clams appeared very nervous.

"Sure, Mikey, of course. What's the problem?"

Spano told him what he wanted. He made no mention of Joe Rizzo.

"So tell me, Sally. Black van, three guys, five-eight or so, one or two maybe had accents. Ring any bells?"

Sally weighed his options, his mind reeling. He looked into the deceivingly innocuous gaze of Herc Davilla. Suddenly, Sally Clams needed to urinate.

"I think I know who it could be, Mikey. That asshole Afansi and his two sidekicks. They work the jobber break-ins for Boklov with the other guy, Peter, the alarm guy. These three guys are donkeys, they just load the truck and drive."

"Well, I gotta wonder here," Spano said pensively, "what the hell were they doing at Anwar's? Besides shootin' two cops and draggin' *me* into this fuckin' mess. What'd they figure they were gonna do with those twenty-two cases, Sally? And who authorized the job? Got any ideas?"

Sally began to perspire. He avoided Davilla's eyes and found no refuge in Spano's.

"Jesus, I just remembered. A few weeks back, when Boklov shut it down and started to lean on us for more percentage, right around then Afansi came to me, him and the other commie prick, Gerb or Gleb or whatever the fuck his name is. Afansi said he could start to score some product on his own, not much, just a little at first, till he got the bugs worked out, then maybe he'd start to deliver more. He said he'd do it without Boklov, just him and his crew."

"And you told him . . . what?"

"I said no, I couldn't move product just between him and me, not without runnin' it by you first. He said to forget it, if I tole you, you'd tell Boklov and he'd wind up dead. This guy Afansi's got a real problem with authority, a real big problem. Anyway, I told him no, he said okay and that was the end of it."

"But you never mentioned it to me, Sally. Why's that?"

"I forgot about it, it was just a bullshit two-minute conversation. I forgot all about it. I *never* thought he'd go through with it on spec, not in a million fuckin' years."

Spano sat back in his seat, tapping a finger lightly on the table-top. He was being lied to, and that made him angry. But he was in a precarious position. Spano knew Rizzo was not to be taken lightly. He remembered how, over the years, Louie Quattropa had dealt with the Bensonhurst cop on more than a few occasions. Once, after Rizzo had just left the Starlight Lounge, Quattropa's headquarters, Spano had come in to see The Chink. Somehow the conversation had briefly turned to Rizzo.

"Try and avoid that cop," Quattropa had counseled. "If you ever do need to deal with Rizzo, play it straight. He'll always do the same. If it ever does become necessary for you to fuck him over, do it *only* as a last resort. And afterward, you better clip him. If you don't, the son of a bitch will find a way to get back at you and make you pay."

Now, years later, Spano recalled the old man's advice. He turned hard eyes to Sally Clams.

"I need you to answer me, Sally. I don't want no explanation, I just want answers, unnerstand?"

"Sure, of course. Whatever you need."

"If it *was* these three guys pulled that job, who'da been the driver?"

"Afansi. He's the wheel man. The other two, they're just muscle. Afansi's always the wheel."

Spano recalled the *Daily News* story about the cop killing on

Atlantic Avenue. He remembered it was the driver of the van who had gunned down the female cop.

It had been Afansi who shot Rizzo's daughter.

"I WON'T give up any more of my people because of your police, Mikey. My answer is final."

Mikey Hammer and Oleg Boklov shared a small rear booth in a neutral territory bar on Flatlands Avenue. Herc Davilla and Boklov's personal bodyguard sat together twenty feet away at the bar, sipping at beers. The meeting had been hastily arranged after Spano's questioning of Sally Sexton.

"They tried to fuck you, Oleg, went right around your back. Mine, too. They were gonna grow their thing and gain strength, then come after you, the boss. Believe me, I've seen it a dozen times. Russians, Italians, Jews—hell, even the stupid micks did it back in the day. You can never let anybody get away with tryin' something like this. *I* won't let them get away with tryin' it. This thing risks putting us all in a fuckin' mess with the cops. The whole situation changed once those two cops got shot. Believe me, we got a real fuckin' problem here. We gotta take these three guys out and dump 'em in the cops' lap, message delivered. They won't know who or why, and they won't care. Their dead get avenged."

Oleg shook his head. "The police have no way of tracing this back to us."

"No, not yet. But once a cop gets whacked, they never give it up. They'll start leanin' on everybody in sight. We can't take a chance on some smart cop getting a lead to Afansi. He'll give us both up to cut himself a deal. He fucked us, Oleg. He went independent. We don't nip this in the bud, we'll have guys pissin' on us at will. I was making good money from that cigarette scam. Now these assholes jeopardized everything with this scheme of theirs."

"And you are sure it was Afansi?"

251

"Sally Clams came to me. He got it firsthand from Afansi himself. There's no room for error."

"I have already allowed you to kill two of my people. Don't take liberties here. You Americans cater to these police far too much. Kill one of their own, or kill one of their women. Then they will not be so insistent in matters such as this."

"You listen to me, Oleg, this ain't Shitstainia, this is fuckin' Brooklyn. When I go to your country, you tell me what I should do. Over here, you take my advice. For both our sakes."

Oleg's eyes were hard. "I will not allow them to be arrested. Under no circumstances will I cooperate with that."

"They're loose cannons, Oleg, the three of 'em. We can't risk them getting arrested, I explained that. We only got one option here."

"Also unacceptable. As I said, you've already pressured me to sanction the killings of two of my people to appease these police of yours. No more."

"Damnit, Oleg, you listen to me: I know these fuckin' cops, they'll find a way to get Afansi and then maybe me and you, too. You wanna know the truth, they're already on Afansi's trail. I've got ears in the police department, I hear things, I'm told things. Afansi fucked up. We both know it. He betrayed you, he tried to cut us both out of money that was ours. My ass may be on the line here, and the way I see it, I got nothin' to lose. I want Afansi and his two guys dead. And if I have to, I'll take you on, too. If you force it, I'll come in heavy."

Oleg pondered it, a sharp anger beating at his temple. Anger not caused by this distasteful American gangster and his threats. No, a far worse anger.

An anger caused by betrayal.

He turned flat, distant eyes toward Spano. "I will not give them up to the police."

Spano nodded, gently patting the clenched fist of Boklov on the table before him.

"I understand. Like I told you, that's not an option. Just leave them to me." Spano stood, preparing to leave.

"They won't suffer, Oleg. You have my word."

Chapter Twenty-four

ON FRIDAY MORNING, May 22, just before the start of the long Memorial Day weekend, Carol Rizzo was discharged from Long Island College Hospital.

It had been eight days since the shooting.

Early that evening, she lay in her own bed, sister Jessica sitting beside her.

"You look great, Carol. Really. If I didn't know what happened to you, I'd never suspect you'd been in the hospital at all, let alone almost . . . you know, really badly hurt."

Carol glanced at the bedside clock, then addressed her older sister.

"Thanks, Jess, but you look *horrible*. Did *I* put those bags under your eyes? Sorry. And it's almost seven-thirty, don't you have a date with that guy from the museum tonight? What's his name again?"

Jessica smiled at her sister. "His name is Fred. Can you imagine . . . Fred? Daddy's already yabba-dabba-dooing about it and calling me Wilma."

"Well, at least the guy's Italian. That should be good for something with Dad."

Jessica nodded, also glancing at the clock. "But you're right, I've gotta get my face on. Are you sure you'll be okay? Do you want some company? I don't have to go out, you know, I can—"

"No way, go. Mom and Dad are home, and I'm fine. I'm just kinda beat. I can't believe how tired I am, it's not even eight o'clock. I'm gonna read for a while, then get to sleep. I should feel better tomorrow."

Jessica stood. "Okay, then. If you're sure." She bent down slightly, getting closer to Carol and lowering her voice as she spoke again. "And Carol. What I told you about Mom and Dad, that's just between us. I don't think we should get involved in whatever's going on. But believe me, it's not just about you. Mom seems super pissed about *something*. And I've never seen Dad act like this—he looks like a puppy who just peed on the rug. I've overheard bits and pieces of it, and I don't think I want to know any more. But you can relax, it's *not* because of you."

"All right. Thanks. But whatever it *is*, I bet it *started* with me. I'm sorry about that, really, but what can I do? I can't live my life—"

Jessica raised a hand to silence her younger sister. "I know, I know. And you're right." She smiled broadly. "And besides, pretty soon you'll be off the hook." Her smile turned conspiratorial when she spoke again.

"Marie told me she's seeing some resident at the hospital. Are you ready? The guy's *Irish*. Wait'll Dad hears about this. You'll be *way* off the hook."

JENNIFER RIZZO sat in the living room, grading her students' final exams. She watched as her husband entered the room. He joined her on the sofa and took the papers from her hand. He placed them down on the coffee table, squaring off their edges and turning his eyes to her.

"We've got Carol home, Jessica's out on a date, Marie's over in the city—probably just finishing her shift at the hospital. Everything's starting to get back to normal, all can be right with our world again. But we need to hash this out, honey, we gotta put it to bed. Let's just lance the friggin' boil and move on. Okay?"

"And just how do you propose we do that, Joe?"

"The only way we can. You make your case, nice and reasonable, nice and logical. Then I get my turn to defend myself, and we can leave out the swearing on our kids and the cross-my-heart hope-to-die bullshit. Let's just do this face-to-face and straight up."

Jennifer held his stern gaze to hers, the lighting in the room angling across his face, shadowing his eyes. She sighed and began to speak.

"You were never home, Joe. Between working double shifts, making arrests, court appearances, you were never home. Plus, there was an awful lot of beers with the guys going on. I had two young kids to take care of. I was tired a lot, remember? And changing diapers and mopping up vomit didn't help my libido much. Our sex life was practically nonexistent. But, as I recall, you were perfectly fine with that. Big, macho, virile cop, just fine with two, three weeks of abstinence. Remember that, Joe?"

Rizzo shook his head. "I was workin' one of the most active precincts in the city. Every other mope on the street was either packin', usin', dealin' or all three. Me and Johnny were *tripping* over collars. They were runnin' the arraignment part at criminal court twenty-four seven just to process all the cases. *That's* why I wasn't around much. And when I was, do you remember how I'd try to help out with the girls? Give 'em their baths, take them to the pediatrician, try and help you out? I was pretty friggin' tired myself, and tell you the truth, sex wasn't on my mind much, either. When I had a chance to hop into bed, *sleep* was on my mind."

Jennifer sighed again. "My cousin Rose saw you, Joe. She saw you and a woman wearing nurse's scrubs come out of a bar on Ralph Avenue. You had your arm around her, and you were both laughing. And when I asked what had kept you that night, you told me you had made an arrest, that's why you were late. I'm sure you don't remember it. It was probably just one of, what, a hundred nights?"

Rizzo furrowed his brow. "That's it? Are you kiddin' me? You've been sitting on that all these years?"

She shook her head. "I began paying a little more attention after that. I saw the pattern. And I knew."

"Jennifer, listen to me: I have absolutely *no* memory of any nurse in a bar somewhere. I don't know what your friggin' big-mouth cousin Rose thinks she saw. But I probably did make a collar that night. You crack a guy's head, he goes to the hospital. If they can't patch him up and discharge him, you gotta sit on him till the arraignment. Me and Johnny spent half our lives in an ER somewhere. Between the aided cases, the gunshots, the stabbings, we practically lived there. So, yeah, we mighta bought an ER nurse a beer someplace once or twice to thank them for some favor. But that's *it*. And as far as Carol's situation's concerned, I did my damnedest to keep her off the job, and for reasons you can't even *begin* to imagine. But she did it anyway. So, yeah, now I am on board with it, now she does have my complete support. And you want more truth? Yeah, I am feelin' some pride, I am feeling good about it. Her first day on the street, she took a gun, one less gun out there to kill some poor bastard. And I wish you could've seen the face on that abducted woman's husband when I delivered her back home from that shack out in The Hole, delivered her back safe and sound to her family. Only a *cop* gets to see a face like that, Jen. Maybe, no, for *sure*, Carol will see a face like that someday. So, I'm fuckin' proud. There. You got me. You wanna be pissed about it for the rest of our lives together, I guess I can't change that. I'll just have to learn to live with it, same as you're gonna have to learn to live with Carol bein' a cop, 'cause if that *bullet* couldn't change her mind, *you* sure as hell never will."

Jennifer sat silently, her eyes beginning to well. Rizzo moved closer on the sofa and draped an arm around her shoulders. He spoke softly.

"You can't toy with the fates. Look at what happened *here.* I called in favors to reach into the Academy. *I* had Carol assigned to the Eight-Four, *I* set up that ride for her with Espo, so she'd be safer, safer than if she was in the Seven-Five or the Seven-Three or twenty other houses in this city. And look, look what happened anyway."

He raised her chin up, lifting her face to his, and smiled kindly.

"You can't toy with fate, Jen," he repeated. "You just got to deal with it."

AT TEN p.m., Rizzo walked into the upstairs master bedroom, car keys in hand.

"I need to go out," he said. "I should be back around midnight, maybe one."

Jennifer glanced at the clock, and turned to her husband.

"For a guy who's trying to convince his wife how faithful he is, you've been going out on some strange errands lately. What's going on?"

"Just business, that's all."

"You're out on leave, Joe. What business can you possibly have?"

Rizzo shrugged. "I wasn't planning on this time off. Mark and I were getting very close on a coupla cases. I'm just trying to keep my hand in. I don't want any leads running cold before I get back on the clock."

Jennifer stood by the bed, studying him. After a moment, she spoke, the resignation in her tone clearly apparent to Rizzo.

"Alright," she said. "We'll just pretend that you're not lying to me."

Rizzo answered with narrowed eyes. "Don't, Jen, okay? Don't start with the accusations. I already told you, it's just business."

After a moment, Jennifer sighed softly. She crossed the room and kissed her husband lightly on the lips. It was their first real contact in over a week.

"I hope you find him," she said, her voice a mere whisper. "I hope you find the animal who shot our daughter and he gets locked in a cage for the rest of his miserable life. And I hope he dies there and then burns in hell. For eternity."

She stepped up against him, her arms going around his body, pressing herself to him.

"I hope you *find* him, Joe."

"SO, YOU got some names for me?" Rizzo asked, once again alone in the rear room of the Pompeii Club, Mikey "The Hammer" Spano seated across the table from him.

"I got some names," Spano replied with a small shrug. "It remains to be seen if they're for you or not."

"You know, Mikey, I was never a hundred percent positive it was you behind this cigarette scam. I was pretty convinced about the Russians, so I figured you were most likely involved, but I wasn't dead positive. I wasn't sure if The Chink was in on it, either. But, I guess now I know for sure."

"Yeah? And why's that?"

Rizzo shrugged with his answer. "You got the names already. If you weren't involved, it'da taken you more than two days to come up with them. But I knew either way, you'd get 'em, even if you had to crack some heads to do it."

"Yeah? What makes you so sure?"

"Well, Mikey, the other night I saw it in your eyes that you believed me. You *knew* I was tellin' you the truth about Lombardi having the tool he needs to bring you down. And you wanna know what it is, no?"

Spano remained impassive for a moment, then reached for the bottle of Johnny Walker Blue Label. He poured two generous drinks, sliding one glass across the table to Rizzo before responding.

"So tell me. What is it?"

"So it *was* you behind the cigarette boostings all along?"

"No. But I found out who was. And I also found out who shot your daughter."

"Alright, Mikey. I'll make like I believe you; you're innocent. It don't mean a fuckin' thing to me anyhow. I'm not here about that."

They raised their glasses, each man sipping the scotch.

"Good," Spano said. "But just to set the record straight, the cigarette scheme, that was all The Chink's doing. I only inherited it. One of the first things I did after Louie died was to shit-can that whole operation. It was disrespectful to Manhattan. The Chink, he never had no respect for the boss. If Manhattan did find out about it, it was them whacked him. Maybe your Captain Lombardi should be spendin' his time across the river on Mulberry Street."

Rizzo looked over the rim of his glass, Spano's lies without meaning or significance to him.

"You know," Rizzo said, "when I was a rookie, I worked with an old-timer who was just waitin' out his pension. I remember two things that old cop told me to always keep in mind. One, a man must pay for his sins in this life as well as the next, and two, all men are liars and all women are tramps. That was his advice to me."

Spano sipped more scotch. "So fuckin' what?"

Rizzo shrugged. "That little speech you just gave me reminded me of that old cop. Was even *one* word of that true?"

After a moment, Spano smiled, his eyes cold. "Yeah. The part about that old scumbag, Quattropa. Son of a bitch really didn't have no respect for anything."

"Okay," Rizzo said, laughing. "Just so we're clear."

"If word was to get out that I'm givin' up people to the cops, my health could take a serious turn for the worse. I know you understand that."

"I do, Mikey."

"And far as Manhattan goes, if the cigarette thing ever did get out, I had it arranged so that it would be nice and deniable. Right now, far as I'm concerned, I could probably *prove* it was The Chink and the Russkies all along and that I had nothin' to do with it."

"Sounds feasible."

"So, Joe, here's my problem. I give you the names of the shooter and his pals, you lock 'em up. Then it all becomes public. You gotta show the D.A. how you made the case. And now the shooters are talkin' to lawyers. Maybe my name comes up and Manhattan hears it and somehow comes to the conclusion it was all *my* idea to start pissin' on Tomasulo and the old man on Mulberry Street. I can't let any of that happen."

"You just gotta keep this simple," Rizzo said, his voice taking on a harder tone. "Real simple: you give me the names; I give you Lombardi's threat. Very simple. I don't give a shit about the rest of it."

"I understand that. I'm not a fuckin' idiot. But no way can I go along with an arrest. I got people I gotta negotiate with on this, and an arrest is a deal breaker."

"You know, Mikey, Quattropa was always a prick, I'll give you that. But among the cops, he was always considered a straight shooter. He was respected. More than once, he stepped up and helped us with a neighborhood situation. He scored his points, which was the only thing he really gave a fuck about, but at the end of the day, some good got done. But you, you got a different rep. The cops view you as just a scumbag, half a psycho and a loose cannon, a guy who won't help anybody, ever. If you're really runnin' Brooklyn now, you gotta polish that image a little. Work with me here, and I'll get the word out where it'll do you some good."

Spano's face darkened as he spoke. "Let me handle this. Your daughter gets avenged. Guaranteed. And the dead cop, too. You give me whatever Lombardi's got, then go back to the precinct and eat some doughnuts, relax. *I'll* handle the rest. And it'll be more than you could ever do, lockin' 'em up for a few years, if you even *got* a fuckin' conviction, that is."

Rizzo sat back and raised his glass. He took a long swallow of scotch. As he allowed the smooth liquor to wash down his throat, he realized exactly what he had to do.

It all ran through his mind and a cold, passionless pragmatism asserted itself within him. When he spoke again, his resolve was steeled, his decision fully embodied.

"Conviction? Did I ever say anything about a conviction to you?"

He put his glass down and leaned forward, closer to Spano.

"This motherfucker shot my daughter. He shot her *twice*. The first shot, that was business. But when he bent over and fired the *second* shot, that was different. That made it personal. He don't know it yet, but the second shot, that's between him and me. And now he's gonna answer for it."

After a moment, Spano sat back in his seat. He shook his head slowly, his lips pursing.

"Jesus Christ," he said softly. "I gotta tell you, Joe, I didn't see that comin'. I knew you wanted this guy bad, I knew you were going over the line with this Lombardi thing to get him. But I swear to God, I figured you were just gonna lock him up. But you're gonna *kill* the guy. Jesus fuckin' Christ."

"Just give me his name, and tell me where I can find him. Once it all checks out, I give up Lombardi's info."

Spano remained silent, turning it all over in his mind, sipping his scotch. After a moment, he reached for the bottle and poured two fresh drinks. He tasted it, then scratched at an eyebrow.

"With all due respect, Joe, I gotta say no. I can't afford to sponsor another amateur hour. Look what happened that night in the Hi-Fi, those two asshole Russians fucked it all up. Wasn't for that, this Lombardi prick woulda never been so hot and heavy on this. What would he care about The Chink and his flunky, Lentini? It's the dead citizen pissed Lombardi off. No, Joe. My hands are tied here. I can't allow you to arrest them *or* take a chance on you clippin' them. No. Let me handle it."

"I want this guy, Mikey."

"Sure you do. You think I don't know how ya feel? You ever hear the story about that prick who raped my niece? You familiar with that? The guys used to call me Mikey C-man before that, 'causa all the broads I fucked. But since that night with the rapist, I'm Mikey the Hammer. I *know* you want the guy, Joe. I can relate. Trust me. But you gotta let me handle it."

"Listen to me, Mikey . . ."

"No, *you* listen to *me*. You ain't thinkin' clear here, and I can't afford to deal with a guy workin' on emotion. Besides, you're a fuckin' *cop*. You can't whack this guy, it ain't right. We got rules here, Joe, not like the Russkies, not like those mick assholes, not like the niggers. *We* got fuckin' *rules*."

Rizzo reached for his scotch and took a long swallow. The bitter taste in his mouth remained untouched by the smooth liquor, and he drank more.

Spano smiled across the table. "Do the *right* thing here. Let me handle it. The people I gotta appease will be okay with it, and everybody's secrets will be safe. We keep all this between you and me, nobody ever knows you were involved. I get Lombardi off my ass, and you and your daughter get justice. It's the *right* thing, Joe. Believe me."

Rizzo considered it, draining his glass before he spoke. Spano reached for the bottle and once again filled their glasses as he listened to Rizzo's answer.

"Okay. You handle it. But remember: we got DNA here. It *better* be the right guys."

Spano nodded. "My word on my children. The right guys."

Rizzo stood. He picked up his glass. Spano stood. They toasted one another silently, then drained their glasses in single swallows.

"Far as what's right, Mikey, let me tell you something about that. Somethin' you oughta know already.

"There *is* no right. There *is* no wrong. There just fuckin' *is*."

CHAPTER TWENTY-FIVE

MIKEY SPANO sat behind the wheel of his red Cadillac, Herc Da-villa beside him in the passenger seat. The car stood parked diago-nally across from the Pompeii Club, in shadow between two rings of light cast by streetlamps.

"So, we clear on this, Herc?"

"Yeah, we're clear. But I gotta say somethin'."

"What?"

"If we boost a black van and leave the bodies in there for the cops to find, they'll run the plate. It'll come back as bein' stolen long after those cops got shot. They're gonna *know* it ain't the same van used on that job."

Spano nodded. "I understand that. But Sally Clams told me Afansi used a van he stole on Staten Island, then he put phony Jersey tags on it. After the job at Anwar's, they crushed the van at that Russkie-owned salvage yard in East Flatbush. We're just sendin' a message, that's all. Let the cops find these three shitheads inside a black van. They got DNA evidence. They'll make the connection. The black van just shows somebody's deliverin' the cop killers, nice and neat. And I want you to dump the van in the Six-Two Precinct, maybe offa the Belt Parkway somewheres. Lombardi was workin' outa there, he'll understand. I don't give a fuck what any of the other cops think. This is all about appeasin' Lombardi."

"Okay, Mikey, I get it."

After a moment, Davilla spoke up once more.

"What about Sally Clams?"

Spano's eyes narrowed. "Sally tried to end run me, and on a nickel-and-dime scam, too. I ain't gonna forget that. But for now, I'm givin' him a pass. He earns too good, I don't wanna waste that. Plus, I can't afford to get too much of a hard-ass rep with the captains. They gotta feel safe with me, secure. I *need* them, especially with this fuckin' prick Lombardi in my face now. If he ever starts squeezin' guys, makin' heat for everybody, and puts the word out it's 'cause he's after me, I need the captains to stand up till I get a handle on all this. Sally's safe for now. The day he starts walkin' into the Pompeii with a light envelope in his hand, that's the day I throw the motherfucker into his own fuckin' lobster tank and let the little bastards eat *him*."

Davilla nodded, remaining silent. After another moment, he turned his soft, kindly looking eyes to Spano.

"What about the other one? Boklov?"

Spano looked into the man's face, and even after so many years of association with this robotic killer, he was still amazed at the kindly, grandfatherly appearance of Hercules Davilla.

Spano smiled coldly. "Boklov's not a problem. When I first went to him with the situation about that dead citizen in the Hi-Fi, he sanctioned the hit on his two people. Now he green-lights me takin' out three of his earners so's I can do P.R. with the cops. No, Boklov's not a problem. He's a cunt, and I can run him however and whenever I need to. You think I'd ever let him whack five of *my* people? I'd be wearin' his fuckin' eyes for cuff links first. No, Oleg Boklov stays where he is. Let him bitch slap the other Russkies for us. If he ever *does* step on my toes, I'll make him wish he was still back in Russia wipin' his ass with yesterday's newspaper."

Again Davilla replied, "Okay, Mikey." Then, shifting in the passenger seat, he more fully faced his boss.

"So when you need this done?"

"Yesterday. Between the task force lookin' for the cop killers and this guy Lombardi lookin' for results, somebody may be gettin' close to me. And I don't know *how* close."

"Okay."

Spano reached to the ignition key and twisted it, firing the engine, an indication that the meeting was over. "All this will cement things. Nobody will have to wonder who's runnin' Brooklyn and why. Set it up."

Davilla opened the door to exit the Cadillac.

"Okay, boss."

ONE A.M. Monday, Afansi Gorban, wearing only his boxer briefs, stood inside the kitchen door of his small Brooklyn house, a Beretta nine-millimeter pistol clutched in his hand. He cautiously moved the curtain aside and peered out into the darkness of the rear yard. Standing on the small porch was Sally Sexton.

"Open up, Afansi," Sexton said softly. "It's me, Sally. Open up. We got a problem."

Afansi swore softly, tucking the heavy weapon into the waistband of his shorts. Using both hands, he undid the locks, then swung the door inward a foot, again reaching for his weapon.

Herc Davilla stepped from the darkness and raised a forty-five to Afansi's forehead, immediately squeezing off a round. The silencer reduced the gun's heavy boom to a slight, anemic *pfffft*.

Davilla and Sexton entered the kitchen, followed by a third man, Mikey Spano.

"Go check the house," Spano said to Davilla. "Make sure there's nobody else here. You find anybody, kill 'em and leave 'em where they fall."

The man left the room, his weapon raised. Spano turned to Sexton. "Go out on the porch. Get the bag."

Sexton, still pleasantly surprised to be alive on this night, stepped out into the darkness and returned quickly, a Vietnam-era military body bag in his hands.

Spano took the bag and opened it, spreading it out on the vinyl floor beside the body, trying to avoid the rapidly widening pool of thick blood forming around Afansi Gorban's head. He turned to Sexton.

"Go get the car. Pull it into the driveway, no lights. Shut off the engine, then come back in here."

"Okay, Mikey."

After Sexton left, with Davilla still off somewhere checking the house, Spano looked down at the body. Brushing gloved hands together, he smiled, then reached into his waistband and withdrew his pistol. Bending slightly, he carefully fired a single silenced shot into each of Afansi Gorban's frozen, staring eyes.

Spano straightened, the weapon dangling from his hand. He looked impassively at the corpse, then spoke in soft tones.

"Joe Rizzo sends his regards," he said.

JUST BEFORE dawn, a blue-and-white radio car from the Six-Two precinct pulled off the Belt Parkway and onto the grass shoulder bordering the westbound lanes. The driver, a young cop named Charles Goff, stopped the car twenty feet behind a parked black panel van. He turned to his partner, Benny Godini.

"Whatdya think, Benny?"

Godino, twenty-eight years old, shrugged. "I can hear the engine runnin'," he said. "But I don't see anybody in there."

Goff smiled. "Somebody gettin' laid, probably."

Godino shook his head. "That van ain't rockin', buddy."

Goff opened the radio car driver's door and unsnapped the

retention strap on his holster, slipping his flashlight from its belt hoop.

"Blow job, maybe. Let's check it out."

Godino keyed the radio, quickly informing dispatch of their location and intention. He stepped out of the car, standing in the crook of the open doorway, providing cover for his partner. He smiled over the car's roof as Goff prepared to approach the van.

"I hope it's not your sister in that van, Charlie," he said pleasantly.

Goff laughed. "More likely your uncle Angelo."

He moved to the van and peered into its rear window.

A moment later, Goff, his weapon now drawn, his face blanched, turned his eyes back to his partner.

Godino, noting Goff's reaction, quickly drew his own weapon. "What?" he asked, his voice tense.

"Call for backup, Benny, quick. And a supervisor. And a fuckin' ambulance—*fast*."

IT WAS later that morning, Memorial Day, and Joe Rizzo sat at his kitchen table sipping coffee and leafing through a *Daily News*. Jennifer was showering, daughters Carol and Jessica still asleep upstairs. Rizzo's cell, charging on the small table near the side door, rang. He rose and crossed the room, answering the phone absentmindedly.

"Hello?"

"Joe? It's me."

Instantly, Rizzo focused on the call, his eyes darting to the kitchen doorway, making sure no one was about to enter the room.

It was Mikey "The Hammer" Spano.

"How'd you get this number?"

Spano laughed. "Yeah, good mornin' to you, too."

"How'd you get this number?"

"What do you think, you're the only guy with friends? Relax.

I'm on a pay phone. Anybody ever takes a look at your cell record, this can't come back to me."

"Good. Let's keep it short so I can say it was a wrong number."

"It's done. Our little issue. All resolved. Now you tell me what I need to know."

Rizzo paused, a coldness seeping into his chest. "Fast work. You a little nervous about all this?"

"Tell me what I need to know."

"Don't take this personal, but I'll tell you when the DNA checks out."

There was a cold moment of silence before Spano spoke again.

"Sure. I understand. I can wait a couple a days." Another cold silence. "But keep somethin' in mind, Rizzo. I'm pretty good at resolvin' issues. So don't you become one of 'em."

The line went dead. Rizzo returned the phone to its charger. He crossed the room and sat down, once again taking up his coffee and newspaper.

It was oddly disturbing to him how blank his mind seemed.

LATER THAT day, with the cloudless blue sky and warm, late May sun warming the Memorial Day holiday, Rizzo stood before the old-fashioned charcoal barbecue grill in a corner of his backyard.

He flipped burgers and gently nudged chicken and sweet Italian sausage to the far side of the grill. Taking up his can of beer, he crossed to the open kitchen window and looked in. Jennifer, Carol, Jessica, and Jessica's boyfriend, Fred Valero, sat around the table, sipping beverages and chatting. Rizzo called through the window.

"Two minutes, Jen. Everything ready?"

Jennifer rose from the table. "Yes, the side dishes are all set. We'll move into the dining room."

When he carried the meats into the room, he smiled at Fred.

"Sorry, Fred. No brontosaur burgers, just regular ones and some sausage, chicken, and portabellos."

Jessica sighed. "*Enough* with the Flintstones jokes, Dad. *Please.*"

He placed the tray on the table and took a seat. "You see? This is why I miss Marie. She's the only one of my girls who appreciates my sense of humor, but now she lives in the city."

"Too bad she had to work at the hospital today, Mr. Rizzo," Valero said.

Rizzo spooned some pasta salad onto his plate, then raised his eyes to the young man.

"Yeah, Fred. From what I'm seein', interns aren't much more than highly skilled slave laborers. I think they could use a better union." He reached for his beer before continuing. "And since we're sharing a meal together, maybe you should call me 'Joe.' Every time you say 'Mr. Rizzo,' I feel like my grandfather just walked into the room."

Carol leaned to her left, closer to her sister's boyfriend. She smiled at him.

"That's a lot of progress for just one meal, Fred," she said, then sat back and glanced at Jessica. "Yabba-dabba-doooo!"

LATER, IN the darkness of the evening, Rizzo carried a trashcan out to the street. As he placed it down near the curb, a dark police department Ford pulled to the driveway in front of his house. Lieutenant Vince D'Antonio was at the wheel.

Rizzo walked to the car and bent to the open driver's window, his arm braced atop the car's roof.

"Hello, Vince. Happy Memorial Day."

D'Antonio nodded. "Yeah. Can I get a word with you, Joe?"

Rizzo noted the coldness in D'Antonio's blue eyes, the slight blush of color beneath his fair skin. The lieutenant's nickname danced across Rizzo's mind—The Swede.

"Sure. Shut if off, come inside the house. There's some coffee still in the pot."

D'Antonio shook his head. "No thanks. Actually, it's good I caught you out here. Avoid any awkwardness with Jen."

Rizzo pressed his lips, considering the man's words, then shrugged. "Whatever you say, boss."

He walked around the car and climbed in. D'Antonio switched off the ignition.

"Strange thing happened today. Very strange. Just about dawn this morning, a Six-Two blue-and-white checks out a van parked by the side of the Belt. It's just sittin' there, engine running, no visible occupant. So the cops take a look. Know what they found?"

Rizzo studied the tight anger on D'Antonio's face. Again, he shrugged.

"From the look on your face, I'm guessin' it wasn't two teenagers fuckin'."

"You're right, it wasn't. It was three dead males. Shot to death, all of 'em."

"No shit? You I.D. them?"

"Yeah, we I.D.d them. Three Russians, two with known ties to Oleg Boklov in Brighton Beach. The third guy checked out clean, no criminal record, but he just got to the U.S. about nine, ten months ago. We put through an overseas call to the Russian National Police. They'll get back to us."

"And you came out here to tell me this personally? Why?"

"It was a black panel van, Joe. Just like the one the perps used the night Carol and Espo got shot."

"Really? It was the *same* van? How'd you determine that?"

D'Antonio shook his head. "No, not the same one. Matter a fact, this van was just stolen out of some rental yard in Queens, the place didn't even know it was missing until we contacted them. So, no, it's not the same van."

"So, what's your point, Vince?"

D'Antonio shifted in his seat, facing Rizzo more fully. "This is my fuckin' *point*. Somebody wanted to get our attention here. Black panel van, three guys inside, see what I'm sayin'? And doesn't something else strike you as a little coincidental? Carol and Espo are shot over in the Eight-Four, but the message is delivered in the Six-Two. *Your* precinct. Carol's *father's* precinct."

"Yeah, so what?"

"So this, Joe: the homicide task force is all over this. They already got a preliminary confirmation on the DNA. The guy that just got here from Russia, he's a match. A match to the blood found at Anwar's, the blood the shooter shed after Carol's bullet or the flying glass winged him. That makes *him* the shooter, the one who killed Espo."

Rizzo nodded. "Good. Good for the prick. But what's all this gotta do with *me*?"

"One of the other bodies, a stupid hood named Afansi Gorban, he had *three* slugs in him. One in his forehead. And one more in each of his eyes. Somebody shot his fuckin' eyes out, Joe. Old-world wiseguy stuff. Whatever he did, whatever he saw, has now been erased. It's all over with, all squared."

Rizzo gestured with his hands, indicating indifference. "Okay."

"This was a message. A fuckin' message to *you*, and it couldn't be any clearer. The black van, the Six-Two dump, the fuckin' eyes blown out. And something else. Afansi had a piece tucked in his shorts. Ballistics matched it as the gun Carol was shot with. Stupid fuck, he never even ditched it."

"Am I supposed to be sorry about any of this, boss? Am I supposed to say, 'Oh, my goodness, justice has been denied' like some intellectual asshole on the debating team? Is that what you're waiting for? What's your fuckin' point here, Vince? If you've got some kinda accusation to make, make it."

"No. I've got no accusation. Neither does Santori, but he was squirming around like a bug fryin' in the sun while he was workin' this today. He's thinkin' exactly what I'm thinkin'. I don't know how you angled this, Joe, and I sure as hell don't wanna know. You avenged your daughter, you avenged Espo. If I wanted to do my fuckin' job here, I'd be takin' you in for a paraffin test on your hands right now."

Rizzo shook his head. "Take me. You think *I* shot these three pricks? Take me in. Let's do it."

D'Antonio turned back in his seat, staring through the windshield as he spoke, his hands clenched white knuckle on the steering wheel.

"No. I'm sure you're alibied real solid for last night. But I figure you're behind it all somehow. This is old-world guinea wiseguy shit, message delivered. Delivered right to *you*."

"Vince, you're outa your fuckin' mind."

D'Antonio turned slowly to face Rizzo once more. In the dark interior of the car, their eyes met. When he spoke, the lieutenant's voice was soft, reflective. His anger seemed dissipated, replaced by a heavy, soul-touching sadness.

"You been walking around the precinct for three years talking about retirement, sayin' how it's time, how you want out. Well, it *is* time, Joe. In fact, it's *beyond* time."

D'Antonio started the engine and pulled the gearshift into drive, his foot pressed tightly on the brake pedal.

"You waited just a little too long," he said softly. "You let the job beat you, Joe. You let the job win."

LATER THAT night, Rizzo entered the bedroom. Jennifer sat propped against two pillows, reading a novel. Rizzo undressed silently, then climbed into bed. He turned to face his wife.

"Vince swung by tonight. I saw him when I was putting out the garbage."

Jennifer closed the book, holding her spot with a thumb. "Oh? Why didn't you ask him in?"

"I did. He said no."

Jennifer's brow furrowed. She assumed the lieutenant had come to visit Carol as he'd done at the hospital. Now, she studied Rizzo's face.

"What's going on, Joe?"

"The guys that shot Carol and Espo. They turned up early this morning. Along with the third robber."

"Turned up? Turned up how?"

"Turned up dead, Jen. Shot to death and left in a van off the Belt Parkway." He allowed some seconds to elapse, then continued. "Inside the Six-Two boundaries."

Jennifer considered it before replying, her eyes suddenly guarded. "Oh. Did Vince say when they were killed?"

Rizzo offered a tired smile. "Funny, but I was figuring you'd ask if Vince said *who* killed them, not *when* they were killed."

She held his eyes for a moment, then continued.

"When were they killed, Joe?" she repeated, her voice void of inflection.

Rizzo nodded. "Okay. Vince said they were killed shortly before they were found. Make it either side of midnight." He reached a hand out and laid it gently on her forearm. "I was here. Layin' right here next to you at midnight last night."

Jennifer shook her head as though freeing it of some unseen encumberance, such as a spiderweb.

"Of course you were. I wasn't implying—"

"Well, Vince was. He thinks somehow I engineered this—that dumping the bodies in the Six-Two was a message sent to *me* personally."

"But how can they even be sure who these men were? What makes Vince think they're the ones who—"

"It's them alright. The task force workin' Espo's murder pushed the forensics through. They got a preliminary DNA match from the scene and a definite ballistics on a gun they found inside the van. It was the same gun Carol was shot with."

Jennifer's eyes widened. "My God," she said, her hand slipping out of the book and rising to her lips. "My God."

"Yeah," Rizzo said. "It does kinda seem like an act of God, doesn't it? These three guys fallin' out of the sky like they did. But, it's over now, Jen. It's over."

Jennifer sat up straighter and turned more fully to her husband. "Is it? Is it really, Joe?"

"Yes. I've been out on leave, visiting Carol in the hospital and putzin' around the house, at home every night, with you. Whatever happened has nothin' to do with me. These guys just pissed off the wrong people, that's all. And they got what they had comin'. End a story."

Jennifer sat silently, studying his face. After a long, awkward time, she reopened the book and dropped her eyes. Idly, she began searching for her place, turning pages slowly, speaking with her eyes still focused on the novel.

"Now you can stop. You can stop sneaking out of here at odd hours looking for Carol's shooter. And I guess we'll just have to skip the part where he rots in a cage. He can go *straight* to hell now, can't he?"

Jennifer raised her eyes from the book and met his.

"You're right, Joe. It *is* over."

Jennifer found her place and began to read once more. Rizzo, thoughts now suddenly jumbled in his head, emotions unsettled, turned and switched off the bedside lamp.

"Good night, hon," he said.

"Good night, Joe."

CHAPTER TWENTY-SIX

WEDNESDAY, MAY 27, was Rizzo's first day back to work. He reported for his four-to-twelve night tour, managing to avoid contact with Vince D'Antonio, who had gone off duty just before Rizzo arrived.

Early that evening, he and Mark Ginsberg were seated at Rizzo's desk.

"So I took a few days off myself while you were out," Ginsberg said. "I was making some progress on a few of our cases, but that kid Vince had me working with was a real pain in my ass. The kid's lookin' for his gold shield, and he figured if he worked me to death, maybe they'd give him mine. So I grabbed some annual, and me and Paula spent an overnighter in Atlantic City."

"So how'd you do?"

Ginsberg shrugged. "You know me, Joe, I'd rather spend twenty bucks for a hamburger than lose a nickel gambling. I didn't play, just caught a coupla shows and had some nice meals. Paula won a few bucks on the slots."

"Jeez, I haven't been down there since Jen and I saw Tony Bennett at the Taj about ten years ago."

Ginsberg's lips turned down. "The Taj? I hate that fuckin'

place. We stayed at the Trop. You know, they got a restaurant inside the Taj called the Calcutta Café. Imagine that? Might as well call it the Diarrhea Diner, for Christ's sake. Who'd wanna eat in a place called the Calcutta fuckin' Café?"

"I don't know, Mark. Lots of people, I guess."

"Yeah, well, I'm not one of 'em."

"Anything new on that scam artist workin' the seniors?"

"Not really. Guy just hit on an old man last Friday, by the bank on Sixty-fifth and Eighteenth. Conned the old guy outa two hundred bucks."

Rizzo shook his head. "We gotta get on that one. This guy's really pissin' me off."

Ginsberg glanced around before continuing. They were alone in the squad room.

"Word around here lately is that pissin' you off isn't such a good idea."

Rizzo's eyes narrowed. "Meanin' what?"

Ginsberg sat back in his seat and raised his hands, palms outward, toward Rizzo. "Take it easy, partner. I just think you should know I've been overhearing things, that's all. Those three stiffs in the van, the shooters, word is you worked a little magic there. Now, *I* personally don't believe it. But, tell you the truth, if some asshole capped my daughter, the guy'd have a problem with me, too. So I'm not judging. Just informing. I think Santori put a bee in Vince's ear, and most of the guys in the precinct aren't real big on coincidences, you know? The heavy money's on you here. Just so you know."

Rizzo considered it. "Yeah. Actually, Vince came by the house to confront me."

"No shit? What'd you tell him?"

"I told him the truth. I've been on the sidelines for two weeks, either in the hospital or at home the whole time. What could I possibly have to do with this? They think I'm a fuckin' magician? I pulled these guys out of a hat and then imported a coupla zips from Sicily to clip them? Who am I, fuckin' Al Capone? Come on, Mark, give me a break. I don't care what the word around here is: I had nothin' to do with this. I wish I *had*. And I'm glad the sons of bitches are dead."

"Okay, partner. Whatever you say. Lucky for you I'm pretty damn stupid. You can ask my mother, she'll tell you. So I personally believe you. But you might wanna make sure D'Antonio's convinced. Maybe Santori, too, while you're at it."

Rizzo shook his head. "I don't have to do squat. Anybody has a beef with somethin', let them prove it."

"Okay, Joe, I get it."

"Good. Do you remember that morning when you came to see us at the hospital? While Carol was still under the knife? Me and you went outside and I bummed a smoke. Remember?"

Ginsberg thought for a moment, then his face brightened with a smile. "Is this about your fuckin' parakeet? You gonna start with that again?"

Rizzo laughed. "No, not the parakeet. That morning, while I was smoking, I was watching people. People movin' past the hospital, walking by, driving by, whatever. I remember thinking how arrogant they all were, how fuckin' smug. They just moved along, oblivious to everything that was going on inside that hospital, oblivious to all the death, all the pain, all the sufferin', all the fear. Just movin' along in arrogant good health, nice and comfortable. Same as those people who like to make moral judgments from their safe, secure positions, judging some scared, threatened, violated person's actions. See, nobody *knows*, Mark. Nobody really *knows*. Not till it's them in that hospital, or worse, one of their kids. So I don't really give a *fuck* what anybody thinks about those three dead pricks in that van, or about how they got there. I wish it *had* been me who killed them. I wish it *had* been me that engineered it. But it *wasn't*. So, end of story."

Ginsberg stood, nodding his head. "End of story," he said, glancing at his watch. "Feel like takin' a ride? Monday night somebody lit up some kittens in the schoolyard over at Shallow Junior High. The custodian found them when he came in Tuesday morning."

Rizzo, his face still flushed with a lingering, unexplained, nearly explosive anger, pushed his chair back and stood up.

"That asshole cat killer DeMarco again?"

"I wouldn't be surprised, partner. Fuckin' psycho's killed enough cats this spring to open up his own Chinese take-out joint. I think we oughta go talk to him, him and his mother. Get the old lady to double-up on his meds. And maybe we can scare the kid a little. I don't even *like* cats, and DeMarco's startin' to piss *me* off. You can imagine how the pet-lover citizens are reacting to this."

Rizzo nodded. "One a these days, some lunatic animal rights activist is gonna chill that kid DeMarco. Permanently."

Ginsberg smiled broadly and slapped playfully at Rizzo's shoulder.

"You mean, take the fuckin' law into their own hands? My God, Joe, that would break the social covenant. Wouldn't it?"

"Yeah. That it would. And we can't have any of that, can we?"

AT TEN-THIRTY p.m., Detective Angela Paulson crossed the squad room to Rizzo's desk. She sat lightly in the chair beside him.

"Got a sec?"

"Sure, Angela. What's up?"

She handed him a sheet of paper. "I made this for you. Copy of a fax that came in a few minutes ago. It's an FYI that went out to all precincts, citywide. You can keep it." She stood, smiling at Rizzo. "As a souvenir." She turned and went back to her desk in the far corner of the squad room.

Rizzo dropped his eyes to the fax. It was a department memo updating the forensics progress on the bodies found in the black van, and it originated with the homicide task force created to investigate the murder of Sergeant Joseph Esposito and the shooting of Police Officer Carol Rizzo.

The body of one victim, Gleb Karin, in addition to two bullet wounds in the back of his skull, bore a partially healed wound at the frontal deltoid area of the right arm. It was consistent with a laceration caused by a grazing projectile such as flying glass or a fired bullet. The wound had been treated with butterfly sutures and appeared to be ten to fourteen days old. There were no signs of prior or current infection.

Rizzo was aware, as were all law enforcement personnel, that a variety of doctors, some stripped of licenses, others still practicing, were available to underworld operatives suffering injuries which required clandestine treatment. Others, such as pharmacists, dentists, ex-military medics, and even the occasional veterinarian were also sometimes utilized for that same purpose. As part of the investigation into the police shooting at Anwar's, the task force had been systematically interviewing individuals known to provide such services. Apparently Gleb Karin had been treated by one such person.

The report went on to state that the preliminary findings regarding blood found at the scene had now been finalized and positively identified as having been that of Gleb Karin.

The second body, identified as Vadim Pilkin, had sustained two bullet wounds to the head, either one of which would have been fatal.

The third man, Afansi Gorban, had suffered three gunshot wounds from two separate weapons. One, a forty-five-caliber bullet matching those found in Karin and Pilkin, had been fired into the center of his forehead at extremely close range and in and of itself would have been fatal. Two more bullets, both from a single nine-millimeter weapon, had been fired into each of his eyes, most probably after death had occurred.

Rizzo knew those last shots were meant to forever erase Afansi's vision of the prostrate Carol Rizzo, rain falling down upon her near lifeless body, her blood running into the gutter.

Rizzo dropped the report down on his messy desk and rose. He crossed the squad room to Paulson's desk.

"Hey, Angela, can I get one of them Marlboros of yours?"

She smiled up at him. "Sure. Still tryin' to kick it?"

"Oh, I already kicked it. This is just to *prove* that I kicked it."

"I understand," she said, laughing. "Over there on the coatrack, the light blue linen blazer, right-hand pocket. Help yourself."

"Thanks, Angie. And thanks for the fax, too. Very interesting."

She turned back to the report she had been working on.

"You're very welcome. I thought you might like that."

Rizzo went downstairs and out onto the sidewalk. He savored the cigarette and watched traffic as it went by on Bath Avenue. After a few moments, he reached into his pocket and took out his cell, pressing the speed dial for home.

"Hi, Jen. It's me. How are my girls tonight?"

"I'm fine, Joe, and Carol just went up to her room a little while ago. Her favorite movie is playing on TCM—*The Maltese Falcon*. She's going to watch it before turning in. She's absolutely fine. Jessica is out with Fred."

"Good. By the way, I'm gonna be a little late tonight. I've had some evidence stored in the precinct locker, and it's gettin' stale. I need to run it down to the property clerk's office. First I gotta finish up some backed-up paperwork. Figure I'll be in about one, one-thirty, okay?"

Jennifer was silent for a moment before responding. "Okay. I appreciate your calling so I won't worry."

"See you later, hon, if you're still up."

"Alright." Again she paused. "Be careful."

"I'm *always* careful, Jen. Always."

He closed and pocketed the phone, then took a last drag on the cigarette, flicking it ten feet into the gutter. He turned and walked back into the precinct.

JOE RIZZO slowly drove southbound on Seventh Avenue, scanning the sparsely parked autos along the darkened stretch of street. For well over a quarter mile, this section of the avenue was lined on the west by the unlit athletic fields of Poly Prep Country Day School and on the east side by sprawling, manicured fairways and greens of the Dyker Beach Golf Course. At its extreme southern tip, Seventh Avenue terminated with the secured entrance gates of one of the oldest continually operating military bases in the country, Fort Hamilton.

After sunset, this roadway was normally the most deserted place one could find within any residential area of Brooklyn. The avenue was a popular lovers' lane, with only rare pedestrian traffic, usually voyeuristic dog-walkers.

Rizzo noted the red Cadillac parked in the near blackness of this moonless night. It sat against the west curb, lights and engine switched off. Rizzo angled his Camry to a space behind the Cadillac and shut it down. It was twelve twenty-five a.m., and he was five minutes early. Before exiting his car, Rizzo scanned the surrounding area once more. Some forty yards ahead sat another vehicle, apparently unoccupied or, more likely, holding young lovers sprawled across its backseat. Diagonally across the wide, two-way avenue, a Lincoln stood parked on the east side, the dark outlines of two men barely noticeable in its front seat. Rizzo unconsciously dropped a hand to the right pocket of his sport coat, touching at his old throw-away Ruger revolver, once again confirming its presence.

He climbed from his car and moved to the red Cadillac.

"Are those friends of yours in that Lincoln over there, or did you let yourself get tailed?" Rizzo asked as he dropped heavily onto the plush leather of the front passenger seat.

Mikey Spano smiled, his teeth showing whitely in the dim interior.

"You noticed, eh?" Spano answered pleasantly. Then he reached a hand to the light stem on the steering column, briefly flashing the Cadillac's headlights. The Lincoln responded in kind.

"No feds, Joe, relax. That's just my associate, Herc Davilla, and his apprentice, Danny DeLuca. Herc is my, what, insurance man? Yeah, let's call him my insurance man. In case you got anything stupid in mind."

"Stupid? Stupid how?"

Spano shrugged. "Stupid smart. Me and you are the only two people who know how this thing went down. *Why* it went down. Everybody else, they're gonna figure it's just payback for those three assholes tryin' to fuck with me and that Russkie, Boklov. But, me and you, Joe, we know better. So, if something was to happen to me tonight, if I was to decide to eat the gun here, kill myself in my shiny new Cadillac, you'd be home free—last man standing. This way, if my guys see a muzzle flash in this car, you're just another dead motherfucker."

Spano turned in his seat, fully facing Rizzo, smile still in place. "Insurance. I'm a big believer."

"Good for you, Mikey. But if I wanted to kill you, wouldn't I'da set this meeting in Riis Park parkin' lot, or out in the boonies on Staten Island and not a hundred yards away from an Army base?"

Spano nodded. "Yeah. And if you'da tried that, I'da known for *sure*. Then maybe Herc and Danny woulda come to meet you without me."

"Well, relax. You're safe."

"Yeah, Joe, I know. I'm *real* fuckin' safe."

The two men sat silently for a moment, Spano turning back in his seat, looking out the windshield to the car parked forty yards ahead. He chuckled.

"I been sittin' here for ten minutes. I like to get to these things early. When I first got here, I saw two heads in that car up there, neckin'. After a minute or two, the guy's head disappeared. Just as you were pullin' up, the broad's head went down. Must be returnin' the favor." He laughed again. "You grew up around here, didn't you? This is sorta your old neighborhood, right? You ever get laid along this avenue?"

"Maybe once or twice."

Spano nodded. "I figured. When I was a kid, I used to go over to Canarsie Park or the pier, the old pier, before the yuppies started turnin' it into another Brooklyn Heights promenade."

"You wanna swap ass stories from the old days?" asked Rizzo. "Or you think maybe we should get to the point here?"

"Yeah," Spano replied with another laugh. "We should get to the point. We probably look like a coupla fags sittin' here."

"Usin' that black van was a mistake. So was the Six-Two dump. What are you, a fuckin' Hollywood director?"

Spano shrugged. "Relax, who's gonna know? *Suspect,* yeah, but so fuckin' what? That Lombardi, he pissed me off. I was supposed to have squared my problem with him when the Hi-Fi shooters got delivered. But he's still carrying a hard-on for me. So fuck Lombardi. I figured I'd send another message an' let everybody know I ain't scared a him. I do whatever the fuck I gotta do, whenever I *wanna* do it. You oughta keep that in mind, too, Joe."

Rizzo nodded. "Yeah, I know. You grew up in Canarsie, you're a tough guy. But you keep somethin' in mind, too. *I* grew up in Bensonhurst. So maybe you oughta watch out for me a little."

"You makin' threats, Joe?"

"Yeah, I am. After tonight, our business is over. Don't ever start to think you got some kinda license here. You and me are done after tonight."

"I know, Joe. I always understood that. But let's try and keep this civil, okay? Don't fuckin' threaten me, don't start to piss me off."

After a few tense moments, Spano continued, his tone free of the anger it had held, now businesslike and calm.

"Tell me about Lombardi."

"First, let me tell you this. Far as Lombardi's concerned, he does figure you square for Maggio. *That's* why he hasn't been all over your captains lately, pressurin' them, costin' them money. If he'da gone that route, eventually the big boys woulda figured it out. They get rid of you, they get rid of Lombardi. You bought your life when you took out those Hi-Fi shooters. But you didn't buy your freedom."

Spano shook his head, exasperation on his face. "What is this guy, a fuckin' Boy Scout, for Christ's sake? Maybe he should find himself a hobby, maybe he's got too much fuckin' time on his hands."

"Maybe he does, Mikey. But it is what it is."

After another silent moment, Spano turned again to face Rizzo.

"So what's Lombardi got on me?"

His eyes flicking briefly to the Lincoln parked across the darkened avenue, Rizzo sighed, the Ruger in his pocket now useless.

"You know, it's a little insulting you bringin' those two hitters along with you."

Spano shrugged. "I apologize, I'm a suspicious scumbag. That's how I managed to reach the ripe old age of forty-four."

Rizzo hesitated, imagining the emaciated face of Johnny Morelli smiling at him sadly from beyond the Cadillac's darkened windshield.

"You know a guy named Ralphy Avena, Mikey?"

Spano's brow furrowed. "Yeah, up 'n' comer I got my eye on. Real good earner. Why?"

"How come you got your eye on him?"

"Coupla the guys are gettin' old, talkin' about Florida and the grandkids. There might be a coupla slots openin' up. Maybe Ralphy'll fill one of them."

"Well, Ralphy already found himself a slot. With the feds, and Lombardi. He got grabbed on a major beef, and he's workin' out all the details. In another coupla weeks he'll be waltzin' into the Pompeii strapped with a wire. Even if you sweep the place every time you walk in, he can still get you a recording contract. And Lombardi's just chompin' at the bit."

Spano blanched. Even in the dimness of the car's interior, Rizzo could see the vein throbbing heavily in the man's neck.

"How good's this information, Joe?"

Rizzo shrugged. "Horse's fuckin' mouth. No room for error."

"Anything else?"

"Not that I'm aware of."

Spano turned suddenly hostile eyes toward Rizzo. "How do I know I can trust you? You're still a fuckin' cop."

Rizzo's face held no expression, but his eyes were telling something, something Spano could not quite fathom.

"No," Rizzo said softly. "Not anymore I'm not. That's over as of right now."

Spano looked puzzled, then shrugged. "Whatever. Is there anything else you gotta tell me? You holdin' anything back?"

Rizzo shook his head. "No. From now on, I'm your biggest fan. I gotta hope you never take a fall, 'cause if you do, you may wind up using me as a bargaining chip. I got that hangin' over my head forever, Mikey. Or at least until somebody starts lookin' at you with those same hungry eyes you looked at Chink with."

Spano reached for the ignition and fired the engine. "On my children, Joe, this stays between us. I'm old school. I *swear,* it stays between just the two of us."

Rizzo reached for the door handle.

"Good-bye, Mikey. It was good doin' business with you. And do me a favor. If anything should happen to Avena, see he don't get mailed to the Six-Two, okay?"

Spano smiled. "On my children. You got nothin' to worry about."

Rizzo quickly climbed from the car and returned to his Camry. Once again, he was surprised at how blank his mind seemed—just as it had been when he received Spano's call informing him that Carol's assailant had been dealt with.

IT WAS just after one a.m. when Rizzo walked through the rear entrance of his home. The house was dark, quiet. He dropped his car keys onto the small table by the door, then plugged his cell into its charger. As quietly as possible, he climbed the stairs to the second-floor bedrooms. Softly, as he had done when they were children, he first entered Carol's room, then Jessica's. He kissed each daughter lightly on the head, smiling at their peaceful, sleeping faces. Noting the darkness and silence of his own bedroom where Jennifer lay asleep, Rizzo turned, making his way back downstairs to the small liquor cabinet in the dining room. He removed a half-full bottle of Dewar's and a small glass, then sat heavily down at the table. He poured himself a drink.

"Here's to you, Johnny," he said softly. "Wherever the fuck you are."

CHAPTER TWENTY-SEVEN

June

MONDAY, JUNE 1, was Ralph Avena's thirty-third birthday. At eight p.m., he stood before a full-length mirror in the master bedroom of his elegant home on Avenue L. His wife, wearing only a thong, stood behind him, her arms crossed tightly in anger across her breasts, her dark eyes fiery.

"You got some fuckin' nerve, Ralphy, goin' out now."

Avena adjusted his open collar and slipped into his jacket. "I tole you, Jeanette, it's business, it can't be helped. I gotta get goin', I'm runnin' late already."

"Yeah, big fuckin' hurry. You managed to make time for me to give ya your birthday present. For *that,* you had time."

Ralph turned and smiled at her. "I know, baby, I know. Look, I'll be home in a coupla hours, I swear. We'll go out then, I promise. We'll go up to Cheech's place, have a few drinks, somethin' to eat. But this is important, believe me. *Very* important."

Jeanette relented a bit, her arms relaxing somewhat.

"Promise?" she asked. "Swear-on-your-eyes promise?"

Ralph nodded, stepping closer and patting her bare buttock. "Promise. Hope-to-die promise."

She smiled. "Okay, but you better mean it."

He kissed Jeanette on the forehead and turned to leave.

"Nothin' can keep me away, baby. Coupla hours, you'll see."

Ralph left, heading toward the driveway and his dark blue BMW. It was just a mile drive to the meeting with Captain Dominick Lombardi and the police department technicians who would brief him on the operation of the transmitting device he'd soon carry into the very heart of Michele Spano's Brooklyn crime organization headquarters.

This night would represent the demise of a very promising career, and Ralph Avena had strongly conflicting feelings about it. Since his preteen years, he had watched with envy and fascination as the wiseguys of Canarsie moved through his world. It had been his sole aspiration in life, to someday join their swaggering ranks.

And, after a successful stint with the Avenue M Boys street gang, Ralph had managed to make the transition. By age twenty-one, he was a valued member of the old Grassi crew, working on various enterprises with the older, more entrenched rising star, Mikey Spano. It was a sanctioned hit made by Ralph that had ultimately solidified his status and helped gain Spano's trust.

But lately circumstances had conspired against Avena, and his fate was now painfully clear: betray Spano or fall on a mandatory life sentence for narcotic trafficking.

He simply saw no other option. Captain Dominick Lombardi was to be his new don, the recently crowned Mikey Spano finishing a distant second.

Now, he climbed into his BMW and started the engine, resigned to this evening's unpleasant task. As he prepared to back out of the driveway, Ralph idly wondered how he and Jeanette would fare living an anonymous, run-of-the-mill existence in some godforsaken corner of the country. He sighed.

There simply were no other options.

★ ★ ★

THE LAST thing Ralph Avena saw was the kindly, grandfatherlike features of Hercules Davilla gazing from behind the looming bore of a silenced forty-five automatic.

"Go get his car," Davilla said to Danny DeLuca after firing a single shot. "We'll put him in the trunk. You drive his car over to the yard on Utica, I'll follow you. The Russian's expectin' us. He's got a crusher waitin' for this guy."

LATER, AT two-thirty a.m., Rizzo returned home from his extended four-to-twelve, an aggravated assault case having kept him beyond end of tour.

Despite the lateness of the hour, he was sharply awake, too much coffee and activity having imposed a second wave of energy upon him. The night had begun to turn stormy around midnight, and a heavy, steady rain still fell. Rizzo could hear it pounding frantically on the roof of the covered porch at the front of the house.

He opened a fresh bottle of Dewar's, crossed the living room, and sat by the window in a plush, high-backed upholstered chair that had once belonged to Jennifer's grandmother. He poured three fingers of scotch into his glass and placed the bottle down on a side table. He sipped the Dewar's.

The old house was still, except for sounds of rain beating atop the portico and a rythmic ticktocking from the stately grandfather clock standing against the room's far wall.

Rizzo gazed out the wet, darkened window to the tree-lined street, soft circles of light from streetlamps glistening against the rain, parked automobiles lining each curb.

As he sat sipping scotch, the street Joe Rizzo had lived on for so very many years was a mere blur. Through a haze of unsettling, tormented thoughts, he envisioned the long, dangerously dark road he and Johnny Morelli had stepped out upon almost three decades earlier.

It was not the same, he told himself. Johnny had been motivated by weakness and selfishness, by self-serving cowardice.

And although their actions had been chillingly similar, so ironically tormented, Rizzo knew that his own motives had been different from Morelli's, so much more . . . what?

What had his motives truly been?

He wished he still knew. He wondered if he had *ever* really known.

Joe Rizzo sat by the window, drinking scotch. And in the blurry reflection of his face in the wet glass, he saw something else; he saw himself as a very young man, climbing into a radio car with his partner, John Morelli, about to face a long and dangerous night on patrol.

Together.